The Nelson Boy

To Peter Hunter Blair, loving partner in the search

THE NELSON BOY

An Imaginative Reconstruction of A

Great Man's Childhood

Pauline Hunter Blair

———◆———

CHURCH FARM HOUSE BOOKS

CAMBRIDGE

Copyright © Pauline Hunter Blair 1999
First published in 1999 by Church Farm House Books
Church Farm House
Bottisham
Cambridge
CB5 9BA

Distributed by Gazelle Book Services Limited
Falcon House, Queen Square
Lancaster, England LA1 1RN

British Library Cataloguing in Publication Data
A catalogue record for this book is available from the British Library

ISBN 0-9536317-0-2

Typeset by Amolibros, Watchet, Somerset
This book production has been managed by Amolibros
Printed and bound by T J International Ltd, Padstow, England

Contents

Preface

This family story of the mid-eighteenth century is set in a North Norfolk still in its rural parts very much the same. Great houses, some inhabited today by the same families, stand in their acres of corn, carrots, turnips and parkland. (And long before 'Turnip Townsend' and 'Coke of Norfolk' were turnips grown and crops rotated.) Village churches provide registers of village people, from gentry and big farmers, doctors, attorneys, and schoolmasters, to shopkeepers, faithful servants and the very poor, humble or sick helped by the parish. All the details in this village are actual, from George Gogg's wife's superior reading skills to Richard Tidd's shirts: and from Peter Black, the rectory man's smallpox inoculations (well before Jenner) to the midwifery and nursing of Goody Black, who I believe may have been his mother.

We are in the most famous of the seven Burnhams, Burnham Thorpe, where the rector, Edmund Nelson, is to be papa to eight youngsters, and his wife, Catherine Nelson, (of the Suckling family, a smidge higher perhaps in the social scale) is the busiest of mothers. She had eleven babies, but two had died in infancy and the very youngest was to die in this story. From amongst this quiverful of children there begins to fly one, outstanding in spirit, wits, and character, who was going to fly far.

Horace, as the family called him, came almost plumb in the middle, sixth of the whole brood, living and dead. His feeling for his father appears in many letters between them of adult life. But so far as I know not 'a scrap of a pen' survives from his mother. I have suggested a huge bond between them, such as sets a person up for life. His relationships with his brothers and sisters, his tender love for Maurice, his and William's child-time devotion due to their near ages, not likeness; his recognition of the staunch faithful dullness of Susannah (Sukey) contrasted with the potential social brilliance of little Catherine (Kitty): these have been drawn by looking backwards from how he speaks of them, and to them, in later life.

Six well-authenticated anecdotes put milestones across Horace's childhood and boyhood: losing himself at Hilborough (where his paternal granny lived): going to school through deep snow with

William (his village school is shadowy, but there was one at Burnham Market, it advertised for a schoolmaster); finding the 'rare' bird's nest (a green woodpecker seems to suit the place and the circumstances, a flashy bird, which would thrill any boy, probably not all that rare then.) The sprig of yew picked at dead of night from the churchyard tree nearly a mile away does pose a problem of motive, and has been taken to be a 'dare', which seems likely. At the Paston School at North Walsham (still flourishing and well documented) he caught the measles (the young woman who nursed him told about it later). He also (most famously perhaps) stripped the headmaster's pear-tree and never owned up. Perhaps his nerve and boldness on this occasion, and his schoolmates' loyalty to him (no one told) are a cameo of his future. Nevertheless it was a conscience-less act, typically school-boyish and impulsive, and probably he suffered afterwards. Conscience would have presided at the rectory: Papa is said to have 'left it to their honour' as to whether they could get to school through that great snow. Also, was the pear-stealing one reason why he was so keen to leave school at twelve and a half and go into the navy? I have dated these incidents more exactly by common sense and deduction and set them into plausible contexts.

The Norwich Mercury and *The Norfolk Gazette* of the time have provided an actual background tapestry of events (in the great snow year, for instance, it is reported in shock that the post from London did not arrive till *noon*), but the family's participation in them has to be largely imagined. No where have I described Horace's involvement in an event if that were circumstantially impossible. We know the people Horace was fond of when a child from the letters he wrote, the messages he sent, the enquiries he made as an adult. I have let them people his childhood. This is to say that nearly every event is actual, and all the people playing a pivotal part existed.

The family are surrounded by relations in the county, in Norwich, and in London, uncles and aunts, cousins, grandparents and godparents, many ordinary, some 'grand'. Mr Nelson, Papa, concocted a *Family Historicall* (sic) *Register* which forms the bare bones of my account of the articulated families. Nelson's own *Memoir of His Services* (written when he was famous) and his letters, were my starting points for these years when he was growing up. He must have looked back in happiness to a time which seemed golden, if he could call his village 'Dear, dear Burnham'.

A contemporary memoirist of Lord Nelson, W Blagdon, proves that the hero industry was well under way in 1806 when he says crushingly that it is not his object 'to record the relations of puerility'.

It is certainly mine: in fact, however impossible a job, I have tried to give Horatio Nelson a detailed childhood, to bring Horace down off his column, where (as was once remarked) we can none of us see him.

Pauline Hunter Blair
Bottisham
Cambridge
1999

CHAPTER ONE

The Parsonage at Burnham Thorpe

'Mamma! Papa says, please to come at once! The newspaper is here! About Uncle Maurice! And the Frenchmen! Last year!'

Mrs Catherine Nelson, a dark-haired, full-figured woman of thirty-three years, had been sitting perfectly still by the west window in her chamber watching the sunset. It was a pale evening in late February. There were pools of snowdrops in the orchard and behind the winter trees bands of startling green upheld a layer of luminous dove pink cloud. The sun's fire set all aflame. The features of her firm face, the high forehead, the full lips, the ample cheeks and chin, had settled into a look of mild pleasure as she accepted the familiar condition of expectancy: another child was to come.

She had heard the wagon wheels along the road from Creake crinkling into the stillness: the carrier from Norwich bringing her husband last Saturday's paper. A dog barked from Gogg's farm across the valley behind her, where the swollen river Burn idled along in its flat meadow, brimming and black. Into this peacefulness burst her eldest son Maurice, running up the stairs calling. 'Please to come at once, Mamma!' he cried again as he rushed into the room. He was a quiet child, excitement had fired his tongue.

'Maurice!' she now whispered, hushing him. For next door Sukey lay quietly asleep, fat-cheeked and flushed, and in the cradle one fighting fist was visible from the baby William. Maurice was nearing five.

They crept down the stairs together, over the hall, through the parlour and into the study.

'My dear?' she said eagerly.

Her husband stood over by the window to catch the daylight, his eyes screwed up over the newsprint. Edmund Nelson wore his silky brown hair almost to the shoulders, and no wig. His mouth was amused. He was a slight man, scarcely taller than his wife, and much thinner.

'It is arrived at last, my love, a prodigious long account.' An earlier report had mentioned the *Dreadnought*, her brother's ship, but had given no word of him. She had suffered anxiety for a month.

'Here is a letter from Admiral Coates himself on board HM ship *Marlborough* in Port Royal Harbour, Jamaica. He has heard from Captain Forrest...of the *Augusta*...of an action on the twenty-first October...between three English ships and seven French! The English are the *Dreadnought*, your brother Suckling, the *Augusta*, Captain Forrest; and the *Edinburgh*, Captain Langdon...Now here speaks Captain Forrest.

> At seven in the morning the *Dreadnought* made the signal for seeing the Enemies Fleet coming out of Cap François...At noon saw with great certainty they were four Ships of the Line, and three large Frigates. I then made the signal for the Captains Suckling (—that's your Uncle my boy) and Langdon, who agreed with me to engage them;...the Action began with great Briskness on both sides and continued for Two Hours and a Half, when the French Commodore made a signal, and one of the Frigates immediately came to tow him out of the Line and the rest of the French ships followed him. Our ships had suffered so much...they were in no condition to pursue them. Both Officers and Seamen behaved with the greatest resolution the whole time of the Action...

And there is a good deal more...So now, my boy, you had best raise a huzzah for Captain Maurice Suckling your gallant uncle, for whom you were named.' The rector smiled down quizzically: he could not encourage his son in huzzahs, but his wife could.

'Come, Maurice, come to me, three cheers—not too loud—three cheers for brave Uncle Maurice, who chased off the Frenchmen! One, two, three!' Maurice participated with joy. He was to remember it always: the light still green at the window pane, Papa reading about the ships and he alone with his parents.

'Oh, confusion to the French. We hate the French, do not we, Maurice?' said his mother hugging him.

'Now here is another letter, from a sea captain arrived at Falmouth which says our ships had sent repeated messages to Admiral Coates at Jamaica for assistance...But none arrived: because, listen here.

> One of the vessels being taken by the French, the Letters...fell into their Hands, either by the Neglect or the Villainy of the Master.

'Listen to this about the council of war:

When upon the Quarter Deck they held a Council of War…the whole debate lasted but thirty seconds…the Commodore said: *You see, Gentlemen, the Force of the Enemy: is it your Resolution to fight or not?* Upon which they both answered *it was*…To it they went, the *Dreadnought*, Captain Suckling, leading, received the fire of all the ships as he passed, till he came up with the headmost ship; the *Augusta* next, Commodore Forrest, and after him the *Edinburgh*, Captain Langdon…never was more undaunted courage and Resolution shown in the Officers and Men…'

'He must know, husband,' Mrs Nelson interposed, 'if any of the captains had been wounded? We should have heard?'

'Yes, for at the end he gives the number of killed and wounded. Now I question if this be true, or a wild exaggeration after the event?

It was observable that never Anxiety equalled that of the Seamen, till they knew their Officers' Determination, which when they heard, they were ready to run mad with Joy; huzzaing, throwing up their Hats and Wigs, and seemed like Men inspired…

'Could any poor wretch do you suppose, embrace the probability of blood or death with such transports of abandon?'

'He has his King to serve,' his wife said with decision. 'His King and Country are his stars.'

'Evidently,' admitted the parson, a trace of disbelief in his voice. 'For your brother's ship had twelve killed and thirty wounded, and the other two somewhat less. But the French, he says, had upwards of six hundred killed and wounded, including a great number of gentlemen's sons, put upon the booms with small arms, poor wretches, to catch the fire. This Captain thinks that the memorable Council of War should be wrote in letters of gold in every great Cabin aboard the Fleet…

and not let us think that any Force is too great for Englishmen, when bravely commanded.'

'He is right, so it should, and neither is it!' Mamma cried. 'We are proud of Uncle Maurice, are not we, my little boy?'

'Well, my love, we must thank God that in all the fire he thought to spare your brother.'

'Indeed we must. We must remember the day, husband, we must make the day a festival. October the twenty-first!'

3

Thereafter, February resumed its grey and usual aspect. It blew sometimes so bleakly from the grey north sea that the old and the poor sent their sons or their neighbours to the farm where George Goggs disbursed the parish money which supported them; and in his indecisive hand kept the present parish account book which had begun in his father's time. (His father had laid perpetual claim to the book: 'William Goggs, his book', he had written in 1707 on its flyleaf). This spring George Goggs entered all up to the end of March and was glad to hand the book to the other overseer, Isaac Emerson, a somewhat younger man who kept the accounts boldly and clearly. Isaac's people had farmed the manor farm above the church at Thorpe for a long while, and Isaac's grandfather, Jacob, figured on the flyleaf with William Goggs. The reverend Mr Edmund Nelson got about his parish on his mare or on his legs, according to his own mood and that of the weather: he had a mile to traverse to Thorpe church, along beside the river and over the town bridge and up the hill; and more than another from there to Burnham Ulph, and a half mile more should he have business at Burnham Norton too. For he had a half-share of both these last parishes, which he served with William Smith, the rector of Burnham Market, who had a handsome Yorkshire wife and some daughters.

The year of 1758 was an indifferent year for weather. In March it blew so hard that Edmund Nelson's man, Peter Black, had difficulty in sowing his seed evenly; and the new lambs were buffeted despite their fold of whins and dry heather. There were some days in April when the sun shone, the valley looked all green and gold, the sky was a penetrating blue: but the wind was still as keen as a blade. All through June blew that cold north-easterly. 'There aren't agoing to be no summer, parson, not so's you'd feel it, not nohow,' said the rector's man in a plethora of negatives, as they surveyed the sodden hay, the stalky wheat.

It was June before the village midwife's professional eye took in Mrs Nelson's condition. Coming away from her nursing in the townhouse, Ann Black met the parson's wife bringing broth. (Goody Black, Peter's mother, was the woman ever in demand in illness or childbirth, or death.)

'Well, my dare. So you're in the way, again. And when is it to be?'

'Late September Ann, all being well.'

'So soon as that, eh? Mebbe tha's a shrimp yew do have. Will you be having the doctor?'

'Dr Murray is glad I am smaller; he says you and my mother should manage.'

'Then do you send a message by Peter so soon as you want me, my beauty.'

The children lay in wait for Mrs Suckling, their grandmother, who was coming to live for good in Burnham Thorpe. She was removing from Beccles, near which she had lived since she was widowed (her children all under five and Catherine the eldest, for her first son had died). Edmund Nelson had served his first curacy at Beccles and thus had he and Catherine Suckling met.

Mrs Suckling was going to live in a dwelling by the shooting lodge which lay beyond the parsonage on the road towards Burnham Thorpe and belonged to her Walpole relations. Her stuff, and her housekeeper with it, had all arrived yesterday by a special carrier; their granny was coming in a hired chaise from Norwich today. Maurice had marshalled the babies on the grass by the road and was trying to explain who came. It was one of the summer's rare fine days and the sun was hot.

The chaise arrived and Mrs Ann Suckling descended with a certain air, as if it were her own carriage that brought her. (As indeed it would have been, if the good Lord had not seen fit to strike Doctor Maurice Suckling dead in the pulpit, preaching to the people with more warmth than usual—or as near dead as made no odds.) She was a well-made woman like her daughter, and in her middle sixties. Her mother had been Mary Walpole, sister to the prime minister; her father Sir Charles Turner, a baronet latterly of Warham near here. She was in a sense coming home when she came to Burnham.

The discreet feathers on their granny's beaver hat bobbed as she held out her arms. She was not forbidding. Maurice ran into them.

'Well, my fine boy! Well, little Sukey! And who, pray, can *this* be? Can this be my grand-son William forsooth, all mud and eyes? What have you been doing, my child? It is I who should stare!' She took him firmly by the hand to bring him in.

Mr and Mrs Nelson came from the front door, waving.

'Mamma! I am so glad to see you!' she cried.

'You look well and happy, my daughter. But what an atrocious summer, dear Mr Nelson, is your corn in? I am glad that the sun shines at last.'

It was an easy birth, being Catherine Nelson's sixth (for her first two sons had died): on a Friday, the twenty-ninth of September, the little boy was born. All laughed at his smallness but loved him the more.

'I told her she had a shrimp,' said Ann Black, her sleeves rolled up over the crock of warm water. 'And she hev and all! But all the more easy.'

'St Michael and all his angels,' Edmund Nelson said, stooping over them. 'A good day to be born.'

Later, the rector's wife lay listening to the delightful sounds of the day, the child in the crook of her arm. Four children she had now, she reflected; quiet, sensitive Maurice, happy, easy Susannah, demanding William. Her mind dwelt on William with a little guilt and sorrow, she had had an effort to love and fondle William, and his greedy feeding, his demanding self-will grew ever the stronger. What would this fourth be like, so small and grave-eyed? What should they call him? She thought without' sorrow now of her first two, born at Swaffham, dying within four months. They had called the eldest, naturally, Edmund. The second they had called Horatio, after Catherine Nelson's great-uncle, Horatio Walpole, who had stood godfather to the child. Edmund was a proper enough name. But Horatio was more positively grand, a heroic kind of name and still fashionable. Was it perhaps too grand for this little creature? Horace, they would call him. Horace Nelson sounded well. Lord Walpole of Wolterton (for this he had become two years ago) was dead, But his son was also Horatio, he perhaps would sponsor the new baby. She let herself think of her child as Horace.

The rector was delighted with his new son, thinking privately that his fragility proclaimed him Nelson rather than Suckling, he himself had always been somewhat frail as a child. He smiled down into the cradle, as he stooped to put two coals on the fire.

'Pass me little Horace,' she said, 'if he is awake.'

'Oh, that is what he is to be, is it?' her husband laughed.

'Unless you would rather he were Edmund? He may be one or the other now, dearest, I think.'

Edmund Nelson lifted the child from the cradle and looked at him. 'Will you be Edmund,' he said, 'or Horatio? There, he yawns upon Horatio. Horatio it is! And if he is Horatio, perhaps your cousin Walpole will be his godfather.'

'I thought the same. And, my love: the first little Horace died on November the fifteenth, seven years ago. If Lord Walpole would agree, and if we might choose November the fifteenth...!'

'For the church christening? A capital plan, my love, indeed. The robe of the first Horace shall descend upon the second; and the second Lord Walpole shall sponsor him.'

The girl knocked and came in, carrying William in his night-shirt bellowing for his mother. It was as much as she could do to hold him being but rising twelve herself.

6

'Now my young man, kiss your mamma. Hoity toity, your nose is properly out of joint,' said his father, 'and accept it you must.' William's red face disappeared back to the nursery, howling above his father's shoulder. Sukey went amiably to the bed and leant upon it.

'There he is, your little brother,' her mother whispered.

Next in the procession came Granny, with Maurice by the hand.

'What do you think to another Horatio, Mamma?' said Catherine.

'I should think it very well.' There were Horatios in the Suckling family too. The Walpoles were a deal richer than the Nelsons and had been good to them: and what was the use of being well-connected if you failed to remind folk of the connection?

So the child was baptised privately by his father ten days after his birth, and when his mother was recovered, Mr Nelson chose a day in the second week of October and rose earlier than usual.

'And do, sir,' said Mrs Suckling, 'do pray remember to ask after Lord Walpole's sister, Lady Mary, will you not?' Lady Mary was the only surviving sister and not in the first bloom of her youth; but she was wooed patiently and ardently by Mrs Suckling's son, Maurice (he who had distinguished himself so recently in the *Dreadnought*). It was difficult to bring a lady who proved so shy to the point, from a ship at sea.

'Indeed I will, ma'am,' the rector promised. 'And if I have a scrap of a chance I shall rehearse your son's bravery.'

The rector waved to his wife upstairs, rounded the house, and set off into the sunrise for Wolterton.

His way was across country. He went, guided by spire or tower, by lanes and green ways and drove roads that he knew, where other men's sheep flowed along in a rippling current, their fleece tinged pink in the misty sunrise, their feet making a subdued throbbing before ever they hove into sight. On the brambles swollen blackberries still hung beaded with moisture, briars flaunted brave sprays of scarlet hips in the air, finches wheeled from the crimson hawthorns in crowded flurries, fieldfares rose from the pale stubble. The smooth leaves of elder bushes, cream and pink and crimson, dropped at a breath; woods were still green with the wet season, with here and there a yellowing birch or bronzing beech or golden chestnut spilling brilliant nuts. The fading bracken was like a light on the floor of the deep groves. The parson, a poetical man, savoured the colours and scents of autumn, making his way through Wighton and Hindringham, Brinton and Stody, Hunworth and Edgefield and Barningham. At length he saw Wickmere church tower and knew that due south lay Wolterton land. From the woodlands came that immemorial sad smell of wet leaves and damp wood, as piercing to the heart as ever are the smells of spring. To this traveller it was more so. He emerged from the trees to look across the expanse of shorn grass. Neat and foursquare, Lord Walpole's house at Wolterton was of rosy brick, warm in the October sun. A flight of stone steps led up to the entrance porch and the plain and regular windows of all three storeys were outlined in stone, pleasingly contrasted with the brick. As he watched, a little party came round the house: the children, three or four of them, and a nursemaid with a push-cart and a baby. He saw it all like the painting of a house, a landscape with figures. Below him on the right lay the round-towered church which would be ruinous enough in a few years to fulfil that romantic function which less fortunate landowners must devise by art.

He descended to the house with the instinctive modesty which became a somewhat poor clergyman approaching the residence of his patron's son. For the first Lord Walpole, seeing in Mr Nelson a devout and regular churchman and a Christian gentleman, had presented him to the parish he now held in the year of 1755.

On a November day they had moved from their small house at Sporle in a wagon (Maurice two-and-a-half, Sukey barely six months) their mother delighted at the prospect of a parsonage, a garden and land: and all near to her mother's old house at Warham. About Edmund Nelson, however, there was no pretence at a humility he did not feel. He had come of middle-class and educated folk himself, his wife from people on both sides slightly richer and grander. He was grateful for this, but his sense of obligation to his wife's cousins was entirely balanced by his own sense of fitness for the task he did, and his consciousness that he did it faithfully. Like other men, he accepted his station. The first Lord Walpole himself, returning here from his brother at Houghton or his brother-in-law at Raynham, was wont to say that his 'own little place' was like a humble but decent cottage, as what was his *should* look.

The children had seen Mr Nelson and broke away to find out who the horseman was. There was a little girl of seven or eight which would be Kate, he thought. There was a boy about a year older than Maurice who would be the new Horatio. With the red-cheeked nursemaid were two more little boys much the age of his own Sukey and William, and in the push-cart a baby.

'Papa! Papa! Here is Mr Nelson come to see you all the way from Burnham!' called Kate to her father by now standing at the top of the steps.

Lord Walpole was a man of about Edmund Nelson's own age, the middle-thirties, and after the fashion of his family he was already a little portly. He had a genial square face and broad forehead, the brown hair brushed back and falling almost to his jaw line which was a determined one, its determination already softened by the beginnings of a double chin. His mouth was firm and full and his nose round and regular. He wore a dark green coat and breeches, silvery grey stockings and a handsome waistcoat of clove-coloured stripes.

'How d'ye do, Mr Nelson! You've chosen a warm day to ride to Wolterton,' he said, shaking his hand squarely.

'How d'ye do, my Lord Walpole. I've been brought on my way by two little escorts...'

'Katy and Horatio,' said Lord Walpole, laying a broad hand on each. 'You left Burnham very early, I dare say?'

'Soon after daybreak,' the rector admitted, following his host up the steps and into the entrance hall. The floor was a grey-green marble like the sea on a windy day, the ceiling patterned with rich cornice and frieze.

'When were you last at Wolterton?' Lord Walpole asked quickly, not knowing whether his guest had ever been there.

'When we came to see your father about the living of Burnham Thorpe, my Lord.'

'Then he will have shown you the rooms on this floor of which he was prodigiously proud,' said Lord Walpole laughing, 'and I may conduct you downstairs to join the family.'

They sat in a sunny sitting room on the south side of the house looking out upon the broad grass lawns in front, and the lines of oak, Spanish chestnut and beech planted by Lord Walpole's father.

'And I hope Mrs Nelson is well?' Lady Walpole asked.

'She is well, my Lady, and happy in the acquisition of a new son, but two weeks ago. She plans to call him Horatio. Your father, my Lord, stood sponsor to our first Horatio who died. I come to ask you if you will perform the same duty for this child? It will make my wife happy if you will.'

'Gladly, I will. When is it to be? I will come myself if by any means I can.'

The rector explained about the date, and saw that the circumstance touched his hosts as he had hoped it would.

The November day was still and quiet, with weak sunshine behind the pallor of the sky, and the sense of falling everywhere: moisture falling, leaf falling, sap falling. Maurice swayed against Granny Suckling's fur muff and back again to his mother who held the bundle in the shawl. He liked blowing the fur, parting it into rosettes with naked middles. From this occupation he looked across at Granny Nelson, small and wrinkled and dark-eyed, who was laughing at him, and Aunt Mary beside her, her face as pale as the sky, and Aunt Alice pinker and younger. The wagon driven by Peter rounded the corner by Thorpe Common, passed Thorpe Hall below the church, and fetched up at the church yard: the rough grass round the gravestones was in tussocks of damp, faded gold.

The square church tower was softened in the misty light. Inside, it smelt damp and felt cool from the stone and the light was poor. First they sat and then they knelt and Maurice heard his father's voice saying prayers. Then suddenly everybody rose up and trooped to the back of the church and stood in a closed crowd in front of the stone font near the tower, so that they could all see his mother with the baby and his father saying the prayers. But he could see nothing. He slipped quietly away from Granny Suckling's skirts and met next a pair of fat stockinged legs. These belonged to Lord Walpole who smiled down at him, feeling the soft grip of a hand on his calf. Maurice then came to a long black cloak which belonged he knew to Dr Horace Hamond, the other godfather. He hurried past it (for Dr Hamond was not so certain to be friendly as Lord Walpole was) and at length he came to a soft brown cloak, where a gloved hand was held out to meet him. He looked up, saw a smiling lady whom he half-recognised and took the hand.

It was Mistress Joyce Pyle, come over from Lynn where her father was rector of St Edmund's church, to be the godmother to Horace. She was feeling a little overwhelmed by the grandeur of Lord Walpole's name and the hauteur of Dr Hamond's bearing as she stood empty-armed near the font, seeing the baby in Mrs Nelson's arms. Then she felt Maurice behind her. She sat him comfortably astride her hip and felt the family circle enfold her. Maurice was pleased that he could now see. He saw his mother nod at him and wave. His papa now had the baby in his arms and surprisingly turned to Lord Walpole and Dr Hamond and did not forget Miss Pyle and asked them what the baby's name was: which Maurice thought very odd since he knew. But they all three said 'Horatio' clearly and Miss Pyle coloured as she said it. Maurice watched her pale cheek with interest.

Back at the parsonage the circle of relations, after dining on good broiled mutton, sat till the light faded in the parlour, the ladies over a dish of tea, the gentlemen with some Madeira which Lord Walpole had thoughtfully brought and furnished themselves with the latest news about their close-knit families.

Lord Walpole enquired after his cousin Hamond's wife, who had lately had a son also called Horatio; Mrs Hamond was well, said the prebendary of Norwich and rector of Great Bircham, and had it not been for her own baby would have come to see Mrs Nelson's Horace christened. For she was Catherine Nelson's first cousin, and had been Dorothy Walpole Turner, daughter of Granny Suckling's dead brother

John. And Dr Horace Hamond was Lord Walpole's cousin, by virtue of his mother being Susan Walpole, youngest sister to the late prime minister, to Lord Walpole's father, and to Catherine Nelson's grandmother, Mary Turner. So there was no end to the cousinships of Walpole and Suckling and Turner which spread their network over the whole of Norfolk and beyond. It was, perhaps, from his mother that Dr Hamond took his sense of position: he kept himself informed of the doings of the nobility and his bishop informed about himself. In this he was as unlike Edmund Nelson as it was possible to be: and while neighbouring parsons such as he and Miss Pyle's father were called upon to preach in the cathedral in Norwich, no such summons ever (to his profound relief) reached Edmund Nelson, content to philosophise and poeticise in his own quiet parish by the sea.

So the gentlemen over their Madeira heard about the latest poaching outrage at Wolterton, when various malicious persons had killed an Indian cock pheasant 'of the gold sort'. And the ladies talked of the season, of the preserves, of the children. Miss Pyle sat between quiet Mary Nelson and her sister Alice, noticing the animation and happiness, the unexpected late blooming which had come over the younger. For it was said that Robert Rolfe who had followed Edmund Nelson at Hilborough church, was beginning to show a liking for Alice Nelson.

When the party showed signs of dispersing, Mrs Suckling lifted Horatio from the cradle whence William had been evicted, and carried him round to be drunk to, crooned over and fondled.

'The child's an angel,' she avowed. 'Not a sound, barely a gurgle, the whole day, I do protest.'

'May he ever stay so satisfied with life!' Lord Walpole said.

CHAPTER TWO

The Year Fifty-Nine

Maurice studied the sugary ice on a stone trough that stood below the pump spout. Peter's saw rasped rhythmically in the wood shed and the old man who came to help him trundled by with the wheelbarrow.

'They do say the smallpox be in the town then,' he called to Peter. 'Hev yer ma been called out?'

'I han't been at hers a week or more, I ought to have went yesterday, but my Mary keep me at home these days.'

Maurice saw William tottering from the back door, and waited until he was near.

'See me break the ice,' he said, and lifted his boot and crunched beautifully through it. William, aware that he had missed something, bellowed with frustrated rage. It was a few days before Christmas; his mother and his granny, wearing large white aprons, were standing at the scrubbed table in the kitchen. There were windows on both sides, one looking out on to William, forlorn at the pump, the other on to the grass courtyard enclosed by the two wings of the house. The sun shone on to copper pots and pans and skillets hanging on the wooden dresser, and upon blue and white china below them. In the great chimney-breast was the hearth and all the cooking gear and the oven in the wall. Sukey sat by the hearth with her doll; Granny rolled more pastry with a pale green china pin enamelled with dark green flowers, and the cat, whom Maurice loved and William tormented, sat on the window sill, looking down longingly on to Horace's cradle.

'Mamma.'

'What is it, Maurice? We're busy baking.'

Both stopped their fussy activity and looked at him.

'The old man told Peter the smallpox be in the town. What is it?'

'That's ill news, daughter.'

Maurice walked over the square red floor tiles and put his hands on the table and his nose over it. The air near some new baked pies was hot.

'What is it?' he persisted.

'It's a bad illness, Maurice, a fever. You are covered in spots and you ache, much worse than your earache.'

'And then you get better?'

'Sometimes. But many people die.'

'My coz Townshend died,' said Granny. 'I call her coz for there was but five years between us. But in reality she was my aunt. She was my mother's youngest sister, Maurice, and her name was Dorothy Walpole, and she married Lord Townshend, and went to live at Raynham with him.'

'What happened next?'

'Why, she had seven children, five sons and two daughters, Dolly and Molly. They are my cousins, Mrs Dorothy Cowper and Mrs Mary Cornwallis. When she was about forty she died of the smallpox...left all her fine children, that was very sad, was it not? But the same thing happened to me when I was a child of ten. My mother died. And I went back to live at Houghton where I had been born (not the grand place it is now, the earlier house) because my papa was much in London. Several years I was there, with Galfridus and Dorothy and Susan Walpole.'

Maurice was silenced.

'Go and fetch William,' suggested his mother quickly.

'People always said,' went on Mrs Suckling, trimming her pastry, 'that when Aunt Townshend died, things were never the same again between her husband and her brother, Sir Robert. Not long after, Lord Townshend quarrelled with his brother-in-law for good, and came down to Raynham to farm the land. And left public life altogether.'

'People say she was a beauty.'

'She was. She was mighty civil and affable too, eager to please, with everybody. Did I ever tell you the story of the alderman? Some city ladies came to call upon her in London, while Lord Townshend was secretary of state. She asked them where they lived, and one said, near Aldermanbury...'

Her daughter burst into laughter, remembering: 'And Aunt Townshend hoped Alderman Bury was very well!'

'Just so! She was Lord Townshend's second wife and much loved I believe. I heard a strange tale once that she walks sometimes. In a dark brown gown.'

'So should I walk, should not you, if I had left seven children?' said the rector's wife fiercely.

The rector came in, comically sniffing the air.

'My dear, Maurice has heard the men talking of smallpox.'

'Oh? I shall hear soon enough,' he replied, going over to smile at Horace and stroke his cheek.

As soon, he did. George Goggs, whose turn it was with the book, paid out sums to the families who had been struck. The rector prayed in church for the sick by name thereby impressing it upon his people to use caution in avoiding infection. Mary was forbidden to go home to Deepdale, Peter was advised to keep out of the inn for his wife's sake, who bore a son on the eve of Twelfth Night.

Last year's wet summer had caused a battle to begin in the paper as to the girth of roots and turnips, a subject of passionate interest to any Norfolker. Mr Roger North of Rougham was said to have a radish with a root of two feet sixteen and a half inches...a horse radish indeed.

'That newspaperman means three feet four and a half!' said Mamma laughing, while Horace lay kicking before the fire.

But a worse effect of the wet was the distemper amongst the horned cattle since the autumn: there were those in the county whose herds were destroyed and who never recovered.

This year there were fine and lovely days in February, and March came in like a lamb gently, the earth was dry and warm, crumbling in the hands and smelling strong as Parson Nelson kneeled to sow his seeds: peas and beans and radishes and onions, the sun hot on him like the hand of God. His wife would walk up with the children, Horace against her shoulder, his face twitching with interest and pleasure. But if the month came in like a lamb, it went out like a lion, blowing a violent storm and driving a ship on shore near Wells.

'She were called the *Catherine* ma'am, and the master and all the crew perished in the sea, they bring 'em all up into the church all dead,' reported Peter. Maurice was shocked about the dead sailors and by the name of the ship too.

'Here is my good Uncle Thomas's house at Sporle up for the letting again. This is the third week I have seen it advertised,' remarked Edmund Nelson one April evening. 'Cousin Bartholomew's affairs have gone ill, he is bankrupt, and I fear Uncle Thomas must remove to save his son's fortunes.' He was fond of Uncle Thomas who was the eldest brother of three, his own father having been the youngest.

'He will be about seventy-six, poor old man.'

'My dear, it may be that Uncle Thomas feels that large house too empty for him? Do you remember how proud he was of his vines?' she added.

'I do. His furniture is to be disposed of "being plain and useful". It smites me to the heart.'

'But my dear, we all grow old. He is going to live in the small house. Or with Bartholomew. To be cared for.'

'I remember it thronging with people, my love, that place! All Uncle Thomas's family, Mary and Barbara who kept house for him (for their mother was dead already you know) and his sons, Thomas and Bartholomew and William, and little Edmund. And all of us from Hilborough, *our* Mary and me and Alice and Tam'sin and Papa. Mamma was not there, for John was only just born. All gathered for a harvesting we were. And the great wagons bringing in the grain until the moon was up. And the noise in that barn where the supper was for the men, beef and dumplings and beer!'

His wife saw into his feelings and sympathised. 'Such a large family, and only Cousins Bartholomew and Edmund left,' she said. Cousin Edmund, who had like her husband been at Caius College, was now rector of Congham, having married the lady who was patroness of that parish.

'It was a terrible tragedy about the daughters. They were suffocated, were not they? Mary and Barbara?'

'Both in a night. It was the charcoal fumes from the brazier set in their bedroom. One parching cold night. It was while I was at Cambridge. And then that William! Sent to Eton, did no good, proved very irregular. Went off to sea.'

'A life at sea will make or mar a man.'

'Uncle Thomas had many connections with the ship-masters round here. I wish he might have been spared Bartholomew's failure.'

'Nobody will remember for long,' Catherine said, more worldly-wise than he.

She shook out a garment diminutive but broad, which she had made for William soon to be breeched.

'Talking of difficulties, my love: have you heard aught of your brother John lately?'

'Not a scrap of a pen. There is another of them. He is twenty-three now, and nothing to show of achievement.'

'I wonder he does not go for a soldier. He is said to like change and adventure.'

'He dislikes hard work and regularity! But I wonder too that he does not, there is plenty of opportunity while this war goes on.'

Gradually, secretly, as April and May drew on, 1759 declared itself to be the most gorgeous of all summers, a summer that fired the imagination and coloured all memory. Catherine Nelson gloried in it: Horace was blessed with heat and sunshine, slept for hours outside, crawled upon dry safe grass scented with thyme and waving with meadow flowers, finally raising himself to his uncertain legs to follow a vivid late butterfly, an Admiral, upon the bergamot.

A field path due east of Edmund Nelson's church at Thorpe brought one to the confines of the great estate of Holkham, and then joined the quickest bridle path to Wells, an old track said to be Roman. The rector took it often upon his mare, glimpses of the huge Palladian house appearing (strictly classical, and to him severely charmless) with the innocent sheep feeding the lawns between. Close neighbours though they were, the parson of Thorpe knew not the family at all. In May this year the earl died. Holkham Hall, built to display the treasures of his Italian travels, was as yet barely finished inside: and alas for the hopes and griefs of men, his only son Edward had died childless before him.

As the glory of the summer unfolded, Parson Nelson, with Peter and other willing hands, cut his sweet-scented hay and saw his sheep sheared, gathered his fruit and watched his vegetables swell and was betimes in hiring horses and harvesters for the reaping. Other activities were equally blessed in the fairness of the season. Though the celebrated Mr Handel had died in London in April (having taken to his bed after conducting *Messiah* two weeks previously)—though the master be no more young Mr Charles Burney the organist presented his usual June concert and ball at King's Lynn. Mrs Suckling visited her Aunt Susan Hamond at South Wootton whence together they might enjoy the concert.

And all over Norfolk the militia were gathering. Brigadier George Townshend (of the family at Raynham) had got his Militia Bill through parliament in 1757 with the help of his brother Charles and of William Pitt: was it not better to raise Britons to defend their country against French invasion than to rely upon German mercenaries from King George's Hanoverian domains? In Norfolk, despite some outcry, the scheme had gone bravely ahead, General Townshend being ably assisted by Mr William Windham of Felbrigg, by Sir Armine Wodehouse, and by the young Lord Lieutenant at Houghton, the third earl of Orford. Opposers like Lord Townshend (the general's own father) and the late old Earl of Leicester pointed out the dangers of a standing army, the difficulties of training country labourers and artisans to be of any martial use at all. (It was rumoured that the hot-headed young general had been so incensed at the opposition of the earl that he had actually challenged the poor old man to a duel: he had protested with frail laughter that he was not likely to turn duellist at his age, who could not hit a barn door with a gun.)

Now the Norfolk battalion was mustering in earnest: the Norfolk men were for London and Portsmouth and who knew where? The Earl of Leicester's 'blustering' bands of 'rude militia' were become tolerably trim troops: and the honour had fallen to them of being the first militia to march for duty outside their county, to take the place of regular troops needed abroad.

> Her brave *MILITIA* shall abroad be fear'd
> And by her sons at home with gratitude revered

wrote one of the rhymesters in Edmund Nelson's newspaper.

Young Maurice, in Burnham Market with his papa one day, was entranced to see a small company with fife and drum set forth for Lynn: he was given a suitable hat and sword-stick by his patriotic mother and paraded often that summer up and down the grass outside the parsonage windows. William would follow, unconscious of the reason but happy in the role; the baby, Horace, not able to keep up, would watch with rapt attention and crow with approval.

When the column of nigh on a thousand men set off from Norwich in the sweltering heat of that early July, their drums rolling passionately, and with George Walpole, Earl of Orford marching on foot at their head, a frenzy of pride and patriotism swept over the county. The extreme warmth of the weather soon drove them to march by night and to rest by day. In Hyde Park, His Majesty himself reviewed them, calling out often, 'They are brave fellows. They are fine fellows.' He enquired the name of every officer as he passed, and condescended to pull off his hat to each: Captain de Grey, Captain Henley and many another. But the heat! They were almost melted with heat! The people stood with full tankards in the road to treat their parched heroes with beer. Norfolk was in the highest esteem for its loyalty and readiness to defend its country.

Moreover Lord Orford himself attracted that kind of aura which makes the hero. Behind him was the grandeur of the vast palace at Houghton which his grandfather, the great Sir Robert Walpole, had built: and although he himself had been totally insensible to his situation of impoverishment when he succeeded his father, and had talked of selling Houghton with a coolness masquerading as philosophy, nevertheless the palatial seat remained and the political reputation of his grandfather still stood high in the estimation of all faithful Whigs in Norfolk. And, despite his insouciance the third earl's older relations had to admit that his figure was charming, that he had to perfection the easy, genuine air of the man of quality. He had begun to show signs of adding to these advantages the kind of eccentricity which gives richness to a man's reputation. Had he not once driven a team of four stags from Houghton Hall to Newmarket? A pack of hounds had picked up the scent and joined in frenzied pursuit. The ostler of the inn had slammed the yard doors to in the very jaws of the slavering hounds. A pretty story which was embellished in repetition. Then too, he was interested in the mediaeval sport of hawking and kept a mews. Now at the golden age of twenty-eight he led his men out of London to

Hammersmith, Kingston and at last to Portsmouth where they arrived on July the twenty-fourth of this memorably hot summer. The following week a wave of great rejoicing broke over the country, for Prince Ferdinand of Brunswick, ally of the great Frederick of Prussia, had won a victory over the French between Petershagen and Minden: and he had won it with the help of English soldiers and English money (far too much English money, as many said).

Life was full (the rector often felt as he read his newspaper) of diversions and good will and scientific progress, more pleasing than the frenzies of war. This summer were called the first meetings in Norwich to consider erecting a county hospital like the excellent Dr Addenbroke's in Cambridge. Then someone had invented a surprising machine that travelled without horse or horses about the rate of five or six miles an hour: and what was more they were to make one that would carry two tons' weight upon a rail way. And late in August the reverend Mr Wesley, the Methodist, announced his intention of being (God willing) in Norwich. Now had he have been coming to Lynn, Edmund Nelson said to himself slipping into the tongue of his native county, I would have went off quietly out of interest and curiosity to hear him.

In the event, Mr Wesley preached to a congregation in his Norwich tabernacle which he found as rude and noisy as a bear-garden: in his opinion, he informed them, they were the most ignorant, self-conceited, self-willed, fickle, untractable, disorderly, disjointed society that he knew in the three kingdoms. His eyes blazed, his long locks shook, his great nose brooded over them hawk-like, as he hissed out the dreadful words. They were abashed and cowed and disappointed, a band of noisy cheerful good-hearted citizens become Methodists, enjoying their meetings mainly for the warmth and the company: and their goodness was proved in that not one took offence. A sun with the strength of midsummer blazed upon the evangelists as they rode back to Colchester.

And General Wolfe had taken the town of Quebec in Canada! He had scaled the heights to the west of it and had died most gloriously in the assault on the thirteenth of September, Brigadier General George Townshend himself had survived to receive the surrender of the town. Hot-headed and quarrelsome though he was—(and an accomplished satirical cartoonist who offended his superiors from dukes to generals)—to Norfolkers he was the first begetter of their much cried-up militia. On their return, Norwich rejoiced with a bonfire and illuminations, General Townshend's regiment being drawn up in the market-place and firing several volleys. The day after Christmas he appeared himself in the city and was made a freeman at once: along with George Earl of Orford and Colonel Armine Wodehouse and not least Colonel William Windham.

Catherine Nelson hearing the brave news decided to drink all deserving healths. It was Sunday the twenty-first of October, it was the second anniversary of her brother Maurice's victory at Cap François! It was a particularly wonderful still hot day, like summer, as if we had plundered the East and West Indies of sunshine!

'My dear, it is the twenty-first of October!' she announced. 'There are Sucklings, Townshends and Walpoles to toast! Run along little Maurice, and beg your grandmamma to come!'

The brave events of the year inspired many rhymesters: the effusion Catherine loved best being called The Year Fifty-Nine, a bombastic jingle excellent for dancing children upon the knee. There were nine spirited verses boasting of deeds in India, at Senegal, Minden, Quebec, Crown Point, Ticonderoga, and in the Channel. She soon had much of it by heart.

"'Whilst Rodney and Hawke watched the flat-bottomed boats
At Paris Belle-Isle cut poor Englishmen's throats..."

'The cruel, bloodthirsty Frenchmen Maurice, but we were a match for them, listen to this.

"Hawke burnt 'em and sunk 'em and 'twas mighty fine
To see how they ran in the year fifty-nine!"'

and she gave Horace an extra big bounce upon the couplet. The rector laughed quietly, watching from the window.

'I think you must take it from your father,' he remarked meditatively.

'Take what, my love?'

'Why, you are as fiery as any man against the French: and it reminds me of the character your mamma sometimes gives your papa!'

'You are thinking of Papa's famous quarrel with the squire?' she laughed.

'I am, I love to hear your mother tell it, it soars so far beyond my capacity. "Doctor," said the squire after they had had hot words, "your gown is your protection." "Is it so?" retorted your father, "but, by God! It shall not be yours!" And he flung it off and thrashed him! I never heard that he thrashed you children!'

'We were not of an age. I was the eldest and only five when he died. I can barely remember him, but that he used to toss me up when I ran to him. Now come quick, Maurice, see how they run in the Year Fifty-Nine!' And she clapped her hands and drove him laughing up the stairs.

CHAPTER THREE

The Nelsons of Hilborough

With the new year came Alice Nelson, the rector's sister from
Hilborough, a mature but none the less excited bride, to be married
by her brother from her sister-in-law's home. She was not beautiful
(she had a slight cast in one eye) but she was illuminated now with the
glow of a happiness unexpected to herself. That it was unexpected to
her mother would be questionable. Mrs Mary Nelson was a little woman
of great character and determination, which showed itself in her bright,
dark eyes and active manner. She had been the daughter of a prosperous
baker in the Petty Cury in Cambridge and had grown up in that keen
atmosphere of ambitious self-betterment: Mary Bland herself had
helped in the wholesome, hard family business before she had migrated
to London, and was later repaid with some of its rewards. For very soon
after her marriage to Edmund Nelson (the elder), her father John
Bland had purchased the presentation of the parish of Hilborough.
When the living became vacant in 1735, he presented it to his son-in-
law, who moved there from East Bradenham with his family. To
Hilborough too Grandfather Bland had retired, after the death of his
wife Thomazin. (Edmund Nelson the younger well remembered this,
for it had occurred while he was at Cambridge, a time when he haunted
the Bland bakery often.) It was natural that when her husband died
Mrs Nelson should give her son the Hilborough living, now hers to
present. Edmund and Catherine Nelson had held with Hilborough
the vicarage of Sporle, given to his father by the provost and fellows of
Eton his old school and now granted to him. Edmund Nelson had not
touched the income from Hilborough, needed to pay his father's debts
and to maintain his mother and the rest of the family, Mary, Alice,
Thomazin and John; and when Lord Walpole had offered him Burnham
Thorpe he had accepted it gladly with an eye on his increasing family,
not lavishly provided for by the eighty pounds-odd from Sporle. The
widow determined that her choice should provide not only a worthy
incumbent for Hilborough but a husband for one of her daughters.
For the eldest, Mary, there was little hope: at her mother's beck and

call from her girlhood and shadowed beneath her personality she had passed the age of asserting her right to marry almost before she was aware. Thomazin the youngest had married by this time a prosperous shoemaker called John Goulty from Norwich. Alice was the marriageable daughter. Robert Rolfe had taken his time, had been perfectly prepared to remain single or resign the living, had he found himself unable to like either young lady. He was a mild and not very strong man, well-connected, the son himself of a parson. What is more, as Mrs Nelson assumed, he would inherit some fortune. Robert Rolfe proposed to Alice towards the end of 1759, the beauty of that glorious summer having helped the ripening of their affections: Alice Nelson accepted him, and was on her way to Burnham to prepare for her wedding on January the twenty-second and to spend the requisite time beneath her brother's roof.

When the wagon stopped at the turning down to Creake Abbey Alice Nelson knew that her long journey was nearly over: when you had passed Creake ruins, the Nelsons used to say, you were not far from Thorpe parsonage. To be sure, Alice could see very little of the ruins in the falling dark of this winter afternoon, but she knew how they lay, tumbled and ivied over near the old Abbey farmhouse, lofty enough to give the beholder a shock if he saw the sky suddenly pale through their blank windows. Now a few lights glowed from the house, as Mrs Powdich prepared to alight with her baskets. She had joined the carrier at Fakenham, as Alice Nelson herself had, and she had very soon made herself acquainted with Alice's name, relations and important business: and of course she knew the reverend and Mrs Nelson along at Thorpe.

Very soon, the lights of the parsonage bestowed upon Alice the same primaeval welcome. The family had been waiting and the door was flung open. Light, warmth, screams of excitement and Mrs Nelson's motherly arms greeted the anxious bride.

'Oh my dear, come in, come in, you must be so cold and weary!' said her sister-in-law: while her brother brought in the precious portmantle and box, and Maurice and Sukey seized her hands and William her skirts, and in the parlour a little creature smaller than them all stood swaying in his smock and gazing at her. It was Horatio, fifteen months old. His mother swept him up and put him in Alice's arms.

'There now, my precious, you kiss your Aunt Alice! Do you not long for some of your own?' she whispered.

Alice nodded mutely, nursing Horace. She was five years younger than Catherine Nelson whose warm easy certainty gave her the reassurance she now needed. To be the centre, the mother, of so delightful a small world! Of course she longed for it.

The marriage was a quiet family one. The journey in January had been deemed too cold for old Mrs Nelson, so Aunt Mary too had been left behind. Mrs Smith, the wife of Edmund Nelson's good friend, the rector of Burnham Westgate, came with one of her handsome daughters, Everilda, both ladies (for want of any closer relations) signing the register. For Mrs Nelson and her mother stayed to supervise affairs in the kitchen, and watch over the children. Catherine Nelson believing herself to be pregnant again, was pondering the mixture of unaccountable joys and inescapable difficulties of motherhood. She had loved Horace's babyhood so much, the little boy was so entwined still with her heart, that she found it hard to conceive that anyone should follow him and demand that place. Yet she knew that there might be many, that for each she must try to be the fountain of trust. For Horace, a great natural love had overwhelmed her like a grace from heaven, the moment she had set eyes upon his tiny defenceless form.

Mrs Rolfe, glowing in her fur-trimmed mantle, drove off with Mr Robert Rolfe next day, back to the rectory at Hilborough. It was empty for them: Mrs Nelson and Aunt Mary were moved to a smaller but charming house of rosy brick (upon the other side of the main road at Hilborough) soon to be dubbed the nunnery because of its exclusively female inhabitants.

Maurice would be seven on the twenty-fourth of May. For a year or so now he had gone to Papa's study in the mornings to learn his letters, his numbers, his catechism and his creed. When the spring came, the rector took him into Burnham Westgate, where one William Holsworth kept a not too large and perhaps not very prosperous school: Mr Nelson had decided it must do for a beginning, it was nearer than Wells. Through the summer, Maurice would set off on his own for the two-and-a-half mile walk, his satchel with some food in it on his back. But sometimes one of the farmers picked him up, Mr Emerson, or Mr Goggs, or Mr Powdich, or a labourer with a cart, and then he delighted in spinning along the lanes shoulder-high with lady's lace, and hawthorn so near he could lean out and touch it, scattering its fading petals like snow.

The rector turned his attention to Susannah. He began by dancing her on his knee, and telling her that a little girl whose godpapa was high sheriff of Norfolk must of necessity learn to read. Sukey, who had not met Mr John Berney, her mother's cousin who had sponsored her, had held for many years a dim impression of a godfather as tall as a tree. She was a sensible little girl and not averse to application and soon made headway with her letters. Her grandmamma gave her a sampler to sew: when she could spell a word, she might sew it. Sukey became very quickly devoted to her needle: and was not unknown to use it as a weapon of immediate efficacy against William: for William had reached the acquisitive and destructive age which spreads disaster, and if he offended, tried to regain favour by clowning. He was a large, hungry little boy of three-and-a-half; his father would give him the fattest dumpling, his mother the largest piece of cake, in almost unconscious propitiation.

'You over-indulge that child I fear,' Mrs Suckling would remark when William's yells had achieved their usual reward. There was something of envy in Sukey's needle. Horace, amenable and sunny-tempered, and so sensitive to blame that the tears would start to his eyes and the blood to his cheeks at any mild rebuke, was as yet unaware of these stresses.

The usual procession of quiet events filled the summer before the birth of Catherine Nelson's fifth child. Yarmouth longed for visitors for its new sea-baths, the most complete in the kingdom: but the widowed countess at Holkham, on the other hand, made it known that that place was to be viewed only on a Tuesday. Edmund Nelson's neighbour at the church of North Creake died and was succeeded by the honourable and reverend Dr Poyntz, a learned man from Christ Church, Oxford, and very highly-connected.

Peter arrived one day with a tale of French prisoners escaped from York Castle. They had taken a coble in Bridlington bay to go over to France, but the wind had forced them to put into Brancaster, where they had been quickly surrounded by local fishermen jealous of their rights and unable to understand the men's story. They had surrendered, and they looked right bedraggled, Peter said. Maurice was sorry for the Frenchers but he did not say so to his mamma, tired as she was within a month of her new child, and little as she liked the French.

The child was born on Saturday the twentieth of September, and Granny Suckling was delighted to see a little girl. The rector agreed it was time for a little girl and said at once that she should have her grandmother's name, Ann. Her grandmother was her godmother, and her new uncle, Mr Rolfe, her godpapa. She was a pale little creature at first, but she soon began to look bonnier: and Sukey adored her and was allowed to nurse her. Almost before Mrs Nelson was up, little Horace had his second birthday. He was brought to her bed to see his small sister and smiled with some curiosity and reservation.

The rector lifted both his smallest sons, William and Horace, under his arms and bidding Maurice follow led them all to his study. They were four male, four female now (counting Granny). He must consolidate his help with his sons. He would tell them a story of buried treasure.

'A day or two past, Maurice,' he began, 'a labourer was clearing a ditch at West Wretham, and do you know what he found?'

'A dead corpse,' said Maurice, whose mind ran on French prisoners and drowned sailors.

"No, no, no. A pot, Maurice—William, leave the poker, no. You'll hurt Horace! Can you guess what was in the pot?'

Maurice considered, and understandably replied: 'A rabbit, a rabbit stew.'

William's attention was happily caught by this and he left the poker and began to listen.

'Not any kind of stew, it was not a cooking-pot. It was a pot containing treasure: it had nearly six hundred coins in it, about the size of groats, you know, threepenny pieces...'

'Were they gold?' asked Maurice who thought this the only ware for treasure.

'I don't know that they were gold, but they were *Roman* coins, Maurice, that is what I am trying to tell you, buried hundreds and hundreds of years ago by the Romans!'

'Who were the Romans?' his son asked, defending himself against William who had now lost interest in this pot.

The parson smiled ruefully. His own sense of history was keen and poetical, he would have loved to find the pot of coins, just as he loved the ancient records of his parish and the keeping of his own faithfully for the generations to come. But how could he put the Romans in perspective to Maurice, and communicate his own excitement? Being a father was uncommonly difficult.

But before long an event occurred which was much easier to explain to Maurice, and who was to say it was of less historical importance? George II, aged seventy-seven, had a fit of apoplexy and died, and the new King, his grand-son, was proclaimed the same day: a solemn, earnest, impressionable young man, too much (some folk said) beneath the sway of his guardian and tutor, the Marquis of Bute, but anxious above all things to understand his duty to his country and perform it.

Other endings and other beginnings echoed the start of the new reign, like rising and falling chords in the symphony of human life. The ancient Norfolk family of Paston, ruined with mismanagement and intractable circumstance, was called into mind again by long lists of the creditors of William Paston, Earl of Yarmouth, published in the newspaper: thirty-two years after his death his debts were at last to be paid. In Norwich Cathedral a new organ was opened at the end of November with a new anthem. Edmund Nelson had news that his ineffective cousin Bartholomew had lost his wife Dorothy at Congham; and that his prosperous cousin William, rector, had lost his bay gelding from Hillington. And in a garden at the Hole-in-the-Wall in St Andrew's parish in Norwich, a pear tree burst into blossom in late November. The superstitious said it was for the new King, but the more scientific looked back at last year's long and torrid heat, which had no doubt thrown Nature out of her usual placid but relentless order.

CHAPTER FOUR

Cousin John Turner

The earth, the grass, the trees gave off that sweet, promising scent which is April.

'April showers brings May flowers, that's what they say my little Horace,' Mrs Suckling said, jumping him along beside her, as they walked through the budding orchard trees towards the house. William ran up from behind and seized her other hand roughly in his.

'Jump me, jump me! Like Horace,' he asked.

She endeavoured to do so. 'I cannot my boy, you are too heavy. Now where's Mamma?'

'Getting ready for cousin John,' called Sukey. 'These flowers are for the table.'

'Should you not call him "Sir John", my child?'

'Mamma calls him cousin John,' she said.

'Ah, but Mamma is not a little girl. He is my cousin, and Mamma's second cousin.'

'He's my cousin,' said William loudly and acquisitively. He repeated his claim many times. Horace smiled, having no opinion on the matter.

Sir John Turner arrived from Warham in time to dine at three. Mrs Suckling's cousin John who lived at the hall at Warham, where Catherine Nelson could remember visiting her grandfather Turner, was a handsome, melancholy man of pale countenance, deep-set eyes and hair now greyed. The details of his inheriting the property were a little unusual. Catherine Nelson's grandfather, Sir Charles, the first Turner to own Warham, had died in 1738 leaving his brother John as heir: for his own son had died before him and left only daughters: and both his own daughters (Mrs Suckling and her sister Mrs Fowle) were married. Sir Charles's death however being followed swiftly the next January by his brother's, his *nephew* John had come into the inheritance. And this was he.

He had followed his uncle, moreover, into parliament as one of the members for King's Lynn. Indeed for many years a Turner had been member for Lynn and there had been one occasion when the two brothers, Sir Charles and John, had been members together. Turners had been merchants at Lynn now for several generations. Having married into the prosperous wine-importing business of the city, they had come south originally from Yorkshire.

'Well, cousin, so you and Mr Horace Walpole bear Lynn once more into the new Parliament,' remarked Mrs Suckling, as they sat around the large mutton pie. From the kitchen across the passage quickly subdued pandemonium reached their ears from time to time.

There had been a general election towards the end of March in this year of 1761. Just after Easter Lynn had welcomed, proclaimed and feasted the same two members as before.

'Aha, yes. Was you there, ma'am?' he replied.

'I was, by chance I was. I spent Easter with my Aunt Hamond, at South Wootton, you know…'

'And how is the old lady? A Walpole still? Still as mighty as ever? Lord, she must be advancing in age by now, cousin? How does she do?'

Mrs Suckling's Aunt Hamond was the last of Sir Robert Walpole's sisters to survive. Mrs Suckling's own mother Mary Walpole had died first, and Sir Charles Turner had taken another Mary, a widow, to wife in his later years. Aunt Dorothy Townshend had died of the smallpox. Aunt Susan Hamond lived on, outliving all her own generation and many of the next partly because she was last of a very large family. Her son was that Dr Horace Hamond who had come to be godfather to Horatio.

'She does remarkable well, sir, considering she is seventy-three. But I must tell you this tale of the late election. It was a fair day, not too cold, and she must needs go she said, to see how her young nephew comported himself. "Upon my word, Madam," said I, "your nephew Mr Walpole is no longer to be considered young, and watched over,"— he being as you know a man in his early forties, and moreover with all the civility of manners which you may expect from a life in the city and the moving in court circles…'

'He is a literary man, is he not?' the rector asked with interest.

'I believe he is so.'

'Do you know him, cousin? Did you know him before this occasion?' Edmund Nelson pursued.

'I think I saw him but once before at his father's funeral,' Sir John replied, 'which was sixteen years ago now: this is the first time he has been at Houghton since. He seemed melancholy at the changes there; his nephew, Lord Orford, does little to discourage encroaching brambles and splitting stone.'

'I've heard as much. What is Mr Horace Walpole like?' the parson said.

'He is a slight pale oval faced man,' Mrs Suckling went on, 'his hair receding from a round high brow. Much intellect so they say, and a rapier tongue. His lips are precise, pursed up. Almost, it is a womanish face: he has never married you know. When we first reached Lynn the people were so thick, I thought we should never make our way through them. But Aunt Hamond leaned out, and waved her cane, and proclaimed herself a Walpole with a right to hear her relation. We heard little of Mr Walpole's address, but afterwards thousands of people carried him up to the market-place. Aunt Hamond seemed much ruffled about something, and was tossing her head and clicking her tongue and so soon as he was safe inside the inn she confronted him and came straight out with it. "Child," (I distinctly heard her call him "child".) "Child, you have done a thing today that your father never did in all his life; you *sat,* as they carried you; he always stood the whole time." He only looked amazed for an instant and then he answered as cool as you please "Madam, when I am placed in a chair, I conclude I am to sit in it."'

'Oh , what a wit!' Edmund Nelson said, laughing. 'I wish mine served me so.'

'He remained perfectly grave, you know, the whole time, though that mouth was pinched up more than a little.'

'And was Aunt Hamond much put out?' asked her daughter.

'Oh, he covered it quickly with smooth civility. He went on to say that as he could not hope to imitate his father in great things, he had no ambition to mimic him in little. So you talked with him, cousin?'

'I did, yes, when we could hear ourselves. There was much huzzaing and drinking of bumpers and singing of songs and pipe-smoking, and six-penny whisk and a ball as usual. I dare say it all seemed rude and noisy to a gentleman of his refined tastes,' said Lynn's other member, 'but I never once catched him looking bored or disgusted. He said all ministers begin to long for peace, except Mr Pitt. He himself thinks we must have peace soon for we cannot afford much more of war...'

'Oh but we must have victory, peace only with victory, I agree with Mr Pitt!' Mrs Nelson affirmed. Her husband smiled to himself.

'Mr Walpole implied,' went on Sir John, 'that talks go on now with the French as to peace. If we can keep what we have gained, then I hope it will come soon.'

And Mr Nelson and Sir John proceeded to arrange the terms of the peace in the far corners of the world.

When they were in the parlour, Maurice's pale smiling face appeared flattened at the window.

'Come and say how-do-you-do to Sir John, and bring the children in, Maurice,' his mother called.

Sukey came first, her round pudding face red from the too-hot kitchen; she bobbed prettily and gave Sir John her hand and some primroses.

'Well my little maid, are those for me? And how do you do? So, Maurice, you are now the schoolboy. And here is the stout William whom I have met once before. Now who is this?'

'This is Horatio,' his mother said, holding him by the hand, 'and he has not met his cousin John and wishes to say how do you do?'

'Now then, Horatio,' said Sir John, whisking him briskly on to his knee, and beginning to trot him with such vigour that he could scarcely say the words quickly enough.

> ' "The man in the Moon
> Came down too soon.
> And asked his way to Norridge;
> He went by the South
> And burnt his mouth
> With supping cold plum porridge!" '

And he let the child down through his knees so suddenly that his mother feared for his dinner.

Horace's cheeks went scarlet and his blue eyes as round as speedwells but his spirit held. When he had recovered from his surprise and was safely enthroned once more, he laughed.

'There's a brave, mettlesome lad. Horace, you must grow a little, catch up with William. How old are you?'

Horace was not sure.

'He's but two and a half, cousin.'

'Ah, then he has time to grow. Now, William, what are you saying? You wish to descend from the moon too? You are another proposition altogether. A Norfolk dumpling to be sure, you need no plum porridge!'

'And this,' said Mrs Suckling proudly, 'is your cousin Catherine's latest daughter and my namesake, little Ann. Six months old. Is she not beautiful, sir?'

'She is, ma'am. Like her mother and her grandmother,' said Sir John, bowing. When the visitor prepared to depart, Mr Nelson bore him on his way to the overseer, to sign the parish accounts. Isaac Emerson had the book at the Manor Farm, and it had not been signed for four years, since old Mr Lee Warner had died at Walsingham. It must be done every year, by one of the Justices, as was Sir John.

That year of 1761 Isaac Emerson and George Goggs, in charge of the book, recorded the death of Goody Craske early in March, and a pair of linens for her boy left unpaid for at the draper's, and the subsequent illness of old Craske, who used to mend up the highways. Isaac and George differed about Craske's name; George asserting it was Craske and Isaac spelling it as Crasp, or, even more wildly, Crast: but when he asked the old man himself whether he took a 'k' or a 'p' or a 't', he shook his head in bewilderment. Then there was the question of the Bees. Thorpe swarmed as Isaac put it with Bees, 'if it warn't one Bee, 'twere another. If they was busy bees, Parson, worker bees, I wouldn't mind,' said he, pleased with his joke. 'But they aren't that.' Last year they had had to set up Bee's boy, when he was apprenticed, with shoes and stockings and shirt and frock and hat: then it was Bridget Bee's turn for shoes and caps and those essential articles of country wear in winter which Isaac called 'pattings'. And when it came to paying the widow who looked after William Bee and his family when his wife lay in, Isaac entered slyly 'for William Bee's being.' George Goggs laughed in a high falsetto as he read this, and carried the joke on.

One sultry day, when the heat even at Thorpe pressed down upon them, when William was furious and Horace fretful and even Sukey sighing and irritable, the rector put his family into the wagon. His wife held Ann, and mopped her own brow and the baby's with a kerchief. They would drive down to Overy, have a breath of the sea, let the children play, and collect Maurice.

A cool breeze blessed them from the sea. The tide was low, but returning: in the channel glittered a cool sparkling strip of shallow water. Horace, feeling the wind upon his hot face, set off at once to reach it. He tripped over piles of sharp empty mussel shells, stumbled upon strong-smelling seaweed, was thrown on his nose by anchor ropes, but nothing hindered his determination. The child reached the edge, flung himself down, and put his hands into the cool water, now beginning to swell. He put one hand to his mouth, tasted salt, and wisely withdrew it. He lay gazing upon the channel.

Catherine Nelson had collected herself and seen him.

'Horace! Come back!' she called. 'Run quickly, Sukey. Fetch Horace. Mr Nelson, look at that child, right at the edge of the water.'

'Intelligent Horatio,' he said, loosening his stock.

'Yes, but...Ah, he's heard. He's coming.'

'He is usually obedient,' said his father. 'Let us go further down, then he can indulge his taste for salt water.'

The whole afternoon, till Maurice was fetched and they ate cake and drank elderflower water by the bank, Horace played by the sea. William must be played with, Sukey preferred her mother's and the baby's company, but Horace was content dabbling his hands, collecting cockles, throwing pebbles, floating pieces of wood, watching the tide creep slowly inwards to dissolve his edifices of mud and shells, learning the behaviour of this huge mysterious and delightful element.

'Horace likes the sea,' his father observed. 'Is it the first time he has seen it?'

'I think it is the first time he has taken note of it,' his mother replied.

CHAPTER FIVE

The Coronation

The young King had taken everybody by surprise that year of 1761, and announced to the privy council on the eighth of July that he would marry the Princess Charlotte of Mecklenburg Strelitz. (Everybody had thought, so Mr Horace Walpole said, that the council would be to do with the negotiations for peace with France.) An emissary had been requested to send her measurements so that English seamstresses could make her wedding garments in an English fashion. Later on in July, King George himself caught the chickenpox. So it was not until late August that the princess put to sea, playing 'God save the King' upon her harpsichord to keep herself in spirits as she set out for her new life, with an unknown husband in a strange country. She was bravely and romantically hopeful. King George the Third of England so the messengers said, was young and good-looking and amiable and eager for his bride, and had been delighted with a lock of her soft, dark hair. She was not as good-looking as she would have liked, but she was young and strong and healthy and had a trim figure, and the best will in the world to please.

They landed at Harwich on the seventh of September, at three o'clock. The king's coach met her at Romford on the eighth, and she reached St James's Palace (where her bridegroom waited for her in the garden) exactly twenty-four hours after setting foot in England. (She prepared to curtsey but he raised her up, embraced her and led her in to meet his family and to dine.) She was married the same evening, in the Chapel Royal over the road from the palace, wearing the bridal dress she had never seen, its train held up by ten unmarried daughters of English dukes and earls. No wonder she trembled a little as she walked in the procession, encouraged by the king's two younger brothers, and given away by his uncle, the Duke of Cumberland. The festivities were not over until two or three in the morning.

'Oh! How tired she must have been, must she not, Sukey?' Catherine Nelson said, when she had read her daughter the story. But Susannah could only think, her eyes bright and her cheeks flushed, how wonderful to be a princess and to come to England and to marry the King! The next week her father bade her read the latest account for herself.

'Her Majesty yesterday appeared at Court in a little Cap, entirely made of diamonds, in the Centre of which was the Form of a Crown... Her Majesty is of middle stature, at present what may rather be called short than tall, but as she is not much turned of seventeen, it is very probable she may grow taller...She discovers great Vivacity, Amiableness, and Affability in her Disposition...Her Majesty can speak no English, except God save the King...'

'Well read' said her father. 'You go on well. You may take it and read it to your grandmamma.'

Before September was out came the coronation, upon which the whole country made holiday. In London the King and Queen went quietly in chairs at nine o'clock in the morning, from St James's Palace to Westminster Hall. Here a large diamond, new set, fell out of the king's crown: an event which an earlier age might have thought ominous, but to this religious young King seemed merely tiresome and to the unobserved onlooker, comical. As they proceeded to the abbey to be crowned, the king's herb woman went ahead with her six maids, strewing sweet herbs in the way. They were not back until seven o'clock, when they dined in the utmost magnificence in Westminster Hall.

In Norwich there was a great triumphal arch in the market-place where all manner of fireworks were played off, sky rockets, and tourbillons and passionflower trees, and Chinese suns, and cascade fountains, and branched fountains with changes of fire, and a furrilony, and a large sun with forty-foot rays. In Lynn the mayor had drums and music and the 'Engins' for which the town was famous played. There was an elegant dinner and beer for the people; and as night fell a tender of a man-of-war in the harbour appeared like a tree with all its branches full of light.

Catherine Nelson looked longingly from the top windows of the parsonage as dusk fell, and saw all around the glow of bonfires.

'Husband! It is a fine night, let us get out the wagon and go to Wells, the children will love to see it, a King and Queen are not crowned every day! Get ready Maurice, and help William! Sukey, help Horace, we shall go and see the harbour at Wells!'

Maurice had longed to go somewhere.

'We're going to Wells, we're going to Wells, come you on Horace, William, we're all a-going to see the fires!'

'Going to Wells, going to Wells,' yelled William.

Horace said nothing, though his heart swelled with excitement.

'Come along, Mary,' Mrs Nelson called to the little nursemaid. 'We all go to Wells! Bring Ann, take your shawl, it may be cold coming back!'

Peter had the horse in the wagon so quickly, the rector wondered if it had stood ready.

They crossed the Burn and took the wide grassy drove road, dry as a bone in autumn, winding its way between pale stubble fields in the falling light, and high hedgerows of rose, hawthorn and bramble, where late fingers of honeysuckle still scented the air. They reached the old Roman track which ran along by Holkham land and down to the coast road. Horace lay with his head on Mary's shoulder looking at the pale sky, his nose assailed with the sun-dried scent of autumn stubble, the evening wind carrying the far-off tumble of waves to his ears. Never had he been out so late. Ann slept in her mother's arms. Papa held jiggetty William whose excitement could not be contained, while he looked across at his wife in her old shawl, her hair escaping from her cap, her lips tender, her eyes bright, and loved her with all his soul. He loved her force and her sudden plans and her exuberance. She seemed to be his sun, golden bright and warm; to himself, he seemed her moon, pale and silver. So be it. She caught his glance and smiled with pleasure. The smell of the sea, the glow of bonfires, the laughing of crowds grew stronger as they took the lower road down towards Wells quay.

'Look, Sukey! Look at the candles in the windows!' In every window a golden candle strained upwards. Small, private fires in lokes and yards showed up children dancing. The gentlemen of the town had dined at the Fleece, entertained by the Countess of Leicester. One of his Majesty's cutters still discharged a few salvos from the harbour.

'Listen, Horace! It's the guns from the ships!'

Down on the quay was a huge fire, just lit, making a roar and a crackle which rivalled the guns. The flames lit up the laughing faces of the people. Stall-holders sold candy and toffee apples and twisted rock, barrels of beer were broached, cockles and mussels and whelks and winkles were called, and hot pies and sausage rolls. Horace had never seen so huge a bonfire before.

'It is hot, my love. Do not you go too near. See, here's Papa with some rock for you!'

They walked along towards the sea, to look at the ships. There were fishing boats, and cargo boats come in to fetch grain bringing coal from the north; and lighters and tugs. But every boat as she lay at anchor had lit her lanterns and run these up to the mastheads and many had decked their rigging all over with lamps. As it grew darker they blossomed like glow-worms, outlining the ships as they bowed gently on the water. Horace gazed, unable at first to understand it.

'Do you see the ships, Horace? All the ships have hung out their lanterns! Because the King is crowned!' his mother said.

As he made out their shapes, a rush of wonder filled him. He held out a fist sticky with rock.

'Ships! See the ships,' he repeated.

'Look at the lights in the water!' said Papa.

The child could scarcely take this in: the lights turned somersaults, danced, ran together in the water, as dreams run into reality and realities into dream. As the wagon jogged back along the coast road he saw for the first time in his life the stars prickling through the clear chill sky, before he fell to sleep in his mother's arms. She wondered if Horace, a week short of three years, would remember it! His senses and his soul had suffered a great joyful bombardment upon this night.

Maurice, who with increasing fluency was becoming an ardent reader of Papa's newspaper, found a tale much to his taste. 'Here's a story about a jolly tar,' he said. 'I can't read all the words.'

'Try now, Papa will help.'

'A jolly tar...'

'What's a jolly tar?' Susannah put in.

'A sailor! With sticky tar about his breeks, to keep out the sea-water!'

'Go on, Maurice,' William ordered, affronted at the explanation though he had needed it.

'A jolly tar, seeing the awk...awkwardness which the men showed in taking down the Awning for the procession (as the weather had cleared) cried out Hollo, what are ye about there, ye landlubbers? You reef a sail? You be damned, avast, let me come – jumped upon the platform and did as much in half an hour as six men would have taken six hours to perform. The people were much pleased, and gave him a great many shillings and sixpences.'

His mother cried: 'Your jolly tar shouts like this, Maurice,' and she bawled in broad Norfolk the words of the jolly tar.

All the children leapt to their feet in instant pandemonium, producing their own versions of the jolly tar, until the study echoed with hallos and avasts, landlubbers and reefs and sails and damns anything but faint. Edmund Nelson sat dissolved in silent laughter until the stamping and shouting had changed to giggles.

'May I be a jolly tar?' asked Horace distinctly: who had joined in the romp at the end.

'I'll show you where to sail a boat,' Maurice offered, 'on the stream, outside.'

'So you shall, but not now, it's nearly bedtime. What has Papa found now?'

'About their Majesties going to the theatre.'

'Read it, read it' implored Sukey, whose taste for royalty was insatiable.

'They went to Covent Garden to see *The Beggars' Opera*. Their box was of cherry velvet...and in the centre were two hymeneal torches enclosing a Heart, and in a Scroll the motto Mutuus Ardor...' That means, they love each other,' Papa explained. 'The King wore purple and silver, and the Queen was in pink and silver. Her hair was done up smooth behind, with two ringlets down the face...Now, Miss Sukey, you know how to do your hair.'

Susannah's simple feelings were well expressed in the lines of a rope-maker of Harwich, put up amongst the lights.

> In two great points has George his skill displayed,
> A war well managed, and a Match well made.
> So young, so wise! The Neighbour Nations say;
> If thus the Morning breaks, how bright the Day!
> Then, Britons, pray the Evening Close may crown
> This darling King whom Britain calls her own;
> That Choicest blessings in his cup may swim;
> Soft Peace for us – conjugal Bliss for him.

But a soft peace was the last thing Mr Pitt wanted, without a sweeping victory. Aware that the French, even while discussing peace with Britain, were secretly trying to bring Spain into the war as their ally, he believed in taking the initiative, attacking a Spanish treasure fleet, cutting off Spain from her colonies and opening up more for Britain. Lord Newcastle thought that Britain could ill afford an extension of the war. The Duke of Bedford wanted peace at any price. The Marquis of Bute was against Mr Pitt and not far from Lord Newcastle. Mr Pitt hated contradiction, so they said, and amidst all this warmth of feeling for the newly-crowned King and Queen, he resigned from the government on October the fifth. The King did nothing to entice him to return, but saw him paid a pension and let him go. People were taken aback: Mr Pitt's conduct of the war had brought him popular acclaim and glory. Yet the text of the coronation sermon, preached by the Lord Bishop of Sarum, and drawn from the Book of Kings, had 'Because the Lord loved Israel for ever, therefore made he the King to do judgement and justice.' Edmund Nelson, along with many another parson and country gentleman, was inclined to trust the Lord God to guide the King. The King, so folk said, was sincerely religious, hated political parties and wished to be the King of all his people. Take it all in all, he seemed a promising King and a good sort of young man.

Meanwhile, Colonel William Windham had died, 'so indefatigable in pursuit of his darling scheme the Militia' that his application to it had hastened his death. And on Christmas Day there died at Lynn old Lady Turner, in her eighty-eighth year, mother of Sir John. 'She must at that advanced age have been happy to go,' remarked Mrs Suckling, as she prepared to pen her cousin a sympathetic line.

Early in the New Year of 1762, the mayor proclaimed in Norwich His Majesty's declaration of war with Spain, thereby proving Mr Pitt to have been right. During the late negotiations of the differences between Britain and Spain, the Spaniards had suggested the French be arbiters. The French! Britain's bitter enemies! Moreover when the Spaniards were asked to deny rumours that they had a secret agreement with the French, they refused. The British ambassador returned and war was declared. The rector felt doubtful pleasure in this and prayed each Sunday with particular fervour for God to guide the King and his ministers.

His wife's patriotism was of the bolder sort. 'Since we are at war with Spain,' said she, stirring the stew in the great iron pot, 'I heartily wish your Uncle Maurice were still in the West Indies in the *Dreadnought* chasing the Spaniards out of their possessions.'

'Where is Uncle Maurice then, Mamma?' asked the sea-captain's godson.

'Your Uncle is in the Channel Maurice, in a ship called the *Lancaster*, in a fleet under Admiral Sir Edward Hawke,' said his mother.

Horace sat cross-legged on the floor beneath the table, where the glow of the fire struck him agreeably.

'Where is the Channel, Mamma?'

'Why, Maurice, the Channel is the strip of sea between us and France! The Channel is what keeps the French their distance, never forget that!'

'But what is Uncle Maurice doing?'

'He is cruising up and down, waiting for the French to put their noses out, so that he can give them a good hiding as he did off Cap François.'

'In the West Indies on October twenty-first 1757,' said Maurice, to please her.

'Just so, the day we keep festival.'

'But when will the French put their noses out?'

'Ah, Sir Edward gave them such a beating off Belle-isle in fifty-nine, they have not put their noses out since. So Uncle Maurice sails back and forth with nothing to do. That is no life for a brave sea captain, is it, little Horace?' she said, as the child now put *his* nose out from under the table. 'I missed you, there you are. Your Uncle Maurice, Horatio,' said his mother, judging the time now ripe and using his proper name to impress him, 'chased seven French ships with only three English and shot them to rags and tinder! And, I'll tell you this, Horatio: Uncle Maurice led the way!'

'Led the way,' the child echoed, inspired with his mother's excitement.

'He did. Shall you do that one day Maurice?' she asked, stirring the pot, her dark eyes flashing. Maurice smiled shyly, but William was ready with his boast.

'I shall, I shall! Rags and tinder!'

Horace said nothing more, hearing again his mother's warm voice declaiming: shot them to rags and tinder!

Peter brought news of a great whale, washed ashore in one of the February storms and captured at Dersingham, nearly fifty-seven feet long and thirty-five round. And Maurice heard at school of the woman found dead on the road from Burnham Market to Burnham Deepdale. Maurice had a peculiarly tender heart. Supposing he or his mother or Sukey were just to *die* walking along the road, with no-one to care for them?

'Why did not she knock at someone's door?' said Maurice in anguish. 'Think, Mamma, walking along till you fell dead,' he sobbed.

'Yes, there, hush now.' His mother could only put her arms round him and enfold him, she could do nothing to explain the cruelty of life and the swiftness of death, as Maurice confronted them for the first time.

His granny sought to distract him by telling him of the Cock Lane ghost, an apparition which was setting all London in a stir: it tapped out answers to those bold enough to ask questions. The house in Cock Lane became a haunt of sightseers credulous or cynical, and even her coz Mr Horace Walpole was amongst their number. Maurice was not comforted.

'So Lord Orford has lost his gerfalcon,' said the rector one evening, looking up from his *Mercury* with a laugh.

'What's a gerfalcon?' said Maurice.

'He tells us exactly.

Houghton, March 23 1762. *LOST A GER FALCON* the property of the Earl of Orford. She is a much larger bird than the slight falcon, of a bluish colour on the back, her breast white, mottled with black spots; has Bells on her legs. She is supposed to have flown to the Lincolnshire coast in pursuit of a Heron...

'He then gives instructions for her capture. You are to fling up a large dead Fowl or Turkey (though why his lordship thinks a person will have such items about him, I cannot tell) and you are to approach gently and lay hold of the thongs on her legs, put her in a dark room with a glimmering light to see her food, and send notice to her owner immediately. What is more, you may expect twenty guineas reward!'

His wife said, 'I think he appears a trifle eccentric, my love, do not you? And Sir John says you remember that in his Uncle Walpole's opinion he neglects his estates.'

'Too interested in his hawks and his hunting. Though he made his mark, my dear, with the militia.'

Late in April, Edmund Nelson's uncle Thomas died at Congham with his youngest son's family. Too late to uproot an old tree, the rector thought, riding to Sporle to his funeral.

But the public news was agreeable: Martinique had been taken from the French, followed by Grenada, the Grenadines, St Lucia, St Vincent, and Tobago. Mrs Nelson thought how vexed her brother, Captain Maurice, would be to miss all this: and won general acclaim herself by producing her next son on His Majesty's birthday, June the fourth. He was called Edmund after his father in place of the son born twelve years ago in Swaffham. Granny came in to help, Ann toddled in her care. Sukey learned to feed the babies and read to her mother in bed. The rector pondered on his increasing brood, read of the window tax, envied carefree shepherds in windowless huts, and was to be seen (with many another modest householder) perambulating his property, anxiously counting windows.

And on August the twelfth there was born to Queen Charlotte her first son and heir, hailed with bells and guns and bonfires through all the towns of England. With more modest rejoicings, Edmund Nelson christened his little namesake, when his wife's brother Mr William Suckling could spare time to come from London to be godfather. The young Nelsons had not met this uncle before, a laughing, chaffing gentleman who arrived in a fast fly and was in far too much hurry to take the slow carrier back to Norwich. (This was James Raven the Burnham Market carrier who now advertised his days and his ways to Norwich, and solicited passengers and parcels.)

With October came in violent storms, which forced a Yarmouth shallop ashore near Overy harbour. Her master was one John Crow and she was bringing coals from Sunderland. Maurice ran into the kitchen (where the children were and his mother sewed and Mary spat upon the flat iron) and declaimed this story with drama.

'They were all lost, the ship and the cargo and the crew! All lost, but John Crow's son!' he cried breathlessly.

Horace was just turned four when these tales from the sea invaded his heart of ships that were tossed about, driven ashore, sunk, the sailors drowned. All lost, but John Crow's son. The refrain sank into him like a knell. For years he was to remember Maurice's pale face, the fire flickering, the smell of the scorching linen, the daylight nearly done in the kitchen, and the anguished bell-like voice of his brother singing that dirge, All lost but John Crow's son! He would wake up on windy nights, hearing it.

All the month gales raged. One night a violent wind sprang up, followed in the early hours by a vast, sudden inundation in Norwich from the river, which flooded many houses and eight churches in a rise of water near twelve feet. At the coast, the *Mayflower* of Lynn bringing coals from Milford, had been lost on the long Overfall, Blakeney church bearing south-half-east, Wells south-west distant about five miles. A Wells coble had rescued the master, all the rest had perished.

Maurice, engrossed one day in the ship news in the *Mercury*, called out in excitement: 'Papa, one of the ships stranded at Cley is called the *Adventure* and her master is John Nelson! Is he our cousin? Our family?'

'What ports, Maurice?'

'London to Hull.'

His father considered. 'My youngest brother, your uncle, is John: but he is gone to the wars, we think. There is a John among my cousins at Dereham, but not a seaman. No, I do not think it likely.'

But the story the children remembered longest was of one George Commin, a red-haired ship's master described by a Cley merchant from whose ship he had perished. He had a watch with his name round the dial plate in great letters instead of hours, the first letter beginning where the twelve is. Five guineas was offered for news of George Commin. Mr Nelson saw in this a good chance for instruction.

'We will make a dial like George Commin's only large, out of stiff paper. And whoever's name makes up twelve letters shall be wrote around it,' said papa.

So they fell with excitement to counting the letters of their names.

'Papa, it's Horace!' shouted Maurice and Sukey together.

'By rights he is Horatio,' Papa said, winking at Horace.

So Horace Nelson's name went on the clock, though the rector was obliged to put the numbers on as well. Sukey and William and Horace all learned their hours with this dial. George Commin's watch, however, was found upon a man at Salthouse by a Jewish silversmith and hawker who (very unjustly, Maurice considered) got the reward.

The rector had decided that he would teach William and Horace their letters together. William was slow to apply himself, Horace seemed the sharper, and there was only eighteen months between them. Against William's disinclination to learn anything at all, he began with mild persuasion.

'But of course you must learn to read. Just suppose you want to be a parson, like Papa. How would Papa manage, if he could not read the service and the prayers, and all the people's names?'

'How do I be a parson?' William scowled.

'You learn your letters, go to school, and then to college.'

'Where?' pursued William, while Horace listened intently.

'I dare say you may go to Cambridge. I went to college in Cambridge. And so did your grandpapa, and your godfather, my cousin William. Why, you might even become a bishop, which is very grand.'

This seemed better to William, who liked things to be grand.

'When you have learned your first few letters, both of you, I will read you a comical story about your grand-papa's college.'

Sure enough, as Edmund suspected, Horace learned more quickly than William, and William's annoyance at this delayed him still further. But he soon learned to use the situation and to demand and get help from his younger brother.

'Now then boys, listen to this.

> On November twenty-fifth a fox was put up near Cherryhinton (that is a village quite near Cambridge) by the hounds of Christopher Anstey, Esquire, and being hard drove near this town, took into Emanuel College...

(that is where your grandpapa was)

> went through the cloisters, round the fish ponds, and afterwards leaped over the College wall and made his escape.

'What do you think of that, William, will you go to college and meet a fox?'

'I think I'll be a bishop,' pronounced William.

His father regarded him with amusement. 'And what will you be, Horace?' he asked.

'George Commin,' said Horace. The name, the story, and the home-made dial had appealed mightily to him.

'A sea captain? Poor George Commin!'

'Poor George Commin,' Horace echoed, nodding.

CHAPTER SIX

Uncle Maurice Suckling

Peace (which had become a certainty by the end of the year of 1762) meant different things to different people. It meant disbanded soldiers from Yarmouth on the march for London in ruffianly mood, girls cozened and deserted, goods stolen, employment urgently sought. In Norwich they organised a Fish Society to press all roaming tars into the catching of fish and the carriage of it by land into the city. The rector wondered about the black sheep of the Nelson family, John, his youngest brother: and what he could do to help him to employment? But his wife thought with pleasure that perhaps her brother Captain Maurice would leave ships and come ashore for a spell, and set himself up with this long-promised wife and visit them again at Burnham. The sea-captain's visits were necessarily rare. She remembered his shy delight at his godson's christening in the summer of 1753, before they left Swaffham. There had been a brief visit at the time of his being commissioned captain of the *Dreadnought*, at the start of the war. Then he had sailed away to the West Indies for six years, to earn himself some glory. He had made a summer visit to Burnham before the excitement of the royal wedding and the coronation, but of the children only Maurice and Sukey had any real memory of him. Then he had taken up command of the *Lancaster*.

As for herself, she had passed her thirty-eighth birthday a few days ago, and then the anniversary of her marriage, the eleventh of May 1749. It was fourteen years since they were married! The years seemed gone in the twinkling of an eye, what a great distance she and her husband had travelled together!

'Husband, is it not strange that time, when we are young, saunters so slowly that we do not mark its passing? And when we are older—' She stopped, her hands falling on her lap.

'Ah, when we are older he gallops away, one year after the other, as fast as pages turning!'

'It is ten years since Maurice's christening, and my brother must be thirty-seven! I hope he will come this summer…But these children are not aware of time!'

Hearing his name, Maurice had cocked his ears. 'I am, Mamma,' he said. 'Sometimes, time goes slower than other times.'

'So you have marked that already, my son?' said Papa. 'It seems impossible to believe that time goes ever at the same pace. However regularly the clock ticks, the sand flows, the water drops, to us mortals caught in the flow, time is a variable stream, sometimes swift, sometimes idle.'

'You put it more poetically than I could do,' his wife said. 'Yet: there's the clock. Tick tock. Even and regular. It is how *we* feel that varies? It must needs be.'

'It is a mystery. And so are the fields of space. There is little Horace, out there amongst the grass, the flowers and the butterflies, busy about his own absorbing concerns – and within ten minutes the picture will be past, and he will be in here!'

Mr Nelson was looking from the study window on to the May morning. 'Or within five Maurice may walk out and join him and be no longer here!'

Maurice did so, the mysteries of time and space which had brushed him with their wings being quickly banished by Horace's collection of wood, twigs, feathers and leaves to be sailed upon the stream.

The lilacs smelled strongly through the open window, as Catherine Nelson held the baby, Edmund, in the sun upon her lap.

'Yes, it is time we saw Captain Maurice again,' her husband said, his hand on her dark hair. 'I must go a-hoeing. Will you come?' Her temples were threaded with silver.

'It is washing-day, my love, I must be down here.' Washing-day happened but once a month. Sukey Bee and Jane Clark had come from the village to help Mary, and chattered in the wash-house like rooks in the trees. Already, cloths and linens and shirts lay over the bushes in the sun, absorbing the scents of rosemary, lavender or hawthorn as they dried. Susannah, with little Ann in attendance, was now spreading kerchiefs from a basket over a low box hedge.

'Where's Horace?' wailed William.

'I think he and Maurice may have gone down to the stream.'

William grunted and turned, charging off anxiously to catch up with his brothers. They often played together, Maurice being idly content to stick to childish games, while Horace had notions beyond his years. All the frail boats of bark and feathers were floating on a pool by the bank.

'You didn't wait for me,' complained William. 'I was in the necessary.'

'Do you like them, William,' said Horace eagerly. 'All my ships?'

'They 'ont sail,' said William in disparagement.

'They will,' said Maurice. 'In the middle of the stream.'

Horace blew gently and patiently upon his fleet, William puffed too wildly, and sank most of his share.

'I think Uncle Maurice may be coming,' his godson announced, lying on his back, one bare thin foot over the other knee. 'You know, Mamma's brother who chased the French ships in the West Indies.'

'He shot them to rags and tinder,' Horace stated as if by rote.

After the grace, Captain Suckling looked round the table, his eyes diffident in his fleshy, weathered face, his generous large lips on the verge of a smile. He found himself uncertain how to act with these little strangers, who seemed to treat him like some sort of a god or hero. At the end he saw his sister, always more buxom than he remembered her in her stern elder-sisterly girlhood, blooming with happiness at his visit, milder, rounder, gentler and more talkative. On her right sat Granny (as he had learned to think of her: and the years had changed her so markedly that this was not difficult). Opposite his sister, this slim, frail parson with a sometimes sardonic curl to his lips but kind and friendly eyes. His godson Maurice sat beside him, a quiet boy of sensibility, mostly Nelson he inclined to think; plump, calm-faced Susannah on his other side, a good mixture of Suckling and Turner. Young William's fat, assertive countenance might almost say Walpole? He was watching his mother serving the plates with greedy attention. Captain Maurice's gaze came to the smallest, young Horatio, right opposite him: an infant when he was last here, now a little boy, frail and slight. Horace was regarding him with such intensity in his blue eyes, his cheeks flushed, his fair hair wispy round his head, that his uncle was baffled in his catalogue of family likenesses, for the lively gaze was more alert and distinct than that of any of the others, and seemed like no other than itself already. Uncle Maurice received Horace's attentive stare, winked his eye, and smiled. Horace went scarlet to the roots of his hair, his lower lip faltered before he smiled widely back.

'Your journey to Norwich yesterday was easy I hope,' the rector began, handing his brother-in-law a crock of home-grown beans.

'I came in that one day Flying Machine, sir, from the Two-Neck'd Swan in Lad Lane...' replied Uncle Maurice.

'It does not actually leave the ground, Horace,' said his father in a loud whisper, seeing his son's round eyes and open mouth. Horace smiled and looked consciously around as the others laughed.

'Then I spent the night in St Andrew's Street, and hired a chaise early this morning. And surprised my mother at noon. And here I am!'

'And happy we are to see you!' his sister said. 'Are we not, Mamma?'

Mrs Suckling nodded, gazing fondly at her son.

'The children are longing to hear more particulars of how you chased the French ships.'

'Shot them to rags and tinder,' whispered Horace, though he knew a child should speak only when spoken to at the table.

'Speak up, Horatio, what have you to say?' Papa questioned, kindly.

'Mamma said, Uncle Maurice shot them to rags and tinder,' repeated Horace softly.

Captain Suckling's eyebrows went up and he laughed. 'Why, it was nothing to what they did to us!' he exclaimed. 'The old *Dreadnought* lost all but her foremast! Your mamma has told you but one side of the affair, I see I must tell you the other!'

'I cannot be expected to extol the doings of Frenchmen,' she laughed. 'Boys, remember to keep your uncle to his word. Now brother,' she continued somewhat teasingly, as if to return his fire, 'is it your intention to visit the family at Wolterton while you are here?'

Young Maurice saw his uncle flush and smile bashfully. Something had been meant by his mother's question, something more than was said, but a child might not ask.

'I hope to pay my respects to Lord Walpole, and his family while his mother – and his sister – are there,' Captain Maurice said, bowing to her.

'Good,' she replied briskly. 'How goes your suit?'

'But slowly: the lady is like a frigate, for ever bobbing about a ship o' the line, even when the ship bids her be gone.'

'Why, brother, you must catch the wind of chance, bear down and board her!' his sister exclaimed. 'You have much to offer. You are too modest.'

Both men laughed at her exuberance and young Maurice watched them with interest, while Horatio looked from one adult to another with round, puzzled eyes. Sukey and William remained unconscious of anything but their dinners.

'Little pitchers,' Mrs Suckling now remarked.

'Sit up, Maurice, do not slouch in your chair,' Papa said: he had been heard to announce that no child's back should touch his chair.

'Papa, may I tell Uncle Maurice about the poacher's letter and Lord Walpole?' said his son sitting up straight.

The rector assented, wondering what was coming.

'By all means let us hear what Lord Walpole wrote to the poacher,' said his uncle to Maurice.

'No, it was the *poacher* who wrote the letter, sir! No one knows who the poacher is, he wrote it without a name. Anon…anony…'

'Anonymously,' Papa put in. 'This happened in the winter. Maurice has been watching the paper for months. Go on, boy,' he said, surprised that Maurice had remembered what he had long since forgot.

'This poacher wrote a most bloodthirsty letter, that is what Papa said, to a man called Everard Hearne Esquire, but Lord Walpole was in it too, and so was Mr William Bulwer and Mr Thomas Durrant, and do you know what this poacher said, sir?'

'I should greatly like to hear.'

'He said, "Mr Hearne take Notes that if you make any more Fuss about your House and the Game as you have done and go on to take up pepel and carry them to the Justis we will blow out your Brains and burn down your house over you. And if Buller or Durrant or My Lord send any body to prison they shall meet with the same Saufe by God for we are strong enough to do for you all so take care How You behave!" And this poacher, he spelled it all wrong!'

'A poacher might not be very good at spelling, I dare say.'

'Maurice was better,' Papa said.

'Blow out your brains and burn down your house,' remarked William lustily and surprisingly, before addressing himself to his pudding.

'Strong enough to do for you all so take care how you behave,' piped Horatio.

'Oh-ho, it is clear that a regular play has gone on about these poachers. And what was the event?'

'They caught one, his name was John Bacon, he was setting hare snares in Heveringland woods! They took him to the castle.'

'Alas, poor fellow,' Catherine Nelson said.

'When we play, I am Everard Hearne, William is William Bulwer, Horace is Lord Walpole (since my Lord is his godpapa) and Sukey is the poacher when we can capture her!'

'Who invented it, Maurice?' Granny said.

'Horace, ma'am. I read the letter to them, but Horace thought of it!'

'Valiant Horatio!' said Uncle Maurice, laughing at the child's giggles.

'He shows the fighting spirit,' said the rector, amused. 'He has it from his mamma, and she from your late husband, ma'am! Not from me, I declare. Now you may get down, children. William, leave scraping your plate, the treacle is all gone.'

When the door was closed, Mrs Nelson said, 'Horace's smallness belies him, he is a bold, active little boy. I have seen him account for William in a fight!'

'But he is very loving-hearted,' the rector said. 'And he is eager and not indolent. He is quicker than William at his lessons, when he is well.'

'Is he often sickly?' the captain asked.

'He is a little delicate as his father was, so he has had much cherishing, which he repays with ready affection. We all love him. But indeed we love them all. Your godson, now, is the most tender-hearted child I ever knew, and would certainly weep for the poacher could he see him languishing in the castle,' his mother said. Mrs Suckling assented: she dearly loved Maurice.

'And Susannah is a dear, commonsensical and womanly little maiden; and William, though hard to teach, may probably do well, he has so strong a will! As for Ann and Edmund, they are innocent babes as yet. You see, brother, what we tell you: seek the joys of a family, a quiverful of children as the psalmist says, no happiness is so blessed!' the rector averred.

The captain nodded his head. 'Each so different, each so interesting! Yes, I envy you with all my heart. But I begin to despair of success.'

'Nonsense, you are only now beginning. You cannot woo from a distance. She must capitulate to a strong sea-captain!' said his sister with assurance. 'You will not be going to sea for a while, now there is peace?'

'No indeed, it looks as if they intend to diminish and neglect the navy to save expenditure, though I cannot believe it wise.'

'Nor I' she agreed, 'but it offers you your chance.'

'Uncle Maurice, Uncle Maurice! Where are you?'

Captain Suckling brought his eyes down from the rustling green heights of the great elm he leaned against at the edge of the rector's highest field and looked towards the orchard and the parsonage.

'Uncle Mau…rice!' shrilled young Maurice's voice again.

How lonely was the sea-captain's life compared to this! But four or five days in and out of the parsonage, and he had found himself opening as a flower does to the sun.

'Ahoy there!' he called.

The troop of children saw him and galloped joyfully upwards.

'Mamma says,' Maurice began breathlessly, flinging himself down, 'will you please to tell us about the West Indies and the sea-fight sir, as you said!'

Horace arrived panting, and sat down affectionately close to his uncle. William attempted to dislodge him.

'Come the other side, master William, I am as wholesome one side as t'other!'

The West Indies! Still enfolded by the spirit of the cool English tree in the July meadow, a pile of silver-edged clouds high in the sky and the mild calls of woodland birds in the orchard, the sea-captain thought of the West Indies and found the thought strange. Those monstrous trees of fleshy brilliant green, those creepers like tangled rigging, the unyielding sun, the heat like a tangible wall, the rain in solid torrents, the huge garish flowers, the lavish tasteless fruits, the flights of chattering bright parrots and the million other darting screaming birds, the crabs, turtles, palms and blue lagoons!

Sukey flopped down and began to pick daisies.

'Come, Nanny,' said Uncle Maurice, lifting Ann and her troublesome skirts on to his knee. She was nearly three. He thought her delightful, with her delicate face and silken hair, and pictured his own daughter like her. 'As to the West Indies,' he said looking at his godson, 'what do you wish to hear?'

'Uncle, Mamma says it is always hot?'

'Ah yes, it is customarily hot in the tropics. But then there may be a cool breeze from the sea. And when it rains, it rains as if the heavens were open. And the thunder is louder and longer, and the lightning is brighter. And there's a great whirling wind called a hurricane that picks up whole houses and blows them into the sea.'

'And Uncle, what about the flowers and the birds?' Sukey said.

'Why, the flowers are bigger and brighter. The birds are all colours, red and yellow and blue and green, and noisier, and greedier! The parrots come chattering down on the coconut palms and the plantains and strip off the young fruit...'

'They cannot be greedier than our pigeons,' the parson remarked as he and his wife arrived, 'coming down upon my pease.'

'Bigger and greedier! Everything in the tropics is "more so",' Maurice Suckling said laughing.

'Are there any apple trees?' Sukey asked.

'There are trees called mangoes and you may see one side covered with green fruit, while t'other is in blossom. But the fruit is oily and tasteless compared with an English russet! And then you will see oranges growing upon a tree. And limes upon bushes, yellow-green and rounder than lemons.'

'Marvel upon marvel,' Catherine Nelson said, leaning against the elm with the baby on her lap. 'Now, Horace?'

'Please to tell us about the ships! The sea-fight when you chased the Frenchmen, sir,' Horace said softly. Horatio was not quite five and still shy.

'Ah, those Frenchmen! Where shall I begin?'

'Tell us it all, all!' said Maurice eagerly. 'Please sir!'

'Well, now it happened like this. Our admiral heard that the French were collecting a fleet of trading ships for Europe, at Cap François on the island of Haiti which lies to the north-east of Jamaica where we were, and belongs partly to the French. To protect these traders, our admiral thought there would be a small squadron of French ships no more powerful than we were, We were three ships, the *Augusta*, Captain Forrest in command, the Edinburgh, Captain Langdon…'

'And the *Dreadnought*, Captain Suckling!' cried Maurice, with his uncle.

'…And we were sent to cruise off the northerly coast of Haiti to catch the French ships when they should come out. Now at seven o'clock on the morning of that day, my look-out roared that he could see ships coming out of Cap François…'

'Where *was* he?' Horatio whispered.

'Why, right up aloft, Horace,' and Uncle Maurice waved his arm towards the leafy heights of the elm, 'in the foremast rigging, looking through his spy-glass. By noon we could count what they were…Four ships of the line and three frigates. Then Captain Forrest signalled us to go aboard him. So my gig is lowered and down the side I go and am rowed to the *Augusta,* and up her ladder I climb, and as I put myself aboard her port side, so does Captain Langdon too the starboard side, and we both stride to the gangway together, and there is Captain Forrest on the quarter-deck above us.'

'Go on, sir, pray go on!' Horace whispered, pushing at his uncle's leg.

'So Captain Forrest says, "Gentlemen, you see the force of the enemy, come out hoping to drive us off the coast: shall we engage the fellows or not?" (Or some such words as those.) And Captain Langdon shouts, "Ay, let us." And I shout…' Uncle Maurice paused at this moment of suspense.

'*What?* What did you shout, sir?' urged Maurice.

'I dare say I shouted, "By all means," though it might be prettier to think I had said, "It would be a pity to disappoint them," meaning the Frenchmen. So Captain Forrest looks satisfied and he says, "Then get you back to your ships and clear for action." So back we go, and clear the decks the people do so that the guns have room, and everything is lashed down hard or stowed away so that it cannot break loose and roll about. Oh, and here's a whimsical thing, will make you laugh. While this was all a-doing, the monkey got loose…'

'The monkey!' said several voices together.

'Ay, there was an officer of mine had a favourite monkey, it was a comical animal and entertained us all. And by some accident he got on deck and I heard a shout and a laugh and there he was running up the mizzen shrouds, and not even his master could coax him back! But I dare say they'll not know the names of the masts of a ship, sister? In a three-masted ship, Maurice, the foremast is in the bows, or in front as landlubbers say: the mainmast is amidships, in the middle, and the mizzen is right aft, at the back. So where did the monkey run, Horatio?'

'He ran up the mizzen mast right aft Uncle,' said Horace at once, the picture in his mind.

'What was his name?' put in Sukey, more concerned with the monkey than the masts.

'Upon my soul, I cannot recall that monkey's name after all these years, but he ran up the shrouds to the top of the mizzen and there he sat upon the truck, as cool as you please. Well, by now it was mid-afternoon, and Captain Forrest gave the signal to bear down, which we did. I led in the *Dreadnought*, the *Augusta* was in the middle, and the *Edinburgh* last.'

'Sir, why did not Captain Forrest lead?' Maurice asked.

'Why, one reason I took the van was that the other two ships were both extremely foul on their bottoms at the time, and this means a ship sails less well, do you see? So away we ran with the wind behind us, and there they came all seven in a double line, with the frigates on the leeward side...'

'Uncle Maurice?' It was his godson again who interrupted.

'We shall never get this battle fought,' Papa remarked.

'Yes, my boy?'

'Were you...were not you...sir, did you not feel frightened?'

'Roused, rather. When you are in command of a ship going into action, you must needs think hard all the time, keep your wits about you. This drives away any qualms you may have felt. Now the first thing I see as we approach is a smaller ship astern of their leader shooting up with the wind, so near her that she looked like to fall on board her!'

'Uncle Maurice, sir, do you mean they bumped into each other?' said William.

'I mean they very nearly did. It was the *Greenwich* was the villain, and so she was all the way through, so mark her. She was not a French ship at all, as you can tell by her name: she was one of ours, and she had been taken a prize by the French about six months earlier. Now whether her crew knew not quite how to handle her, or whether it was pure mischance, or whether a ship knows her own and fights for them, I am not prepared to say. But the *Greenwich* had turned too sharp into the wind and was like to be drove on board the stern of the *Intrépide*: that was the French commodore's ship, leading. So this threw them into confusion. And when I observed this I hastened to make all the advantage I could of it, as any, captain would.'

'What did you do, sir? What did you do?' Horace whispered.

'Why, I bore down on to the *Intrépide's* bow, that means fronting her, boys, like this,' and Uncle Maurice used his two hands to show the two ships. 'And then I put my helm hard on starboard (that means to the right, this way) and kept it there and the *Dreadnought* swung round, so, broadside on to the French ship, so that our guns could rake her. Or if she had proceeded then we would have fallen on board her in the most advantageous situation and taken her.'

'And did you, Uncle?' said Maurice.

'No, no, for so soon as we were within range and the *Dreadnought's* guns had opened fire—Boom! Boom! Boom!'

'Boom! Boom! Boom!' roared all the Nelson boys at once.

'So soon as the fight was fairly joined, she chose to bear up, and not come on. She bore away out of the wind and we went after her, and we raked her and she raked us, till our rigging was cut to pieces with their devilish French shot, and our sails torn to shreds and would not answer, and our mizzen top-mast went, and the mizzen-yard was shot down, and indeed every mast, yard, sail and rope were damaged by the end of it. But *she* was so damaged she could do no more and she fell astern disabled. But meanwhile...'

'Uncle Maurice?' whispered Horatio. 'Sir?'

'What, my boy?'

'What about the monkey? You said the monkey was up the mizzen-mast sir!'

'Why, a monkey, he's at home in the ropes and the rigging, he swung away, he took care of himself I promise you, for I saw him at the end of it. He was a small fellow, he had the luck not to be hit. Nine of my men were not so lucky, nine were killed, thirty wounded. When the *Intrépide* fell astern disabled, their next ship the *Opiniâtre* shot up into her station, and in the doing of this the *Greenwich*, still in confusion, and in avoiding the *Opiniâtre*, got on board their ship the *Sceptre* which lay behind. And there they were entangled and a fair target for the *Augusta* and the *Edinburgh* who furiously cannonaded the whole group...'

'Boom! Boom! Boom!' began the boys once more.

'Pray let Uncle Maurice finish!' their mother commanded, laughing.

'Why, the *Edinburgh* fairly drove the *Sceptre* out of the line, before the action was over. We were at it full two and a half-hours. Thrice I saw the *Intrépide* set afire by her own powder! And her rigging and sails were so much damaged, she had signalled for a frigate and was being towed away. But, bless you, we were in almost as desperate a case. And our other two ships were near as bad. We were obliged to bear up for Jamaica, to get our damages repaired.'

'What about the *Greenwich*, sir?' Horace asked.

'Ah, she was damaged in the masts and yards and rigging and I heard she had thirty shot between wind and water. And she came to a bad end. I heard about it later. When the Frenchman had got his squadron repaired he sailed off for Europe with his convoy and they met a severe storm near the coast of France, and three of them parted from their anchors in Conquest Road, and drove ashore and were wrecked: and the *Greenwich* was one.'

'So that was the end of the *Greenwich*,' said Catherine Nelson.

'Perhaps her heart was broke,' said the rector. Little seemed to have been achieved, many men had died, in this particular encounter. What a useless, wasteful business was war!

Horace sat, his eyes on his uncle, his hands detaining him, as if he still lived in the battle.

Maurice said: 'If you had boarded one of the ships sir, must you have fought her sailors?'

'Ay indeed we must, had they not surrendered at once. And I should have wielded the sword of Galfridus Walpole!' their uncle said with a flourish of his hand in the air.

'Who is Galfridus Walpole?' asked three voices together.

'He was my great-uncle, so perhaps he is your great-great-uncle. You should ask your honoured grandmamma about him, she knew him at Houghton as her youngest uncle.'

'Uncle, how did you get his sword?' Maurice said.

'He left me his sword when he died. He was the first to suggest I might enter His Majesty's Navy, do you see? Why, that sword has seen stirring deeds.'

'Tell us, sir!' the boys shouted.

'My great-uncle lost his right arm by a cannon ball, while he fought with that sword! In a sea-battle.'

'Where? Where, Uncle?'

'In the Mediterranean Sea. It was called the battle of Vado Bay, and I think it was in 1711.'

'How long ago is that, Maurice?' Edmund Nelson said quickly.

'Fifty…fifty-two years, Papa.'

'What will happen to the sword when you die, Uncle Maurice?'

'William. That is not the way to speak to your uncle,' the rector said with anger. 'Beg his pardon at once.'

'I beg your pardon sir,' muttered William surprised.

Uncle Maurice bowed his head with a smile. 'I shall leave it to some young man who will make good use of it,' said he lightly.

'Uncle Maurice, sir, had you rather have captured the French leader?' his godson asked.

'Of course. But we were far outnumbered.'

'So was it not a victory, sir?'

'It was not the complete victory which perhaps your mamma had led you to suppose,' he said smiling up at her. 'But it was an inconvenience to the Frenchmen all the same.'

He had surprised himself at the ease and pleasure with which he had recalled the tale, for he was not a man of words. But every man, they say, can tell one tale: and this was his.

'It was a brave bold action,' said she, risen to her feet and stooping to pick up the baby, 'and I am sure the boys will fight it many a time. It has more matter to it than chasing poachers!'

'Yes!' William said, jumping up. 'Come on, Maurice, come on Horace, I'm Captain Suckling, you're Captain Forrest, Horace is Captain Langdon, I'm Captain Suckling!'

'No, Maurice is Captain Suckling!' Horatio was heard to argue as he ran off after the other two: 'Uncle Suckling is his godpapa!'

'A well-developed sense of justice,' remarked Papa.

Chapter Seven

The Turners of Warham

'Now then, here we all are to be sure, a wagon load of little Nelsons, like a wagon load of monkeys!' said cousin John Turner as he lifted down wriggling, sun-bonneted girls and straw-hatted boys. 'Cousin Catherine, my dear!'

'Cousin John, I long to walk to the camp again, there is always a breeze at the camp! Here is brother Maurice!'

'Well, well, Captain Suckling, much water has flowed in Stiffkey river since you last were here? I am heartily glad to see you!'

'And I you, Sir John. I had a longing to see our grandfather's home again, and the camp and the church.'

'It was a capital idea, and I have arranged a picnic...'

'Huzzah!' shouted all the children.

The rector arrived, pink and hot upon his horse.

'What a day, Mr Nelson sir, what a day!'

'And a good day to you, Sir John. What is it, what is it, William? Hush, Horatio...'

'A picnic, Papa!' they breathed in loud whispers.

Sir John led the way round the house to the front court which was paved with narrow red bricks and pungent with thyme and other sweet scents. Warham Hall was a Tudor house, neat and not large, but so delightfully inviting as the sun shone full upon its warm brick and twinkling windows, that Catherine Nelson sighed with pleasure at the memory of childhood visits.

'It is a dear house, brother, is it not?' she said. 'Oh you could never pull it down, cousin!'

'I doubt I could not, though we have all talked much about it.'

'It is one of the fairest aspects in all Norfolk, is it not?' Captain Suckling said, looking across the gently sloping country to the river Stiffkey in the valley, which looped its way brightly round one side of the strange, circular earthwork which folk called the Danish camp. At the bottom of the meadow below the house, the river was dammed up into a double ornamental water, crossed by a rustic bridge. Cattle grazed the meadow. Beyond the river stretched a varied prospect of distant enclosures, scattered with villages, churches, little hills. Above them to the north-east the church of Warham All Saints peeped through its trees over the vale. Almost a mile along the Wighton road lay the other church, St Mary Magdalene. Behind them, a crescent of trees sheltered the house, planted and nurtured by Sir Charles Turner.

'Why, visitors often avow that it is as much worth seeing as half the greater houses where folk run. The house itself is homely and ordinary and old-fashioned, none of your grand Palladian about it: but it is comfortable enough to me. Since I am used to it and inhabit it alone.'

Sir John's wife had died fifteen years past and his daughters were long since married. He was looked after by a housekeeper, Mistress Mary Fisher, a steward, and a modest number of servants and labourers.

The rector always noted a trace of melancholy in him, though he covered it with good cheer for the children. These now shouted from behind them: 'Mamma! Papa! Here is the sundial! May we tell the time of day, Mamma?'

'Oh they have found it, I have told them of it lately,' their mother said.

Cousin John went over to the cluster of eager children round the old sundial.

Catherine Nelson entered the familiar porch, thinking of the genial presence of her grandfather, whom she had clung to the more particularly after her father's early death. Upon this event he had settled them all in a house at Brooke near Beccles, and provided for them. But they had often been welcome visitors here. His warm cheerful tones (she could hear them in her mind as she stood there) had eclipsed those of her own father. As they paused there, the Knibb clock struck from the end of the passage, its two bells, big and little, denoting the hours in Roman figures. She remembered her grandfather explaining it: she had never forgotten the maker's curious name.

Later, they sat upon the crisp, short turf within the grassy walls of the earthwork. There were two great circular grass ramparts with a deep ditch between them, on whose outskirts grazed Sir John's cattle. Twice or thrice in their expanse the banks and ditch were breached, as it were with a drawbridge over a castle moat, forming an entry into the central high meadow where a few trees grew. They had walked along the driveway which led from the hall to the Wighton road, crossing the river in its way, and turned aside to enter the so-called camp. Cousin

John's servant, Charles, now packed up into the hamper the remnants of the picnic feast.

'Folk commonly call it the Danish camp, cousin,' began the rector, 'but had you ever stopped to wonder how any pack of sea-faring Danes raiding upon the coast for plunder, food and beasts, should have the respite, the tools, or the men, to raise such a considerable earthwork?'

'I had not,' Sir John admitted. 'All I was concerned for was to keep so notable and perfect an antiquity from being ravaged by the ploughs of my ignorant tenants. Crabbe's Castle on towards Wighton was a similar entrenchment much defaced. Wighton Mill stands upon what remains of another.'

'Your concern was an excellent thing for all lovers of antiquity,' Edmund Nelson agreed. 'But is such a vast fortification only as old as the Danes?'

'One of the meadows is still called Sweyno's Mead, over there. They take it to refer to Sweyn, the Dane.'

'Oh, I allow that a settlement of Danes must later have used it, as a safe stronghold from the people of the country: and the countryside remembers. But I contend such a work is more likely the legacy of the Romans? Or of those shadowy folk before the pen of history?'

'Certainly it may be. You have the antiquarian's vision, cousin.'

'Papa,' whispered Maurice now. 'What were the people here that the Danes attacked?'

'Why, our ancestors, the Saxons! Off you run, children, and play Danes and Saxons round the walls!' The children rose gladly to their feet and were gone.

'Remember you cannot run down the steep slopes, you will fall,' their mother called.

'I will go,' said her brother. 'I always liked the view of the whole from the banks,' and he strode off after the screaming children who were already running along the skyline. The rector followed him.

'Little Nan shall stay with us,' said cousin John. 'She is too tender to fight the Danes. You remind me of my own Nan, little one. You are named for your grandmother, are you not?'

Ann nodded seriously, settling in his arm.

'How is your mother, cousin Catherine?'

'Well, cousin. She sent her respects but begged to be excused, it is too hot. She was bereft of both sister and aunt in January, did you know? My Aunt Elizabeth Fowle followed quickly after my mother's Aunt Hamond.'

'Ah, I heard of Aunt Hamond's death! The last of her generation!'

Shrill screams came from Horatio as he topped a bank behind them, waving a stick at his father and his uncle. 'We are the Danes! You are the Saxons! We are the Danes, Papa,' the tiny, fierce figure yelled and danced against the blue sky, looking smaller than ever upon the high rampart.

Before they left Warham, Mrs Nelson and her brother walked up through the trees to the church. Maurice followed, eager to be with his godfather, Horatio came holding his mother's hand.

In the porch, quiet and hot, Catherine stopped to remind her brother of the old servant, Dorothy Forster, who was buried there.

'Do you remember her, brother? She was old when we knew her. She sat in the kitchen in a rocking chair, with lavender in her lap...'

'I can have been only nine when she died: the stone is 1736. I think I do...'

'A great cap she had, spotted muslin.'

'Who was she, Mamma?' Maurice asked.

'A faithful old servant of Sir Charles, your great-grandpapa. So he put her here to remember her.'

'But we tread upon her,' Maurice objected.

Horace clutched his mother's hand the harder. Despite the hot day, the church was cool and smelt dusty and enclosed. In the small square chapel on the left of the main altar lay the graves of the Turners. There were eight, in three rows of three, except that the first place in the middle row where one entered the chapel was an empty space, waiting.

'There,' said their mother softly. 'There lies your great- grandmother, Mary Turner, sister of Sir Robert Walpole. And in the middle, lies your great-grandfather Sir Charles Turner. And next to them lies their only son, John, who died before his father. And behind him lies his wife, Anna.'

Horace stared, silent, appalled. 'Do they like it, Mamma?' he whispered.

'It is but their bodies,their bones here. Their souls are quite elsewhere in heaven,' she explained. 'Would not you like your bones to lie near all your family, when you are in heaven?'

'Come, sister, they are young for such notions. Let us get out into the sunlight,' Captain Suckling said, suddenly seizing their hands and hurrying out, a cold shadow invading his whole frame.

The children long remembered the summer of Uncle Maurice's visit. There were visits to Wells, where he walked the boys down to the quayside, teaching them the parts of the ships. Fat William would sigh and puff as they came back through the lanes towards Burnham, and Horace's small legs, though he made no complaint, would ache with tiredness. Maurice showed his uncle how Burnham Thorpe church tower standing in the Burn valley would peep suddenly over the high clover field before it, as you walked along the path from Holkham. And the first to see it would cry out in triumph.

In the village, life and death, sickness and health, youth and age, luck and loss rubbed shoulders. William Bee had died in May and so had Mrs Gilberd, the sexton's wife. Richard Gilberd did not dig his own wife's grave, but handed over to William Scott. In July, Peter, Mr Nelson's man, bought a coal grate and a pail from an empty house for six shillings and took them home to his wife. That spring the overseers' accounts had been signed by the new Mr Lee Warner from Walsingham, and by Mr Pinckney Wilkinson, squire of Burnham Market. And this year George Goggs' daughter Catherine, who could not write but made her mark, married one Thomas Buck: and George Goggs himself fell ill in late October and his wife, a superior and lettered lady unlike her daughter, took over the books and kept the accounts for him.

'No school for Maurice!' Papa had announced one day in September, coming home from the Market.

'Why? What? Huzzah!' Maurice yelled, before he waited to hear more. No school at the end of the harvest holidays, because William Holsworth had gone bankrupt, a notice nailed on the door said so. His father could not but worry about this. For it was nearly time for William who was six and a half, and even sharp little Horatio just to be five, to join Maurice at school. Other parents worried also, and very soon the town advertised for a schoolmaster and mistress, properly qualified, who would meet with encouragement.

This year for the first time the family festival of October the twenty-first went home to the heart of Horatio, for he had now met its hero and heard his tale. Uncle Maurice himself had gone three weeks past, back to London in good heart to pursue his now hopeful suit.

Sometimes, the echoes of the great world approached more nearly. One bright Tuesday morning in late October the three boys, idling down by the stream because their father was not free to teach them, heard the sound from Creake of many wheels and horses approaching: a grand carriage bearing arms, two smaller chaises and several horsemen. The boys smiled shyly, took off their hats, waved: the very fat elderly man in the carriage bowed! Who was it, who? And where, but Holkham, could he be going? It was soon whispered who it was: it was the king's uncle, the Duke of Cumberland, coming to see his late friend, the Earl of Leicester's great house and his lawns and trees set out new last year by a gentleman who was referred to by fashion as Mr Capability Brown. Edmund Nelson reflected with amusement that the Duke must surely be the most honoured guest to come, yet came he upon the right day, a Tuesday.

One of Maurice's favourite pastimes was spotting putative cousins or distant connections, were they grand or humble, in the weekly paper.

'Papa,' he began one day, 'one of your cousins at East Dereham sells a particular stuff for the bite of a mad dog.'

'Does he now? Which coz is this?'

'Mr James Nelson. It is called Herring's Norfolk Antidote for the bite of a mad-dog. Is he your cousin?'

'I think he must be, yes, a substantial mercer I believe, but I do not know them well. It's a poor thing if we must go all the way to East Dereham when we are bit.'

'Oh, but our Mr Raven the carrier sells it too, at Burnham!' Maurice discovered, pleased.

'Now all we lack is the mad dog,' observed Papa.

Maurice had lately announced a Mr John Nelson to be wanting immediately 'a young man who knows the Hardware business' at his Ironmonger's shop.

'Now, which of you young men knows the hardware business?' Papa had asked his sons. 'Be off at once to East Dereham and earn your own living!'

Maurice had once also in great delight saddled his mother with a discharged smuggler.

'Mamma! One of your cousins...' he began in a tone charged with meaning, 'My granny says you have some relations named Henley?'

'True, a Miss Suckling married a Captain Henley long ago. Old Mrs Henley is still living in Norwich and her daughters. In St Andrew's street. Your Uncle Maurice stays there.'

'Well he's a smuggler, Mamma, listen! Tuesday was released after a confinement of near Ten Years in the City Goal...'

'Gaol, Maurice, is how you say it.'

'No, it says "Goal"..."one Henley, alias Captain Henley, a *smuggler*! A collection was made by the gentlemen in the city of fifteen pounds, to procure his discharge."'

'The Captain Henley I spoke of died years ago. I do not think I have a cousin who is a smuggler,' his mother said reasonably, as if willing to be persuaded.

'Oh, Mamma, it would be vastly more diverting if you had!' Horace piped, and was pleased to hear his father laugh with surprise.

As the winter drew on, Farmer George Goggs from across the valley died of his sickness and his wife handed over the account book she had kept so well and the cash in hand to Isaac Emerson for his turn. And at the end of November Peter's father, old James Black died, and Goody Black told Mrs Nelson every detail when she called to enquire of her lying-in next year. And old Craske who mended up the highways died too.

But in the first days of December all village happenings were swept from every mind, as the relentless tide rushed over the coast and the marshes, a fierce gale from the north-east whipping it from behind. From Snettisham and Hunstanton to Cley and Mundesley and Waxham, came news of sheep drowned upon the marsh, ships washed far inland. At Mundesley the cliffs were washed away. At Wells it was said to be the highest tide observed since 1737, the fishermen's boats were staved, ships at the quay damaged, the *Resignation* loaded with corn for Newcastle driven more than a furlong on to the marsh: and upon cousin John Turner's saltings more than a hundred of his tenants' sheep lay drowned. In Holkham Bay the custom house smack was ashore. Mr Nelson and Peter took the three boys to see a vast expanse of churned and roughened water where there had so recently been land. Ships lay like stranded arks upon inland banks, wreckage danced by on the flood, swollen bodies of sheep and dogs and pigs lay in the mud where the water had retreated. Through the film of tears raised by the cruel wind, Horatio surveyed the grey ravaging sea and spoke no words: for the wind took the breath. In enclosures where the tide had now ebbed Maurice noted the drowned worms: in the hawthorn and elder bushes the clots of grey sea-wrack, lodged like huge birds' nests, amazed the staring William.

CHAPTER EIGHT

Horatio at Large

So it happened that Catherine Nelson's new son was born on the eve of Twelfth Night into a cold, cruel world. (They called him Suckling, with a warm memory still of Uncle Maurice's visits and at Mrs Suckling's suggestion when appealed to.) Following the great tides, the fens were in dire trouble: from Peterborough to Wisbech the poor cattle had hardly a resting place; farmers lost their stock, families were driven in the greatest distress to their upper rooms, and everything wore a face of horror in that flat and fenny country. Two Swedish ships were wrecked the same night upon Burnham Flats: causing the three boys to hurry to Overy the next morning by the footpath way to get a sight of them. They had come back so exhausted, cold, wet and muddy that their mother had wept with anxiety and tiredness. Sixteen wagon-loads of dead sheep were taken out of the Lincolnshire fens in a day, and many farmers in the east were ruined.

Cousin John Turner's man, Charles (whom the children well remembered from the picnic), was clapped into the castle in Norwich for stealing five guineas from Mistress Fisher the housekeeper's locked box in her bedroom. And Charles, third Viscount Townshend, hurried home from Bath feeling recovered from his late illness, only to die at Raynham. This spring too the Earl of Orford's advisers found it necessary to sell off many of his famous grandfather's estates at Houghton.

By the end of February came snow: and little Horatio took a feverish chill and was ill all through March, until Catherine felt distracted with her sickly infant and her ailing boy. And finally there was to be an almost total eclipse of the sun, on Sunday, April the first in the morning.

'And perhaps *that* will be the end of all these disasters,' Mrs Nelson cried. Everybody was ready before church with their smoked glasses, or their tubs of water strategically placed, or their horse-ponds cleared as reflectors. Certainly by ten o' clock darkness was falling, it was cold, birds went to their roosts, Horace (up from his bed) gaped shivering out of the window with the others, and thought it the strangest thing he had ever seen; the cats came indoors and shook and bristled their tails: and the parson alone in the church knelt coldly, with that sense of awe which strange natural phenomena always aroused in him. But as to seeing the sun as a luminous ring nearly blotted out by the moon, alas: cloud covered the sky and no sun (or stars) appeared.

'Even the eclipse was a disappointment,' Catherine Nelson wailed that night.

'My love,' her husband said, 'my mother has written from Hilborough, she and sister Mary will have Horace and the three elder ones for an Easter visit. Dry your tears, for that you should cry at the perversity of an eclipse is sign enough you are too tired!' And he rocked her in his arms, mocking her gently until her tears turned to smothered laughter.

Seven o'clock on a tender April morning: it was Horatio's first long journey and he was quiet and almost sick with excitement. He clung to his mother and she to him before Peter lifted him into the wagon. Maurice was bright-eyed and pleased, he loved a wayfaring and he and Susannah had been to Granny Nelson before. William was glum with sleep but Sukey flung her arms round her mother's neck.

'I wish you were coming, Mamma!'

'Yes, my lamb, but the babies are too young. Now, you and I have put up all the clothes and things you all need. And pray, Sukey, keep an eye on Horace, see that he does not get too tired or cold or wet. I make it your trust, you are old enough,' her mother bade her. Susannah nodded in solemn obedience.

While the four excited children waved and called, their father leaned out to watch his wife and the babies until they turned and she was out of sight. It was only for two days, but the melancholy, the fearful echoes, of departure! The anguish of all partings swept over him, partings which could only presage a final parting. He pulled himself up, spoke briskly to Horatio.

'Now Horace, come and sit with me and share my big cloak. There, that is capital. Look at Creake ruins, where the monks used to live!'

'What are monks?' demanded William, who had quickly come to his father's other side to share his attention.

The parson did his best to describe to his sons the monkish life, hampered by the disparity between his prejudice (as a clergyman of the Church of England) and his predilections: he felt a nostalgia for the quiet regularity of the abbey life which disturbed yet delighted him.

Almost, he could fancy himself amongst their number: he thought that perhaps it was his sense of history.

'One of these days when your legs are all longer we shall walk along the ancient Peddars Way across Massingham Heath to the priory at Castle Acre, there is more of it left there,' he said.

'What is the Peddars Way, Papa?' asked Maurice.

'It is a footpath, a green way. It starts at the coast, right up at Holme, beyond Brancaster. The name is from the Latin word for 'foot', I should suppose. Why, a peddler is a foot-traveller, is he not?'

'Where does it go to?'

'Oh, down and down into the midlands somewhere, I do not know. It is an ancient way made generations ago.'

'Like the camp?'

'Good, Maurice, yes. Probably people as ancient.'

North Creake: and there was Canon Poyntz below his church, upon a fine horse. The two clergymen greeted each other, Mr Nelson explaining their journey.

'You have a long way but a fine day,' the Canon called, bowing them off in courtly style.

'Papa, he is a very grand gentleman, Canon Poyntz, is not he?' Sukey said.

'He is Sue, he is. Grand connections, and rich I believe.'

Sukey gazed at her own father and decided she liked him the better, poor and homely though he be.

Fakenham and the wind mill: here they stopped for some of the food Mamma had packed for it was now after nine and a bright warm morning. Horatio was warmer and happy and full of the excitement of the adventure.

'Raynham, children, there lies Raynham. Where Lord Townshend has lately died.'

They stood in a row to look at the great handsome hall in the distance. Maurice had seen it before. It always recalled a memory of a cold morning and his granny telling of her aunt Townshend with the smallpox; and with the memory mingled the smell of fresh pies.

'Who'll be Lord Townshend now?' he asked.

'Why, the Brigadier his son, who led the men at Quebec with General Wolfe, do you remember?'

Next Edmund pointed out where lay Castle Acre and they gazed over to the ruined, ivied castle on its hill, and the priory lying lower in a loop of the river.

'We will rest a bit here,' he said.

'Papa, I would love to go up to the castle!' Maurice sighed.

'One day you shall. Not today.'

Horace climbed down, glad to jump and stretch his legs and eat one of Mamma's pies. Mamma was left behind at Burnham, and he was happy and enjoying the journey! He was overcome with sudden pain and guilt and longing for her. He choked.

'What is it, Horace?' the rector said, seeing his son's eyes bright with unfallen tears.

'Mamma,' he whispered.

'Only think,' his father said gaily. 'She will have six less hungry mouths to feed at dinner time! She will bless the peace and quiet!'

Horace smiled, comforted.

Before the journey was over, he had fallen asleep. He was roused by the shouts and bustle of the busy town of Swaffham.

'In less than an hour, we shall be there!' the parson told them, excited himself at the old market town and the direction post to Sporle and faces he still knew strangely older and turns in the road which meant nearing home. His children he supposed would forever feel this about Burnham. He reflected upon the strong aching pull of home, to him the symbol of the soul's ache for heaven.

Round twisting corners, uphill and down again, through woodland, over breckland and heath they went, until the rector shouted out at the sight of Hilborough Inn with the initials and the date he remembered upon it: H.R.M. 1718. Not far beyond it on the other side, the red brick wall of old Mrs Nelson's rosy brick and flint house came into sight, with the small round window in one gable at the front.

'There it is Horace, that's my granny's house!' Maurice shouted. There were trees behind it, and a gateway in the wall too small for the wagon, and a larger opening further along where they turned in up a short driveway. The horse tossed his head and stamped and blew, as Peter threw his reins across and leapt down. The ladies ran out of the front door, little Mrs Nelson in black, larger Aunt Mary in dark blue, their caps and aprons frilly and crisp.

'Me Peter, me,' Horatio cried, with unusual shrill insistence.

. 'You, my man,' Peter said, swinging him down by the armpits on to the grass, amongst the chickens and the ducks and the cats.

Horace stood on the grass and jumped and jumped, in a frenzy of excitement and freedom, till he was almost faint with jumping. Old Mrs Nelson slapped both her hands on her thighs and laughed, her merry dark eyes in her round face like plums in a bun.

'Look at that child, Mary! Let out of the wagon! Horatio,' she said pulling him against her, 'be you so pleased to be visiting your granny, now?'

He nodded gasping, his face pink. He beamed at her, he was filled with joy.

66

'Yes I be, I be, Granny!'

'Bless the child,' she said, kissing him. 'We'll soon have you well and strong. Now master William, have you a kiss for your granny? And Susannah, dear! Maurice how you have grown, like a bean, my man! Well, my son, you will be glad to be here at last. Aunt Mary will take the children.'

Sukey and Maurice had hurried to Aunt Mary, standing quietly in the background. They loved her, she was quiet but sweet, she would giggle with them and play with them and have secrets with them, she was one of them. Their granny was a little frightening. Hung around with bags and baskets they all trooped in at the porch.

The house was two sides of a rectangle, the front wing broadest, with a double gable at the side, the narrow back wing extending from it. Inside there was a twisty staircase going up, and a room each side of the front door, and behind these a long dark passage with several rooms off it looking on to the back courtyard, with a way to the back door in the middle. At the end of the long, dark passage was another stairway.

In the wing which lay at the back were the kitchen quarters, very like home and ending in a wash-house and a scullery. Aunt Mary let the older children take the new ones all over it without hustling them. In a day or two Horace was as much at home as the puss upon the hearth, and the warmer, drier climate of Breckland soon served to round his cheeks and turn them pink again.

Before it was dark the rector took his children up the village street and over the field path which led to the rectory and the church. He loved the first sight of the long low house just visible from the road, and beyond it the grey flinty gleam of the church tower through the still unclad trees. Aunt Mary walked with them and Mr and Mrs Rolfe came out to meet them, she with her young son Edmund in her arms and little Ellen who was nearly three clutching her skirts.

'Well brother, here is your little namesake.'

'Here he is, to be sure, and a fine lad. How are you all at Hilborough rectory? This is little Ellen, Horace.'

Ellen stared solemnly at Horatio who smiled, held out his hand and edged up to her. Alice Rolfe suddenly remembered the friendly little creature thrust into her arms on a cold winter evening before her marriage.

'Now Horace, you have come to Hilborough to get well,' she said. 'Ellen, here are all your cousins from Burnham, pray do not be shy, run and play with them!'

Ellen doubted, but Sukey and Maurice, used to Ann's silences, seized her hands and bore her away.

'Sister Mary will have her arms full,' remarked Robert Rolfe to Edmund Nelson, leading him into a study he knew well, and weighing the joys of peace against the warmth of children. His wife and her sister took the baby to bed, and all the children followed.

'There, Horace, this is where your papa slept when he was a little boy. Is not this a dear room?'

Horace nodded and ran to the window. 'Come and see, William!' William followed his brother and the two children stood there, arms round each other, gazing out at the paling sky and the village in the distance.

'Horace and I sleep together,' William said huskily. 'Who did Papa sleep with?'

'Why, there was a little John who died. Then when your father was fourteen or so there was your Uncle John,' explained Aunt Mary standing behind them, her knobbly red hands gentle on their shoulders.

'Where is my Uncle John?' asked Horace, who had never heard of him before. Aunt Mary was silent.

'He went for a soldier the year I was married,' said Aunt Alice.

'Where is he now?' Horace persisted.

'Why, he never writes, so we cannot know.'

'Aunt Alice,' Maurice began. 'In the paper I found a John Nelson, master of a ship that went aground at Cley. But Papa did not think Uncle John could be a sailor.'

'Why, it might have been the making of him, to be a sailor,' Aunt Mary said. 'But I think he is dead.'

Horace turned and looked up at Aunt Mary and thought that she was sad that Uncle John was dead.

'Come and see where Aunt Alice and Aunt Tam'sin and I used to sleep,' she said taking the little boys' hands. 'It is Ellen's room now.'

'Sukey may help with Ellen.'

Sukey lifted Ellen up and staggered with her to the door, while Maurice stood still at the window wondering why nobody would say much about Uncle John.

Horatio was watching the chickens scratching up the dirt for things to eat, and then running quickly backwards so that the things did not escape. (Aunt Mary had showed him this the night before.) The still, hot April day around him was full of activity. The bees made a hollow distant humming round the cherry tree, and a loud hungry buzz upon the red velvet wallflowers. He had seen a glossy blackbird harassed by three open-billed fledglings of bright speckled brown. He liked birds, and he loved birds-nesting, when Maurice took him: Maurice had gone over to Uncle Robert for some special lessons he was having to do with accounts. Sukey was folding linen with Aunt Mary. They had all had warm creamy milk from a cow at mid-morning but it was a long time until dinner. The sun was high in the sky. Horatio thought of the tumble-down stone chapel in the middle of the field on the way to Cockley Cley (not the same Cley as the seaport, for he had asked: another one). They had climbed up the walls and jumped off into the grass last night and he had greatly enjoyed it. He set off up the street to make his way back to it.

In the chapel field there were some cows grazing and against the pilgrim's chapel in the sun leaned the cowherd from the manor eating his noon bite. They had earlier made friends with him.

Horace ran over the grass and flopped down in the sun next to Fred.

'And what may you be a-doing of in my master's cowfield,' said Fred, handing Horace a wedge of cheese on his clasp knife.

'I came to play. We climb up and jump off the walls. Is it your master's cowfield?'

'To speak trew, that be'ant, neither. That belong to some old person miles away, that do.'

'Then what be your master's cows a-doing of in it?' said Horace giggling, his mouth full of cheese. Fred laughed. 'You be a right cute younker,' he remarked, 'for a shrimp.'

Horatio pushed him. He was tired of people calling him a shrimp. If only he could be suddenly as tall as Maurice and as fat as William.

'Trewth is,' said Fred, 'my master he say that be a wicked sin to waste all this 'ere good grass, and no one 'on't be none the wiser no how. That old person...' – he pronounced it 'parson' – 'he 'ont know nuffen about it.'

'Your master could buy it,' Horatio said, scrambling up the wall, and on to the high corner. 'Here I come! Whee-ee-ee-ee!' he gasped, flying through the air, with his arms spread and his knees bent ready to land and his wispy pale hair on end.

'I dessay he will an' all,' said Fred. 'Take care you doan't break your legs. I dursn't do that no how, that be a high jump,' he added in prudish disapproval.

'I dare jump off much higher than that!' boasted Horace. 'Where are you going?'

'Down t'mill, wi' a message. These cows'll stay while I goo I reckon.'

The cows were busy, heads down, twisting off the juicy April grass with noisy enjoyment.

Horace trotted along, keeping up with long lanky Fred's slow strides. They regained the main road and took the lane which ran down to the church and the mill. Each side the celandine reigned with the primroses in attendance.

'Look! Up there. There she goo!'

The startled thrush, unable to outface Fred's peering, flew off her nest with a sound of soft wings and a chuckle of alarm. Fred lifted Horace, up to the hawthorn bush. He put his small hand through the twigs and gently into the nest. Eggs! Warm! The thrill of it!

'May I take one?'

'One then. Happen she can't count.'

Horace laughed softly and stole an egg from the side of the clutch.

'Can you blow it?'

'Maurice can. I can too, I expect,' Horatio added confidently.

'You, there aren't nuffen you can't do an' all,' teased Fred.

There was a greenfinches' nest from which waved four pale diamond-shaped beaks, open for food. Horatio laughed. They passed the church. He thought he would take Maurice to see the nests when he came home.

Horace loved the mill. As they approached they could hear the grinding clack of the wheel, the splash and tumble of the water, the roar and gurgle of the river as it flowed under the brick archway and into still reaches again. There was a high wooden platform built out from the handsome south face of the large mill, where the grain sacks were loaded off the wagons on to the granary floor. There was a wagon there now. Horace could hear the men shouting. He flung himself down on the river bank, his small body half over the water.

'Watch out, doan't you goo a'falling in now,' Fred called with some anxiety. The boy seemed to pay no heed to any danger. 'Do you'll drown,' he warned.

Horace hung with his head sideways and his pale hair flopping, fascinated and deafened with the shapes and the leaps and the drumming of the rushing torrent, until it seemed to rush through his head. He sighed, pulled himself back, and rose to go on. He passed a barn where a man greeted him and then pursued his way up the river. There was a great deal to see along the river: there were wild ducks and smaller birds, there were water-rats, and frogs making croaks, gurgles and plops, there were bays where he could float boats, and small overhanging cliffs. There were marsh marigolds and reeds and rushes, whose woollen middle you could pull out, Sukey had showed him how. Every now and then Horace sat down and tried to think of a way to cross the river.

❦

A most appetising smell came from the great black stew-pot on his grandmother's hearth, Maurice's sensitive nostrils quivered with expectation. He had worked hard at Uncle Robert's lessons and was hungry. His granny polished a huge serving ladle upon her linen apron.

'Did you call William? Ah here he is. Are you clean, child? Show me. Black. Go and wash,' she decreed sharply. 'And call Horatio.'

William did so, in the yard whence he had come. 'Horace!' he bawled over his shoulder, hurrying back to the stew. 'He's not there.'

'Then where *is* Horace?' old Mrs Nelson demanded, looking at Aunt Mary.

'He has not been with us,' Aunt Mary said, 'has he, Sukey?'

Susannah had laid the table. 'No, not at all,' she said.

'Then where has he been? William, when did you last see Horace?'

'When we had our milk, ma'am.'

'Did he walk over with you, Maurice?'

'Only a few steps. He came back here to the garden.'

Their grandmother started to serve stew. 'I dare say he will be here directly. Just run and look over the house, Sukey. I've known a child fall asleep after noon, before now.'

Sukey hastened to do so. She wished so much Horace would come. It was hours since she had seen him, it was three o' clock! He was not in his room or hers, or anywhere else upstairs. He was not in that little nook under the front stairs where he sometimes sat. He was not in the parlour or in the dining-room (they were having dinner in the kitchen).

'He's not anywhere in the house, ma'am,' she said.

'Go and call in the garden and up to the trees, Maurice.'

Maurice did so, inwardly cursing his little brother. His hunger was great. 'There's no answer, ma'am,' he said on his return.

'Then where is the child?' the old lady said, beginning to feel some alarm.

'He's always wandering off at home,' Maurice grumbled.

'Daughter, why are you looking so solemn? What have you to suggest?' snapped old Mrs Nelson.

'Only that...not long ago ma'am...I heard the gypsies go by,' Mary Nelson faltered. 'I wondered if Horatio had been in the street...'

Sukey, who had turned first scarlet and then pale, burst into tears. 'Mamma *bade* me,' she sobbed, 'Mamma made it my trust to look after Horace, and see he didn't get cold or wet or...' Her sentence ended in sobs. 'And now he's lost,' she wailed.

'Come child, we do not know that he's lost yet. Aunt Mary, what time was this you heard the wagons?'

'Well after noon I think, going the Swaffham way.'

'Yes, into the market. Well, they'll not have gone far beyond the town. James,' she called from the back door. 'Young Horatio has disappeared. Do you get on the horse and follow those wagons that went through for Swaffham and make enquiries. Maurice, poor boy, eat this plateful up, and then you go along the Cockley road, where you all were last night.'

Aunt Mary had already put her shawl on. 'I'll go and ask at the rectory and the mill. He may have turned up there.' She was suddenly thinking with horror of the mill pool.

Sukey still cried. She had heard tales of gypsies stealing children, especially fair children. Horace *was* fair; it seemed to her inevitable he should have been stolen. It was all her fault.

'Come Sukey, go with Aunt Mary, it will make you feel better.'

Sukey sprang up to do so. William ate, though not undistressed. His quick tears, induced by Sukey's, mingled saltily with his stew. Maurice scraped his plate, gave a deep sigh, and hurried out wiping his mouth.

Coming from the chapel field was Fred, driving his cows back to the manor. He told his tale, although fear made him refrain from mentioning how he had last seen Horatio.

Maurice hurried after Aunt Mary and Sukey. The Rolfes knew nothing. Maurice ran on down to the mill. One of the men, eating cold food in the barn, had noticed Horatio trotting away along the river. Maurice set off urgently. Ten minutes later he heaved a great sob of relief, seeing Horace at last on the bank beyond a tributary stream. For his torturing imagination had already taken him home to his mother to tell her that Horace (of all her children) was drowned.

'Horace!' he yelled. 'What are you doing?'

Horace had followed the stream which led him into a spinney in a most exciting way. Here he found a small tree fallen across, and over this bridge he had gone. He had wandered far after this, and when it occurred to him to re-cross the stream he could not find the tree. He had followed the stream back to the main river. Bubbles rose in the river, there were fish! Maurice's yell made him jump up.

'Hullo!' he called. 'There are fish, Maurice, huge ones!'

'Why did you not come back? It's late, it is long after dinner, we are all out searching for you, my granny is in a right old way, and Sukey is roaring with tears, and I don't know what all!' Maurice's voice was unusually cross.

Horace stared, startled and puzzled and guilty. He looked about him. 'I cannot get over.'

'But how did you get over *there*, in the first place?'

'There was a fallen tree. Somewhere back in that wood. I lost it.'

'Well, we must needs find it. Come on, I'll go this side.'

72

When the log was found and his brother safely over, Maurice, usually so easy and good-tempered, seized his hand and hustled him. 'Now come you on. No more loitering,' he said sternly.

Horace panted along, half running. He could not understand all the fuss, he had been so happy. 'Is my granny cross?'

'Not so much cross, as anxious. Aunt Mary thought you had been stolen by the gypsies.'

'The gypsies! Why the gypsies?' Horatio said with interest.

'They steal children sometimes.'

'Do they?' Horace thought this would have been mighty agreeable, to go with the gypsies.

'Anyway you were lost, so she's anxious.'

'I was not lost,' Horace stated, surprised.

When they reached home, Granny stood in the doorway.

'He's been along the river,' Maurice said.

Mrs Nelson threw up her hands. 'I wonder, child, that hunger and fear did not drive you home! Why, it is four of the clock and after!' exclaimed she, profoundly relieved to see him. Horatio was still puzzled. Why did they all think he was lost and afraid? He tried to explain to his grandmother that fear never came near him, as he was not lost, and he did not know it was so late. As to hunger, he had not thought of it. But he was beginning to think of it now. She led him in, and served all the hungry with large plates of stew. William, who had eaten his fill, sat watching his brother with a kind of envious, furious admiration. How bold, how cool Horace was! He wished *he* were so adventurous.

On Easter Saturday which was the twenty-first of April, Uncle Robert and Aunt Alice took everybody for a drive. Good Friday had been William's seventh birthday and the expedition was his birthday treat which his uncle thought better executed upon Saturday. Aunt Mary had made William a plum cake: she was sorry for the boy (having an inevitable tendency to pity the downtrodden and unattractive) with his awkwardness and his clowning and his reputation for greed, his dull unloveableness, which contrasted so sharply with Horace's eager spirits and Maurice's quieter sensibility. William had been loudly delighted, and protested he would eat it all himself (quickly pretending this was a jest when it was taken to be one). They carried the rest of the cake with them on Saturday. Uncle Robert drove the ladies in his chaise, Mrs Nelson's man brought the five children in the wagon. William lorded it over them all, telling them where they must sit, since it was, as he declared, his expedition.

They took the road to Bodney and made for the woods around Merton, where the children could pick primroses and look for birds' nests and play hide and seek to their heart's content.

'So Colonel de Grey is the member for the county in place of Lord Townshend,' Mrs Nelson remarked, as they sat watching the children munching William's cake.

'Who's Colonel de Grey?' William, unwontedly talkative, asked the question with his mouth full.

'Wait till you have finished eating before you speak, William, and address your grandmamma with respect,' said she. 'Colonel de Grey lives here in the hall at Merton, as did his father before him, both named Thomas de Grey. Do not you stray too far away, children, or you may meet a keeper.'

'Granny? Why has Colonel de Grey taken Lord Townshend's place, ma'am?'

'Why, because when you become a high and mighty noble lord, you go up to the House of Lords. Brigadier Townshend became a lord when his father died t'other day, so we have to have someone in his place in the House of Commons, do not we?'

'There was an election, Maurice,' explained Uncle Robert. 'They set out at six o'clock in the morning from the Hall here, to get to Norwich by eleven. There was a good crowd went with him to vote him in and they all had dinner at the Maid's Head.'

'So I heard,' Mrs Nelson said. 'Several went from Hilborough. Good sort of people, the de Greys. Old Thomas de Grey was a member fifty years ago. Now children, run away for your play,' she added.

'Bring me some primroses,' said quiet Aunt Mary.

'And watch that Horace,' called Uncle Robert, 'he has a way of losing himself!'

The four children disappeared into the trees. Ellen stayed with her mother.

'Let's see if we can find the hall,' Horace said as soon as they were out of hearing.

'They told us not to,' objected Sukey.

'They did not. They said we might meet a keeper.'

'But they meant...'

'May we, Maurice?' Horatio asked.

'There's no harm in creeping up to see it I suppose.'

'Come on then,' Horace said eagerly, leading the way. 'This is where Granny pointed.'

They soon came to a grove where the trees were thinner and there ahead lay the lake, and the hall beyond it, and stables and farm buildings behind that. It was a handsome place.

'There it is!'

Horace gazed. There it lay in the sun, the shining water before it, the haze of trees making it seem distant and unreachable, like a paradise. How splendid it would be to live in such a place! Colonel Thomas de Grey of Merton Hall: the names seemed to him delightful, quite as good as Lord Walpole of Wolterton, his godpapa.

'Should you care to live there, Maurice?' he asked.

Maurice considered. William said yes at once. Sukey said: 'It is very large and grand. There would be a lot of work. It is bigger than Warham where cousin John lives.'

'Why, the servants would do the work,' Maurice said, 'but you must have a great deal of money to live in such a place. Should you care to live there, Horace?'

'Yes!' Horace said, his eyes shining. 'And have a boat and sail on the lake!' There was an old punt tied up by the lake.

'And a chaise like Uncle Robert's,' said William huskily.

'Grander than Uncle Roberts,' Maurice said. 'A carriage like that Duke's we saw. With arms upon the door.'

'Yes! And with footmen.'

'Where will you get all the money, Horace?' Sukey asked, quite willing to indulge his fantasy though prosaic herself.

'When I grow up, I shall make my fortune. I shall earn plenty of money! For all of us!'

'How?' Maurice asked, laughing at him.

'Oh somehow,' Horace said confidently. A high and mighty noble lord, his granny had said!

'May I live there with you?' William requested.

'Yes, you all may, but it shall be my house!'

'We shall all require houses of our own,' Sukey said. 'When we get married.'

'Then you shall come and visit me and William.'

'May we fish in your lake?' Maurice asked, amused.

'Yes you may! Now, come on. I shall find a nest first, I wager!'

They turned about, and went off laughing into the wood after Horatio.

CHAPTER NINE

The Mariners of England

In June, 1764, Captain Maurice Suckling was to be married at last to Lady Mary Walpole. Catherine Nelson longed to go. To dress up in style, to go to London upon the Lynn diligence with her mother to the fashionable church in Hanover Square, to see brother Maurice take his bride!

'Oh, Sukey, how I wish that you and I could go! It will be a grand wedding, every lady and gentleman in brave clothes, depend on it. And delicious things to eat at the dowager's London house...'

'Oh Mamma,' pleaded Sukey, her eyes filling with tears of longing, 'can we not go? Oh, pray can we not go with my granny, Mamma?'

Her mother sighed as she smiled, all her responsibilities and her tiredness flooding back upon her. 'My lamb, it is so far, a long day's journey. And this poor child is not yet weaned,' she added as she dried little Suckling upon her lap.

'I suppose in truth it is Maurice who should go to his godfather's wedding,' Mamma deliberated.

'It will be nearly midsummer, he will be at home for the hay-making, you said it was the nineteenth of June!'

But Maurice was far from wishing to sacrifice the hot sweet-smelling hours in the hayfield, his midsummer holiday, to the sitting still all day—two days indeed—in a stuffy conveyance and the doubtful pleasure to one so quiet of a fashionable gathering in London. He said so.

'Little Sukey, would you enjoy such an adventure?' her papa said, smiling at her round flushed face.

Susannah looked at her mother, having a brief struggle. 'Oh yes, Papa!'

'You shall go and represent us all,' Papa said. 'Mamma shall make you look a picture!' Sukey dashed to her father and hugged him.

Susannah would be nine a week to the day before Captain Suckling was married and Mrs Suckling was delighted to have her company. Catherine and Sukey chose muslin and silk and ribbons and slippers and a new straw hat, at Westgate, and were busy for a week: and Peter drove the travellers to Lynn early on a June morning to catch the London coach. They were to stay at the house in Hanover Square whence Uncle Maurice was to be married and which belonged to his mother's cousin, Admiral George Townshend.

So Captain Suckling was married on a day of heat, and following such a thunderstorm that he hoped that his lady bride was not lying awake imagining it to portend something disastrous. They took their wedding journey into Suffolk and Norfolk visiting relations. At Woodton (home of his cousin Denzil Suckling's widow, to which estate he was heir) Captain Suckling sat for his portrait to Mr Bardwell. And one summer day he drove his bride to Burnham. But she seemed a shy, formal, quiet lady, and neither Catherine Nelson's warmth nor the children's muted zest for their uncle detached her from her reserve. Horace and William agreed that they would rather have the Uncle Maurice of last year with his battle and his booms, and Maurice and Susannah went so far as to say so.

'Oh, she will be different when she is better acquainted with us,' said Mamma, 'and when she has children of her own. She has lived her life with an ageing mother, you know. Why, Aunt Alice is pleasanter and more agreeable now she has her own children, is she not?'

Sukey looked doubtful. 'Yes,' she conceded. 'She was very kind. But we like Aunt Mary best,' she confessed. 'She always lets me help her…'

'And she makes us laugh, she has secrets with us,' Maurice added. 'From my granny.'

His mother smiled at this.

'And she does this Pig went to Market with my toes. And she sings rhymes like you do,' added Horace. 'Boys and girls come out to play,' he warbled suddenly and not very accurately.

'She made me my plum cake,' William stated: a fact he would never forget.

'Dear Aunt Mary! Papa, the children love your sister Mary.'

'Do they so? I am not surprised, so do I, she is a dear creature,' said Papa. 'What other rhymes did she teach you?'

'She taught us A was an Archer…'

'S was a sailor, a Man of Renown,' Horace remembered. 'What is renown, Papa?'

'Oh, it means a man is famous, well thought of, everybody looks up to him. Do you understand?' Horace nodded.

'Like Uncle Maurice,' he said. Of this the parson felt doubtful.

'Here Edmund, let me show you: "This pig…"' Horace said coaxingly to the little boy crawling round the room in his night-shirt. Dear God, their mother thought, looking at little Horace playing the father, how they grow, how quickly they grow! Her husband saw her thought and they smiled. He seemed to have grown from child to boy in the few weeks he was at Hilborough.

This summer, the three boys began to play at collecting the names of the ships and shipmen at Burnham and Wells. You must be first to see the ships in the harbour: and if you discovered the master's name too it went for double. Uncle Maurice had suggested it last year: and Papa approved of it as a sharpener of the memory. Long recitals of names were often to be heard issuing from upstairs at night.

'*Resignation,* Pentin; *Plough,* Henderson; *True Friends,* Oldman; *Sea Nymph,* Bloom; *Elizabeth and Ann,* Wabon,' came Horatio's piping voice.

'*John and Elizabeth,* Mattsell; *Hopewell,* Story,' called Maurice from his room.

'*Success,* Brin,' stated William huskily, as if trying his luck.

'You did not see the *Success,* William,' Horace argued. 'I did. And her master. And so did Maurice.'

'I did,' roared William. 'I did see the *Success* first!'

'No you did not, did he, Maurice? It was the day he was not there.' Horace's memory did the work of two.

'Hush boys, it is nine o'clock,' Papa called up the stairs. 'You will waken the children.'

This summer too, Maurice tried to teach his small brothers to fish. It all arose from the salmon of Downham Bridge.

'Papa, Papa, pray just listen to this! "...a Salmon leap'd out of the River near Downham Bridge into a Boat lying there, which weighed nineteen pounds and was sold for eight pence per pound"!'

'Now then, let us see what your uncle's lessons have done for you. How much money did the great salmon bring to the fortunate owner of that boat?'

Maurice did the sum in his head. Horace tried but failed. William did not try.

'Maurice, do pray let us go fishing! *Tomorrow!* You said you would teach us,' demanded Horatio.

So they would be off down the River Burn to the stretch above Overy Mill, where the teasels grew for the wool-combers. And Maurice would try to teach them to cast, and they would sit for hours in the sun waiting for a bite. Sometimes they went to the harbour at Wells to join the boys at high-tide fishing off the quay. On windless, warm, moonlit nights the fishermen at Burnham Overy would put out their seine nets for the salmon trout at low tide, and gather them up when the sea brought the fish in. Once, Maurice was invited to go. He came back with stories of great silver fish in the moonlight, heaving upon the sand, neatly killed with a stroke on the back of the head.

In Burnham Thorpe the townhouse was mended up that August: and the rector persuaded John Humphrey junior to take a turn at the overseers' accounts after George Goggs' death. And the letter posts were altered for the better, to the rector's satisfaction: there was to be a post six days in a week instead of three between Thetford and many places in north Norfolk, including Wells and Burnham. In Westgate, Edmund Powdich, who kept a grocery and drapery store (where Catherine Nelson had taken Sukey to buy her wedding muslin) went bankrupt; and the inhabitants of the seven villages hurried to buy up stuffs from his store being sold a pennyworth to pay the creditors. Perhaps his downfall, people said, was because of the importing of clothes and lace from France:

> Such Art and Perfection, such elegant Taste
> Our own Manufactories grace
> 'Tis pity our Nobles their money should waste
> In buying French clothes and French lace,
> This custom pernicious, ye Britons oppose,
> Consider how hard is the case
> To see British subjects arrayed in French cloaths,
> Bedizen'd and daub'd with French lace.

Mamma and Sukey would link hands and skip round the parlour declaiming this rhyme, Mamma's voice rising in a hiss at the 'custom pernicious'; but Mamma grew so breathless so quickly these days, it quite frightened her.

"'My father had a small estate in Nottinghamshire; I was the third of five sons. He sent me to Emanuel College in Cambridge, at fourteen years old, where I resided three years, and applied myself close to my studies...'" began Edmund Nelson, in the satisfied tones of a father beginning to share a feast with his son. Horace stood at the study table upon a stool that he might the better see Lemuel Gulliver's map. There were two islands, one called Lilliput, t'other which he could not read, and two small three-masters in full sail which he greatly liked, and other pieces of land at the extremities, but the largest part of the page was blank white sea, giving him a sense (though in miniature) of the vastness of oceans, which he had not felt before. In Burnham parsonage the sober, regular new year season which the rector loved was in, and work

80

was to begin. (Maurice envied the prolonged Christmas festivities of Norwich, where those of delicate ear might attend Mr Cartwright's demonstrating the musical glasses; and you might see a grand piece of machinery, The Lilliputian World, according to Dean Swift.)

But no. Maurice and Sukey and William must go daily to school, and Horace must learn his lessons. The rector enjoyed teaching Horatio, who was lively and apt and eager to please: the boy should have six more months at home, for so often the nameless ills of childhood struck him, sore throats and aches and coughs, fevers and chills, when his eyes would look huge in his pale face and his smallness seemed simply frailty. Reminded of Dean Swift the rector had produced *Gulliver's Travels*. Surely this was a tale Horatio would enjoy.

'Now then, here are two things in the very first page to interest us. Who do we know who is the third of five sons?' said Papa, pulling down the sides of his mouth in a comical smile. Horace looked up quickly, thinking and counting.

'I am, Papa! I am. Not counting Sukey. And Ann.'

'Quite so, for they are daughters. And who went to Emmanuel College?'

'My grandpapa! *Your* father?'

'So. Now listen a little and then you shall read.'

But when Gulliver laid out some of his money in learning navigation and other parts of the mathematics useful to those who intend to travel, Horace interrupted. 'Papa, I should like to learn navigation.'

'Would you so? Many schools teach it. Do you intend to travel?'

'Yes. Like Uncle Maurice!'

The story delighted Horace, and what he did not understand he hurried past. Mamma once found her son poring over the book alone, little bursts of satisfied merriment escaping him from time to time.

'What does he do now, Horace?'

'He's captured the whole enemy fleet, Mamma! He made hooks and cables and put them through the prows of the ships, and tied all the cables together! And they kept shooting their tiny arrows at him, but do you know what he did, Mamma?'

'No, tell me!'

'He put on his spectacles!' Horace rolled from side to side, giggling: Ann toddled over to join in.

'And then he had to cut all the anchor cables. And then he waded over the sea, pulling the ships behind him. Between where the enemy lived and this island where he lived. You know he was a giant to these people?'

'Yes, I remember.'

'Well, he pulled fifty men-of-war after him, Mamma! Only think of it! This is my favourite tale Mamma, I *dote* upon it. I think Papa likes it very well too!'

His mother smiled to hear him chatter on in his increasing mastery over words; although he still read slowly and uncertainly, he would sometimes talk with abandonment.

'What a tremendous thing it would be, Horatio, if some British giant strode over the Channel and did the same to France! How the French would squeal, I warrant.'

Horatio stood up at once and strode about. 'I wish there were a way to turn myself into a giant! I could fix the hooks and pull the fleet over the Channel!'

'So you could, and the King might make you a baron for your pains. There,' his mother said, putting Suckling down to join Edmund and Ann, 'watch the children, Horace, while I go to the kitchen.'

Horace tried to impress the babies into an enactment of the stealing of the enemy fleet, but had scant response. The house was merrier and noisier when the others came home from school: Horatio loved it. As they lay side by side in bed, Horatio would tell William about Gulliver's latest adventure. In return he would demand to know what William had done at school; but more often than not William was overcome with sleep first, while Horace lay later awake, listening to his brother's breathing.

One day in February, the rector looked up from a letter and said: 'My cousin Edmund bids us go, and lie at Congham, and visit the Lynn Mart. What about you, my love? Does the Mart tempt you?'

'It is plain I cannot go, dearest, much as I would. But you shall go, and if it is fair weather take Horatio with you. He will be the better for a little change.'

'Could we ride both upon my old mare, do you think?'

'Horace will make little difference! But it is a long trot for the mare. Why do you not bear Horace to the Hamonds at Bircham and show him to his godpapa? I will write to my cousin Dorothy, and ask if Dr Hamond will carry you on to Congham. You may leave the mare at Bircham a day and then ride home upon her.'

Horace was listening eagerly, the prospect of a journey with his father filling him with excitement. Papa smiled at him.

'Well, Horace, will you accompany me to the great Mart at Lynn? It is a brave sight I promise you. Bigger than our market. And you must be on your best behaviour with your godpapa,' he said, his eyes twinkling at his son. Horatio was aware that his father was for some reason a little amused at the prebendary of Norwich. As to cousin Edmund, he could not for the moment remember who he was.

'Yes Papa! Papa, who is your cousin Edmund?'

'Why, you know cousin Edmund, he came last April when little Suckling was christened,' his mother reminded him. 'After you all came home from Hilborough. At Bircham you will meet your namesake the other Horace, much your age,' his mother went on.

'And at Congham he will make the acquaintance of James, Elizabeth and Charles. That is a fine beginning for a boy who intends to travel,' Papa said.

'He must not go if it blows from the north-east or if it snows, my love. Show Horace the Custom House and the Market Cross and the Duke's Head in Lynn, husband: they were built at the expense of his Turner forebears.'

'Which forebears built which? Pray listen, Horatio, to your family history,' Papa said with a smile.

'Well, now. You know that your great grandpapa was Sir Charles Turner of Warham, do you not?' Horace nodded, he remembered Warham.

'He had two uncles, great merchants in Lynn. One of them, another Sir Charles, had the market cross put up; the other, Sir John, had the Duke's Head built for the use of the merchants who came to his exchange. There, that's some family history for you.'

Horace, to the manifest disgruntlement of William who was jealous, began to pray nightly that it would neither blow from the north-east nor snow, and could hardly believe his fortune when he found himself pressed warmly against his father, his thin little body jolted mercilessly by the mare's quick trot.

'Now, Horace, remember what I have told you, rise with the horse as I do, or she will shake you to death. Come the spring I shall purchase a pony or two at the fair, it's high time you boys learnt to ride.'

It was far from Horatio's first trip upon a horse, but he had never gone so far as this. They had left behind Creake Abbey ruins and turned off between some light brown winter plough lands for Stanhoe, and the Birchams which lay up against Houghton land. Dr Hamond lived in a fine parsonage and he came out on to his steps to greet them, holding up his broad hands as if he blessed them. At his side hopped small Horace, come to greet Horace Nelson.

'Well, godson,' boomed the doctor, enclosing Horace's small hand in his great paws. 'How do you do?'

'How do you do, sir?' Horatio replied. 'I hope you are well, godpapa?' He had asked his mother what he should say and was repeating it exactly.

'Run in with Horace, and you shall have some refreshment.'

The boys had not met before. Hamond took Nelson's arm and

hustled him in towards his mother. Mamma's cousin Dorothy was a niece of Mrs Suckling's: she kissed Horace and gave the boys and her daughter cups of hot chocolate and little cakes. Horatio longed passionately for more chocolate but Hamond and his sister bore him away.

'Where will you school your boys, Mr Nelson? We think of sending Horace into Norwich as Dr Hamond is so often there.'

'We have taken no decision yet, ma'am. The older ones go daily to Burnham Westgate. Horace goes after midsummer.'

'I hear there is a fine new school house to go up at North Walsham this year for the Paston foundation, you know. The Paston debts being at long last paid, I heard the school gets over a thousand pounds.'

'Is that so? We were shocked to read of young William Walpole's death at the school in Norwich.'

'Ah, it would be happier not to have to send them away at all,' Mrs Hamond sighed.

'It would not be good for them,' said her husband unequivocally.

The rector supposed that this was true, it was an axiom upon which the English always acted: but he felt his usual doubts.

Before twelve they were off in Dr Hamond's chaise, which Horatio climbed into with the utmost satisfaction. Young Hamond begged to be allowed to go too. The rector watched the two boys with pleasure, entertained pleasantly with a lively account of the adventures of Gulliver which the other Horace had not yet read.

'But have you read *Robinson Crusoe*?' demanded he. Horatio admitted that he had not. The journey towards Hillington and Congham passed in Hamond's recital of shipwreck and palm trees and parrots and goats and sand, to which Nelson added some colourful details from the West Indian adventures of his uncle Maurice Suckling. Mr Nelson could scarce claim enough attention to show Horace the church at Hillington of which another cousin, the reverend Mr William Nelson, was parson. This was food for thought to young Horace Hamond.

'And now you are going to a third reverend Mr Nelson at Congham?' he piped after a moment. 'What a quantity of reverend Mr Nelsons there are, sir.' The truth of the remark made the rector laugh, despite its pertness.

At Congham the little boys parted as if they had known each other all their lives, and hoped to meet again.

And here were cousin Edmund (with Papa's long nose) and cousin Elizabeth Nelson, and little Lizzy who was Sukey's age and Charles who was about Horatio's. James was away at school. Horace's cheeks were flushed with the excitement of the day: there was little shyness about him and he seemed happy and at home with each family. His father watched him fondly, comparing him with quiet, indolent Maurice and awkward William, and thought that this was the easiest of his sons. But soon after dinner he flagged and cousin Elizabeth bore him quickly away upstairs.

Horatio awoke to a yellow dawn pierced by the jagged cry of the cocks in the yard, and the realisation that something more than usually agreeable was to happen. He was going with Papa and his cousins to the Lynn Mart!

February, the dullest month of all the year, was always enlivened by the Mart at King's Lynn. As well as a great influx of traders from as far away as London, it was a time for special assemblies, or for balls given by schoolmasters who desired to please parents and impress more pupils, or for the freedom to be presented by the mayoralty to some man they wished to honour: and for many entertainers.

As cousin Edmund's conveyance wound along St Nicholas Street and emerged into the handsome Tuesday market place, Horatio hardly knew where to look first. The square throbbed with people, with chatter and shouts and the cries of traders, with the clop of hooves, the clink of harness, the creak of wagons. Many of the regular shops, bedizened with new stock for the occasion, burned flares at their doors which glowed in the grey February morning: while in the middle of the square, shouldering the handsome octagon of the domed market cross as if they would shoulder it out of the way, were the movable booths and stalls of the traders.

(In due course, Papa was to point out to Horace the Market Cross, the Duke's Head Inn, and the Custom House.

'Why, you quite own the place Horace, do you not?' he said solemnly.

But Horace giggled, knowing he was twitted.)

'Hop down, Lizzy and Horace and Charles,' said cousin Elizabeth now. 'I shall go first to Mr Jones, that London linen draper.'

Mr Jones sold Irish linens and hollands, Russian and Irish sheetings, dowlasses, huckabacks, damasks and diapers, cloutings and tablecloths, and very much else. The rector took Horace and Charles on, while cousin Edmund waited impatiently to carry the purchases.

At the corner of King Street stood the Globe Inn (Horace caught sight of a great licking fire and a hurly of people already drinking ale) and next to it was the glass warehouse of Mr Jonas Phillips, open every year at Mart time. In the light of the lamps twinkled cut glass, candlesticks, toilet bottles, glass lanthorns—'very neat for halls and staircases,' Horace read.

'Shall we buy Mamma a toilet bottle? Or a new candlestick?'

Horace chose a toilet bottle, prettily cut, with a silver lid: Papa purchased also some flour of mustard from Durham, not often found in Burnham Market.

They walked right round the square, passing saddlery, or ships' chandlery, coaches a-making or furniture upholstering, and re-met the others. All turned along High Street, where Mrs Nelson and Lizzy disappeared quickly into Sarah Pawlett's, a silk mercer; and the gentlemen by common consent were making towards Thomas Hollingsworth's bookshop, when Horatio cried out:

' Papa! Pray wait, Papa! Here is a shop called *Robinson Crusoe*, Papa! Is it the same? That Horace told me of?'

Could the adventurer after all his travels have been washed up in Lynn? Was he sat behind his counter, with his parrot upon his shoulder and his goatskin cap? Horace longed to go in and see. The two men turned back, looked, and then laughed.

'He has taken his name from the book, Horace! He has been here some years, I have seen the shop often. Upholsterer and auctioneer.'

Horatio's face showed his disappointment.

'You did very well to mark and read it,' said his father.

'He is a dull dog, Horatio, compared with real Crusoe.'

Mr Hollingsworth's bookshop smelled of leather and paper and ink and glue (for Mr Hollingsworth was a binder as well as a bookseller) and as well as books and quires of paper, there were chap-books and broadsheets and maps and newspapers, and quills and pen knives and sand in glass trays. And books of music for the harpsichord and the German flute, and books of airs for the fiddle, and songs for the family, and gentlemen's pipes and tobacco pouches. There were medicines too and Herring's Norfolk antidote for the bite of a mad dog (which made the rector smile). They bought three neat leather notebooks for Maurice and William and Horatio and a ladies' pocket companion 1765 for Sukey, with all manner of information in it including recipes and tables and a picture of the Queen.

'What will you write in it?' Charles urged as they hurried along the street. Horace's fingers were over the book in his pocket feeling its smoothness.

'I might write the names of the ships in it,' he said, remembering the old game.

'What ships?'

'All the ships that come into Wells and Burnham. We learn their names and their masters and count who has seen the most.'

'Wells, and Burnham!' Charles scoffed. 'I'll show you some ships! Papa, may we go down to the quay? There may be some big ships in, Papa!'

They came out into the Saturday Market Place, watched over by St Margaret's Church, turned up into Queen Street, past overhanging houses, ancient colleges and courtyards, then walked down by the Custom House towards Purfleet Quay. Horace could smell the water.

They reached the River Ouse. How broad it was! How dark and deep the water, how far off the churches and houses on the other side! It was much, much wider than the channel at Wells, and dear Burnham Overy, with its mud flats and sunny sand dunes and narrow channel seemed a castaway place fit only for Robinson Crusoe. And the ships! Several lay there in the channel at anchor, the bare masts of others criss-crossed the sky above the wharves at the common staithe.

'Take care now, mind the ropes and chains, watch out for the bollards, beware of the tumbrels, keep away from the edge!' called cousin Edmund briskly. 'It is quite safe,' he added. 'Charles often comes here and knows his way about.'

Thus for the first time Horatio took in the sights, sounds and smells of a bigger port than Wells. Mountains of coal from the northern ports, thickly stacked barrels of wine from France and the Channel Islands, piles of timber from Russia and the Baltic, tall baskets of local fish, all waited in their appointed places. On to a ship, gently heaving in the dark water at the staithe, men loaded baskets of cargo into the hold. They laughed up at the two little boys. There were smells of pitch and wet wood, of ropes and fish and salt and sea, there was the tap, tap of blocks against each other, the creaks and murmurs of wind in rigging, the rumble of wagon and tumbrel wheels over the cobbled quay. Horace stood rapt, looking up at the huge furled rolls of the sails, and started when his father's hand touched his shoulder.

CHAPTER TEN

The Poor of Burnham Thorpe

'Papa, may I write with a pen?'

'Why would you write with a pen? You have your slate, or your pencil.'

'But Papa, when I write in my new notebook I must write with a pen—and not allow the ink to splutter.'

'That you must,' Papa smiled, entirely understanding the pleasure of a clean page in a new notebook. 'So you wish to practise. And so you shall.'

He opened the ink pot, took a pen from his stand and tried it. 'I will sharpen it for you, make a new point…There. Try that.'

Horace wrote, a large A and a small a with great care.

'Write me an alphabet. Before you go to school, Horace, we must have you writing and adding up your numbers. Your reading is good already.'

Horace copied the alphabet the rector had made for his children: the hand was bold, comely, rounded and almost upright. The hand they had taught Maurice and Sukey and William at school was much less good to Mr Nelson's eye, a pointed, sloping copyist's hand with many loops. However, he could only hope each child would impress his nature upon his handwriting as he grew.

Horatio's face was intent, his lower lip protruding: the pen scratched circumspectly. Fate overtook him upon the k: the hole filled, the tail left behind a trail of ink spots.

'Oh, Papa!' he wailed.

'Never mind, never mind. Practice makes perfect. Try, try, try again. Write k anew.'

When he had done, Papa gave him the newspaper.

'Here, write about this forward German boy. He is not much older than you, about William's age. Only fancy, if William could compose tunes, or Maurice play solo!'

And the rector sighed, at the lack of achievement of his boys.

Horace wrote:

One Wolfgang Mozart, a German Boy, of about 8 years old, is arrived here, who can play upon various sorts of instruments of music in consort or solo, and can compose music surprisingly; so that he may be reckoned a wonder at his Age.

London, 23rd February.

His father commended him. He had not yet learned to join up his characters but formed them well and boldly.

Before March was gone the rector had acquired a couple of ponies from Isaac Emerson. Maurice had already learnt to manage a horse, now the parson put Horace and William up and began to teach them their paces. Horace got on the faster being the most at home, and within a week or so was able to accompany his father. To trot along the spring lanes high enough seated to be able to see! To wave at his grandmamma over her wall! To see mad March hares boxing up on the ploughland, to look right over the Burn valley to Whitehall Farm and East End Farm and the cottages, and the town bridge and the church in the distance! This expanded Horatio's little life in a great leap. All seven Burnhams were within reach of a child, if he did not have to trudge. Horace and William loved the ponies: and Horatio's desire to excel led him to bend his mind so ardently upon managing his mount, that he would find himself trotting and cantering in his dreams.

One Monday morning in April, the rector produced the leather parish account book, and gave Horace his first lesson in adding up pounds, shillings and pence. The book had been brought to him on Sunday by young John Humphrey. Old Mr Humphrey had been a churchwarden for years and years, and had agreed with Mr Nelson it was time his son took a turn. The Humphreys lived at Whitehall Farm: their daughter Jane had married Robert Beeston, a miller from Wighton, last December, their other son William was still a lad.

The book was tall and narrow, fifteen inches by six: and Horace had to crane his neck to see the top of the first page: 'William Goggs, his book'. He would write this, he decided, on the first page of his new notebook: Horatio Nelson, his book. Papa picked out a few items and began to show him how to add up money. Horace's mind was elsewhere, he was reading from the top of the page:

The Disburstments of John Humphrey junr from the 21st of October 1764 untill the 7th of April in the Year 1765.

'Horatio, you are not attending,' Papa said, giving him a smart rap on the knuckles with his desk ruler.

Horace flushed scarlet. 'I beg your pardon, Papa, I was reading the top of the page.'

'There is no call for you to read it now. You are to learn to add up the items. Now, then. Go through it with me.'

Horace added two and then three and then four and more items, until his father could see that he had begun to master the wayward idiosyncrasies of pounds, shillings, pence, halfpence and farthings.

'Now you may read through the accounts, and then I will ask you some questions.'

'Thank you, Papa.' Having to read the accounts was perhaps a kind of penalty for being too eager to read them before: but he struggled on.

...gave Margaret Shapherd when sick o.7.0...gave Ann Black for Nursing Margt Shapherd 0.0.9...pd for a Shirt for Richard Tidd 0.2.6...pd for a shift for the Widow Scot 0.2.5¼...pd for a pair of Breeches for Rich. Tidd 0.2.9...pd John Seels the Certainty 0.3.0...pd. for Richard Tidd's coat mendg 0.0.8...then pd the wid^w Dean 24^w Collection at 1^{sh} p.w. 1.4.0...Mr Jacombs Bill for Coals for the Poor 5.1.8...for a Rate Makeing 0.1.0...

At last he reached the bottom.

'Are there any words you do not understand?'

'Yes Papa. What is the collection?'

'The collection is what the poor may collect each week, but the overseers give it them for six months at a time, usually. It is easier. What does Richard Tidd get a week?'

'He...may...have...' Horace's finger sought the place. 'Two shillings a week. But Widow Dean only gets one shilling a week...'

'They are given what they need. Now, how much more did Richard Tidd's shirt cost than Widow Scot's shift?'

Horace found the place and considered. 'Three-farthings...Papa? Has not Richard Tidd any money at all of his own?'

'No, Horace. Unless he may earn a penny or two, in the summer time in the fields. But he is old.'

'It cannot be very agreeable, Papa?'

'No, it cannot be agreeable to be so poor. Often there is not enough to eat. In winter you are cold.'

'But they get some coal, Papa!'

'Yes, they have some coal. And some wood if they are strong enough to collect it.'

'Papa, what is the Certainty?'

'That is a fixed sum, that goes every year to a person who needs it. It may be the same person for years.'

'And what does a 'Rate Makeing' mean?'

'Why, someone has to work out how much we need to help our poor, and how many pennies from each of their pounds the richer people shall give, to make this sum. Do you understand?'

'Yes, must you pay some?'

'Yes, all the people of a certain income pay the rate. This year, it was ninepence per pound. Now Horatio, can you add up that great column? Or shall we do it together?' His eyes twinkled.

Horace laughed. 'Pray let us do it together!'

Papa put the figures on to a spare sheet as they laboured up the column.

'Tomorrow, we will take the book to Simon Simpson,' he said.

Simon Simpson of Thornage had married Sarah Goggs, George's widow, at a decent interval after his death, and was perfectly willing to step into George's shoes as overseer too. After lessons on Tuesday they set off towards Creake, crossed the Burn by the road bridge and turned back towards Thorpe. East End Farm is a neat house at a corner, where the Overy and Thorpe and Walsingham lanes meet. It was then the last dwelling in Thorpe on that side of the river, as the parsonage was on t'other. As for Mr Humphrey at Whitehall Farm, he was upon the road to Walsingham and barely in Thorpe at all. There is a sundial upon the front of East End Farm with the date 1729. Simon Simpson, pale, tall and long-nosed, hooded his green eye at Horace and poked him in the ribs. In the parlour Mr Jacombe waited, and young Mr Humphrey standing first on one foot and then on the other.

'Good morning, Parson. Good morning, Horatio.'

Simon had already taken the book and was busy making his own tally: which agreed with the rector and his son. Mr Nelson then took a pen and wrote out the accounts, what had been paid out, what was left over, what had come in by the rate. Beneath the sum, Papa wrote:

Ap: 9th 1765
These accounts examined
and approved
By us   E Nelson Rect.

and handed the pen to Simon, who signed beneath him. Then Papa turned over, smoothed down the new page and wrote at the top of the left hand sheet:

Ap: 9th 1765
For the year ensuing
We appoint Isaac Emerson Junr
and Simon Simpson Overseers of the poor.
                                                        E Nelson Rec^{tr}

Underneath, signed Robert Jacombe and John Humphrey Junr, the churchwardens: and left the book and the money box for Mr Simpson.

Papa and Horace went towards Thorpe town. Over the town bridge, past the townhouse and the flint cottages, past the forge, on past the inn and another farm, and then along the mile of open road to the Market. They came to Ulph Church at the east end of the town, and Edmund glanced at it anxiously as they passed.

'One more wild winter and it will be as bad as Sutton,' he said, 'which no one dare enter unless he cares to risk his neck.'

'Will they fall down, Papa? What will you do?'

'I wonder if we may not rob Peter to pay Paul; let Sutton go, sell the materials to provide some money and make Ulph secure.' He nodded to himself, approving the idea.

Horace loved Burnham Market, as the town of Westgate was often called. The town green was bright with April grass, the goose beck full and rippling, the geese and ducks plodding its edge, hunting. Standing well back from the green in a handsome line each side curved the houses and inns, flint and red brick, some with handsome pillared porticoes and fanlights; the shops with bow windows and lanterns and modest signs, with doors which rang mild bells as you entered and steps leading down to dim counters. The wide loop of the street met in the church at Westgate end. On its south side the street ended in Burnham Polstead House, one of the handsomest in the town: on the north of the church lay the park of Burnham Polstead Hall where Squire Wilkinson lived, and whence the rippling beck issued.

Burnham Market was a flourishing little town. There were two attorneys, Mr Matthew North and Mr Nicolas Raven (whom the rector always consulted for church or family business); there was Mr Charles Dewing, land agent, and Mr William Suckerman, surgeon and apothecary. There was Thomas Cranefield the watchmaker, straining his eyes in his window mending a clock: and Dent's shop, agent for chemists and herbal remedies, and snuff and tobacco, behind which was a carpenter's workshop where Thomas Dent and his son pursued their prime occupation of joiners, making many articles as well as coffins. There was Mr John Raven's, newsagent, chemist and carrier (gone off early this morning on his usual trip to Norwich). There was a fine malthouse and dwelling house with it, which belonged to the Powdichs of Creake Abbey.

Papa made his own and Mamma's purchases, and rode back to the Turf ground (which lay between Westgate and Norton parishes) to survey the sheep, a quarter of this flock being his, and Peter being even now preparing to welcome some hoped-for lambs. On up over the fields to Norton Church, its neat, round, castellated flint tower glistening in the sunlight. From Norton tower you would certainly see the sea: Horace made a vow to climb it as soon as chance permitted.

Horatio rubbed impatiently at the dusty glass of the tower window with his shirt cuff. He wished to clean enough of the small panes to enjoy the view before his brothers came and elbowed him out of the way. He liked being first, fastest, ahead on his own. He had scrambled almost on all fours up the twisting stair.

He caught his breath at what he saw. It was one of those clear, piercingly blue, chill summer days in late June, with the north-easterly wind still blowing. The tide was brimming high. A vast expanse of sparkling blue water lay over the distant marshes, over Deepdale Marsh and Norton Marsh and Overy Marsh. Below him, nearer at hand, he could see the Burn wriggling its blue way to the sea. Halfway towards Overy Staithe, it was crossed by a bridge where a mill stood. Overy Staithe and the channel to the sea were brimming too, the dunes of Scolt Head looked far away over a wide strip of dancing water. In the places where the marsh had been drained, he could see it patterned with full dykes and sprinkled with the tiny white balls of the grazing sheep, like toy sheep. Over the saltings was the purplish, fluffy haze of the coming sea lavender. The open sea was trimmed with crisp frills of brilliant white foam. The air was diamond bright. Toy ships took the lovely wind in their sails, far out on the horizon. Horatio saw it all as some undiscovered land glimpsed from the main top by a sea-adventurer.

'Come on, move over, let us look,' William urged, pushing his brother aside. Horace squatted on a step higher up, patiently waiting for a chance to renew the dazzling vision.

'I've never before climbed up here. What gave you the idea?' Maurice said.

'I thought we should see the sea.'

'What a great tide!'

'I can see one...two...three ships,' William croaked.

'Let's ride back by the friary. We can eat our pies there, out of the wind,' Maurice said, turning to go down.

'Yes,' William agreed with enthusiasm.

Horace leaned over and looked his fill, until he heard the others calling impatiently from below.

There was a footpath over the fields to the old friary meadow, which lay between Overy town and Norton parish. Only the great flint gate-house was left, which in an earlier time had been made into a dwelling-house, but was beginning to be ruinous. In the farmhouse lower down the field were pieces of the monks' old refectory, built into newer walls. Lower down still towards the river was a holy well, which people said was dedicated to the Virgin Mary. The boys went into the field, hitched the ponies' reins over a post, flung themselves down in the sun and began to munch their mutton pies. At the bottom of the meadow were the remains of the old friary walls, and beyond them ran the River Burn.

These were Horace's last weeks of freedom. The midsummer holiday would soon be over, the first cut of hay was in; then he would take his way with the others to school. He was excited but a little fearful. He did not think, no child does, of the end of freedom.

Maurice shied a stone at a clump of thistles, dislodging a rabbit which bounced away over the grass.

'Shall you like coming to school, Horace?' he asked.

Horace nodded, still munching. 'Yes,' he said without hesitation.

'How do you know?' William put in. 'It's not so agreeable as you suppose. Will you sit next to me?'

'Why do you want him to sit next to you?'

'He can tell me the answers to things.'

'He'll sit where he's bid,' Maurice said shortly.

The rector encouraged Horace, helping him on to his pony on the first day of school.

'You have no need to fear, my son. Your reading is good, you can add up, and subtract, you have the first rudiments of accounts, you can write a tolerable hand. Indeed you may be better ready than William was in some ways,' said Papa.

'Why, Papa? Why is he better ready than I was?' William said gloomily.

Papa came round and patted William's knee and looked keenly at him. 'I think that perhaps he has more confidence in himself than my son William,' he said.

'We're off!' Maurice called, his brown cheeks fat, his smile cheerful.

'I cannot hold her in any longer!' He was on a sturdy farm horse with Sukey up behind him. 'Come on, a regular cavalcade today!'

Mamma came hurrying out almost too late and took her husband's arm. She was pale and tired, six months and more pregnant.

'O, my lamb! Are you happy to be going?'

'Yes I am!' Horatio called, trotting off cheerfully beside William, his school bag bouncing on his back.

The rector supported his wife to the house. 'You are tired, my love.'

'Yes, I am very weary now.'

'How much longer?'

'Two and a half more months.'

The school was not a large one. A new master and his wife had come, to the advertisement of the Burnham citizens. He taught the older boys, while a pupil older than Maurice sometimes looked after the younger. Sukey went off with the girls to the parlour, where the master's wife, though spending a cursory time upon reading and arithmetic, mostly taught her charges plain and more elaborate sewing. Horace's first friend was Charles Boyles, already a friend of Maurice's. His father was collector of the customs at Wells: his grandfather was supervisor of the riding officers on the Norfolk coast, and had handed on to his grand-son many tales of smugglers caught and as many of smugglers escaped. When Charles began on one of these, he quickly collected an admiring audience. Within a few weeks Horace had begun to forget the hours in the study with Papa.

The greatest excitement in Burnham Westgate this August was a wedding. On Monday the fifth, Sir Mordaunt Martin (a cousin of Canon Poyntz) who had been marshall of the vice-admiralty court in Jamaica, but had been living in Norfolk for some time now and interesting himself in the progressive agriculture of the neighbourhood, married Everilda Dorothea, the third daughter of the reverend Mr Smith (she who had witnessed Alice Nelson's marriage to Mr Rolfe) and carried her off joyfully to North Creake. Mrs Nelson could not go, she was too near her time; but Mr Nelson went to help Mr Smith whose health had for some time been failing: and the children were allowed out from school in time to jump and wave and huzzah as the bridal carriage drove away from St Mary's, Westgate, to the rectory. The new Lady Martin waved back: her bridegroom surveyed them with happy pleasure, hoping for such a brood himself. It was not a fair day, but the couple though rained upon were undismayed.

Before the end of the month, poor Mr Smith was dead.

'Hey William, Horace, listen to this,' said Maurice one August evening, as they leaned against a barley stook in one of the enclosures of the rectory glebe.

' "A gentleman new arrived from the East Indies lost a large Brilliant Diamond out of a Ring upon his Finger…which 'tis said was a present to him from the reigning Nabob…" It was picked up by a boy who received fifty pounds reward!'

'If I am ever in the East Indies I shall make friends with the reigning Nabob,' Horace declared grandly.

'You shouldn't boast,' Maurice announced. 'You think you know everything, Horace, and you always say you can do everything. The reigning Nabob might cut off your head.'

'I don't say what I can't do, do I, William?' Horace appealed to his loyal brother.

'No,' said William staunchly, 'because you can always do everything you want to. What is the reigning Nabob?'

Maurice laughed, not knowing. 'And there's smallpox in Swaffham again.' he said. 'Lots of people have been inoculated.'

'What's inoculated?' William asked. 'Papa,' he called, 'what's inoculated?'

Edmund straightened himself from his work, removing a tickling barley head from his open shirt neck.

'Are you boys given up? There is plenty more to do.'

They scrambled to their feet ashamed.

'Inoculation is when the surgeon gives you a small dose of the disease, and you are then enabled to fight the disease at its worst. Some people disapprove, they think it spreads it.'

Sukey came up from the house. 'Mamma has made some potato cakes for you,' she called.

'Dear, kind Mamma,' Papa sighed. 'She is never done!'

'You are to come when you tire, or cannot see.'

Maurice noted pale dusk, scented sweetly with hay and flowers, fold silently into silver evening. The moon had risen. Idle though he sometimes felt when faced with the tasks of the land, Maurice was to look back upon such evenings as lost paradise.

Mrs Nelson's new son was born on Friday the thirteenth of September, a puny little mite (from whose birth his mother took longer than usual to recover).

97

''Tis unlucky, ma'am,' Mary choked to Mrs Suckling in the kitchen.

'Fiddlesticks, girl,' said Granny Suckling, relieved that the birth was over. Nevertheless, she resolved privately to beg her daughter to have no more. The difficulty was, they were such love-birds still. It was too delicate. She could not interfere.

After five days little George was privately baptised by his papa. He did not fatten very fast or feed very well and his mother had much anxiety for him. Before the weather became too cold, the child was taken to church, his family around him, and jovial Sir Mordaunt Martin stood sponsor with old cousin John Turner and Mrs Ann Amyas. Horatio, sitting on the floor in the parlour afterwards between the two gentlemen agriculturalists, heard them pursuing the contemporary controversy about carrots as winter feed for the animals: did they not make horses sweat and weaken them? On the other hand, they seemed less likely to fail as a crop than the turnip.

That November, Maurice read to his brothers how two women dressed as countrywomen brought a covered basket to a butcher near the Mansion House one Sunday evening and left it with a lad for the master as 'pork, from Epping'. But the master on his return found to his great surprise a fine chopping boy about three days old. Maurice snickered, looking up from the paper. 'I reckon she was not married and the baby was a bastard.'

'She must have been married if she had a baby.'

Maurice laughed again. 'Well now, think now, the dogs and cats and beasts and sheep and horses don't go to church and be married, now, boy, do they?'

Horatio and William discussed this matter in private, adducing many wild theories about bastard babies.

Just before Christmas Maurice triumphantly read out that Papa's true cousin, Mr James Nelson of Dereham, had married Miss Anne Hales of Tasburgh.

Soon after this a long, long winter, a four months winter, set in.

Chapter Eleven

The Great Snow

An aromatic scent, bitter yet sweet, filled the air. Horatio's small nostrils twitched, first encountering it in the morning and not recognising it at once. The parsonage was full of the smell of that fruit which a Norwich grocer, to the rector's delight, had advertised this week as the civil orange. His wife, with Mary's, Mrs Suckling's and Sukey's help, was making marmalade. Little George was crying in the cradle, Maurice was helping his father bring in more wood and coal, Peter could be heard straining at the frozen pump-handle in the yard. It was very cold.

'"As the days lengthen, So the frost strengthen,"' murmured Mrs Suckling. 'No break in the weather yet.'

'Horatio,' said Papa briskly, 'what is a civil orange?'

Horace smiled. 'An orange from Séville,' he repeated, having been shown this the night before.

'And what is a civil answer?'

'A polite answer, Papa.'

'An answer that turneth away wrath,' added the parson.

'And where is Séville?' Mamma put in, joining without hesitation in the catechism of new knowledge which formed the daily education of the children.

'In Spain, Mamma!' Horace said, a notion of heat, strangeness and enmity entering with the word. 'Is it a hot country?'

'Yes, it's hot. Oranges do not ripen here, except in hothouses.'

'Orangeries,' put in Mrs Suckling reminiscently. She knew one, at Blickling.

'Now little Ann, where does the sugar come from, think you?'

Ann knew not.

'The West Indies, Papa,' said Susannah, as she watched her mother stirring slowly the heaving, dark gold mixture.

Maurice dumped down the log basket in a corner, retrieved a piece of peel that had escaped the cooks, and cut himself a row of white pithy teeth. He proceeded round the kitchen wearing these and grinning vacantly at the family. William bawled with laughter and at once fought him for them, knocking into the cradle. George cried the harder. Maurice gave William the teeth without further ado.

'Oh take care, Maurice, William,' Mamma shouted. 'Take care of that poor babe. There are too many people in this kitchen, husband,' she said helplessly, hurrying to the cradle and rocking it. Mrs Suckling possessed herself of the spoon and stirred the marmalade.

'Poor lamb, poor mite,' his mother said with anxiety to the screwed, waxen face. She was afraid she might not rear him. If only the two months' cold would break! But it closed its grip, harder and tighter, like a relentless hand.

'I beg your pardon, Mamma,' Maurice said full of remorse, watching the baby.

'Mamma,' said William, plucking at her, 'pray look at the teeth, Mamma! Look at the teeth Maurice made!' William had still an obscure jealousy of babes in cradles. His mother looked at him and laughed in spite of herself, pushing his shoulder.

'William, you are such a clown, such a baby,' she said with a pale smile. 'Sukey, my love,' she went on, 'set the large skillet on the hearth with the ale, it will warm us all up. Here are some pieces of peel I kept back. Put in a stick of cinnamon.'

Sukey hooked down the wide shallow pan, Papa measured out the ale from the barrel in Mary's scullery. She put it carefully next the fire, added the lemon and orange peels and the cinnamon from the old black spice box, and stirred it gently. When bubbles strung the edge in a line of scum, she moved it away to mull. The pewter mugs were fetched to stand ready and be warmed. Horace kneeled expectantly on the hearth, smiling up at his granny who was still stirring. She had made them a plum cake for Twelfth-day and there was still some left. The thick sweet wedges, one each, allayed the bitterness of the mulled ale providing a pleasant contrast. Horace received his mug with pleasure and, looking round at the others, was overwhelmed with happiness as with a warm wave. Little Edmund and Suckling, still milksops, left their ale but gobbled their cake: Maurice and William quickly seized upon the children's mugs. Mamma was refreshed, and brought George and put him to her breast. In the warmth of the fire and her arms he pinkened and fed a little and slept.

'He needs coaxing, coaxing all the time,' she murmured.

It had been uncomfortably cold for a long time and people knew that the winter had not finished with them yet. Mamma let the children undress downstairs. Maurice, Horace and William would dash shivering upstairs, flinging off their clothes and their linens in silence with chattering teeth, struggling breathlessly into their night-shirts, the bed sheet icy beneath them, the two youngest glad of each other's warmth. Each morning, furred patterns of leaves and flowers, tendrils and ferns, gloriously idiosyncratic, had grown over the bedroom window panes from the edges, to be melted only with warm breaths or later sunshine. Through the privy porthole his breath achieved, Horace looked with screwed eye over the frost-bound valley, to East End Farm and Whitehall Farm, to the black curve of the frozen Burn, to the grasses and winter weeds drooping with cold beneath the window. There had been snow intermittently. Coming and going, it had never thawed completely, but left always a patch to come back to as the country people said. The boys chased, snow-balled and sleighed down slopes upon hurdles, Horatio slid fearlessly along frozen tracks in the yard until his mother forbade it, anxious for those of them older and less agile. There were chapped hands and split fingers, cracked lips and sore noses, running eyes and chilblains, chilblains, chilblains. Peter blew on his hands, Rector took to his mittens, Grandmother to her muff.

On the twenty-ninth of January, Edmund Nelson rode off booted and caped and muffled for the induction of the new parson at Burnham Westgate, who had been presented by Squire Wilkinson to follow Lady Martin's father. When the sun was red behind the orchard trees he returned, his breath and Peter's billowing like steam from two opponent kettles on to the frosty air as they put the mare in. Papa joined the family round the fire in the parlour, for he had dined with the party at Westgate.

'Well my love,' his wife said, enjoying the hour she loved most: the day's work done, dinner over, the children not yet in bed, 'is he agreeable, the new clerk?'

Susannah fitted her father's slippers over his black stockings, patting his feet with affectionate care.

'Very agreeable, I think,' the rector nodded. 'Very brisk and sprightly, he is quite a youngish man. That is to say, he's a deal younger than Papa, about eight-and-twenty I believe.'

'What is his name, Papa?'

'The reverend Mr Bryan Allott. There is some Irish there, I should say. He's ruddy-cheeked and fiery-eyed and he walks with an almost martial swing. So that I was not surprised to learn he had been a soldier.'

'A soldier, Papa!'

'Yes. It seems the late war overtook him, after his third year at Cambridge, at St John's. He put by learning the law and hurried off to join the army! He has not been long a clerk, was ordained priest in Norwich in December. An unusual man for a parson, but I think he will be an active one. He is already planning to help restore Ulph chancel. As to the ruinous Sutton, he snorted and said, "A ruin is only of use in a nobleman's park. We'll have no ruins here!" So I hope at last we shall achieve something of my ideas.'

'Admirable,' his wife agreed. 'I think I shall like Mr Allott.'

'So shall I,' said Horace fervently, sitting cross-legged and nodding his head.

'Why, my boy?' his father asked, much amused.

'Will he not tell us about the war?'

'Ah. He may. Yes.'

'And his wife, my love?'

'She is a Scottish lady, very pleasant, and there is an infant or two, they were married in 1761.'

'And is poor Mrs Smith, and her remaining daughter, settled?'

'Yes, they are in their new house in Burnham. She took the tithes, I gather, up till Christmas and will make a settlement with Mr Allott. But a strange thing has arisen which we shall hear more of. Half the tithes of Burnham and twenty-five acres of the glebe belong to Christ's College in Cambridge. It has been leased for generations to the incumbent or to some gentleman in trust for him. Christ's have unexpectedly decided to grant the lease to one of their own body, a certain Dr Shepherd, who is now claiming his share.'

'And what does our martial friend say to that?'

'That he has no intention whatsoever of yielding any moiety! "I shall find the way round it, Mr Nelson sir, the law is a circuitous labyrinth, but I shall find a way round," the rector quoted, laughing.

'Is he within his rights,' his wife asked, 'to withhold the moiety?'

'I'm very much afraid not. I advised him to beg the college to restore the lease to him as incumbent. It is his only hope.'

Catherine Nelson felt an immediate sympathy for Mr Allott, and secretly hoped he would fight.

The long hard winter claimed its victims. At school one day early in February, Horace and William learned from his grand-son, Charles, that old Mr Valentine Boyles had died. In their own town cold had taken Richard Tidd upon whose breeches and shirt Horace had had his first lesson in accounts. Granny Suckling prayed for snow again.

''Twill release the frost, my dear. Nothing else will.'

But all the snow did was to come in small, hard whirling showers (which pricked the boys' cheeks as they rode) add itself to the layers upon the ground and freeze. Until one morning the silence, the cold white light, and the shadow of a great furred cliff overhanging from the roof brought Horace out of his bed and to the window in one leap.

Snow! All earlier snows slipped from the memory. Never could Horatio remember such snow as this. The world was blanketed, smoothed and muffled: the lane, the stream, the hawthorns, the valley, the river had disappeared. The bushes were glistening mounds of crouching whiteness, the distant woods were like piles of clouds, the farmhouses winked half-closed eyes, like men in mufflers with broad hats pulled down, the pump was a hunched long-nosed dwarf in a white sea. He ran to the other window. The washing line was a thick white rope like a bell-rope, a bank of snow lay half-way up the door, and higher than the rounded, white window ledges. Peter came battling round from the yard, digging as he walked, making a track with his spade to the door. Mary laughed at him from the kitchen window; Horace beat excitedly upon his. Peter surveyed them with a rueful smile, his face glowing like a rose with the cold.

'What is it, what's the matter?' groaned William.

'Wake up, wake up, William! Come and see the snow! You've never seen snow like this!' Horace shouted. 'Maurice, have you seen the snow?' he said, opening Maurice's door and shaking the latch. 'Sukey, Suckling, Edmund, Ann, come and look at the *snow*!' he yelled, running from door to door.

'Huzzah,' muttered William, shivering and stamping. 'We shall not be able to go to school! Horace, we shan't be able to ride through this!' And he performed an ungainly caper.

It was Thursday the thirteenth of February. Snow had covered the inland parts of the county, the city of Norwich and the coast lands, in one vast blanket.

'Mamma!' said Sukey in disgust when somebody mentioned the date. 'Tomorrow is Valentine's Day! The poor birds, Mamma. They are supposed to build their nests!'

'No nests for birds tomorrow I fear,' Mamma agreed.

'Papa,' said William slyly, 'we shan't have to go to school, shall we?'

Papa had other ideas.

'We shall see how it is when it is time, William!'

By the time they were ready, a few folk had walked and ridden along the lane and the shape of the road was visible.

'You see, it is not so deep in the road as you suppose. I think you will get through now. Do but try.'

Horace was excited, longing to be out in the new white world, but William was cold and grumpy. The sky was pewter with a tinge of gold, like a mug burnished from the firelight. Maurice, since Christmas, had not come to school for he had learnt all the master could teach him and was helping at home. It was out of the question that Sukey should go. They were alone.

They went in single file in the narrow track that someone had made, Horatio leading the way, blowing upon his right hand while his left, freezing, clutched the reins. The ponies, going down a slight slope, were suddenly breast high in the fluffy whiteness. They tossed their heads and blew.

'Oh come along back Horace, it is no good, it is dangerous, we shall not get through.'

'It's not dangerous,' Horace called. 'I can see where the road lies quite clearly, we keep along my granny's wall.'

'I am frozen, my feet are quite gone, I am going back to tell Papa.'

'Then we lose all the time we've spent! He will but send us forth again, you should know Papa.'

'You can do what you choose, I am going back. And I am older than you, why should I not decide?'

And William clicked crossly at the pony, turned its head out of the drift, and trotted for the parsonage gate, brushing snow from his knees. Horatio sighed: he had been enjoying himself. The rector saw William come, from the study window, and went to the door.

'Papa!' William gasped. 'The snow is too deep to venture any further! There is a great drift before we reach my granny's, the ponies were half drowned in it!'

Papa smiled quizzically and looked at Horace, and up at the sky, and back again. 'What thought you, Horace?'

'We were halfway through it, Papa,' Horace admitted smiling.

'Then try once more, William. I leave it to your honour. If the road proves dangerous, you certainly shall not go, you may come back. But get through if you can. Remember, I leave it to your honour.'

William scowled, turned the pony again and trotted off. Horace waved to his father, his face impish in the clear, cold light.

'Goodbye, Papa!'

'Goodbye, boys. Leave for home in good time, particularly if it snows.'

This time they passed their granny's wall with no difficulty, but near the town the highway to Burnham Market stretched untrodden before them: earlier travellers had turned aside to the right, into Thorpe.

'Very well then,' Horace decided, as William came to a stop, uncertain where the Westgate road opened, 'we will go through Thorpe. We cannot miss the road if we go through Thorpe. Plenty of folk are about and some will have gone on to Westgate. Come on, you've no excuse, we're upon our honour,' he explained in his high confident voice.

William followed silently, his feet aching. Outside the forge they waved at the smith, envying his fire.

'Tha's a cold ride today and all, young masters,' he called.

'Shall we get through to the Market?' Horace called.

'Ay. There's folks been and come already. Thoul't be all right, bor.'

'I told you so,' Horace said smugly.

William's temper was hard tried. 'Oh go on, hurry up, let us get there. I am frozen,' he raged. Why did Horace always know what could be done, and knowing, do it? Why did he, William, not want to do it? Yet it always seemed safe to follow Horace, who was seldom cross with him, always waited for him. William looked ahead at Horatio's small, determined back and his fury was mixed with admiration and an aching love.

Where the ways parted at Thorpe Common edge, one to their father's church, one to Westgate, drifts had again blurred and blocked the way. Undaunted for more than a moment, Horatio led William round by a track others had made, now rapidly being effaced as huge, soft flakes began to float gently down again from the grey sky. Once on the Westgate highway, Horace urged his pony faster.

'Hurry William,' he called. 'It may grow worse!'

William felt a stab of fear. They would be snowed over, stumbling off the road into drifts, and freeze to death tonight, unseen by other travellers! He dug his heels into his pony's sides and made him trot hard. And what good would Horace's courage be to them then? That would teach Papa to send them to school in the snow! But when they reached the outskirts of the town, lit up and cheerful against the grey day, his spirits rose. And when they arrived late but victorious, it was William's voice the schoolmaster heard the loudest, raised in extravagant boast to a crowd of admiring school-fellows.

At the end of school-time Peter was there, waiting: for the whirling flakes, chalk white against the mole grey clouds, had caused Mamma's nerve to break.

The next day, the London Post did not arrive into Norwich until twelve noon, and the city complained of a very thin market owing to the great quantity of snow. For a few days even the sea's edge had frozen, and sandy blocks of solid snow, like miniature icefields, nudged shoulders and danced upon the rising tide round Overy Staithe and Wells harbour and Blakeney Cut.

'Huzzah, huzzah!'

'Bravo, well done! Encore, encore!'

Shrieks, cheers, cat-calls, clapping and stamping made chaos of the great room at the Fleece at Wells, where Mr Herman Boaz a conjuror held his audience enthralled. In one row sat Maurice Nelson, cheeks pink and mouth agape with laughter, William Nelson, who rose frequently from his seat and waved his arms, Charles Boyles (who had kindly invited the Nelson boys) and Horatio, whose appreciation was intense if less noisy.

He was doing the most amazing things. He was turning whole packs of cards into flights of birds, you could hear their wings flutter. He was breaking eggs into his hat, adding flour, salt and fat, drawing out hot pancakes! The children gasped, as much with longing as with surprise. He was eating tenpenny nails and small tenterhooks and wine glasses, and drinking half pints of wine at a toss, and lastly chewing up the decanter 'by way of digestion', as somebody behind Horace remarked. He had just possessed himself of a gentleman's watch and stroking the glass with the ball of his thumb, had stopped it: and stopped it would remain, he boasted, as long as the company chose. He strode along the rows, showing the watch: half past the hour, half past eight. The show had begun at seven. Horace could not bear that it should ever end.

But end it must, and good Mrs Boyles put them to bed after huge hunks of crisp crusted new bread and beef dripping. Only the digestions of the very young (or of Mr Boaz) could have supported it, Papa said, when they told him. When last Saturday's *Mercury* arrived as usual from Norwich, he read out to the family Mr Boaz's advertisement, offering the opinion that it was not only exaggerated but verging upon the blasphemous:

> Ye Sons of Jollity and Joy,
> Sworn Enemies to Grief and Care
> To share delights that ne'er can cloy,
> To Boaz's theatre repair.

'All earthly delights,' said Papa sternly down his long nose, 'are capable of cloying, are they not boys?' Horatio caught the gleam in his eye but did not dare to smile.

'Yes, Papa,' they earnestly agreed (being not entirely clear what the word meant) and continued to chatter happily about the delights of the night before.

With the middle of March a half-hearted thaw had begun: but Catherine Nelson looked at her baby and knew that she had lost. Dr Suckerman came from Burnham but found nothing he could do; she could but keep him warm and persist in the heartbreaking effort to make him feed.

106

The conjuror had gone on to Walsingham. Mr Samuel Mackerell had superseded old Mr Boyles as head of the Riding Officers. In Norwich, the scaffold was down from Mr Ivory's building in Surrey Street, to reveal eleven elegant town houses. The rector went off once more on March the fifteenth to support the reverend Mr Henry Crowe, another new parson, at his induction to Burnham Deepdale. And on the twenty-first, a Friday, with the supposed beginning of spring, little George died. When Thomas Dent arrived, Mary burst into tears and hurried into the kitchen where her grief quickly infected Sukey and Ann. But Mrs Nelson could feel nothing at first but relief that the unequal struggle was over. On Monday their granny took Maurice and William and went with Papa to bear the small coffin to its grave. They buried George within the rails of the altar on the south side, and Maurice frowned hard on seeing the coffin lowered. He seized William's arm and marched him out and pointed up to the rooks, discussing life in the tall trees. The rector entered in the book, under the note of George's birth and private baptism the year before, '1765 Burial of George Nelson Infant Mar 24', and never noticed in his distraction that he had copied the year from the one above, when he should have written 1766. It was the Monday before Easter.

Mamma had kept Horatio back with Sukey and the babies, for he had a cough and she feared the cold wind. He came upon her standing in her chamber looking out over the valley to watch the others go, and saw that at last her eyes glistened with tears. He put his arms round her waist as she turned to him and his head into the softness of her body. Her hands enfolded his head and held him. When she released him from this delicious haven she was smiling again.

'Well my little Horace, what shall we do? Let us go and find Sukey and the children.'

On the day after they buried George, there was another heavy fall of snow: snow hung about the church yard on Good Friday.

CHAPTER TWELVE

Rare Birds

'Hee hee hee hee hee!'

Horace followed the laughter into the wood. He stole forward in the westering sunlight up the hill beneath the trees that lay beyond the parsonage orchard.

The spring was truly come at last. The birds had now been building busily for the past three weeks. The lace of buds was turning fast into full, bright leaf. The windflowers, primroses, dog violets, frozen for so long, were all come out together. It was the last week in April.

For several days the boys had heard the strange, mocking call. This morning, he and William had seen the great green bird in a clearing, hopping along, prodding at insects. When they described his red head and his long bill, Papa had said at once;

'It sounds like the green woodpecker, the woodsprite. I have not lately seen him here.'

'Perhaps he has a nest,' said Mamma. 'They make holes in trees.'

Horatio had determined immediately to find it. He had stolen off alone, without William. He who found the nest was entitled to the prize: one egg.

He crept onwards, stopping frequently to listen and to watch. It was becoming difficult to see.

Suddenly the woodsprite laughed again close at hand. He froze upon the spot. First one, then two of them, came into sight, chasing each other through the trees with a strange looping flight, as if they bounced along. They had flown off towards the edge of the wood where there was a row of tall old trees next to the open land.

A call far different from the woodsprite's reached him from below, away down in the orchard: a noisy human call, strident and cheerful.

'Yoohoo, yoohoo, yoohoo! Horace, master Horace! Where be you? Come you on at once now, wherever you be!' Mary's shrill voice commanded him. His heart sank: the noise would shatter the peace of the wood and startle the birds. He turned and ran quickly and silently down through the trees saying nothing.

'Yoohoo, yoohoo, yoo—oh, there you be you young rascal. Why di'nt you answer me? It's hours past your bedtime, why 'tis nearly dark. You're a quaint boy, daring into the wood in the dark!'

She seized his hand and hurried him along, her ceaseless loud, cross chatter concealing her fears. He was used to people thinking he was lost.

'Off you go now, up them stairs and don't you never dare not come no more when I calls you. I'ont tell yer Ma and yer Pa, it were William said you w'ornt upstairs, or ye'd likely be in them trees yet.' She slapped his behind as he started up the stairs but her voice was perfectly friendly. He was not afraid of Mary Blackett, the silly.

William only grunted as Horace flopped into the bed. Horace fell asleep at once.

When he awoke he thought it was daylight, until he saw the full face of the moon hanging low and close in the sky. It was a luminous pink. It must anyway be nearly day. He remembered the woodpeckers. He dressed, wondering if he would ever get downstairs unheard. The huge key in the door turned easily. He was away into the moonlight.

It was gentle, mysterious and beneficent. An owl called, making him jump, but he was not afraid. This time he ran through the orchard and into the lane and made his way up beside the wood. The row of trees, not fully clad, stood clear and grey in the strong moonlight. He pottered along, hearing mice and rabbits scurrying, seeing the first hedgehog of spring nosing the ground. He was aware that a change was coming over the earth, the light was altering. He looked behind him. Away down the slope and beyond the meadows and the village, a distant streak of light began to rise and grow.

Almost upon the moment, a quiet bird chirped in the wood. Another answered modestly, sleepily. Then another, and another, the whole wood, the whole world was filling with chuckles, chirrups, flutes, calls, the triumphant songs of waking birds. Horatio had never before heard the chorus at the dawn. He stood with his eyes wide, his arms clutching his cold thin body, listening until the sound became so intense that he was drenched in it. He leaned against a tree, and gazed into the colouring wood. Gradually, as the light increased, the torrent of sound waned, and single voices could be picked out from the choir. One of these, quite close at hand, was the subdued laugh of the woodpecker. Horace saw the green bird fly out of his tree just ahead of him. He crept along and slid down at the tree's foot, suddenly so sleepy that he must sit down. He yawned and sighed. He fell fast asleep.

When William woke him, he was warm in the sun. (Mary had told William where to look.)

'I found the woodsprite's nest!' Horace said. 'I shall climb up in a minute, and get an egg or two.'

William accepted this statement without argument. He even lent his back, offering encouragement as Horatio shinned up the tree, hoping ardently that a woodpecker's egg might be his reward.

One still day in mid-May Horace, idling back from school, lingered on the common, where they had lately mended the gate with new iron hinges and new nails. Now two old men were dragging the river, skimming off the weeds and cresses edging the banks, that the stream might run less sluggishly. Horatio squatted, prepared to snap up any unconsidered trifles, when he heard behind him on the highway the brisk approach of a determined pair of feet. He stood up and turned, recognising the now familiar figure of Mr Allott swinging along towards Thorpe, a little cane in his hand which he waved at Horatio as he saw him. He did not slacken his speed by a jot, but called out:

'I hope your Papa is at home, my boy, for I have walked from Westgate to see him.'

His river-wrack forgotten, Horace bounded over the grass and fell in beside the clergyman, sticking out his chin and swinging his arms in an effort to keep pace. Mr Allott smiled sideways at him, amused.

'Do you always walk both ways to school, Horatio?' he asked.

Horace was pleased that he had not mistaken him for Maurice or William (he did not realise how easily distinguishable he was by his size and his manner) and said that he liked to walk in summer. Parson Allot already thought of him, indeed, as 'the lively one'.

'Ah, like me; I enjoy a march on a fine May day and that's a fact,' he said.

They tramped past the forge, where heads turned from amongst the group of idlers round the smith, to see who strode so fast.

'*Halt*, Corporal Nelson, halt, and right half turn and away we go,' said the parson as they took the turn for Thorpe parsonage.

'Did you like marching to a band?' Horatio gasped breathless.

'I did, I certainly did! The pipe tune winds into your heart, and the drums rouse your blood, and away you go and are there before you know it.'

Which indeed was the case on this occasion, band or no. Screwing himself up for a last effort, Horace ran ahead of their guest, found out from his mother where his father was, and led Mr Allott up the hill to the top meadow. Then he collapsed in the grass and looked up at the sky, puffing, unable at first even to listen.

'What I can't find out, Mr Nelson, is where the rest of my own land lies, let alone this twenty-five acres supposedly belonging to Christ's

College. What I have in my hands at Ulph or out to tenants is not enough to account for all that my glebe should be! Westgate glebe should be nigh on one hundred acres! But I have been to Mrs Smith more than once, and she seems to know nothing of it!'

'Mr Smith was no great husbandman,' said the rector, leaning upon his hoe. 'It is quite probable he never worked the land at all, but let it out. What does the squire say? Have you been to him?'

'He says he knows nothing of my land. He says that the incumbent before Mr Smith, one Thomas Groom who died in 1742, left all the glebe to him or to his tenants. But if he did, Mr Nelson, he had no right to! A plague upon these people, who leave away what is not theirs!'

'Indeed, indeed. Are we to suppose Mr Smith never troubled himself to find out where the glebe lay? How did he collect his tithes?'

'Perhaps his moiety of Ulph was all he took. His wife has means, has she not? Mr Wilkinson protests that he knew nothing of the college claim, until after Mr Smith died last August and the matter of the lease arose. Neither he nor his tenants have ever paid any rent, he says. But I can't get him to say which the land is that Thomas Groom is said to have left to him. He swears he knows not the boundaries with his own land, that all is one and has been for twenty years and more. I begin to think he has the larger part of my glebe. How am I to find where the boundaries lie?' roared Mr Allott, brandishing his cane in the air. Horatio saw his father step back and his lips twitch.

'There must be a map, Mr Allott. Mr Wilkinson must have had, must still have, a map. Of the estate and the church glebes and the common land and all. Demand that you see the map. He may be your patron, but he has no right to your glebe.'

'That he has not, and I shall fight it, eh, Horatio?' he said, his fiery eye falling upon the listening child.

'Yes sir.'

'Never say die!' with a flourish of the cane.

'No sir,' Horace agreed, shaking his fair head vigorously.

'But what have you done about the college?' the rector said, uneasy lest Mr Allott should put himself in the wrong as much as Squire Wilkinson seemed to have done. 'I fear the college has the right to grant their lease where they choose. Have you asked if they will reconsider it?'

'They cannot do that, the lease is granted, it is too late now to retract it, but I have offered Dr Shepherd sixty pounds per annum rent for the twenty-five acres and the share of the tithes, if he will allow me to be *his* tenant. From this he may pay his due to the college for the lease, a mere twenty-three pounds, which is what the rent has always been. Thus he has no trouble, I look after the land, all he does is take the profit.'

'And what is his reply?'

'He refuses! He refuses my suggestion utterly.'

'So. What will you do?'

'We shall see. We shall find some way round. Fortunately, I know the law. Cozened, on every hand! Cheated of the lease, cheated of my own glebe, I suspect! But, courage! Troubles are sent to be overcome. Are not they, Horatio?'

'Yes sir!' said Horace, now on his feet, his underlip stuck out, his arms folded.

'Horace, take Mr Allott to Mamma. Pray take a glass with us before you go sir. I will put up my hoe in five minutes and come.' He watched the small figure and the large strut hand in hand down the slope, the same aggressive determination visible in each.

Mrs Suckling's woman, Sarah Bowes, watched her mistress out of the corner of her eye, as she pretended to busy herself with the urn of flowers. Mrs Suckling did not receive letters from London often: Sarah hung about, hoping for a little news of one or other of her mistress's sons. Mrs Suckling looked grave and unhappy (which was all the more tantalising, bad news being usually more interesting than good). She folded the letter and stood up.

'I must walk up to the parsonage, Sarah. Is it warm? Do I need a cloak?'

'It's raining ma'am,' Sarah said discouragingly.

'Then fetch me the light cardinal and the oil silk hood.'

The woman did so, showing her disappointment by her manner. These oil silk hoods were a new fashion. Keep off the rain they may, thought Mrs Suckling, but they destroy the coiffure. She set off abstractedly, hardly aware of the green June day or the rain pattering on the chestnut leaves or the chestnut candles soughing above her.

Sukey and Ann, her darlings, greeted her in the parsonage hall with kisses and pleasure, helping her to take off the wet things.

'Tell Mamma, Sukey love, that I an here in the parlour and want to see her.'

Catherine Nelson came, her hair straying from her cap, her cheeks pink. She was looking better, her mother thought.

'Mamma...? Is anything wrong?'

'Catherine my love...Here, read the letter.'

'Brother Maurice? Oh, Mamma...' she took the letter at once, her smile dying.

'Oh, poor Maurice. So she is dead. He says so little, poor brother. But the last letter made me fear.'

She stepped to her mother and put her arms round her, feeling her lean shoulders, her bowed back. She was no longer plump, the thinness of age had overtaken her. Her daughter had scarcely noted it before. But she was seventy-five. They kissed each other as if for comfort.

'He was never one for many words. He will feel the more.'

'Only two years, Mamma, it's but two years, almost exactly.'

'I know. Poor Maurice. He waited so long.'

'Yes. And hoped so much! That portrait painting at Woodton, the year they were married!'

'And Woodton itself awaiting them soon, one supposes.'

'Perhaps. Mary was difficult to win, Mamma. Sit down, let us talk a little, it's a great grief. I never knew why they did not marry earlier?'

'Partly his being at sea, I suppose. But I always imagined that his being named heir to the Woodton estate must have influenced the Walpoles, her mother and brother, and helped to persuade her at last. And your brother's being heir was confirmed six months later. The present owner, the widow's son, is out of his mind, you must remember?' Mrs Suckling had lowered her voice. 'Robert, the present squire, is to all intents and purposes a lunatic. He is not expected to live long. Though how long his mother will live is quite another matter. No doubt the Woodton visits two years ago were so that his bride might see her future portion. Mrs Denzil Suckling welcomed them with some kindness he said.'

'And it was then that he sat for Mr Bardwell.'

'It was.'

'Is it a good likeness of my brother, Mamma?'

'Yes. It looks very fine in the Park Street house. He wears his full uniform.'

'How long were they promised to each other in secret? Brother Maurice is so bashful, he would never admit to it! How old was she, Mamma, think you?'

'She can only have been a year younger than you, my love.'

'Do you suppose it may have been a child?'

'I have wondered. He has said nothing and she never wrote much to me. She was with the dowager in the Whitehall house he says. I suppose she had gone back to her mother, ailing.'

'We shall hear more perhaps when Maurice comes. They will bring her to Wickmere I imagine.'

'I imagine they will, but I doubt if we shall hear more.'

'Oh poor Maurice,' mourned his sister again. 'Only a family, and warmth and gaiety ever made him talk! You remember the time he came here when he was wooing her finally! He played and talked with the children, he told them all about the sea-fight! He was open and happy almost the whole time! They have adored him ever since.'

'Well he is a proper tar, in his taciturnity. Grief may loosen his feelings, we shall see. I wonder what he will do with that great house in Mayfair where he must have hoped to see a child or two. He will never marry again, I think.'

'Never. He was almost too shy to marry at all, and only achieved it because she was a kinswoman, I do believe, Mamma. How is cousin Turner?'

Sir John had been ill, Mrs Suckling had been over to Warham to see him the day before.

'Recovering, but not very well yet. Unless he gets quickly better, he says he'll not stand for mayor again this year at Lynn. Let them find another, give him a rest.'

'Very wise, too. How old is he?'

'Oh, younger than I by near ten years. But this has depleted him. Shall you tell the children now, about their uncle's sorrow?'

The children, when told, had little memory left of the lady who had been his wife but were dashed upon their uncle's account, whom they dearly loved. Captain Suckling, however, though he came on from Wolterton to see his mother and his sister, seemed hardly to notice his eager nephews and nieces. Catherine Nelson understood why: all his hopes were buried with Mary Walpole in the vault at Wickmere, he could hardly bear her large brood of children, their bloom, their youth, their chatter: their still hopeful innocence a bulwark against the despairs of middle age.

What with the late sowing and a poorish summer, the harvest seemed likely to be bad this year. Even the hay-crop was not abundant. Mr Allott's rage was the more, to discover (one day early in July) that a certain Mr Roger Sherwood, a nearby farmer, had been employed by Mr Henry Case of Lynn, Dr Shepherd's attorney, to collect the disputed tithes. He had actually come and helped himself to a load of hay from one of Mr Allott's meadows!

Mr Allott had stuttered with rage, telling Mr Nelson. The next week he was ready for them, and when they arrived again, demanding wool and lambs, if you please, he told Mr Case that he need collect no more tithes for Dr Shepherd, since he had offered him a decent rent for the rights. But when the lawyer tried to insist (since Dr Shepherd had after all refused Mr Allott's rent) Mr Allott had told him the truth: that not he but the squire was working the twenty-five college acres, and that to the squire he had better apply. And he drove them off his land and saw the back of them, and would do so again if he had to.

The rector looked dubious, finding the truth not so simple to see.

'But have you not,' he suggested mildly, 'admitted Dr Shepherd's right by offering him rent for the college glebeland and the moiety of tithes?'

'I do not deny his right: though it is a wicked thing that glebeland and tithes can be left away from an incumbent for ever, by some benefactor back in the days of Queen Elizabeth hoping to do himself good in the eyes of God and a college. What I deny is that the college acres are in my possession. As to the moiety of tithes, they apply to the old parish of Westgate only, and where its glebelands lie has yet to be discovered. Were not several old parishes consolidated? In any event he has not a jot of right to the *Ulph* tithes, half of which are yours, sir.'

'Did he take the hay from Ulph land?'

'He did.'

'He put himself in the wrong there. Was it Bunting, this old benefactor?'

'Richard Bunting, yes.'

'Well, we have all heard of Bunting.'

Later in the summer came Dr Shepherd himself, chasing his missing acres and tithes. A prodigiously tall, stout, gentleman with a dull face, he drove up from Cambridge accompanied by two female acquaintances of his, sisters, fashionably agog to see something of Norfolk. He called upon Mr Allott, who was (he assured Edmund Nelson afterwards) politeness itself, explaining kindly to the confused doctor that when he had ascertained precisely where the boundaries of Westgate glebe lay in the days when the benefaction was made, he could begin to determine what the doctor's share was. As to the twenty-five acres, he must go over and see the squire. Dr Shepherd drew himself up and walked in all his dignity along to Mr Wilkinson and demanded the restoration of his five-and-twenty acres. Squire, it was generally said, had laughed at the application. The Cambridge party retired discomfited. But Mr Allott wrote a friendly letter, repeating that the glebe question was quite distinct and only the tithes concerned them both. He was as civil as you please (hoping that Doctor Shepherd would forget about it for a little, while he ferreted round in various ancient books trying to prove that Westgate boundaries now were very different from what they were in Queen Elizabeth's days).

Moreover, the quarrel was superseded by much more serious, immediate and practical troubles. The harvest had been so bad that the price of wheat went up, and up, and up. Very soon the poorer people were suffering real hardship. No wonder this summer that Mr Thomas Durrant of Scottow complained of people taking his fish from his waters at Belaugh. Already in July the price of barley had started to rise: by the end of September there were riots in Norwich about the price of all foods and of flour and grain in particular. The shortage was dire, a petition was sent to the King against the exporting of grain; and the principal inhabitants of the city agreed not to send any fowls or provisions (excepting game) to London or anywhere else, from then until Lady-day.

On October the tenth the rector trotted peacefully away from Thorpe church by the top lane, brooding upon what strange forces had caused a Methodist preacher a few weeks ago to break into the church at Gressenhall, and in a fit of Enthusiasm to tear the church bible and all the common prayer books into small pieces. (Mr Nelson had been reminded of it looking at some of Thorpe's tattered books: he must renew them.) He was startled to be overtaken from behind by Mr Allott, galloping his horse as if in a cavalry charge. He reined in with a flying of gravel and a tossing of harness and rode with Edmund Nelson, his breath coming hard.

'I've been right to your parsonage, Mr Nelson, looking for you! We've uncovered a plot...'

'A plot!' said the parson in mild surprise, his mind upon Methodists.

'Yes, a forthcoming plot. There's thirty or forty men in a band planning a riot in tomorrow's market at Burnham. The prices, you know. The high food prices...'

'I can hardly blame them,' the rector put in.

'Maybe not. But this is not the way to arrange things. They've agreed, I'm told, to lower the price of provisions by force! Think of it! We shall have fighting and bloodshed, the shop-keepers and stall-holders will retaliate. Precious food will be stolen, or wasted, or...'

'Quite so,' the other agreed. 'What will you do?'

'I am calling a meeting. At my house this evening. Will you come? Six o'clock. We need every law-abiding citizen we can collect. We will make a proper plan to relieve the distressed and disperse the rioters. Can I count upon you, Mr Nelson, sir?'

'Certainly.'

'Excuse my haste. I must tell Mr Styleman at Overy; I have been to Mr Crowe. Do you think Sir Mordaunt Martin would come from Creake? And Canon Poyntz? And Mr Goodall?'

'Very probably. Shall I send the boys to ask them?'

'I should be most grateful. Good day to you Mr Nelson, I count on your help.'

And Mr Allott galloped off to bear his news waving his whip above his head.

The Saturday market in Burnham began at ten o'clock. Edmund Nelson set off early according to the plan they had all made the night before, accompanied by Peter and Maurice and William (who seemed a little doubtful). 'We may need all the strong arms we can muster,' said Papa. There was no pony for Horatio, but this did not deter him. Despite Mamma's protests he slipped off after the others, by no means willing to miss the riot, and was overtaken by Sir Mordaunt who gave him a lift up, and the canon. Quietly and with little said, the gentlemen, the farmers, the parsons, the shop-keepers and anyone else who had a horse to mount, collected in their stations throughout Burnham and waited. At ten o'clock, the sexton would ring St Mary's bell to open the market: there was a kind of hush over the market-place, waiting for it. Horatio hugged himself with excitement in expectation of an immediate uproar. But, as the bell rang, all these stout well-wishers to the peace appeared on horseback, more than two dozen of them, from behind the shops and between the houses, and started to patrol the green and the streets. The market opened, the buying and selling began, subdued at first, but soon reaching its usual fervour. Prices were kept steady, stocks were shared out, certain provisions were marked down cheap for those who needed them. Horatio, who had longed to see at least one rioter and if possible to trip one up, was disappointed. For all continued quiet as the horsemen quartered Burnham, searching for any troublemakers: Squire Wilkinson and Mr Allott (their differences forgotten), Mr Styleman, Mr Nelson and Maurice and Peter Black, Mr Crowe, Sir Mordaunt Martin, Canon Poyntz and the reverend Mr Goodall from South Creake; Mr William Powdich, Farmer Allison, Farmer Emerson, Farmer Simpson, young Mr John Humphrey, Mr James Lateward, Mr Raven, the carrier, old Dr Suckerman, Mr Fasit and Mr Vertue, the two young apothecaries, Mr Nicholas Raven and Mr Matthew North, the attorneys; and Mr Jacombe and Mr Drake, and Robert Goggs; and various others from Westgate whose names Horace did not know. Round and about they went, some coming and some going but always a fit quantity to keep the peace, until (it was said) twelve o'clock at night. But long before this the rector of Burnham Thorpe had led his party home where even Horace's ardour could not produce one scowl or scuffle, let alone a drop of blood, for the excitement of the family. Mr Allott had arranged things very well: there had been no need for the riot in Burnham Market that day.

Nevertheless, provisions grew scarcer, prices continued to rise, Norwich citizens wrote to their MPs (Harbord Harbord and Edward Bacon) about the shocking price of food; and a Norwich grocer (an alderman) found an ill-spelt threatening incendiary missive pushed under his door, To Mr Pool, Grocher. Nine hundred men (and no Boyes) would rise, it avowed, unless goods were sold at decent rates. And those cynical merchants of inflation, forestallers, regrators and ingrossers, were warned in the press what penalties were due for their transgressions. Meanwhile, if you could not eat bread, you might eat oysters, for you could buy a barrel-full in Norwich market fresh from Colchester for one shilling and sixpence.

From North Walsham, the governors of Sir William Paston's Free School there announced that they intended to elect a new master, and invited applications and testimonials. They described the endowment, worth forty pounds a year to the Master and twenty to the Usher, with a living of about sixty in the governors' gift. He should be a married man and capable of teaching the young boys English before they were ready for Latin. There was a new-built school house and garden in a most healthful and convenient situation, capable of receiving more than thirty boarders. In due course they elected the reverend Mr Jones, recommended by the vice-provost and headmaster of Eton and many another distinguished gentleman.

Edmund Nelson, keeping his eye upon this, had it in mind that he must find a school next year for William and Horace. Maurice seemed very well at home at the present and had no great ambition. But if he could afford it he must send the younger boys away. His wife was overdone, there would be a new baby in March. He thought that Dr Hamond had mentioned the Paston School. He would remember it.

CHAPTER THIRTEEN

The Sprig of Yew

'What's that?' Sukey exclaimed in horror, dropping her darning on to the kitchen table, and fleeing to the other side of the room.

'That's the ghostie what have no head a-kicking his head afore him,' Maurice stated, as a hollow rattling clangour was heard to come bouncing over the yard in a pause in the raging tempest. The girls screamed. Ann ran to her sister and buried her face in her apron. Maurice, smiling, went over to the north-easterly window, picking his way with exaggerated stealth.

'Don't Maurice, don't draw the curtain back, pray don't,' Sukey begged.

William and Horace, playing a game of soldiers before the kitchen fire, had leapt up to follow Maurice. Little Edmund and Suckling continued to build their castle of wooden bricks below the table.

Rattle, clang, bump.

'There it be. That's a good head an all, with long hair and startin' eyes. That's fetched up agin this wall, looking up at me sumthen ghastly,' he teased, in the broad Norfolk accents which he often affected these days, being much with Peter. 'Shall I let 'un in?'

Sukey screamed again.

'Let's see, let *me* see,' said Horace eagerly. 'Yes, I can see all his teeth too, numbers of teeth, aren't there, Maurice?'

'Ay, all rattling about in his head,' Maurice averred, his voice producing one of those surprising breaks to which it was now subject.

William peered out with some apprehension.

'It's only one of the wooden buckets, Sukey,' he said solemnly and gruffly. 'It's not anybody's head to be sure.'

Maurice and Horatio crowed with laughter at the shrinking girls.

'Anyway, who believes in ghosts?' Sukey spat out, sitting down again. 'I don't, I am sure.'

Maurice guffawed.

'I shall not mend your stockings unless you are more polite, Maurice Nelson,' said she primly.

The wind continued to howl. Coming off the sea, tearing up the valley, it roared and blared and whined and buffeted. It gathered up the whole house in a frenzy, screaming as it shook tiles and timbers in its arms. It flung handfuls of stony hail against the glass. It blew sooty wet blobs into the fire. The mugs and plates on the dresser trembled, the doors shuddered, the latches rattled, the boards creaked, rugs rose off the floor. It whistled a high moan of malicious triumph in the tree-tops forcing the trembling twigs to turn upon each other with whip and lash.

It was a Friday evening, the second of January. Mary had set off, the dishes done, on a belated new year visit home; Peter had gone to his cottage. The children were all in the kitchen, their parents in the study. Maurice threw another log on the fire.

'Poor Mary, walking home in the dark,' Ann whispered, drawing herself up to the table again to the little sampler she sewed.

She was only three months turned six, still allowed to be afraid of the dark.

'Why, what do you reckon she's a-going to meet?' Maurice asked, his mood bent upon provoking. He had been pent up in the house for hours because of the weather.

'A skellinton?' he went on, extending his far from bony fingers and dancing them before her eyes, while he opened his mouth in a frightening grin. Ann's fear mounted, she bit her lip. 'Mebbe they heaves up and walks about on nights like this.'

'They do not, they are dead, so you be quiet,' ordered Susannah.

'Mebbe she'll meet a witch on a broomstick, old Mary,' Maurice suggested next. A particularly violent gust whined towards the house and enfolded it.

'There, there be one now a-landing on the chimley, she'll be down on the hearth in a trice.'

'Then she'll fall in the fire and be burnt up. Horace, put some more wood on,' Sukey demanded.

Horatio did so. The flames licked up again and made the kitchen lighter, for there were only two candles, one on the dresser, one by the girls at the table. Ann looked over to the hearth.

'Do you believe there are witches, Sukey?' Horace asked. 'Mary said an old witch killed their pig, her mother told her. She put a spell on it.'

'You don't believe that stuff, Horace,' Sukey said angrily. 'It could have fell ill any way and died. Papa says it's only because they are old and ugly and people provoke them, and then they get cross and mutter things.'

'They used to burn them,' observed Maurice.

'I know they did, poor old women. Nobody could prove they'd done anything, Papa said. Anyway Mary's full of tales.'

'What tales?' Horace urged, eager to hear more.

'Oh , tales about the churchyard. It was the church porch. She said...Mary *said...*'

'Go *on,*' Horace demanded.

'Out with it, girl,' said Maurice.

'I'll pinch you if you don't,' William added, advancing his fingers.

'She said that if you go to the church porch and wait at midnight on St Mark's Eve...all the people that are going to fall ill or die that year come up and go into the church...'

'How do they know they're going to fall ill or die?'

'No, it's not them, their bodies that you see, it's their ghosts, their apparitions. If they're going to get better they come out again. But if they're going to die...' she paused.

'They stay in. Now who believes in ghosts?' Maurice asked, laughing. The wind howled and whistled in a fresh burst of venom around the house. 'Sakes alive,' he confessed honestly, 'I wager none of us dare try that church porch thing and that's a fact.'

'I wouldn't care to try, it's wrong to try to see the future, Papa said so,' Sukey affirmed.

'But would you dare go to the churchyard in the middle of the night? That's what I'm asking,' Maurice pursued.

'No,' said Sukey with a shiver.

'Nor would I,' said William at once.

Horatio immediately felt himself challenged. 'Why not?' he said. 'I would.'

'Alone? Up to Thorpe?'

'Yes.'

'Past the craves?' Maurice meant the meadow on the south side of the church with its strange bumps and hillocks, where perhaps the old village used to be. 'And all through the gravestones? You wouldn't, don't talk so big.'

'I would. I'm not talking big.'

'You are, you always do.'

'I am not,' Horatio yelled.

'I say you durstn't.'

'I say I dare!' Horace stood upright, his fists clenched at his sides, his eyes flashing.

'No you durstn't, you're still a shrimp!' Maurice teased.

Horace lunged towards him, his pride enraged, his temper failing. Maurice sprang up and began to dance round the table, Horatio after him.

'You durstn't!'

'I dare!'

'You durstn't, you shrimp!'

'I durst, I durst, you liar!'

'Horace!' exclaimed Sukey, much shocked.

Maurice seized the shovel and held it before him, dancing backwards; Horatio seized the tongs and brandished them furiously, prancing after his brother. Maurice bumped into William, sending him flying, William bellowed with rage and prepared to add his fists to Horace's tongs. Susannah stood up, her hand guarding the candle.

'Leave off, leave off!' she shrieked. 'Put down the shovel, you'll hurt each other, you've made Ann cry!' Ann sobbed at last for her pent-up fear, not her brothers' rage. 'You'll set things afire, mind the candle!'

Horace's flying feet kicked the children's castle into ruins. Four-year-old Edmund, dark and pale, emerged from under the table, his mouth open in a steady roaring square; Suckling followed, quiet and fair as Ann, and clung to Sukey's leg in silent terror.

Maurice's teasing was perfectly good-humoured. 'You durstn't, you durstn't,' he yelled with breathless laughter.

'I durst, I durst, I'll prove it to you,' roared Horace.

'Look what you've done, you've made all the babies cry. I shall go and fetch Papa...' Sukey screamed making for the door.

'Pax, pax,' Maurice gasped, seizing Horace by the wrist and wringing the tongs from him. 'All right. You durst. How will you prove it?'

'Let go of me! I shall prove it by bringing something back,' Horace panted.

'What?' Maurice gasped.

'I don't know, whatever you say.' And he smote Maurice hard, not to be cheated of his object.

'A piece of yew.'

'Not yew, it's unlucky,' Sukey said. 'Mary wouldn't let me bring it in for Christmas.'

'This isn't Christmas. But he could pick it anywhere, that won't prove it!'

Horace was stung to fury again.

'You know I wouldn't do that!' he screamed, lunging once more towards his brother.

'No he wouldn't,' William affirmed in a roar.

'Sssh.' Sukey suddenly pointed to the door.

William stood looking embarrassed, staring at the door. He could never cover things up. The door opened and their mother came in slowly, she was tired. She smiled at them.

'Oh what a terrible storm! Bed for my babies,' she went on. 'What is it, little Ann? Is it the storm frightens you?' Ann sobbed, saying nothing. 'And Edmund crying too! Come along little one. And Suckling, where are you? Sukey, go and fetch the night-shirts. Maurice, what are you doing with the shovel and the tongs, what silly play have you been up to, frightening these babies? Go and join Papa, boys, while we undress the children.'

Maurice, who was casting the shadow of Snap the dragon upon the wall with his tongs now put them down and loped sheepishly to the door, grinning. Horace caught him up, put his arm round his waist.

'Not tonight,' he whispered. 'I'll not go tonight.'

'No. Wait for a fair night,' Maurice replied. He put his arm round Horatio's neck and drew his head close. 'I'll let you off if you choose,' he breathed in his ear.

'I don't choose,' Horace said jauntily.

'All right bor!' agreed Maurice.

Next day dwellers on the coast looked out once more upon a flooded world. The great north-easterly, pushing a huge spring tide, had caused havoc all along the eastern coast. The sea banks broke at Lynn and Cley and Salthouse, boats were beat to pieces at Cromer and Mundesley, Bacton and Happisburgh, Palling and Yarmouth, Ipswich and Harwich. Aldeburgh in particular had suffered, losing thirty houses. And snow storms followed, greater in some parts than the year before.

This wretched weather did nothing to lessen the plight of those who were hungry and cold. Duty-free wheat and flour were allowed in, people noted the extraordinary reversal of the usual trade, as wheat came in to Lynn for the midlands. Edward Bacon arranged to sell flour to poor families in Norwich at a shilling a stone; Lord Orford, Lord Townshend and many another rich man warm in his hall gave money for firing and provisions; Lynn and Norwich, Holt and North Walsham led the towns in collections for their poor for coals and food; Norwich theatre gave its first night takings; and the newspaper printed a frugal method of making household bread by using a quarter part of boiled potatoes. Good Dr Murray of Wells started a free service for poor people on Sunday mornings. And a plot was uncovered to burn Norwich to the ground and club Alderman Poole into the bargain, on the occasion when two of last year's food rioters were to be hanged in the Castle Ditches. They were duly hanged and Alderman Poole kept himself close.

Horace chose a moonlit night. He had once heard his father say that if he wished to awake he would thump his head so many times on his pillow. Horace chose three and thumped accordingly.

'What are you doing?' his brother complained.

'Putting something into my head,' Horatio replied.

To his satisfaction the device worked. He arose, dressed, and was creeping down the stairs as the grandfather clock struck three in the hall.

It was cold, still, raw, but not freezing. He could see perfectly. His highlows scrunched on the gravel of the road: he moved on to the grass.

Candlelight showed up the square of his granny's window, and he wondered if she were sleepless, or ill. There was candlelight all over the townhouse too: perhaps old people did not sleep much, but sat up talking? He jogged on towards the common, and then turned up to the brooding shape of the church. He wondered if Papa had ever been in the church at night and whether to Papa the church was as homely, as friendly as the parlour? Perhaps all the dead people lying in their cold beds were friendly too? Why should they be anything else? Thus he disarmed them as he walked between them.

He picked a piece of tough green yew from a tree, tugging it against the grain, stroking its wet soft fronds. He started for home filled with exhilaration. He had done it, it was easy. He laughed, running down to the village past the bumpy meadow. Of course he had chosen an easy night, but Maurice had allowed this (he was afraid of his brother falling ill afterwards). You simply made up your mind what you intended to do and you did it. As like as not things said to be frightening were not frightening when you met them. He reached home consumed with a great hunger and took a slice of bread from the crock and a hunk of cheese, which he shared with the importunate cat by the kitchen hearth stones that were not quite cold.

Maurice laughed, confronted with the frond of yew.

'I thought you'd forgotten, bor,' he said tweaking Horatio's long nose.

'Not I,' said that character bridling, drawing back his narrow shoulders and striking something of an attitude. Maurice imagined the small figure traversing the distance at dead of night and was struck by his brother's fearlessness.

Little Catherine was born upon her father's birthday, March the nineteenth, a Wednesday. She was known to be Catherine the minute her sex was seen for Papa had told them all that if it were a girl this time she should bear her mother's name. The circumstance of its being his own birthday added to his joy. He was waiting for William and Horace when they returned from school.

'Little Catherine is here!' he announced.

William looked bewildered for a moment, Horace was immediately aware of his father's mood.

'Oh Papa! Are you glad? Is Mamma well? May we see her?'

'In a little, let her rest a bit, poor Mamma. She's a pretty little moppet with curly hair.'

'Did I have hair, Papa?' Horace asked.

'Did I, Papa?' echoed William.

'Upon my word I cannot remember, boys,' their father admitted. 'But you have turned out very well hair or no, and it is more important that a girl should have plenty than her brothers. Tonight we shall all drink a bumper, not only for your ageing Papa whose birthday it is, but also for your new sister, Kitty.'

Horatio would dearly have liked to ask his father how old he was but did not dare his good humour that far.

When the boys crept up to see their mother the curtains were drawn back round the bed, and firelight flickered in the unlit room. A strange smell, sour but clean, lingered. Mamma opened her eyes.

'Dear Horace and William,' she whispered.

They stood looking at the baby, finding her hair less than they had expected. (William had imagined thick locks.) Horatio went over to kiss his mother.

'Go to sleep again, Mamma,' he ordered firmly.

She smiled, her eyes already closing.

All through April and into May the reverend Mr John Price Jones sang the praises of the Paston school at North Walsham, not only advertising a dazzling array of subjects which included (to Edmund Nelson's interest) navigation, but promising to take the greatest care of the children's morals and pay the strictest attention to instructing them in the principles and nature of Religion.

The day after Easter the reverend Mr Henry Crowe married Miss Haylett of Little Fransham and brought her back to Thorpe Hall. Thorpe Hall, the manor house, lay below Thorpe church behind a loop of the river which wandered over the common. Mr Crowe had taken a lease of it from Lord Walpole of Wolterton Horatio's godpapa, and here he brought his bride. From this day forth a warm friendship began between the Nelsons and the Crowes (who were indeed tenuously related). Little Nelsons trooping out of church on cold Sundays would be hailed into the hall for hot grog before walking home, or entertained on the summer lawns beneath alders or willows. Mamma (tired with the walk from the parsonage) would rest awhile in Mrs Crowe's sitting-room while Papa hurried on into church: and it was not unknown for latecomers, panting and dishevelled, to malinger by the Crowes' stream and not come into church at all.

The price of food stayed high. But the price of rice now imported without duty went down from fourpence to twopence a pound: and the weekly news provided receipts for savoury rice cooked below the roasting meat, rice boiled in milk, rice baked.

Catherine Nelson thought of rice as a French mode, suspect and despicable, but nevertheless bought some from Mr Lateward's and was somewhat triumphant when her family received it with distaste.

> Half a pound of twopenny rice
> Half a pound of treacle
> That's the way the money goes
> Pop goes the weasel,

the children soon sang to their skipping ropes.

One May Monday after school Horatio trotted behind his friend, Charles Boyles, along the bank beside the harbour at Wells. There was a brisk breeze off the sea and they ran to keep warm. They were going to see the wreck. William had declined to join the party, saying he was hungry and did not wish to be late for dinner, Horatio who thought little about his food until it faced him considered this to be of no importance.

'What's her name?' he called.

'Fontayne, of Rotterdam. She's Dutch, she's a dogger.'

'What's a dogger?' Horace continued, always ready to store up information about ships. 'A fishing boat?'

'Ay, but she had deals on board as well. There's a place out at sea called the Dogger Bank.'

'When did she drive on?'

'Sunday morning early, and my father said she broke up last night.'

'Were they all drowned?'

'No, no, they worn't drowned, they got off in the boats, I saw them come up the quay yesterday. They all went into Mr Springold's at the Fleece, they cou'n't say much, they're Dutch!'

'What about the master, was he cross? What's his name?'

'Tha's no good being cross with the sea.'

'He came too close to the sand banks,' remarked Horace.

'Ay, bor, he must've done sumthen wrong. William Kraut he was called.'

Like Maurice, Charles often used Norfolk speech: it made him feel older than he was, a man amongst sailors. They were jogging past the Pool. As they turned the corner beyond the shelter of the marram hills the wind struck keenly over the salt marsh. Gulls shrieked as they rose from the channel and chuckled as they settled again, leaving precise prints over the mud. It was low tide.

'She be on the far side, Papa said. Only think of all them lobsters! I like lobster.'

'What lobsters? Did she have lobsters aboard?'

'Ay, someone said she had ten thousand lobsters! Look, there she be, what there is of her.'

The vessel lay on her side in shallow water badly holed amidships, her two masts pointing forlornly inland in a tangle of shivering rigging.

Horatio regarded her, thinking. He was thinking of one lobster, and then of a hundred. A thousand. Ten thousand!

'Ten thousand lobsters!' he repeated in amazement.

'Ay, so someone said. And some barrels of salt fish too.'

'I don't believe it, do you? Where do they keep them?'

'In the well. There's a great well, they keep fish alive till they land 'em.'

'Those ten thousand lobsters must have been right crowded. Let's go and see if we can find some!'

'Why the well's stove in I reckon, and all the lobsters will have floated out to sea on the next tide. Besides, we can't cross the channel.'

'There might be a few hanging around this side. Come on, let's have a diddle.'

'Not dead, we don't want 'em. And they'd not just sit waiting, they'd go crawling off to the sea I reckon, right pleased to escape.'

Horatio reckoned so too.

'What happened to all the barrels of salt fish?' he said. Salt fish, though inferior to lobsters, was better than nothing.

'That's all washed away, they say. But I know what I think come of some of it. It'll all be hidden in folks' back yards, what the sea di'nt get.'

Horace sadly agreed that this was likely. 'Any smugglers lately?' he asked, turning to go back.

'Ay well, they pick 'em up now and again. I heard my father talking about a desp'ate gang of outlawed smugglers round the coast of Belleisle. Where's Belleisle, eh Horace?'

'"At the siege of Belleisle, I was there all the while, I was there all the while, At the siege of Belleisle,"' chanted Horace, breaking into a wild skip and flinging his arms about as he warbled the rhyme. 'My Uncle Maurice used to say it, he used to dance Ann to it.'

'How do it go on?'

'It don't,' said Horatio. 'That's all there be to it.'

'Was your Uncle Maurice at the siege of Belleisle, or what?'

'He may have been, I don't know. It's an island, I think. Off the French coast. What does your papa do when they catch smugglers with wine or tea or spirits? Drink it?' Horace laughed.

'Drink it! It's sold off at the Custom House. But the sailors that take the ship get half you know. It's a new law.'

'Do they now?' Horace imagined himself boarding a boat-load of desperate outlawed smugglers, fighting for control of the vessel, tying up (with the help perhaps of Charles and a few more trusty friends) the gang and bringing the bottles in. Brandy or Geneva were the usual things he heard Charles speak of. For his papa. The thought appealed to him.

'Because if they know they're agoing to get half they'll give the rest up.'

When they reached the house Mrs Boyles greeted Horace from the kitchen, and handed him something armour-hard in cheesecloth. It was warm.

'There's for your ma,' she said. 'Boiled fresh.'

Horace glanced quickly at Charles but his mouth never quivered. Charles looked blank.

'Oh thank you, Mrs Boyles,' he said. 'Don't you like them?'

'Ay, we like them. We've several,' she said laconically. 'You're welcome.'

Horace rode home excited, with his knobbly prize. An awkward customer, was a lobster.

CHAPTER FOURTEEN

'To the Ocean now I fly...'

The Tuesday before Whitsun, June the second, little Kitty was taken to church for her public christening and Canon Poyntz came along from North Creake to stand godfather. It had been wild weather, no breath of summer about it: Horace and William and Sukey, hurrying back from school, found the party in the parlour with a cheerful little fire, for the guests were to dine at the parsonage.

Canon Poyntz, whose air of rich courtliness had once over-awed Sukey, was a distinguished-looking gentleman: fine-drawn features and dark eyes glittered with a smile of great sweetness. To Edmund Nelson he seemed to shine with the allurement of a keen intelligence. Coming to know him better but lately through his more loquacious and easy cousin, Sir Mordaunt, he had felt an increasing affinity with him; had borrowed from his library and been pleased if ever called upon to lend books in return. As he rode from Creake to Burnham the canon would stop and pass the time of day with the parson of Thorpe if he were working within call in his glebe. Pungent remarks concerning poetry or politics, prices or farming, churchmen or enthusiasts would fly between them.

Horace sat down on the floor by the canon.

'Well Horatio, and what adventures have you had lately?' began Canon Poyntz. Thus invited, the boy turned himself round, sat cross-legged and smiled up at the questioner as he gave him a spirited account of the wreck of the lobsters.

'So I quite suppose, sir, that the fishermen at Wells had been out secretly to see what they could find?'

The canon laughed.

'It is the usual custom of the country with stuff washed ashore. You like the sea, Horace? My cousin tells me that he can always enchant you with tales of Jamaica?'

'Oh yes, sir, because my uncle Captain Suckling was in the West Indies.'

'How old are you, Horatio?'

131

'Nearly nine, sir. All but four months.'

'Then you may soon be going away to school?'

'We have heard Papa talk about the school at North Walsham. But my mamma told me that both my godfathers send their boys to Norwich sir. That is, Lord Walpole and Dr Hamond.'

'What books do you read, my boy?'

'Oh, I like stories about travellers and sea-voyages and ship-wrecks and islands and strange places!'

And Horatio began to describe the delights of *Gulliver's Travels*, and *Robinson Crusoe* and *The Pilgrim's Progress*.

'Every book you read, Horace, is a world of its own. Had you ever thought of that? You enter that world and if the writer knows his skill you are caught and held in it until he lets you go!'

Horace had never thought of this, but he thought of it now and nodded.

'Or they are like gardens, like walking in a gracious garden! Do you know of Sir Thomas Browne of Norwich? He was a famous physician, a cunning thinker, and enticing writer. And Samuel Pepys who will tell you his daily life of a hundred years ago so that you may see it, hear it, smell it...'

'We have some cousins called Pepys, sir.'

'I dare say the very same family, for Sam Pepys had Norfolk cousins as I remember. And the great Doctor Johnson, whose paragraphs soar one atop the other like halls of well-hewn stone!'

Horatio had never thought of the writing of books like this. He understood only that Canon Poyntz loved books.

'And the poets, Horatio! Does your papa read you the poets?'

'He once read us some of John Milton,' said Horace doubtfully, having a memory that it was very difficult.

'Ah, *Paradise Lost*? He should have given you *Comus*! Listen to this now:

The Sounds and Seas with all their finny drove
Now to the Moon in wavering Morrice move,
And on the Tawny Sands and Shelves,
Trip the pert Fairies and the dapper Elves;

Who would have thought John Milton wrote of fairies, eh, Horace? Or this,

To the Ocean now I fly,
And those happy climes that ly
Where day never shuts his eye,
Up in the broad fields of the sky...'

132

He stopped, seeing Horatio transported by the vision of sea and sky.

'There are fair worlds in the poets, Horatio. What about Andrew Marvell, and Sir John Suckling (no doubt a forebear of yours?) and Richard Lovelace?' Even their names seemed silvered to Horatio. 'And Shakespeare, highest of all! Have you read any of Shakespeare, my boy?' Horace had not.

'Do you know much more poetry by heart, sir? Will you tell me some more?'

The canon considered.

'This should please you, it is by Andrew Marvell about the islands called the Bermudas.

"Where the remote Bermudas ride
In the ocean's bosom unespied,
From a small boat that row'd along
The listening winds received this song:" '

As the musical voice proceeded the parlour gradually fell into silence listening.

' "He hangs in shades the orange bright
Like golden lamps in a green night,
And does in pomegranates close
Jewels more rich than Ormus shows:
He makes the figs our mouths to meet
And throws the melons at our feet;
But apples plants of such a price,
No tree could ever bear them twice.
With cedars chosen by His hand
From Lebanon He stores the land;
And makes the hollow seas that roar
Proclaim the ambergris on shore." '

Papa had bade William hush and listen to one of his favourite poems, Mamma rocked Kitty hoping she would not cry, Granny held Ann in sleepy silence, Mrs Church, Kitty's godmother, nodded her head smiling.

' "Thus sang they in the English boat
A holy and a cheerful note:
And all the way, to guide their chime,
With falling oars they kept the time." '

In the pause that followed, Horace still heard the plashing of the oars, the complaint of the rowlocks.

'Papa,' he said into the silence in an amazed whisper. 'Dr Poyntz knows miles of poetry! In his head!'

There was laughter.

Horace thought of the rectory lying up in the tall trees behind the church at North Creake holding all Canon Poyntz's books and wondered whether he should ever go there.

Horatio hovered about, trotting backwards and forwards along the staithe at Overy like a busy little pointer, searching the filling channel for some fisherman of his acquaintance in a small rowing boat who looked as if he might use a boy for crew. Someone, surely, would teach him to row? It looked so easy, the rhythm was so delightful. (What were those English people doing in that poem, rowing along in a small boat on that calm blue sea with the winds listening, and the trees hung with oranges and melons? Miles from England, why were they singing? Was their ship wrecked, had they abandoned it?)

It was the summer vacation from school, mid-June to mid-July. His brothers were in the hayfield. Mr Allott had turned up, stuttering with rage, to tell Papa that Christ's College and Dr Shepherd had filed a bill in Chancery against him in May for the recovery of their tithes and land but that he was not beaten yet. Longing to hear more, Horace must leave, sent for by his mother to ride on an errand to the Market.

He had ridden on down to Overy, his resolve to row crystallising as he saw the blue channel. Was there no one he knew well enough to ask? (What strange things he had seen in Mr Dent's where he had gone to buy the remedy for Mamma's faintness. He had it safe in the saddle bag and the pony was tied near some grass feeding. Essence of Water Dock, Tincture of Valerian, he liked the word tincture, Tincture of Centaury, of Sage, of Spleen Wort, Elixir of Bardana.) He turned and looked up at the cottages and boat barns behind him. A rotund figure with bright curly hair emerged, and waddled across to the water's edge. Mr Woodgett! Going for his boat, carrying oars and his pronged spear!

Horace ran lightly along the shingley mud towards him.

'Mr Woodgett! Mr Woodgett, are you going out in your boat?'

Mr Woodgett smiled down at him, his face as round as his body.

'I am, bor,' he said. 'What be you a-doing of down here, Horatio?' he added, seeing who it was.

'Do you need...? Can I help...? Will you take me with you? Please. Mr Woodgett?' Horace said urgently.

'And what way can you help me I'd like to know?' said the fisherman laughing at this small pale member of the Thorpe parson's brood.

'If you please...I wondered if...' Horace said, hopping from one foot to another 'Mr Woodgett, pray will you teach me to *row*?' he said boldly.

'To row! What made you think of that now, Horace?'

'Oh, I do long to have a try, Mr Woodgett!' he pleaded.

'Well bor, you be a roight totty lad to wield an oar, I don't know as you'ld make to hold that, an all. Least ways not both on 'em. They're heavy, you know.' He was putting his stuff in the boat now and about to pull up the small anchor. He had not taken Horatio's plea with any seriousness. Horace was silent, watching every movement, his underlip stuck out, his face melancholy. Mr Woodgett looked up at him.

'You might balance over and land in the water and what would yer Ma say then? Your clouts wet an all.'

Horace was silent upon the possible recriminations of his mamma.

'I tell you what then Horace,' said the portly fisherman, unable to bear the intensity of the child's desire, 'I'll give you a few turns up and along the channel with one oar, eh? A-sitting wi' me. I'll take t'other. Careful, careful,' he bade, as Horace in his sudden excitement thundered into the boat, rocking it wildly. 'You don't never want to step in no boat that way, bor, do you'll upset un. That's the first thing to larn an all. And now you're a-settin' hind to fore,' he explained as the eager boy plumped down facing the bows. 'Turn you around, that's it, now make room for me, I take a tidy bit of space I do.'

Horace squeezed himself to the extreme edge of the thwart making room for his stout companion.

'Now then I push us out and we're away,' said the fisherman doing so. 'You do nowt but fit your oar in the rowlock, can you lift un to do that?'

Horace did so with some difficulty.

'That's it, now you just hold that steady over the side whiles I turn har around. Now then. See? We don't face the way we're agoing, we face the stern, whiles her bows face ahead.'

Horace nodded, intent. Having manoeuvred the boat so that she was set straight in the channel, Mr Woodgett prepared to teach his pupil.

'Now then. Grab hold o' that there oar with both hands, like you see me do.' Horace's small hands set themselves on the handle exactly as the fisherman's lay. 'That's it. Now we'll practise the stroke afore we put 'em in the water. You've watched us do it? Lean for'ard, as th'oar goo back. That's roight. Now this is the way of it, that oar she goo in the water with her blade stood upright so she push the water away as

135

she come through—that's what make the boat goo. If you lay har flat in the water she 'ont push no sea away, and you 'ont get nowhere. See, bor?'

Horatio saw exactly and said so.

'Let's have you take a stroke, I'll keep har steady.'

Horace leaned forward, looked back over his right shoulder, saw the oar was at the right angle, dipped it to the water, cut into the water cleanly.

'Now then pull hard, and as you pull lean back.'

Horace pulled hard. Horace fell off the thwart, his legs in the air, his oar driving into his stomach. Mr Woodgett smiled.

'That was very good, that oar went in roight clean, save that it got the better of you in the end. A few more tries and you'll have the knack of it.'

They set forth again. Horace splashed, he wobbled, he lost the oar from the rowlock, he slipped off the bench, he caught crabs (as Mr Woodgett called them), he caused the boat to go round in circles, his shoulders ached. Mr Woodgett commended and recommended, encouraged, explained, and kept them going with a shallow dip of his own oar. After about twenty minutes, Horace, scarcely daring to believe it, counted twelve passable strokes to his arm, felt the boat moving beneath him, saw the bank slide past, heard the water slap the bottom. *And all the way to guide their chime with falling oars they kept the time.* He must say it very slowly. He was rowing.

'Well done, Horatio. That's enough for one day and I must fare up to the mouth don't I'll miss all the fish. Shall I put you out here, on this bank? Can you pick your way back?'

'Yes. Oh thank you, Mr Woodgett! Thank you very much! May I come again?' Horatio said, dazed with exertion and success.

'Ay, I'll teach you about feathering 'em next time You did very well, tell yer ma and pa. Goodbye now!'

'Goodbye!' Horace called, waving, and turning to run along the marsh bank to the staithe and the patient pony. (But he was not altogether sure he would tell his ma and pa.) He found himself rowing in his imagination for the rest of the day. He longed to try again and do better. And feathering: what was feathering? He wished he were taller so that the oar did not go in so deeply.

The Custom House smack had one mast, a fixed bowsprit and a jib stay. Horatio watched avidly while her master and crew readied the sails and ran up the jib, as they eased her off the quay at Wells. Once clear and into the channel the mainsail was hoist. Horace and Charles from below the half deck looked up to watch. There was a great creaking and rattling, a banging and a flapping, as the pile of tumbled canvas straightened out, the boom swinging a little: up went the sail until it was as smooth and stretched as could be. There was a moderate steady wind from the east: she would drive down the channel, across the Pool and into the Run, on a broad reach with the wind striking full on the beam.

'Up you come,' called Mr Boyles.

The boys came up, Horatio quiet with excitement. The channel banks were sliding by fast, the water was blue from a blue sky, there was a frill of curling foam at the bows as she cut her way through, and behind (which he must learn to call aft) that shallow, widening trail that they called the wake. Up above was this towering expanse of strong canvas stretched hard in the wind carrying them along.

'Mind your head don't fall off,' called one of the men smiling.

Horatio brought his eyes down from the very top of the main sail and laughed. He could hardly believe his luck: he had watched sails fill often enough from quaysides. Now he was below one, sailing towards the sea. It was a fair, sunny Saturday in August, and he had been spending the day with Charles. Mr Boyles had suddenly appeared to say that the wind was right and they had to drop around to Holkham and Brancaster and would the boys care to come?

It was a high-tide and they had taken it before the full. Horace looked to his left, seeing the bank where he and Charles had run along on their way to examine the wrecked dogger. Now they were in the Pool where several other ships lay at anchor, while two or three fishing smacks ahead of them were making for the sea.

It was cold in the Run. Horatio hugged himself, dressed in an old sailor's slop Mrs Boyles had put on over all his clothes. His skin felt whipped up and alive, his whole being felt alive, with the kind of excitement he had experienced one day from Norton tower. He smiled, licking his lips. They tasted of salt, for the fine spray filled the air.

In the mouth of the Run they met an invading army of brisk bobbling waves, so that the boat rose and fell, rose and fell as if she bowed to the open sea. Outside the channel Mr Boyles began to turn the cutter's head towards the west. Horace saw him give a backward look over the stern, considering. Then he called out:

'I think 't were best to go about…Ready about, haul away!'

The hands were hauling hard on the sheet, the boom swung over, the sail filled quickly on the other side. Now they were sailing westwards towards Brancaster and soon would enter Holkham bay. Horatio could feel what had happened and saw the reason why. Ships rode the seas like great horses, you learned to turn their heads, rein them in, let them run, as you learned to ride a pony. The difference was you must needs learn the behaviour of the wind as well. He would gladly learn. Now they were right out at sea: for the first time in his life he was 'in the ocean's bosom', able to look back at the land. He saw the channel mouth, the town in the distance, the quayside, the church, the mills, the farmhouses, the sand-dunes and trees near Holkham Gap, and above, the park itself dotted with new trees, and a sight of the great house! And on, on to Overy, Scolt Head, Brancaster. All laid out like a map in another life far from theirs on the ocean! His spirit expanded at the sight.

Summer diminished to autumn. At King's Lynn, Mr Charles Turner, a kinsman of cousin John's, was chosen mayor. And to Raynham was returned the body of the right honourable Charles Townshend, late Chancellor of the Exchequer (who had enraged the American colonists so much with his custom upon tea) to be buried in his family vault.

In Burnham Thorpe the family drank Horatio's health on his ninth birthday, and little Kitty was beloved, the darling of all, petted and danced upon every knee. The rector and his wife discussed schools for the boys. The school at North Walsham, having put off its opening until midsummer due to further alterations in the new school-house, had announced itself ready to receive boarders, and, as an additional incentive to its most healthful and agreeable situation, described itself as surrounded by a brick wall, which effectively prevented the boys from having any communication with the town. Mamma was tired and often felt faint with effort. She had too much to do, he must relieve her from some of it, her husband decided, going into his study one early October day to re-read the notices of the schools.

Horatio was there lying on the floor, his head in his hands, reading the latest paper. Hearing his father, he began to scramble to his feet respectfully.

'Don't disturb yourself, Horace,' Papa said. He liked to see them absorbed in reading. 'Go on with your reading.'

'Papa, what is an auctioneer?'

'A man who sells things, usually furniture, or pictures, or even houses. He arranges the sale and gathers the people and asks them to start by giving a price for a thing. Bidding, it is called. Do you remember your friend Robinson Crusoe at Lynn? He is an auctioneer. His job is to push the price *up*. And when no one will bid any higher, he takes his hammer and he knocks it three times, knocks it *down* to the purchaser.'

'And he says, "A-going, A-going, A-going"?'
'So he does, yes.'

Horace sighed and read again the verses he had found. They were about an auctioneer who had died, whose own furniture was to be sold.

Think on the Fate of Auctioneers
(The Fate of Commoners and Peers)
And while your wit you're showing
Think that a King as well as Clown
Think all at last must be *knock'd down*—
A-going, A-going, A-going.

Horace felt stifled with sadness. He wished to think on no such thing, he wished for all his family, his loving mother, his dearest papa, to be around him for ever in this house on this land, where the scent of October came in through the windows from Peter's bonfire, and the russet apples lay in sweet-smelling rows on the shelves. He scrambled up, gave his father the paper, and hurried out to find William and Maurice and Sukey and Nan and the little ones.

The rector read the rhyme in due course and thought that he must remember to tell Horace that Shakespeare had said these things more poetically. But this doggerel was enough to carry its sorry message to the child's feeling heart.

CHAPTER FIFTEEN

'...The High School at Norwich'

Alas for Horatio, change (which he did not yet realise to be the one permanence in this mortal life) had him in her relentlessly wayward hand, would toss him and tumble him now in who knew what direction until he was cast upon the broad sea of life on his own. Perhaps indeed the very sense of this being to come due to rumours of school, had caused him to be struck so passionately by the dying fall of the news-sheet rhyme. (He had talked of it again later.)

Thus ran the rector's thoughts, as he and his sons bowled along in the hired chaise through an ordinary November day just opening into pale sunlight, on the high road from Fakenham to Norwich. He was taking the two boys to school.

It had all at the last been arranged expeditiously and the Free School at Norwich had been settled upon. For not only had his wife favoured it, thinking of young Horace Hamond being there to show them the ways, but Mrs Suckling too had had her say. Old Mrs Henley, her husband's sister, lived in Norwich in a house in St Andrew's Street, and, though to be sure she was an ancient lady, she had two unmarried daughters, nieces to Mrs Suckling, cousins to Catherine Nelson, whom she was sure would keep a motherly eye on the boys. Why, it was near at hand, all they must do was cross Tombland and run up St George's Street! She had written to her relations, who had responded kindly. The rector had likewise written to the master and governors, suggesting that his boys might come now rather than wait till the new year. For it had become imperative, he realised, to relieve his wife. The reverend Mr Edward Simonds had agreed and all had been arranged. William and Horace had bidden farewell to their school-fellows in Burnham at the end of October, not without some sense of importance, William in particular realising himself to be an object of interest and envy. Charles, downcast to lose his friend, was enheartened by Horatio's stalwart affirmation that they should always be friends and that anyway he would be back for Christmas.

Change, the rector thought, glancing down at Horace's arm through his, and William's broad hand upon his knee the other side, mitigated her blows by dispensing the delights of variety. Horace had been quite markedly excited and eager in the last few days, as he had spoken to his sons of the pleasures of the city, the beauty of the cathedral, the welcome of the Henleys. Mamma too had done her best to encourage them, had sorted and mended, and packed their box; had bidden Mary make them a cake and some toffee and pack them up apples and pears. He himself had replenished their school bags with pens and pencils and paper, notebooks and rulers. While the boys nodded on each side of him (they had made an early start and the excitement of being in the chaise on their own had now given place to sleepiness) he thought with fondness and some pain of their festival that year, two weeks ago. His wife had asserted that it was time the little boys knew of their uncle's exploit and bidden Maurice and William and Horatio to tell the tale. Horatio, good child that he was and eager to please, and delighting to play a leading part, had done most of the telling and had coaxed and dragooned his self-conscious older brothers to enact the scene upon the quarter deck. His father smiled down with amusement at him now, remembering his frenzied efforts to arouse some enthusiasm from solemn Edmund and puzzled Suckling. 'I hope,' Mamma had explained with animation, 'I hope that *one* of my sons will follow his uncle.' She had been ill that night, the excitement had quite fagged her out, she had descended into several days of quiet and burdened abstraction when he could see she could scarce keep upon her feet.

'Oh my darlings, goodbye, be good, learn your lessons well, think of Mamma, write to Papa, and come home soon,' she had said this morning, hugging them both as they eagerly clambered up and turning away quickly for the house. Embracing her, he had seen the tears stand in her eyes, swallowed back as she smiled at him.

They entered the city by St Augustine's Street, turned off to the right, crossed the river and came up into St Andrew's past the remains of the old Blackfriars monastery, and the church, refurbished and made into a new hall. Across St Andrew's Street round the corner lay Mrs Henley's house, opposite St Andrew's Church: the yellow mist of the November afternoon was descending as the horses clattered into the stable yard gate at past three o'clock. William sat forward and peered about him, his mouth opening in an enormous yawn which conveyed itself to Horace. Papa stifled his own, saying:

'Yes yawn your fill in here, but pray do not yawn before our three hostesses, I beg of you boys. William, jump down now and give Horatio a hand, watch the step, mind your papa's poor toes. So.'

A side door in the house opened and an elderly man with a face like a benign horse stepped out stiffly to welcome the travellers.

'Come you on this way, sir, and young masters.'

Horatio caught his brother's eye, nudged him and giggled. He was silly with excitement, tiredness and anxiety. But William frowned and hushed him, striding with dignity after his papa, his chin up, aware of his ten and a half years, Horace after all was just nine, a perfect child. A grave maid ushered them into a drawing-room. (It was perhaps, though small, a drawing-room and not a parlour: there were mirrors and gilt and bright brass candle-sticks and a crystal candelabra, Horace thought it was beautiful, but knew he must not stare around him.) Two ladies considerably older than his mother but more fashionably dressed had risen from their chairs, and upon a pretty sofa beside the fire was a petal-faced old lady in a shawl with a little dog near her feet. Her cap and her clothes had the timeless quality of age and not of fashion.

It was the elder Miss Henley who was the spokesman of this family: coming to meet them with arms extended, she gave the rector her hand, then darted her head of auburn ringlets towards each boy, kissing them on their cheeks.

'This must be William!'—William barely forbore to flinch—'And this is Horatio!' but Horace received her kisses with pleasure—'Now here is my honoured mamma whom you have not met before—' Both boys bowed with deference over Mrs Henley's hand: but Horatio smiled too, thinking that for a lady of over ninety (as his mother had told him) she had a very soft, smooth face. 'And this is my sister, cousin Mary.' Cousin Mary was darker than her sister and in face like her mother.

And all through dinner as the grave maid served, cousin Lucy engaged the boys in cheerful conversation, while Papa talked of old times and family connections with Mrs Henley, and cousin Mary watched and smiled; and Horace knew that he sat over a deep, unknown hole, a kind of pit, which would soon swallow him up: that first the exciting journey with Papa and now only the meal and the candles, stood between him and it: that soon Papa would rise and the kind ladies would bid them farewell, and they would enter the gates of school and Papa would leave them, for days and days, and weeks and weeks, and who knew what would be there to engulf them? His stomach misgave him. He knew he must show no sign. He found cousin Mary's kind eyes upon him and her hand on his knee as he trifled with his food.

'Leave the rest,' she whispered. 'You are tired, my child, we will excuse you.'

William's plate was polished.

'And remember my boys, how near we are, think that you may come here as to a home,' said cousin Lucy.

But Horatio could remember nothing but the yawning hole.

Papa took their hands and the man brought the box, and they crossed St Andrew's Street again and wound round by a great elm tree and down the steep, cobbled street which they later learned to call Elm Hill, because Papa wished to show them its picturesque antiquity, lit by a few shop lanterns. They came out into the road which soon broadened into Tombland and a lamplighter passed them carrying his stave and his rushlight. They crossed the wide street and went towards a stone archway on the other side, tall and decorated with a niche above it.

The rector paused, looking up. 'In the niche boys, if I remember aright, is Sir Thomas Erpingham and this is his gateway. You will see him better by daylight.'

Then they were in the Close: and the dark shadow of the great spire of the cathedral soared up to the sky straight ahead of them beyond the west door. The school hall lay on the left, wide stone steps leading up to its porch. Near at hand lay the school-house (the master's) and the usher's house. The boys were to board with the usher, the reverend Mr Nichols.

'Now my children, my dear boys, here we are...' Edmund Nelson spoke with a cheerfulness he did not feel.

'Papa,' Horace whispered clutching hard to his arm, 'shall we see you in the morning?' And William sniffed.

Their father's heart smote him.

'I shall be away early, back to Mamma. Be a man, my good Horatio. Two or three days I promise you, and you will be quite settled. Think how fortunate you are, to have your brother William with you who is older and will protect you, will you not, William? That is capital. You may confide in each other. Write us a letter as soon as you can. You have nothing to fear, I think, Horace but your own imaginings. I shall bid you goodbye here for we may not have the chance inside.'

And he embraced both his sons heartily, before he led them towards the house where they would live. Finding they were to be bed-fellows as they had always been, the boys were comforted. But Horace shed hot tears upon the hard pillow, thinking of his mother and his bed at home, and Maurice, and Sukey and the little ones; and Mary and Peter, and the ponies stamping in the stable. And ever and again of his mother.

When the master entered the great hall at eight o'clock a comparative silence fell. The boys had been there since half after seven; William and Horatio had thronged up the steps with the rest, being stared at and questioned. Mr Nichols, with much clapping of his hands, banging of his ferule and raising of his voice, had at length set each group at each end reciting their particular lessons, some Latin, some tables, some Greek, some geography, some psalms, until the uproar had become at least a controlled uproar, like the water upon a weir. He had then strutted like a jackdaw, flapping his gown, between his own end and the master's end, striving to hear and control each group in turn as they shouted ever louder to hear each other (those who knew not their lessons relying on those who did).

As the reverend Mr Simonds appeared, the uproar faded, and isolated chanting voices wavered into silence, benches scraped and scholars stood and mumbled their responses to his good morning. A collect was said as the boys stood, then the whole school was led into the Lord's Prayer. Horace said it with all his heart, finding in it some link with the days he knew. Now Mr Nichols proceeded to call the day-bill; William glanced at Horace, wondering when their turn would come. It came at last, for Mr Nichols had added their names hastily at the end.

'William Nelson,' he shouted.

'Here, sir,' said William rising and subsiding.

'Who is that boy?' called Mr Simonds, the newness of the name upon his ear arousing him from dazed abstraction. 'I never saw that boy in my life before. Stand up, boy. How did you get here?'

William stood miserably, his face slowly reddening, struck totally dumb.

'How did you get here, boy? Answer me. Who are you?'

'William Nelson, sir. Last night, sir, my father brought us...' William faltered.

'They are the sons of the reverend Mr Nelson of Burnham Thorpe, Mr Simonds, sir. They arrived last night; I did not disturb you. You knew of their coming,' explained Mr Nichols patiently.

'Oh, ah, yes. *Nelson.* Quite so, quite so. Sit down boy,' said the master, as if he had mistaken the name rather than forgotten their existence.

'Horatio Nelson,' called the usher last and somewhat unnecessarily.

'Here, sir,' piped Horace with spirit, determined to make himself heard against the titters which surrounded him.

After this there was breakfast, during which the Nelson boys bore much needling from their immediate neighbours (on the subject of their never having been seen before and having no right to appear now) and then there were lessons until twelve; and as it was Wednesday, a double day, more lessons after dinner from two until five; and then an evening prayer, and then once more the tedious day-bill, enlivened only by the breath of laughter which greeted the Nelsons' names at the end. (Mr Usher had found no time to fit them into their alphabetical place.) Horace giggled with the rest, his nature having little of self-esteem about it as yet; but William's dignity was affronted and he scowled before he laughed. Then there was supper and lessons to prepare, and washing and bed.

Horace and William being but nine and ten were taught by Mr Nichols with the younger boys, and, in those subjects in which their father or their Burnham master had grounded them, fared not badly. But in Latin, coming in at the middle of the term and knowing nothing and the usher making little time to enlighten them separately, they entered a strange world of new words whose meanings eluded them, whose endings changed to mean other things, where *mensa* and *magister*, *puer* and *equus*, *civis* and *liber* were chanted, changing incomprehensibly; and *amare* and *facere* and *habere* and *esse* changed in even more mysterious ways; and they were as likely to conjugate a noun as to decline a verb, having no notion yet of which was which. And in this limbo, for all Mr Nichols cared, they floundered. Their translations from the one tongue into the other (which must be written in a book and shown up every Friday after breakfast to be heard by the master) remained very largely a matter of random guess and luck and earned for both boys the roars and thwacks that William had secretly dreaded. More than once did he raise his hand for permission to leave the hall after this ordeal (only one boy from each end was allowed down at a time, and he must leave by the back door) and cried angry tears in the necessary.

Horace Hamond who had quickly become (as their earlier meeting had promised) a particular friend to Horatio, used to laugh at their troubles (being good at his own Latin) and offered to set them right. But it was much pleasanter on half-holidays to wander into the old cloister beyond the cathedral, and see the stone bench where the monks once played nine men's morris with their marbles; or hear Hamond talk of Sir Thomas Erpingham and Agincourt; or make their way out of the Bishop's Gate and down to the river and see the folk crossing Pull's Ferry; or explore the Cow Tower, or watch the fishermen, or even fish themselves with their home-made rods: all these things were much pleasanter than Latin grammar and very naturally took precedence over it. Until the next lesson, when Horatio would wish with anguish that he could understand what it was he was trying to do.

Every Sunday all the boarders were assembled and conducted across to the great west door and into the shadows of the huge cathedral. The boys' feet would make a considerable clattering as they proceeded to their pews, ladies in bonnets would turn and smile or frown according to their natures, churchwardens would hush, gentlemen would grunt. Horace had never before been in so vast a church, where the chanting was lost in the distances of the choir, spiralling faintly like the voices of angels; where the lofty marble pillars soared up, up, higher than a mast, and on dark days were lost in the dimness of the roof; where the candles on the altar seemed as remote as stars and the side aisles with their chapels and tombs and recesses were like streets, their carved bosses far beyond the ordinary sight; where the nave was a great highway to the altar, and the organ (new and splendid) produced such seas of rich and thundering sound that a boy felt near drowned in them.

Several times upon a Sunday they ran up St George's Street to the house in St Andrew's Hill and knocked with the beautiful brass knocker (which William could reach and Horatio could not) upon the door and were ushered by the grave maidservant into the warmth and cheer and firelight of their cousins' house. Their dinner here seemed a feast after the plain fare at school; and they would play such games as the ladies deemed innocent enough for the Sabbath, or read, or write to Papa and Mamma; and Horatio's lively talk vastly entertained old Mrs Henley, who would become aquiver with laughter as he described Mr Simonds' latest absentmindedness.

One cold Saturday, Mr Nichols informed them that a relation was coming to see them and they should be ready after lessons, at twelve; and ready they were, waiting in the Close by the Erpingham gate, Horace hopping to keep warm, William blowing his nails.

'It couldn't, I suppose…it couldn't be *Papa*?' Horace wondered, the glory of this seeming too much to hope for.

'He would have told us in a letter, and so would Mr Nichols,' William said gruffly.

Horatio knew this was true, yet the lovely dream persisted until a chaise drew up and an elderly gentleman kindly and quiet, got out and announced himself to be their great-uncle John Fowle, whom they had seen when they were younger at their grandmother Suckling's house but did not clearly remember. For he was the husband of Mrs Suckling's sister, their mother's aunt Elizabeth whom again they could only dimly remember. She had died three years since. The Fowles had had no children of their own, but nonetheless great-uncle Fowle was fond of boys and showed it at once.

'If I were your age, my boys, I know what I would like to do in this handsome city, I would like to climb up to the castle. Or have you already seen it?'

'Oh no sir! Yes sir, please sir!' they both said together and were bundled into the chaise in the highest glee, Horatio bouncing upon the seat, and taking his uncle's arm and forgetting the dream of Papa in the pleasant reality which had overtaken him. They climbed up the castle mound and walked around it, entered those parts where the populace was admitted, toiled to the battlements and surveyed the city spread out below them, the churches so many that towers and spires protruded on all hands. From up here the graceful cathedral spire was their equal.

'There are the castle ditches, where the felons are hung.'

'Where are the dungeons?'

'Down below, full of prisoners.'

Of course the castle was full of prisoners, and when people sent them food or drink a message of thanks appeared from the governor in Papa's paper. Horace had often noticed this.

Then great-uncle John gave them chocolate at Saunder's coffee-house in the Gentleman's Walk below the market; and afterwards showed them the Guildhall and the market square and for good measure drove them round and about Norwich, down to St Stephen's and up again to Chapel Fields. Everywhere they saw the lamps lighting up in the shops as dusk fell, and heard the cries of the market men selling off the week's stuff cheap. Then he gave them a fine dinner at the White Swan next St Peter's Mancroft and opposite Thomas Ivory's fine Assembly House (which he bade them admire). He asked them how was Mamma, and how Mrs Suckling, and how fared Maurice and what he was to do in life.

And lest William should still be hungry, they called in at William Hilling's the muffin-baker in St Gregory's church-yard. The boys went back to the Close at last with two muffins apiece hot and dripping with butter, and having thanked and embraced their kind relation who had near fifteen miles to journey back to Broome, lurked in the cathedral shadows to eat them privily before going into the house.

Old Mrs Henley had had several sisters, one of whom had become Mrs Thomas Berney of Bracon Ash. Her son was that Mr John Berney who was Sukey's godpapa and whose position as high sheriff had so puzzled her when she was small. Mr John Berney, hearing from the folk at Burnham, came to show kindness to the boys also and carried them off one Saturday to Bracon Ash to meet his wife and his daughter. And on the way he drew up the chaise and showed them the ancient stone walls round a sloping field at Caister which he said was an old Roman camp or city: and he let them climb down and run along to examine these. Horace made up his mind to tell Papa, for Papa liked such things. Mr Berney and his family asked the young Nelsons what they would do when they were men; and William said that he would be a bishop (he had been much impressed with the bishop's throne in the cathedral). But Horatio smiled and said nothing and was declared to be too young to have thought of such hard matters.

The rector had written regularly to the boys and they had waited eagerly for his letters with news of home, replying themselves in short, comical, schoolboy phrases which had often made their parents smile. On post evenings in Norwich a man who had had the idea of collecting the letters would come into the Close with his tin-box (locked) and ring his bell, and from many a clergyman's or prebendary's house would come a maidservant with missives; and last he would come over to the school and the diligent boys who had written home would post their letters into the box.

One day in the middle of December a letter came from Papa telling the two Nelsons that since Mamma was at times not very well and their grandmamma was ill and confined to her bed, he would not come to fetch them, but that they should travel on the Thursday before the Saturday the school closed, for then they could come with John Raven in his wagon: and that good Mr Raven would come himself to collect them very early in the morning. Papa had, he said, informed Mr Nichols and he looked forward heartily to their return and was their affectionate father.

'William!' Horatio burst out. 'We're going home, William! Can you believe it? Only think, we shall be there next week! Is it not splendid?'

William agreed, his enthusiasm coming more slowly than Horatio's, but, when it came, outdoing it. He began to dance clumsily about, endangering the inmates of their room in the usher's house.

'Give me the letter, let me read it for myself,' Horace said as his brother waved it.

And he was quiet, his father's words chilling him a little.

'Mamma is not well,' he said. 'I hope she will be recovered for Christmas.'

And a slight unease, a fleet shadow, undermined for a few moments his heartfelt joy.

Chapter Sixteen

The Holly and the Ivy

It seemed the middle of the night to William and Horatio when they were roused and bidden to dress quickly in the cold darkness, by the light only of a lamp in the Close outside.

'No doubt we shall see you after Christmas,' Mrs Nichols whispered, her night-cap barely concealing her curl papers above her tired face, which looked thinner and meaner at this early hour. 'A good journey to you,' she said, and bundled them after the carrier as he shouldered the box.

'There y'are then,' said John Raven setting off towards the Erpingham gateway. 'You be half asleep but keep you up wi' me one each side, don't I may lose you in the dark. That's right. You be glad to be going home for Christmas, lads, I reckon?'

Trotting along beside him, they passed their cousins' house in St Andrew's all shuttered, and turned down into London Lane, where Horace must skip now and then to keep pace. Up the hill past the market they went and round into St Giles to the inn called the Black Horse. There John discovered that they had eaten nothing and sat them down to hot chocolate and rolls while he loaded up his last parcels.

As the city clocks struck five, Raven's wagon pulled away. Nodding against William in the stuffy dark tent which the canvas cover made, Horatio had time at last to relish the fact that they were going home. John called each stop, Drayton and Attlebridge, Sparham and Bawdeswell Bell, Foxley and Bintry and Guist. At the Swan at Guist the carrier sat the boys up to the inn ordinary, a plate of steaming stewed mutton, some apple pie and warmed ale.

'Lay to, my boys, you've not long while they change the horses and your pa gave me money for your meal.' William rapidly made clean work of his and helped to finish Horatio's.

Approaching Kettlestone, they leaned out at the back of the cart to see the gibbet. (There was a gibbet above Burnham Market too, they had sometimes ridden to Gallows Hill to see it.) Over Fakenham Common they jogged as the sun began to sink behind a windmill. Now the road became more familiar. Dusk fell over enclosures, woods, uplands whose shape Horatio recognised. He would see Sukey and Maurice! And Papa. And the little ones. And Mamma, *Mamma*! William dozed, breathing loudly. Horace saw the regular heaving movement of the horses' rumps as he peered round the canvas for the lights of Creake Abbey. Then the shadow of the ruins. Then at last their own stream, their own trees! He shook William in a frenzied excitement.

'Wake up, wake up, we're here!' Horace said.

Before John had time to climb down, go round and pull out the steps, Horace had picked his way over parcels and passengers and had leapt into the dark, his school bag banging on his back, and run round the house, through the little white gate to the lights each side of the door. He burst in shouting wildly.

'Mamma, Papa, we're here, we've arrived!' and ran for the kitchen. The latch clicked, the warmth, the firelight, the candleglow washed over him like a blessing. Everybody was there, he took them all to himself in one excited happy glance: Mamma at the table making something with flour, Sukey chopping suet on a board, Nan sitting up in a great sticky mess stoning raisins, the small boys by the fire, Kitty crawling between them.

'Mamma!'

'Horace! Here you are safely back, here, come kiss me, I cannot embrace you, my hands are all flour, we are making the plum puddings, you are arrived in time to stir...' Horace flung his arms about his mother's neck as she stooped, pulled her down, kissed her glistening cheek. 'And here's William!' she said laughing, as she kissed him in turn. 'Quickly Edmund, run and tell Papa!'

But Papa had heard the wagon and came from the study and was there behind them at the kitchen door, smiling his quizzical smile. Horace flung himself upon his father.

'Now then, now then! Here are my two schoolboys! William, you are fatter than ever, I declare. Has John gone?'

'Yes Papa, he gave me change for you from our meal. And here's your paper,' William shouted jumping about, caught up into the general excitement. 'Mamma, guess where we dined? We dined at Guist at the inn on mutton stew, it was very savoury, and a splendid apple pie. I helped Horace finish his, he was so excited he could eat scarce a thing...'

And William proceeded to laugh heartily at his own greed. Horatio greeted Sukey, who smiled in a shy but grown-up way at him, he kissed Ann continuing devotedly with her raisins, he went up to fondle Kitty who was now struggling in Mary's arms bewildered by the sudden excitement. Someone was missing.

'Where's Maurice?' he said.

'He's down with your grandmamma helping them out a bit,' his mother began to explain. She put her arm up to her brow. 'Oh dear me, I must sit down a while, all this stir makes me feel quite faint.' She lowered herself into the rocking-chair by the fire. Horace went over eagerly and she took his hand, holding it on her knee as if to reassure him.

'Your poor grandmamma is very sickly, very ailing,' Papa said, 'and Mamma is quite overdone, trying to help her as well as do all here.'

'So Maurice has gone down to see what he can do to help Sarah,' Mamma murmured. 'Good boy, he is fond of his grandmother. There, that is better...' she sighed.

'Let me fetch you a glass of wine, my love?' Papa's voice sounded concerned.

'Thank you, husband. You see, boys, this is why you find us making the puddings at night, which ought to have been done weeks past. Now Horace, William, are you both well? Have you learnt a great deal? Are you hungry? Mary has some soup for you. Sukey, we will leave it all now. Put it to the dresser and cover it over.'

Papa brought the wine, and Horace watched his mother take it with pleasure. Maurice walked in, hailing his brothers, hugging them affectionately. Papa sat in the high-backed kitchen chair and began to open his paper, loth to retire from the warmth of the family circle. Horace's heart swelled, looking from his father to his mother and around his whole family.

'Oh Mamma, I am so happy to be back!' he said, his eyes filling with tears of joy. His mother noted this as she smiled at him. What a feeling child he was and with what ease he showed his feelings!

When the morning's work was done, Catherine Nelson called Susannah and Ann and set off with them down the road to see her mother. The girls carried the little dishes she had made to tempt the old lady. She could see Horatio up in the bare orchard, quartering the whole place as he had announced his intention of doing. She herself felt better after a good sleep: what a merciful providence was the night, the dark. One could not go on from task to task through the night, one must stop and rest. She had learned by now that when her head reeled she must always rest, sit down, fold her hands and wait. Sometimes it even came upon her in bed, and the pillow seemed to swing in the way she imagined a hammock at sea might swing and she with it. Then it was a strange but not altogether unpleasant sensation. She supposed it might be her time of life, though it was full early for this to be showing signs.

She knew also that she had always too much to do. For her mother was still half the day in her bed and not leaving her chamber. Sarah, not a young woman, was finding it hard to manage without complaint.

'Well, dearest Mamma,' her daughter said cheerfully.

Mrs Suckling was propped up on her pillows, a pretty ribboned cap sitting upon her white hair, her always strong features emphasised by the pale face now so thin. Her daughter could hear at once that she drew her breath hard.

'How are you today?'

'It seems to lodge upon my chest, nothing moves it. It quite pains me to draw breath. How are you, my love, and the family?' the old lady whispered.

'The two boys are safely back from Norwich, they shall come and visit you.'

'Good. And you, Catty?' Her mother spoke anxiously, using a name from long ago.

'I had the dizziness last night again, with the boys' return! I have to sit quietly and rest, naught else for it.'

'Nothing. I hope you will go gently, with the house full over Christmas. You must not think of me, I shall be very well with Sarah. Pray, just leave us. I have put too much upon you, Dear Maurice came last night as usual. Ah, my little doves! Here you are!'

'Good morning, Granny, are you better today?' Sukey said, patting her grandmother's cold hand. 'You are right cold, shall I put more on the fire?'

'Do, my love. But old ladies are customarily cold. And I shall be seventy-seven come March the first. Well, Nan? What have you been doing since I last saw you, darling?'

'Stoning raisins ma'am,' said Ann solemnly, 'for the puddens,' as if this occupation had lasted twenty-four hours: as indeed to her it seemed to have done.

Mrs Suckling laughed, coughed painfully, and gasped. Ann watched with interest while she recovered her breath.

'Would you like to find the old purse, play with the gold medals?' she whispered, seeing the child's wide eyes upon her.

Ann nodded. She went over to the small rosewood table with the china shepherdess on top, opened the drawer, took out the long chamois purse, grey with age, and tipped its contents on to the hearth rug.

'Yes, seventy-seven I shall be, if God spares me so long.'

'Oh Mamma it grieves me to hear you talk so.'

'Well 'tis a good age my dear. I have had my time I dare say. If I could but shift it from my chest, I might be better and see the spring,' she repeated.

'It's cold again today of course.'

'I can feel it is. Easterly winds are bad for the breathing. And what happens in the village? I hear little.'

'They say Widow Bee is six months gone with child.'

'Who will that be, then?'

'They are after some man called Langley, Charles Langley, Papa says.'

'And they will make him marry her and they will live unhappily ever after,' said Mrs Suckling wheezily.

'Perhaps, perhaps not.' Sukey listened hard, gazing into the small fire, her cheeks burning. 'Women have their devices. No doubt Mrs Bee knew what she was about,' her mother laughed, 'and found it better to be molested than lonely.'

Sarah came up grave and fussily anxious, bearing a tray upon which were the parsonage dishes. She was used to feed the old lady early in the hope she would sleep thereafter. The time upon her granny's pinchbeck watch lying with its velvet ribbon beside her bed was near two o'clock, Sukey noticed. She kissed her grandmother and led the way downstairs, thinking of the plain, quite faded Widow Bee molested by a dashing figure called Charles Langley, all ruffs and feathers and velvet, mounted upon a horse.

The Sunday before Christmas the sun shone, the wind blew, the brown earth looked clean and the stream dark and merry, the pattern of the winter trees was fine and beautiful. The rector was marching the older children up to church. He and Sukey danced Ann between them, William plodded just ahead forever under Sukey's feet. Maurice and Horatio burst into a spontaneous run as Maurice kicked a stone, shouldering each other out of the way, contending for it. Boys, boys, Papa heard himself say, yet was glad to see their spirits and said nothing.

What secret was it that glorified the Christmas countryside, made it seem mysteriously endowed with a beauty, a meaning beyond his grasp? The polished holly leaves, the scarlet knots of berries, the pointed ivy with fruit like small pomanders, the crimson haws on the twisted thorns, the brilliant green mould that clothed the old tree stems in the thickets! Was it simply that nature waited in joy for the rehearsal of the miraculous nativity? Regaining afterwards her everyday dullness, as the ancient mystery fled. Each year he felt it in advent more powerfully than the feast itself. He wondered if this were peculiar to him or whether other people shared it. He must ask his wife.

On the way home Mr Nelson took the two boys in to greet their grandmother. Horatio produced a drawing of a ship in full sail upon a bouncing sea and laid it on the coverlet. William added some sprigs of holly with berries which he had just plucked.

'Thank you my dear boys,' Mrs Suckling whispered, scarcely looking at either gift and smiling vaguely upon them as if she had forgotten they had been away for six weeks.

Edmund Nelson was aware at once that she had something upon her mind. Horace was disappointed, he had found it a sacrifice to part with the ship drawing at all. Should he quickly pocket it again, would she ever notice? He feared Papa would.

'Look Granny, ma'am, it is a ship like Uncle Maurice sails in,' he insisted eagerly.

'Why Horace, so 'tis,' she said, picking it up and peering at it. 'Poor Uncle Maurice,' she sighed. And with this Horatio must be content. She did not even seem to realise he had drawn it, nor how difficult it was, nor did she compliment him upon it! Papa pressed Horace to his side knowing his thoughts.

'Shall these boys go down and help Sarah, should she need it?' he said. 'Now that they have paid their respects ma'am?'

'Dear boys,' she said, 'let them do so. Let you come again Horace, William, when I am more myself. Goodbye now.'

'Goodbye ma'am,' they said subdued, glad to be given their dismissal.

'My son, I am glad you have come...' she began the moment the door was closed.

'Now what is it ma'am?' he said at once sitting down. 'I can see something exercises you. What can I do for you?'

'It is my affairs my son, my will. I have little to leave, but I may as well dispose it as I wish,' she said hoarsely. 'And then should I not recover everything will be in order. My son William will be my executor.'

'My dear madam, I have every hope that you will recover when the warm weather comes and be with us a great while. But shall I get Mr Nicholas Raven to wait upon you from Burnham?'

'That is what I wish,' she said gratefully.

'I will send tomorrow. I dare say he will call upon the Tuesday. Is that soon enough?' he asked, uneasily aware that the poor lady might feel worse than she appeared.

'Some time after noon on the Tuesday will be most convenient,' she said with an air of relief and closed her eyes. 'Thank you, my dear son-in-law.'

'I shall leave you now, you are tired. My wife will come later on no doubt. God bless you,' he said touching her hand, finding a slight dislocation between his roles as son-in-law and priest. 'May I say the Collect for the day?' She opened her eyes, smiled and nodded. Edmund said the prayer. She was going to die, he believed. His wife would be distressed at her death, would miss her mother constantly.

'Come boys,' he said into the kitchen. 'Oh, has William gone? Good morning to you Sarah.'

Father and son left together.

'Is my granny very ill, Papa?'

'She seemed so today. She was fretting because she had made no will and that is why she paid no heed to your ship.'

'What is a will, Papa, exactly?'

'It is a document to tell people how you wish your goods and money to be left. When you die.'

'Is my granny going to die then, Papa?'

'It is impossible to say, Horace. It is in God's hands. Any of us may die at any moment. She may well recover. Why, rich people make their wills when they are quite young.' There was a pregnant pause.

'So my granny is not at all rich?' was Horatio's conclusion.

'No. She's of modest means certainly,' his papa said, smiling at the boy's logic.

Mamma was by the fire in the parlour lit early for Sunday, sitting in the low nursing chair, feeding little Kitty. She was weaning her. Kitty, though usually a good feeder, was blowing the pottage in all directions.

'Oh Kitty-katty, naughty baby,' Catherine said with unusual severity, spooning up the messy stuff. 'What is it Horace, cannot you see that I am occupied? Now then let's try again. Come now, lovely dinner.' Young Catherine, diverted by Horatio, blew again. Her mother felt near to tears of rage.

'Go away, Horace!'

'But Mamma, there is something important to tell you about my granny…'

'Unless your granny is dying child, I bid you go away!'

'But she is Mamma, Papa thinks she may be…'

His mother looked up, harassed and startled. 'What do you mean?'

'She is thinking about making a will, she took no heed of my ship at all Mamma—Papa said she might die,' he finished lamely.

Mrs Nelson was unconvinced of her mother's imminent decease and tried to control her irritation.

'Now Horace, go away, close the door, but send Sukey to me, she can sometimes achieve what I cannot. I will go to your granny later on. Go along.'

Horace sighed noisily, was tempted to slam the door, thought better of it and scuffled towards the kitchen, savage gloom upon his countenance, cheated of the sympathy he wanted.

Catherine Nelson felt demented with anxiety. Caught by all the necessities of the day here (particularly on Sunday when Mary must be allowed home), tethered by this wanton child, pestered by Horace (whose self-conceit about his ship was prodigious), she could do nothing to comfort her mother if she were worse. Suppose she were to die while she herself was drowned in cares struggling to keep going! She needed her husband to find the truth of the matter. She could not reach the bell-pull. She sank back after trying. Her head spun. She put the spoon up, gathered the struggling Kitty to her bosom, lay back, closed her eyes, waited. The baby infected by the silence and warmth fell instantly to sleep.

Thus Sukey found them: her mother's cheeks pale.

'Oh, Sukey love. I felt so ill. But I'm better now. She would not feed. Is she asleep?'

'Yes Mamma. Leave her. Let her sleep. I will feed her later,' said Sukey wisely. 'Give her to me, I'll put her in the cradle. Rest you here, now.'

'Thank you Sukey. What should I do without you, my grown daughter. Poor Horace, I was so cross with him.'

'He will survive it, Mamma.'

Her mother smiled, hearing Papa's rare asperity in her daughter's voice. She slept.

It was strange to be thinking about it at last, as if it were next door. Death. All the things she had been told since she was young about light and glory and angels and the huge awesome Presence of God (which had grown the less real as she aged, not the more): all these things seemed tenuous against the bones and the skulls the masons chiselled upon the gravestones. What death seemed to offer now, Ann Suckling thought, as the grey afternoon darkened outside the window, was peace, was rest, was freedom from this pain and struggle, possibly even a blessed unconsciousness like deep sleep. She thought with an odd little shock of her fiery husband, dead so long ago. Was she to face him, would she know him, would they find each other? She knew her duty, she must be buried beside him at Barsham. Even though to lie in the parish where the Nelsons were seemed warmer. She wished her sons would come quickly, after Christmas perhaps. Catherine must have what little she possessed and her daughters after her, except for the parcel of land at Beccles which her son William had best look after. There were one or two little treasures she should devise to the children: would not Maurice like her watch? He had none. Little Nan should have the old purse whose contents would be worth something, it might start her savings, she was a rare little hoarder. Her thoughts rambled on happily, free of her weakening body.

When Mr Raven came upon Tuesday the twenty-second of December the task was soon done, for she had thought it all out and it was a simple document. Sarah Bowes witnessed it and Mr Nicholas Raven himself and John Smithson his clerk.

'There Mamma, you will now cease to fret and grow daily stronger,' her daughter said gaily that day. 'You can forget all about it and get better, if you please.'

❦

'Wake up, wake up! Christmas, it's Christmas! Happy Christmas,' Horace yelled, tossing his pillow into William's fat face, leaping out of bed, wishing to be the first to greet the season. 'Happy Christmas Edmund, Suckling,' he said, rumpling the little boys' heads. 'Happy Christmas Mary!' he bawled up the attic stairs, hearing her faint cry in return. He ran into Maurice's room (where he received only a growl for his pains) and round to the other wing of the house, where he banged upon the girls' door. 'Happy Christmas, Sukey, Nanny, Kitty-Kat!'

'Go away!' said Ann severely and primly.

Sukey groaned, still fast asleep. It was never easy to her to wake up.

Only Kitty greeted him with what he considered suitable fervour, her eyes following him with interest towards his parents' door. Here he knocked more modestly. 'Happy Christmas Mamma, Papa!' he piped.

Edmund Nelson looked at his watch. It was early, but not too early for him to be about. He liked no rush before going to church. 'And the same to you my boy,' he said in a loud whisper, hoping not to wake his wife.

'Is that Horace?' she said drowsily.

'That is Horatio, yes,' he laughed, 'wishing us the compliments of the season.'

'May he come in?'

'Certainly. Come in, Horace!' called his father as he made for the small, cold dressing-room beyond theirs. It faced east, he supposed it was a useful penance.

'Happy Christmas Mamma!' Horace said with excitement.

'And the same to you, my dear child. Why are you so early awake? Is everybody awake? Come, sit on the bed, you have bare feet.'

Horace drew back the curtains and edged himself on to the end of the bed, put his feet beneath the coverlet and smiled at his mother.

'No one except Kitty and she's staring through her cot, Sukey's groaning and Maurice's snoring, and William's grunting. I often wake up early.'

My children, Catherine Nelson thought yawning, smiling at Horatio. (All memory of her anger with him seemed to have fled, he had shown nothing but pleasure and activity over the days before Christmas.) All my children, in their beds, under this small roof! She sighed.

'Go and dress, my lad. Bring Kitty to me, can you hold her? She may like to feed in pretence, though I've naught to give her now.'

Horace let down the side of the wicker cot, picked the baby up with an effort, carried her to his mother.

'There!' He envied Kitty his mother's breast.

'Goodbye Mamma! Happy Christmas!' he said again, flinging his arms in the air and twirling about as he danced for the door in his night-shirt.

'Happy Christmas,' she echoed, loving his gaiety.

Oranges and apples (somewhat wizened), late pears saved for Christmas, nuts, and sugar plums in boxes, pink mice with string tails, scented comfits in the shape of letters for Ann to make words with and a new doll, and toys for the small boys, books for Horace and William, his first high boots for Maurice, a gown for Sukey. Church, with the hymns they loved, William bellowing so loudly that Sukey blushed and nudged him: holly and ivy and bay hung up, rosemary on the table, a garland swinging above it made with Sukey's needle and neat fingers, the great roast of beef, the plum puddings, all Ann's labour vindicated: Mamma in high spirits, her cheeks flushed, hurrying from one thing to the next, with Mary in attendance: Papa proposing toasts with the mulled ale, Maurice drinking overmuch and giggling: Horatio and William making everyone laugh with a dramatisation of the usher and Mr Simonds at Norwich School, and the calling of the day-bill: games for the little ones, ring-a-ring o' roses, hunt mamma's thimble (Horatio finding it), oranges-and-lemons, head-chopping, leap-frogging, races round the carpet for Edmund and Suckling mounted upon Maurice and William: cribbage in a corner, Papa and Sukey contending with happy shouts, Horatio wishing to be taught. A great log Maurice had saved burning merrily in the hearth.

Mrs Nelson went out at last, to prepare a little supper. If they were like she was, none would want much supper, all had eaten too largely at four o'clock. Mary had gone home to Deepdale, the dishes done. Mamma had bidden Sukey follow her out soon to help. The dining-room was cold and dark, after the parlour; she had forgotten the candle, she must go through to the kitchen and light a taper at the fire. She groped, trying to feel her way round the table, unable to find the opposite door. As faintness overcame her she put out her hands to reach a chair, found none, fell to the floor, the hammock swinging, swinging, higher and higher, surely so high she must fall out. This time the roaring waves of the sea came up to meet it and closed right over her head.

Susannah, coming through the dark room some minutes later, stumbled into her mother's body.

'Mamma! What is it?'

Sukey ran back to the lighted room.

'Papa, pray come, quickly. Mamma is not well. Bring a light!'

The rector and Maurice leapt up, the cards, the board, the table flying before them. He seized a candle and followed Sukey. Mamma lay in a lifeless cold faint upon the floor, her breath coming heavily.

'We must lift her on to the couch. Where's Mary, where's Peter?'

'Gone, Papa. No one's here tonight.'

Horace, who had headed the procession of children from the parlour, saw his father, with Sukey and Maurice to help, lay Mamma upon the couch. Papa rubbed her hands, touched her brow. She showed no sign of consciousness, her breath came loudly as if she had been running. Papa tried to raise her head. Sukey took off Mamma's satin slippers, loosened her clothing everywhere, held her cold feet.

'Sukey, fetch the pillows and blankets from our bed. Horace, help Sukey. William, return to the parlour and look after the children. Mamma needs air, not crowding. Maurice, fetch me a glass of water. Or some wine. Both, perhaps.'

'Either you or I, Maurice,' Edmund Nelson said twenty minutes later, 'must ride for the doctor.'

'I will, Papa. You had rather stay with Mamma.'

'Thank you, my boy. Take the mare. Is it dark? Take a lantern.'

'I'll need no lantern. Dr Suckerman?'

'He's the nearest. Christmas night, too, Pray God he's there. If not, young Kerrich. I trust you will not have to go all the way to Wells for Dr Murray. Be as quick as you can.'

Maurice was gone. Sukey fed the children, put the young ones to bed, sent Horace and William after them, went to see that all was well with the sleeping Kitty, tidied the parlour. How sad, how forlorn the decked room looked now, the half-eaten sweetmeats a mockery! She went back to her father who sat by her mother, his eyes scarcely leaving her face.

'Should I not undress her, Papa, make her more comfortable? Oh poor Mamma! Why does she breathe so?'

'We had best wait, Sukey, not disturb her until the doctor comes. You go to bed, try to sleep. I will sit up with Mamma. Good night, little one. It is a sad end to our Christmas.' He felt tears on her cheeks as she stooped to kiss him. 'Take heart, Mamma may be better in the morning.'

Maurice had had the foresight on the way back from fetching the doctor to call in at Peter's cottage: all were still around their hearth sipping their Christmas ale, Peter's mother, Ann, with them. The nurse and midwife of the neighbourhood, Goody Black, came at once, and knowing the ways of women's clothing made 'rector's wife' more comfortable, raised her on her pillows, wiped her brow, moistened her lips, did all that was necessary. Peter came too, re-lit the fire in the room, blew up the kitchen embers, set the kettle nearby for filling the earthenware bottle. The doctor felt Mrs Nelson's pulse, noted that her face was by now hotly fevered, but decided against bleeding her. He said not much, but had shaken his head and told them to disturb her as little as possible. She might rally, he said, and he would come early in the morning.

Ann Black had tried to send Mr Nelson to bed; she would watch over and nurse the dear woman, so many of whose babies she had delivered into this world. Her cheeks in the firelight had glistened with tears. But he was not to be banished. Mrs Black, knowing Mary away home, took herself off to the attic promising to return each hour: which she had most faithfully done.

Edmund Nelson sat now with little hope in his heart at the lowest, coldest hour of the night. There had been some time ago a passage of great restlessness, when his wife's eager right hand, releasing itself from the blanket, had seemed to him to try to perform all manner of tasks, to fold and fetch, to smooth and knead, to stir, to sew. It was like a great miming of the life of a busy woman. He, longing for her to be at peace, to rest, had tried to hold the anxious hand, had spoken her name and words of love, not knowing whether she could hear him or no. (Dr Suckerman had addressed words to her with no response, not even the shake of the head he had asked for, and had therefore thought her to be deeply unconscious.) A slight quiver upon her face had caused her husband to hope that she might know his voice, and at last the turmoil had ceased, her breath had become quieter, her hand still and cold as he put it beneath the coverlet.

He slept not at all, sleep was far from him. He watched her face. Over her face now there passed as if in slow procession the countenances of her own family. First he saw her brother Maurice, his very lineaments: then the less well-known features of William, her younger brother. Then, strangest of all, her mother's face took shape there and lingered longest. He remembered with a shock that Mrs Suckling lay herself near to death, that he and his wife had talked of it, prepared themselves, thinking it very possible her time had come. Did she think of them all in the deep places where she now was? The waters are gone over her head he said, not knowing as he quoted the psalmist that he echoed her very sensations. Was it her love, her thought, that called up her kinsfolk like phantasms, to borrow her own face, to rest there like ethereal spirits, before flitting away? Or was it merely that the family all bore a certain likeness?

He did not know and it mattered little, but that it filled him with foreboding. He found himself shivering uncontrollably, rose up and put more upon the fire. He took some of the wine that he had longed to give her (holding her shoulders against his breast when she should open her eyes) and found it cold comfort. Her breath, which had at first frightened them so with its heaviness and disturbance, had now become so light and shallow he could scarce hear it. Now at this minute it seemed to have stopped entirely. Then it would renew itself. So it went, for the hours before dawn. Ann found her feet cold, ever colder; her face despite the cool cloth she applied ever hotter. The rector heard her sob quietly as she crept out.

Before Ann came again, and when the day was running its pale fingers into the sky, Edmund Nelson thought that his wife was dead. He knelt by the couch, his head against her body, consumed by such grief and longing as he had never known.

CHAPTER SEVENTEEN

'...brings all my Mother into my heart...'

Horace awoke early as usual and blinked at the still dark window pane. It was a moment before he remembered the cause of his unease. Mamma had fainted, was ill, the doctor was sent for, they had heard no more but been sent to bed, Christmas Day ending in confusion and misery. He slipped out of bed and made straight for his parents' room, creeping across the girls' chamber in order not to waken Kitty. He did not knock at his parents' door, but listened. No sound came from within. He lifted the latch carefully, pushed open the door, peered in, saw the bed empty, as he and Sukey had left it, the pillows robbed, the blankets pulled off. So she had been kept downstairs. Where was Papa? He came quickly away thinking of the room yesterday, he sitting upon Mamma's feet. He longed with all his heart that it were yesterday again, Christmas. He came to the top of the front stairs and began to descend into the hall.

From the dining-room came Papa with a candle in his hand which lit up his pale dazed face, his crumpled stock, his untidy hair.

I have had my brief space for grief, Edmund Nelson thought bleakly, I must indulge it no longer, I must now support and encourage all my children. In that half hour before Ann had appeared again and confirmed his fears, he had lived a thousand ages, crossed waterless deserts, become a different person. Death had taken his beloved (but to his children he must learn to say God had taken her) and no grief, no rage, no remorse, no longing, nothing in this world would bring her back.

He tried to smile at Horatio, coming down the stairs. Horace looked at his father's tired swollen eyes with fear, with a choking fear mounting in his throat. Papa was not undressed, had not been to bed. The rector put the candle on a shelf, held out his arms, waited for his son to reach him, grasped his shoulders. The boy's eyes never left him, he saw his cheeks go pale, his mouth drop open as he whispered, 'Papa?'

'Mamma is gone, Horace, she is dead.'

Horatio frowned with lips apart, his face stupid with shock. Then a huge shudder took him, he buried his head in his father's chest and sobbed. His father let him sob, his own tears falling on the child's head for a minute or two.

'Listen, my brave Horatio, this will not do. We are the men of the family, tears are all very well for the girls. Will you dry your eyes and come with me and we will tell the others? I cannot keep it from them, they must know at once.'

Horace took a shuddering breath.

'Yes Papa. Where is Mamma, may I see her?'

'Not yet. Wait until the doctor has been and Mrs Black has finished, then you shall. Come along. Go and waken Maurice and William and Edmund and Suckling and tell them to come at once to the girls' chamber for I wish to speak to them. Will you do that?'

'Yes Papa.'

'Let them not linger, waste no time.' The rector felt they must breast their grief quickly, and he his in the having to tell them. He went into the girls' room, looked across at the door behind which Catherine should be, just bracing herself for another day, took firm grip on his thoughts and roused the still sleeping girls. Sukey woke quickly today, aware of anxiety, and sat straight up in bed looking at her father. He lifted the curtain on the east side: no light as yet. The forlorn procession of boys in their night-shirts trooped in, from Maurice halfway to fifteen, to little Suckling barely four years old. All knew (but Suckling) what Papa was going to tell them, Horace's face had betrayed it.

'My dear children, your mother is dead, God has taken her into peace and rest. She never recovered her senses, she was restless at first, but then she went to sleep quietly and did not wake.'

Sukey sobbed, Ann rocked herself in a silent terror of grief, Maurice and Horatio held to each other in blank silence, William cried noisily with the two small boys. Little Kitty, delighted but puzzled to see everybody in her room and unconscious of the reason, laughed with merriment as she stamped up and down in her cot. Meeting no response, her laughter faded. Her father picked her up and held her in his arms, his anguish assaulting him anew.

'Yes, let your tears flow, it does not do to hold them in. But remember that Mamma is at rest, however bitter is our loss.' He stopped, thinking he sounded as if he were in the pulpit. 'Dear Sukey, when you are better, get dressed, help the children, look after Kitty. It will help you,' he said touching her heaving shoulders. 'Maurice, William, we are men as I have said to Horatio. We must look after the girls. There's much to see to. Good Mrs Black is here to help us, and Mary will soon be back. But we must all busy ourselves. And I must wash,' he muttered quietly, giving Kitty to Susannah and going into the bedroom, past the empty bed with his eyes averted into the chill dressing room. The water in the pitcher was cold, cold, against his aching eyes.

'I have sorry news, ma'am,' Edmund Nelson said walking quietly over to Mrs Suckling's bed. He had been to Sarah first, whose face had expressed total disbelief at his news, who could only sit down heavily upon a stool to recover herself. Mrs Suckling looked at him narrowly as he approached, sat down, took her hand.

'Catherine,' she gasped her other hand going to her throat.

'She is dead, Mamma.' He had never called her this before. He did not trouble to correct the slip, and she noted it with comfort. 'She was took ill about eight o'clock or more last night, Sukey found her in a faint, she had gone to prepare a little supper. We lifted her to the dining-room couch. Maurice fetched the doctor. She never regained her senses, was very restless. I was with her all night. Ann Black kindly came. She died a little before light, peacefully.'

The old lady seemed, like Sarah, stunned and unable to speak. She clutched his hand for minutes. 'Forgive me,' she whispered at length 'I could not take it in, I was dumb. My poor son Edmund, all the children. Oh, I am thankful she had not time to think of it. It was merciful for her, you know.'

'I do know that. Later I shall be grateful for it would have been an agony to her.'

'So. It is exactly what happened to her father, you remember?'

'Yes, I wanted to ask you the details of his death. She had often referred to it, but not lately.'

The details to Mrs Suckling seemed as clear as yesterday, indeed they had become clearer of late.

'Why, he was struck thus, in the pulpit.' She had a sudden clearly-incised view of his very features, in a face quite young but choleric; gone in a second. 'He lingered longer, almost twenty-four hours, but not sensible.'

'Did he have great restlessness?'

'At the first. Then he lapsed deeper and died quietly.'

'It sounds very like. I longed to be able to talk to her.'

'Ay, I remember that, it is a torment. What will you do my son, have you enough help? Here am I, laid low...'

'We shall manage, ma'am. Poor Mary is back and sobbing her heart out over her work. Goody Black stays for a day or two, coming from Peter's, to help. I think Mrs Jacombe perhaps may oblige me sometimes through the week. Sukey is most capable, ma'am, you know.'

'She is, dear child. Poor children, poor children! How do they take it? I long to see them, to see my Catherine's children!'

'You shall, they shall come often, but not all together. I shall send Sukey soon, in her dear mother's place.'

'Thank you. And Ann. As to my sons, I have heard from both for Christmas, they speak of a visit…'

'I have written, I meant to tell you. I have sent Maurice early to Burnham to catch the Saturday post for Aylsham and London. They may wish to come for their sister's funeral.'

'Yes. When will it be?'

'I have said Wednesday. This gives them just time, should they wish.'

'Yes. Thank you. Then I shall not write myself.'

'Pray do not, ma'am. How are you today?'

'I was going to say to Catherine that I thought I was a little better.' Upon this, a few tears flowed at last. Edmund Nelson sighed, smoothing her hand.

'At every turn the loss leaps out at us,' he said.

It leapt out at them all, at different corners according to their natures. Susannah, controlling her grief because she had now much to do and because of the smaller children, would feel her tears start again at the sight of the cake, the pudding, the baby's pottage that Mamma's very hands had made so few hours ago. Dreamy Maurice would be planning to ask his mother some question before he would remember she could not now, or ever, be asked again. William displayed the most grief, Ann the least, but their father was not sure that this accorded with their true feelings. The small boys, bewildered because they had been expecting their grandmother to die, and living more completely in the present, were swept along by kindly time ever further from the shock, and found other people to comfort them. Kitty showed distress, bewilderment and anger after two days without her mother: but she was so used to Sukey or Mary nursing her and to her father's arms, that the loss was bridged.

It was Horace, Edmund Nelson thought, who suffered most after himself. Horace grew quiet, pale and ailing. He ate little, his ready tongue was silenced, his spirits lowered. From Horace a living part of himself had been cut, his father thought, like a limb from a young green tree. He bled and wilted. Horace could never for one moment forget that his mother was dead, either sleeping or waking, any more than a man could forget his leg were off. His father tried to watch over him with especial care as his wife would have wished, he knew. But it was hard to rally a child from his grief when that grief consumed him too.

Mamma came up the lane from Granny's house towards the parsonage, her shawl blowing a little in the blue windy day, her shallow basket empty over her arm. Horace saw her from an upstairs window, she was smiling, she waved, she said his name. He heard her call his name and hurried down and out to meet her. Knowing, as his feet touched the grass within his dream, that he would not find her, she would be gone, she would not be in the road, she would have disappeared. His happy dream could not deceive him for long, the knowledge of her death had bitten too deeply into him. He awoke with wet cheeks into the darkness of the night. William breathed evenly beside him. Mamma was dead, dead.

Edmund Nelson's letter reached Captain Suckling in Park Street in the middle of Monday afternoon. He had not been out of London for the Christmas season but had dined quietly with his wife's mother in Whitehall. Since the death of his wife eighteen months ago, the death of all his personal hopes, he had become even quieter in his habits, his inability to talk (which his sister Catherine and his mother had often laughed about) even more pronounced. Now, even so silent a man leapt up with an exclamation of disbelief and horror, and perforce confided the contents of this distressing letter to his housekeeper. The lady shed sufficient tears for them both at the plight of his motherless nephews and nieces.

Captain Suckling drove at once to New North Street off Red Lion Square in case his brother William was at the Customs Office despite the season. William was in his office and being early from home had not received his letter. He was surprised to see his brother. Maurice waved the letter, with unusual demonstration.

'You have not heard from Edmund Nelson?'

'No. What is it? My mother gone, before we could get there?'

'It is *Mrs Nelson*, Catherine who is dead! Our sister *Catherine*,' the sea captain repeated, still unwilling to believe the news.

'Catherine!' William Suckling said, snatching the letter. 'But it is my mother who was ill!' He read Edmund Nelson's brief account of his sister's death. 'I cannot believe it. All those children of course. She has too much to do.'

'No doubt Ma'am's illness has added to it.'

'No doubt. This will be the end of Ma'am. The funeral is tomorrow—no, Wednesday. One of us should go. Are you free to go, Maurice?...If I come tomorrow and we are then to sit there waiting for poor Ma'am to die also, who may I suppose recover, I shall be too long from my work. What say you?'

'I will go. You come on when we planned in the new year, and let us hope my mother lasts as long.'

'Let us hope so, indeed. It is not that I do not wish to see her. I am her executor I suppose too. I always told her I would be. Will you promise to send at once if you think she is failing?'

His brother promised.

'Poor Edmund Nelson. We must show proper feeling,' he said. 'Indeed I wish to show it, to follow poor Catherine to the grave. I cannot realise the loss…' he went on haltingly with unusual emotion, his cheeks warm.

'Yes, you and she were always devoted. It is proper for you to go. I wish I were not tied…'

'And all those children!' Captain Suckling echoed his brother, his happy visits of four years ago glowing like sunshine in his mind. 'Those poor children. Perhaps I can encourage their father, offer to help with one boy.'

'Maybe so, you have no commitments,' his brother agreed with scant sensitivity. 'What will you do, take the flier to Norwich or go to Lynn?'

'Lynn is the nearer. I had best go now, brother, and arrange it. I shall see you on Friday? Or Saturday?'

'Saturday, as we had planned, tell Ma'am I come.'

'Very well.' They grasped hands and the elder hurriedly left.

Edmund Nelson had had to write so many letters, arrange so many things. He knew that it was merciful, that to have his mind so occupied and pestered was better than to have great deserts of sorrow and despair to wander in unhindered. Yet he caught himself resenting the ceaseless activity, the preoccupations which were separating him from his wife (now lying in the church) from that private place of love and grief where he wished to retreat in an effort to be near her. He must write to Hilborough, to Congham, to Hillington; he must write to Dr Hamond, to Wolterton and to Warham. Messages reached him from his fellow clerks and neighbouring gentry, from the farmers, the churchwardens, all the friends in the parishes. Such kindness warmed his desolation even while it quickened afresh his wound.

All the neighbourhood mourned for Mrs Nelson, rapt so suddenly away, borne to her grave at the end of the dying year. For, despite her many family duties, she had always tried to show warmth and love, to visit the sick, the poor, and folk in distress: and those who came not to the funeral from genuine affection and sorrow came from curiosity disguised as such.

The sea captain walked with his godson, Uncle Robert Rolfe from Hilborough brought William and Horatio, grasping the younger firmly by the hand (which Horace, though he had rather go with his Uncle Maurice, submitted to with a sense of comfort), Dr Hamond and the Nelson clergy cousins followed with Great Uncle John Fowle and the Berney cousins after. The little church was full: Canon Poyntz and Sir Mordaunt Martin, Sir John Turner and Squire Wilkinson and Mr Lee Warner from Walsingham, brisk Mr Allott, Mr Crowe from the hall, Mr Styleman from Overy, and many people from the villages. The rector was glad of the ceremony, the well-known words, the often-performed ritual; it enabled him to see his wife's coffin lowered before the altar with calmness. He lingered when they had all gone, speaking private words to her. He knew that it would be many years before he ceased to speak to her. Now he was pledging her his care of her children. Then he found the register and entered that day's merciless history: Catherine, wife of Edmund Nelson, late Catherine Suckling, Spinster *(never another's, he thought, always and from the beginning, and ever mine)*, was b^d Dec 30th, 1767. By whom the ceremony was performed. He signed it E. Nelson rector as he signed so many other ordinary, unimportant things.

Then he mounted the mare and hurried after the family mourners. Though his sister Alice was there and had undertaken everything with Sukey and Mary, he must nevertheless hurry, hurry away, leave his heart in the cold church. Everything is for you, Catherine, he thought, the irony rising like a hard lump in his throat, yet everything conspires to separate me from you.

Uncle Maurice's coming had roused Horatio a little. It was not only that he was like his sister in face and voice, his presence reminded Horace of happy summer days with Mamma here and tales of ships and battles. Captain Maurice himself, stricken again so soon by an untimely death, did all he could in his shy and clumsy way to comfort the children. He took them for walks, told them tales, played games with them, carried them to Wells, bought them sweetmeats. Horatio's pathetic face distressed (and secretly irritated) him, but the child haunted him, showing a longing to please him, to be well thought of, which Captain Suckling supposed to be better than ever brooding upon his loss. The rector had found his brother-in-law's company both a comfort and a constraint, When he had first seen his mother, he had begged to be allowed to stay longer if it were no inconvenience, for he confessed to Mr Nelson that in his opinion she would not live long. He had found her strangely detached.

'She is casting her moorings, soon it will be up anchor and away,' he said.

Edmund Nelson enjoyed the metaphor.

'And the pilot boat that brought her here is away before her,' he said quietly.

'Ay, the same thought came to me.'

Little Susannah, her twelve and a half years making her seem deceptively adult, had learned hardly, the same lesson. After her mother's death she had hurried to her grandmother hoping to find there the open arms, the warm heart, the comfort she so much needed and which she had always had from Mamma. Her granny had touched her head gently as she sobbed, spoken kind words, listened as she poured out her grief. But the fire was out. Mrs Suckling could not recapture the desolation of youth, she could not properly comfort. She was already on her way after Mamma. Sukey went bravely every day taking one of the others with her, and learnt to hide her grief, ask nothing for herself, cosset the dying old lady for her mother's sake.

Uncle William arrived, whom none of the children knew very well: burly and talkative, sympathetic but somehow (the rector always felt) devious. Sukey remembered him at Uncle Maurice's wedding: but Burnham had not seen him since little Mun's christening, to whom he had stood godfather in 1762, and that was five years ago.

'Come now, don't you remember me, Horatio?' said Uncle William, prodding the child with a plump hand adorned with a signet ring.

'Yes sir, a little sir,' Horace admitted untruthfully but with a tact he learned early and which always surprised and amused his father. Uncle William stayed in Mrs Suckling's house, was a burden and a pleasure to Sarah, teased her, petted her and altogether was better she thought than no company, with mistress a-dying.

It was the strange chance of fortune, the sudden change of position between her daughter and herself, which had dazed Mrs Suckling, causing her to seem to the family so detached already. Why, she need no longer lament to leave Catherine (her chief lament, for she and her daughter were close). Catherine had gone, there was nothing to stay for. Much as she loved the children, especially the girls and Maurice, she could do no more for them were she to live. She had not the strength to take over her daughter's tasks, all she could be was a burden herself, weak and ailing. She had made her modest will, and now she had seen her sons: Maurice, silent, embarrassed, not knowing what to say to his dying mother. She smiled a little, thinking of it. She had had to set him at ease, tell him the situation. I shall not recover, Maurice, she had said, let us admit the fact.

Once more she had expressed her grief at his wife's death, asked him would he not look about him, would he not consider another marriage? He had shaken his head at once, dismissing the idea. Then William: almost teasing, never at a loss for words, trying to rally her, talking of visits to Kentish Town, forsooth, in the spring. She had long since ceased to voice any opinion of William's oddities of life, of his marrying no wife, but consorting with his housekeeper: it was not her affair. She had always loved William sufficiently to accept him as he was and madam as his wife, and her offspring as her grandchildren. William was successful, settled. Maurice, personally sad, was well thought of in his profession, would achieve more yet. She had no reason to worry about either, they did not need her. She was ready to go, and Catherine was gone: but perhaps Catherine was near, she seemed much nearer than her long-dead husband. Faith taught that she might find her, her life's true companion. But age had dimmed all the certainties of faith; she knew nothing, and had not spoken of it to Edmund Nelson. Sometimes in her fitful dreams she found herself walking with Dorothy and Susan and Galfridus in the garden and countryside of her childhood at Houghton; her mind in old age having eclipsed the memory of the present Houghton, the wide lawns, the enormous, ornamented parapets, the stone steps, marble halls and saloons of Sir Robert Walpole's hall. Waking, she reflected that Captain Galfridus Walpole's sword had found its way to her son Maurice. Maurice would have no son. Which of Catherine's children should wield it next? Her thoughts made images for her but her lips could no longer express them to the Nelson children who came or to their father.

In the first week of the new year, the weather turned sharply, bitterly cold. Frost bound all. Mrs Suckling died upon the eve of Twelfth Night January the fifth, little Suckling's fourth birthday, and two weeks exactly after she had signed her will. Mr Raven, the attorney, read out the will in Mrs Suckling's little parlour.

'*I desire to be Buried in as plain a manner as is consistent with Decency and without pall Bearers,*' said Mrs Suckling's frail, prim voice to her sons, to her son-in-law, to Maurice and Sukey who were bidden to be present. Her debts and expenses were to be discharged at once out of the money she should leave and if necessary out of the three hundred pounds now in the hands of her son, William Suckling. Catherine was to have the interest from the rest of this money, and after her decease it was to be equally divided between her grand-daughters Susannah, Ann and Catherine Nelson.

Also I give and devise unto my Grandson Maurice Nelson my pinchbeck watch. Also I give and devise unto my Grand Daughter Susannah Nelson my six Gilt Tea Spoons. Also I give and devise to my Grand Daughter Ann Nelson my Old purse containing some Gold Medals. Also I give and devise unto my Son William Suckling a parcel of Freehold land containing about five Acres lying and being in or near Beccles in the County of Suffolk and to his heirs for ever. Also my household furniture plate China and Wearing Apparel I give and devise unto my aforesaid Daughter Catherine Nelson. Also the Rest Residue and Remainder of my Real and personal Estate and Effects I give and Devise unto my three children that is to say Maurice Suckling William Suckling and Catherine Nelson Share and Share alike...

Sukey could hear her very voice. Maurice was glad about the watch. He loved his grandmother. He would go to Mr Cranefield at Burnham, Papa might give him the money for a chain. The rector wondered distractedly how they should make room for Mrs Suckling's furniture in the parsonage, what they should do with the clothes: Sarah might like them, she deserved something. Ann, when given the purse, clutched it silently to her small bosom, noticing again the strange scenty, stewed blackberry smell of old chamois. It would always call up her grandmamma. She started to save from that day on and never stopped.

Later that week, a conveyance having been hired, a solemn little cortège set out over the hard frosty road from the house near the shooting lodge: Mrs Suckling's coffin going sedately to her long home, followed by the chaise containing Uncle Maurice, Uncle William, in their black hats and black crepe bands, Papa in his black cloak going to perform the ceremony, and Maurice wearing his watch going to represent the Nelson grandchildren. As they passed slowly by the parsonage, William and Horatio, Sukey and Ann, Edmund and the luckless Suckling, Mary with the struggling Kitty, Peter Black and Ann his mother, raised their arms in decent quiet salute. It was strange to young Maurice to be for the first time with the adults leaving the others behind. The rector worried about Horatio in this cold spell. William Suckling wondered whether on the high road they could leave the hearse to come at its own speed and make better time themselves, otherwise they should all freeze. After the funeral he and his brother had planned to make visits to Woodton (to which, when all was said, Maurice was heir: he had no need of five acres in Beccles) and to the Henleys in Norwich. And at the same time they had better put a notice of both deaths into the *Mercury* office, he would speak to the rector of it when he decently could.

'What shall we *do*, Mary?' whined William Nelson when the wheels had ceased to be heard in the distance of the Creake road. The departure of the chaise had made him feel more keenly the emptiness of the house without Mamma.

'You go along o'Peter, eh Peter? Help him out bor, 'stead o' Maurice,' Mary said. 'The rest of you come with me and Mrs Jacombe into the warm kitchen. There's a plenty to *do*. Come now, Horace, coughing like that. Come in do. Poor motherless babes,' she added for good measure under her breath, her stature increasing daily with her responsibility.

Chapter Eighteen

'...removed to North Walsham'

There was most certainly a plenitude of things to do. They crowded in upon Edmund Nelson so soon as he was back and still stunned with his grief he felt overwhelmed. William Suckling would hasten to have his mother's will proved at Canterbury, settle any debts and release to his brother-in-law the legacies: Edmund Nelson thought he might usefully devote them to the boys' and girls' education. Sukey was to be thirteen this year: if she was to go away to school she must go soon. Even more pressing, there was Maurice to settle in life. Mr John Fowle and Mr William Suckling had kindly said that they would see what might be found for Maurice as a clerk under one or other of them in the Customs or the Excise. (Both the uncle and the nephew worked here, and the rector had always supposed they might owe their positions to their Walpole connections, for Sir Edward Walpole, he had heard Mrs Suckling say, had a right by patent in the Customs department for his life-time.) Meanwhile, Maurice must be weaned from his country life on the glebe, perhaps put with one of the attorneys for a month or two. And what about the two younger boys? Even his dear Catherine though amused at Horace's lively accounts of the distracted usher and the absentminded Mr Simonds, had expressed some doubts on that last happy day of her life which he could only remember with anguish. He had the feeling that the boys had not learned very much. Lord Walpole, calling to commiserate about the deaths of his cousins, had chanced to remind the rector again about the Paston school at North Walsham, of which his neighbour Mr Thomas Durrant of Scottow was a governor.

Everybody was exceedingly kind, all tried to help him. Why then did these things, which would have seemed interesting, pleasant and fruitful with his wife to share them, crowd upon him so inimically like a hostile army? A death, he reflected, two deaths in this case, started a landslide. And each new decision he took alone seemed to remove him further from her. Even the ordering of the stone seemed to freeze her into immobility. He longed for the warmth of her heart and her loved body.

It struck him that he should find out the extent of William's and Horace's ignorance.

'Boys,' he called, 'my two Norwich schoolboys! Come you in here, and give your papa the benefit of your new knowledge upon the Latin for your dear mamma's memorial.'

William looked nervously at Horatio. Horatio smiled palely, in his pale thin face. It was no use to dissemble, Papa would discover soon enough.

'We wish to say that the slab is for the purpose of preserving the memory of Catherine Nelson, daughter of Maurice Suckling D D, granddaughter of Charles Turner, baronet, and Mary, his first wife, daughter of Robert Walpole, knight of Houghton,' Papa was jotting down the English words as he spoke, 'wife of Edmund Nelson, rector of this church. Eleven children were born to her, eight (is it eight, you are?) survived her...' That is enough, for a start. William, the word for "purpose", "cause"—there, I have given it to you, do you not know it? Horatio? No? "Causa" is the word, what case must it be in? "For the purpose of?" The dative, boys, the dative. Now I shall write the first line to start you off:

Conservandae memoriae causa

Next comes your mother's name. We wish to say the memory "of Catherine Nelson". The case, William, for your mother's Christian name? Horatio? It is the first declension, the feminine, the easiest, like "mensa", why surely you learned some declensions by heart in your six weeks?'

William seized at a sliding memory.

'If it's of, belonging to, it's...it is...I cannot remember what it is *called*, Papa!' he wailed.

'The genitive?'

'Yes! The genitive.'

'Then what ending must I write to your mother's name?'

William shook his head.

Their father struggled on a few moments. No gleam of light illuminated his sons' faces, they were innocent of cases, conjugations, meanings and agreements, they were totally at sea. Tears streamed down Horatio's cheeks, William wore the glum frown of complete incomprehension.

Papa drew Horace to his side and mopped his cheeks. His tears were not for his Latin.

'Tell me, William,' he said sighing. 'How does this come about, how did you spend your lesson time?'

'Papa, no one taught us, no one explained, the other boys knew it, we came late, we never understood what we were about, Horace Hamond said he would teach us but he never did...'

'And the usher, the master, never saw your plight, never taught you what you had missed?'

'Never Papa,' William was whining now and near to tears himself.

'Then we must put you to a master who will. Take heart, Horatio, William. If you were not taught, it is not your fault. Run away and help Sukey or Mary or Peter.'

William ran gladly, but Horatio lingered with his father who once more attempted to console and establish him.

Traversing the pleasant town of North Walsham, skirting the market square, Edmund and his boys turned east, and not many yards along the road upon their left came upon the new spacious stone building, plain but elegant, which must be the school house. A stretch of inviting grass lay before it, round which curved handsomely a modest driveway to the central door. It was the last week in January and the trees round the school garden were bare, but lamps glowed already from some of the large and regularly disposed windows of the house, and quickly moving figures of boys like shadows crossed and recrossed the illuminated panes. William peered with gloomy interest into the schoolroom. Two boys stared out at him, wondering who arrived.

'New boys,' said one as the Nelsons alighted, 'a thin one and a fat one.'

'Bless me,' said the older under his breath, a new boy himself and come from Norwich, Thomas Taylor by name, 'if it isn't those Nelson brothers again, they haunt me.'

The door was flung open and the rector led his boys into a handsome plain parlour, covered from floor to ceiling on three walls with many leather-bound books. A bright fire danced in the grate on their right, and before it stood a gentleman rubbing his hands: tall, thin, dark, with a sinuous nose and one eye which (Horace remarked at once) did not properly look at you.

Mr Jones advanced to welcome them giving the parson his cold hand.

'Well, Mr Nelson sir, so you bring me your two good boys in order that they may be educated in the learned tongues and in the elegant expression of their own, eh young gentlemen?' (interposed the schoolmaster, showing, as the rector thought, some lack of elegance himself)—'and in geography, navigation, merchant's accounts, writing, and every branch, Mr Nelson sir, of the mathematics. And I beg leave to inform you of the fact sir, that I am this year introducing the French language, Mr Nelson sir: it is to be taught in its purest dialect,' sang Mr Jones, twirling a hand in the air, 'by a native of France. Oh, and sir, I hasten to acquaint you, he is of course a Protestant: have no doubt sir, I expend as much time and care upon the pupils' moral and religious state as upon their lessons, seeing them as well grounded in the principles of their faith as in the Latin grammar...'

'If my boys,' Mr Nelson broke in at last, 'if William and Horatio become as well found in Latin grammar as they are already in Christian principles I shall be well content, Mr Jones. At the moment they know nothing of it but what in the last two weeks I have tried to teach them.'

Mr Jones showed his feelings by stuttering his tongue against his teeth in a frenzy of surprise and concern.

'Ah,' he said knowingly, 'I have other pupils, several young gentlemen, sent on to me from the Norwich school. Indeed one who arrived yesterday, he may know your boys, I will call him in...' he opened the door beyond the fireplace into the schoolroom, 'Thomas Taylor, are you there? Come in here, please. Do you remember these fellow pupils of yours from Norwich?'

Thomas Taylor had every reason to remember them, they none to remember him. His smile was friendly but amused. William was guarded. But Horace smiled affably and returned his greeting. He reminded Horatio of Maurice in being gentle, somewhat diffident, but evidently well-disposed.

'Show them round, Thomas, instruct them where to put their belongings, they will be in the far dormitory with you.' The boys were borne away. 'I must tell you, Mr Nelson, that I teach the Latin language according to the Eton method, the best possible method, you know the school of course...'

The rector admitted with a faint smile that he knew of Eton, that indeed his father had been there.

'Ah quite so, quite so. Here is Mrs Jones now, we would both commiserate with you most sincerely sir, upon the recent sad bereavement you have suffered...'

Mr Nelson acknowledged their sympathy, shaking hands with a lady who had emerged from the room on the other side of the parlour. She was as silent as her husband was loquacious, but her reserve seemed to the rector due to good taste rather than ill-humour. She murmured kindly when he confided Horatio in particular to her care. He took his departure very soon, hoping all would be well for the two boys, that the change of circumstance would carry Horace over his grief, applying his mind to new things. He was paying nigh on fifty pounds a year, eighteen pounds each for board and education, two guineas each for entrance, thirty shillings each for their washing, and they must have pocket money, and there would be extra needed for their travelling. He added it all up again as the chaise bowled through the darkening lanes past Felbrigg, towards the coast road. Of Mr John Price Jones he decided he could make but little, the real man seemed hidden behind a cloud of words and pretensions.

Horace sat in the schoolroom, pressed up against the front of the desk (the desk was too high for him) facing the next interminable stretch of lessons and feeling indigestion. The earliest hour of work, prayers and breakfast was now over, and still the world outside the window panes was only grey. The bread and brawn and warmed ale, wolfed so greedily by William, he often found difficult to stomach: if he ate too much or too fast, it made marbles in his inside. If too little, he was empty. He was still too young to notice and regulate all this. The schoolroom ran the whole depth of the front wing of the house, alongside the parlour where they had first entered; there were windows in the front and the side walls, and a central fireplace in the wall that backed the parlour. The boys were divided into two classes. William and Horatio started off both in the first, the lower class, which occupied the upper half of the room next the front windows. Opposite them in the lower half of the room where the door went through to the parlour, sat the young gentlemen whose knowledge and perseverance had placed them in the second class. The two classes were not so far away but that they could eye each other, exchange grimaces, or enjoy the jokes of the master or the discomfiture of a member of the opposite group. But this communication, if espied by Mr Jones, would enrage that pedant to a fury.

'It is attending to your own lesson you must be,' he would cry, waving his cane, his Welsh tones emerging with his anger. 'Were your minds fixed so, for heaven's sake, you would no more be able to follow what t'other class is about than see through the brick wall behind the school, I am telling ye!' Sometimes Horatio had much ado to understand Mr Jones's Welsh tongue, which would add to his difficulties in mastering the structure of the Latin language; for the reverend Mr Jones (wishing to impress a parent whose father had actually been educated at Eton, that prince of schools where for a brief spell he had been privileged to assist) began at once to instil this into the two Nelsons. Little by little the pattern, the precision, the logic of the tongue revealed itself to them, helped on by arduous hours of learning by rote; and pleasanter times of construing followed, inspired by the Welsh master's romanticism, poetry and eagerness. At last even Horace (halted out of his early lead over William by the shock of his mother's death) began dimly to appreciate the detail of a language so nicely predictable, its scope so variously grand. To William, a painstaking scholar who had not his small brother's far-flung restless imagination but possessed more patience, it was to become a delight.

Far otherwise was it with French, which M Julien Moisson endeavoured to teach. M Moisson was a slight gentleman of uncertain age, with a mincing step, a fluttering hand, a deprecating titter. His irritability would flare up into rapid French oaths uttered chokingly beneath his breath and subside into wounded pouting sulkiness. He now stood, one hand on his hip and his left toe pointing at ninety degrees to his right, his head rolling upon his neck like a puppet's, as he touched up his coiffure and bid Horatio's class good morning, in that utmost purity, elegance, and true pronunciation of his native tongue which Mr Jones had described to Mr Nelson.

'Répétez, répétez s'il vous plaît, mes jeunes gentilhommes,' M Moisson bade them, raising his left hand from his hip and gesturing to them to speak. Some took it otherwise, and rose to their feet. M Moisson's head rolled more and his arms waved.

'Non, non, non, non! Répétez, répondez-vous, mes jeunes hommes, à mes salutations, mes bon jours!'

But the impurity of the few voices which understood enough to reply to him caused him only to sigh. He changed the position of his toes (it was rumoured that he was capable of teaching fencing, a rumour proved true when he took over that instruction from the visiting dancing master). He pursued his lesson with little inspiration and less response, few of these Norfolk lads having any desire to learn French and most considering him and it an object of ridicule. Horace indeed counted it a positive affront, so strongly had his mother instilled hatred of the French into him. Since M Moisson ('old Jemmy' as he soon became) inspired no fear (unlike the fiery Mr Jones) and no respect, Horace made not the slightest attempt to learn his French, despising its delicate pronunciation which was beyond his grasp and deriding what he refused to master.

There were more than thirty pupils in the school, about half of these coming every day, and they were to increase in the next few years to sixty or more. Of boarders there were around twenty, sleeping in the two long rooms at the back of the house where Thomas Taylor had conducted the Nelsons on their first day. Horace could see Thomas

Taylor now, in the second class, flanked by two even older boys who had left Norwich before he and William went there. Thomas Taylor had fulfilled Horatio's first impression of him and been kind and friendly to them. He was the son of a weaver of Norwich, fourteen years old, conscientious rather than fast in his work but gaining Mr Jones's approval by his love of poetry and the classics. He had even, under this encouraging master, begun to learn Greek. Horace had stared at the characters in Thomas's primer in fascination and some horror. On the rare occasions when Mr Jones allowed his pupils into the town, Thomas and the Nelsons would explore together, for he too was new to these parts. Thomas said that his father wanted nothing better than that he should go to Cambridge and be ordained deacon and priest, and he was ready to pay for him. Next to him now sat John Ashmul, a grazier's son from Worstead, a lad of fifteen who had told William that if he went to Cambridge he must go as a sizar and work his keep and his education, unless he were so lucky as to win a scholarship. He was a clever boy, particularly at accounts and mathematics. Eldest of the three seniors and already seventeen was a Walsingham boy, William Booty by name, another good mathematician aiming at a scholarship for the university. These two worked much together and Mr Jones was enquiring for a mathematician who could bring them on further than he could, classicist as he was. Horace had heard them talking about it.

'Nelson! Minor! What have I just been wasting my precious breath to declaim to your worthless ears?' whined Mr Jones.

Horace sat up, flushing scarlet to his unworthy ears.

'A poem, sir, a piece of verse.'

'By whom?'

'Shakespeare, sir.'

'About what, boy?'

'Nature, sir,' hazarded his pupil, who had retained a lasting impression (from Canon Poyntz) that 'nature' would cover most poetry.

'And what were you thinking of meanwhile?' Thus questioned, it never occurred to Horatio not to tell the truth.

'About the three senior boys going to Cambridge sir.'

Taken aback, Mr Jones knew not what to say.

'And may I ask if you intend to go to Cambridge, Horatio? With which seat of learning this school has many ancient connections?'

'No sir. But my brother William does, sir.'

'Why do not you?'

'I shall not be scholar enough, sir.'

'That depends upon you. Attend to your lessons now and do not dream about the future.'

Letters came, from Papa and Maurice and Sukey, all eager to hearten the two small boys exiled from home.

'We have all been about emptying our granny's house,' wrote Maurice to Horatio, causing that exile to long to be there, 'carrying things forth and struggling up the road; the wind took some curtains and landed them in the mire, whereby I got a great lecture from Madam Sukey. Sarah Bowes is fixed and goes from here very soon. I am to go to London sometime into an office. Papa says the more I pen to you the better for my hand is out of use, so I am to copy you verses from the paper. The election is all the noise, Papa says. At Downham the "election issue" seems to be the moving of the butter market to Swaffham. This rhyme goes to the tune of the Dust Cart, you may yell it running round your play yard.

> Butter butter butter butter
> Butter is our staple trade
> If they take away our butter
> Downham Market soon must fade.

'Dr Poyntz has passed on to Papa the *Lynn Magazine*, with all the papers folk have wrote about *The Contest*. Papa says the man behind it is an arrant, ranting, rude young man, calls himself Dick Merryfellow, is in truth Dr Gardiner of Massingham's son and puts it about he's a natural son of the late Earl of Orford (if you do not understand what this means, ask William!) There is a long poem about a militiaman called Sir Dilberry Diddle (Doctor Poyntz says, perhaps Lord Townshend).

> He dreamt, Fame reports that he cut all the throats
> Of the French, as they landed in flat bottom'd Boats:
> In his sleep if such dreadful Destruction he makes,
> What HAVOCK – ye Gods! Shall we have when he wakes.

'There has been a great battle between the excise men and the smugglers at Yarmouth. The smugglers were aided by a gang of mounted men on shore, forty or fifty horse and footmen. So Charles Boyles' Papa must prepare to defend himself. I met Charles in Wells, he sends his love. As so do I and all of us at Burnham...'

Horace was not much affected by elections, but pleased with the two rhymes. As to natural sons, he had long known all about it, what did Maurice think? He had asked Mamma. As Horace thought now of

Mamma, he tried to remember what Thomas Taylor had once said, finding him weeping at bedtime.

'But you are wrong to weep, you are wrong! She is happy, you do not know how blessed she is! We cannot imagine how happy heaven is!'

'How can she be happy, to leave all of us?' Horace asked sobbing.

'You do not know how near she may be, watching over you! But happy she must be, we are promised so! There's no need to weep for *her*. So it follows you weep for yourself.'

'I do. I want her, I miss her!' Horace said in a burst of grief.

'I think she had rather you were not so unhappy,' said this wise boy. Horace was struck by the thought and clung to it.

'That reprehensible Charles Langley,' Sukey had to ask her papa how to spell the word, 'has been taken to a house of correction for six weeks. Widow Bee lay-in and had her child. When he is discharged they will make him marry her. We miss dearest Mamma and our granny all the time. Farmer Emerson has had his sorrel hobby and his pretty black colt with the white star stolen, is it not shocking that we cannot leave our animals out in safety. Maybe in the summer, I go to school! Pray look after Horatio, see that he eats enough and does not get chilled, William. I am sure Mamma would say this…'

And Papa wrote too.

I see Maurice tells you of the noisy nonsense of the Elections which disturbs us not much. But you should know what in a certain sense affects you for they are your distant connections, the two members for Lynn are re-elected against the new candidates put up (for whom 'Dick Merryfellow' made all this shouting), your Mamma's cousin Sir John Turner; and Mr Thomas Walpole who is a brother to Horatio's godpapa, and who takes the place of his cousin Mr Horace Walpole, lately retired. I think you are to have a short vacation at Easter, we all look to have you both home…'

CHAPTER NINETEEN

Poor Maurice

Mr Nelson was at great pains to have his boys home whenever they were allowed to come. He wished to keep an eye upon Horace often, as he knew his wife would have done (her great love for the boy, his grief at her death, impressed upon him the especial bond between them). Also, time and times moved fast: soon the close-knit family would begin to tease apart, its centre already gone. He must keep them close while he might, let the family enfold Horatio who missed his mother so bitterly.

And so it did: Maurice fetching them from Wells in the wagon, Sukey mothering them, Mary boiling them pace eggs with onion skins. Doctor Poyntz called in with books for them, Mr and Mrs Crowe came also and invited them down to the hall. The dread in Horatio's heart of the empty place he must find was healed with kindness, banished gradually with plentiful doings and gossip and overheard talk. Only imagine, said the canon to Papa, that man John Wilkes elected freely with no contenders by the people of Middlesex at Brentford! Could an outlaw, a scribbler found guilty of blasphemy and libel sit in the British House of Parliament?

The lively Mr Allott also greeted Horace with glee. He and Squire Wilkinson had both, this spring, made their answers to the bill in Chancery filed by the college. Mr Allott said not a word in his answer about the squire having the college's glebe lands, as well as most of his: he simply admitted the college's right to them. But as to their share of Westgate tithes, that was another matter.

'Westgate *then* was smaller than Westgate *now*. All they have a right to is a half of Westgate tithes *then*. Its boundaries *then* cannot be by any person set out or abutted.'

'Then how can you prove your case?' the rector mildly enquired.

' Ah, the old map, Wilkinson I believe has it, but declines to lend it to me. Somewhere there will be another copy. Did you never hear of a parish of St Edmund, now? Or of St Andrew?'

'St Albert was mentioned in my presentation to the moieties of Ulph and Norton…'

'That is yet another dedication! I shall find where they lay. Never say die, Horatio, my lad!'

' No sir!'

The whole world was soon in an uproar about Mr Wilkes, he had become a hero, a martyr, the symbol of the freedom of the British people. In Lynn, in Wells, you could buy prints of him. For as soon as he was a member of Parliament, he had surrendered himself to the King's Bench to receive the sentence for his earlier convictions: a fine of one thousand pounds, and twenty-two months in prison where he now lay. On the opening of the new Parliament, a huge crowd clamoured outside roaring 'Wilkes and liberty': a mob made for the prison in Southwark and tried to rescue him. Troops had been called in, fighting followed, a man was killed. Behind all this, the charge which caused it to explode, was hunger, the long-standing high price of food aggravated by bad harvests and cold winters. The seamen refused to man ships in the port of London until their wages should be increased, the coalheavers (thus cheated of their work) turned on the seamen and fought them. Mobs terrorised Londoners.

Remote in Norfolk, the rector welcomed the boys home again in the green and gold of May time. Whitsunday was upon the twenty-second, Maurice's birthday on the twenty-fourth. At the end of the week Maurice, now fifteen, was to travel to London to his job. It was the last time they would see him for months.

Maurice was an accepter, not an arguer: he surrendered, he did not fight. When Papa had suggested to him that it was time that he should seek his living in London, he supposed that this was true. When he must spend hours writing and doing figures instead of pursuing the life he loved, he assumed that it was necessary. He did not fully realise until he was about to lose it how much he loved it. He only knew now, as they scuffed through the lush grass by the river above Overy Mill, that at the end of the week the coach would carry him to London and that he did not want to go.

Along the bank, William led the way, snatching at great handfuls of grass, Horace walked lightly in the middle, Maurice followed in a numbed dreaminess.

'Maurice? What is your job to *be?*' Horace's light voice came over his shoulder.

'I am to be a clerk under Mr Fowle in the auditor's office of excise.'

'Yes, I know, but what does that *mean?* What's excise?'

'Well, it's a kind of duty. You know what "customs" is, what Mr Boyles has to collect from the stuff coming in at Wells...Excise is a duty raised upon English stuff before it is sold abroad, I think. Auditor means checking all the figures, the money you know.'

'So what will you have to do?' pursued his brother, with dawning horror.

'Check columns of figures I expect,' admitted Maurice gloomily.

'All day?' said Horatio, turning about and standing still. 'Add up figures all *day*, Maurice?'

Even William, not very imaginative, was arrested.

'Shall you like it, Maurice?' Horatio said doubtfully.

'I shall not like being in all day. From about seven or eight I dare say, till about six. There will not be any day left.' And Maurice looked out towards Burnham Marsh, and saw the flats, the sea plants, the distant blue water in a blur of sudden tears.

'Poor Maurice,' said Horatio.

'Oh, I must make the best of it,' said his brother. 'It may be jolly at Uncle William's you know. There's madam, and our little cousins. And exciting things happen in London.' But his voice held no real hope. Horatio drew back with Maurice and together they tramped along, their arms round each others' waists, shoving each other off into the long green grass and giggling. Maurice knew it was his brother's way of showing his sorrow and was comforted.

But when he found himself a week later at his high wooden desk in the office near Red Lion Square where the sun only came for an hour or two of the day, scratching, scratching with his pen down the long sheet of paper figures which must be copied exactly, so that the mind must not wander: then he stopped, and thought of a week ago today, the long green grass, the buttercups of enamelled gold, the far distant ocean, Horace and William; and felt a depth of despair which was devoid of all hope. He was a prisoner far from the place he loved. When would he ever be free again?

In Horatio's mind for the next month was just as strong a sense of the imprisonment of school, but growing beside it an increasing determination not to be thus confined.

In each successive season the parsonage was found wanting to Horatio in a different way: Mamma was not here in the mid-summer vacation with her flowered muslins and tabby silks and summer caps: Sukey tied on Mamma's straw hat with the cherry ribbons. Horace frowned, sticking out his lip. And now Maurice was gone too, who had never been away for long before. Peter missed him, welcoming William's and Horace's help in the hayfields. Mary Blackett and Sukey (not many years in age between them) managed in the kitchen, and a little cousin of Mary's appeared, to be lorded over in her turn. Sukey had just had her thirteenth birthday: she organised the washing-girls, the ironing, the mending, the linen, the children's clothes, and Ann was her constant quiet shadow. And Papa: Papa seemed silent, almost as if he were not there, surprised when they arrived as if he had forgotten they were coming. In the hay-field he had worked without words today, resting often, mopping his brow. Now he had disappeared, he was not in his study. Kitty had cried for him that night in vain.

Horace charged in the cool of the evening along the Burn, past his granny's still empty house towards the village, over the bridge and up to the common and the church. The common had a new gate at last. Old Denis Vout was in the churchyard armed with stick and hook and gun, busy about his summer occupation of keeping jackdaws away.

'Evening, Mr Vout.'

'Evenin', young sar. Yer pa's in there.' He offered the information with a slight sad shake of the head.

'I know,' Horace said. He walked into the church and saw his father kneeling up by the altar rail. His father stood up, looked quickly away and back again, stared without smiling at his son and then walked to meet him.

'Horace, is anything wrong? What brings you?'

'I came to find you, I wanted to see you Papa,' Horace said: was not that reason enough?

The rector put his arm round the boy, leading him up towards Mamma's grave.

'And I am glad to see you too,' he said, 'it is little enough I see my sons these days.'

They stood side by side surveying the stone in the fading light. Horace began to read the words: Papa would be pleased if he could now read the words. Six months had made a great difference. He began to translate them and with his father's help construed it all. A loving wife and mother, she was possessed of Christian charity, and true friendship.

'Papa, there are two lines written in English,' he said.

> Let these alone
> Let no man move these Bones

'Why did you have them written in English, Papa?'

'It is often done. To ensure they rest undisturbed. I shall come at last and lie beside her. But we want no ignoramus who knows not Latin, who comes long after we are gone, taking it into his head to move this grave, do we, my boy? She must rest in the quiet grave in peace after all her labours.'

Horace nodded, understanding. No person, surely, would dare to disobey that stern command.

'But it is only her body lies here, Papa, is it not?' he whispered, quoting (without remembering) what she herself had taught him. The man looked sharply at him as if he felt himself rebuked. Only her body! How explain, to this ungrown boy, the enormity of that 'only!'

'That is all,' he said thinly, strangling the irony in his voice. 'Come, we'll walk back home. It smells sweet outside, as if all the hay in Norfolk were garnered, does it not?'

Horatio's hand, warm, living, was in his, he jumped along as he had used to do when he was much younger, pausing to look up at the sky, following a bird's flight with eager head. Edmund Nelson's healing began from that night in hay time. The children, her children! He had sworn to her departed spirit that he would look after the children! He had been near to neglecting his promise. This loving child had recalled him to his task, quite unaware.

Mrs Nelson and Aunt Mary came from Hilborough. We come to help you this first summer, she had said firmly in her letter, we shall not sit about idle. His mother took over the kitchen and meals which he had known in his boyhood graced the table and aroused memories. Aunt Mary took over the housework and the children, and Sukey effortlessly reverted to the girl she was, devoting much excited attention to her school trunk. William took Maurice's place and laboured outside with Peter. So did Horatio, when he was not off on his own down at Overy Staithe, or riding into Creake to visit Sir Mordaunt or Dr Poyntz, or tramping to Wells to find Charles. Ann struck up a great new friendship with her Aunt Nelson. Mun and Suckling flourished under their grandmother's crisp stern kindliness, feeling a hand upon them which they had missed. All, but particularly Papa, devoted themselves to the enchanting Kitty, now walking unsteadily, fifteen months old. How the parson adored this baby, his wife's last child! She reminded him of Horace in her manner, open and friendly, much unlike reserved little Ann. She was often with him, wheedled much out of him.

'Do not you indulge that baby over much now my son,' said Mrs Nelson with one of her sharp, bright-eyed looks. 'It will be no kindness to her. She should not by rights be at table with us. Leave her in the high chair, she may feed herself. Now, where is Horatio?'

Memory swept over Sukey.

'Granny! Do you remember when we thought the gypsies had taken him?'

'I do. Or your Aunt Mary did. He was all but drowned in the river. Where is he now? Do you allow him abroad on his own, my son?'

'He tells me before he goes ma'am. Today he has gone down to the staithe. It will depend on the tide when he is back, but he thought to dinner.'

'He should not be allowed to run wild, my son.'

'He does not ma'am, he was invited to go fishing. Fishermen must use the tide.'

Mrs Nelson sniffed, serving the plates. She liked children about the place, under her eye. She could not do with these roving habits, they put her in mind of John.

They saw him come across the garden, a bag over his shoulder, and heard him run in at the door.

'Papa! Granny! Aunt Mary! We caught hundreds of mackerel, Papa! You can see them come, all green and shiny and silver! I felt sorry for them to be caught! They gave me *ten*, Papa, big ones, enough for us all!'

'Well done, well done Horatio! A good morning's work. Now you are a little late, ten minutes or so. Beg Granny's pardon.'

'I beg your pardon Granny,' Horace said panting. 'I ran all the way.' She smiled at his red face.

'I see you did. Put them in the scullery, child. They will be very tasty. Wash your hands and come quickly. Why did not you go, William?'

Edmund Nelson smiled privately into his plate.

But William had not wanted to go, he had rather stay with Peter, he said. He felt envious now, seeing Horace's delight and success.

Susannah was off to school. Wearing a new bonnet, and a dress and cloak deftly cut down by Aunt Mary out of one of her mother's, she mounted John Raven's wagon early one summer morning, for her young ladies' academy in Norwich. She had shed a few tears kissing them all, particularly for Ann (who would miss her most): but her father knew she was full of excitement. She had worked without complaint, shouldering far more than she was used to since her mother's death; she had needed no telling, she had done all willingly. Now, he thought, she could be a girl again and giggle with the others. All her sewing problems would be solved, for the school taught all plain work and much fancy work too. Her writing and spelling and accounts would be polished up, there would be some drawing and some music, she might learn French and dancing if she wished. They all waved, until she was out of sight round the Creake corner. Mamma would surely have been pleased. Within an hour the boys must be off, Sukey had helped to pack their box as well as her own. Peter took them to Wells to put them on their way, their father going with them. Horatio was quiet, gloomy, bitterly unwilling to leave the sea and the fields of home; the month in high summer had made him love his adventurous freedom passionately. The autumn and winter stretched interminable, with no break till Christmas. William was more resigned, he liked school. Papa bade them take heart, work hard, time would soon pass as time always did.

On his return he surveyed the depleted parsonage with some dismay. Ann, sitting quiet on the step, made a daisy chain for Kitty while the two boys argued over their game.

'Now, little Ann,' Edmund Nelson said, 'I am the father and you are the mother, and this is our family is it not? We shall do very well together!'

She was pleased with this and gave him one of her infrequent smiles. He must comfort her, pet her, he must not neglect her for Kitty, who was so easily loved. When the summer was done, he must set about teaching the little boys, neither of whom showed much sign of cleverness. He picked Ann up under one arm, Kitty under the other, and squeezed his way in at the door amidst screams of laughter.

CHAPTER TWENTY

The King and the Founder

On ordinary days Mr Jones would intone the prayers through his long and rippling nose in the schoolroom before the first lesson: but on Sunday the boys would be summoned by the church bell behind the school. Sir William Paston's scholars would then hasten to the stable yard which lay beyond the headmaster's private garden, and line up by the door in the high brick wall. Then Mr Jones or one of his assistants would unlock the door and the boys would jostle through the gateway, above which a plaque in the wall announced this to be Sir William Paston's Free School founded in 1606. On warm August Sundays Horatio wished passionately he were at home.

Every month, usually upon a Thursday afternoon, Mr Fowke the vicar would have the boys over in the church for their religious instruction, a duty laid down by the founder for which he was paid twelve guineas a year. (Mr Jones secretly begrudged the vicar the task, and could have done with the twelve guineas himself.)

Horatio had so strong a sense of duty and so lively an awareness of his father's hopes that he applied himself to all his lessons, helped in his Latin by his good memory; and in his excursions into English literature and history by the prospect of vividly portrayed people performing deeds of heroism or horror. These fired his imagination. But when he came to lessons which had a practical value, his interest was quickened in quite another way. Both merchants' accounts and navigation were in the curriculum. His horror at Maurice's job had been partly due to his own lack of mastery of the subject. He was determined that he would make money whatever he did, money to help Papa, to help the family. Money was an interesting subject, so was trading! And traders were often sailors. The early lessons in navigation were rudimentary but Horace delighted in them. An old master mariner instructed the boys upon a mariner's compass, showing them the mysterious magnetism of true north and teaching them the names of the points between. Horatio recited these with glee, they reminded him of Charles's Papa, of Uncle Maurice: he seemed to hear them yelled above bluff winds or storms of crashing waves; nor'-nor'east, east-nor'east, north by nor'-nor-east! There was poetry, adventure in the compass points. Then there were some simple lessons about the stars, enough to whet the boy's appetite, to cause him to walk head-in-air on frosty evenings, trying to discern the patterns of those distant, pulsing points of light by which sailors found their way. What fired him most of all was to see Mr Jones twirl the globe and trace the line that a ship would sail, down to those islands nestling between the two great continents of America, the West Indies where Uncle Maurice had been! And Dr Poyntz's voice would sail into his mind reciting... *Where the remote Bermudas ride*...How could ships sail upon this lonely circle, how could the world be a ball, a globe, turning and forever turning! Yet they did, and it was.

The Nelsons had been pleased to find last week's Norwich newspaper in the parlour where the boarders gathered on Saturdays and Sundays, and were often to be found with the paper spread between them.

'Have you read about the *Endeavour* Bark, Mr James Cook,' Horace wrote to his distant brother in London 'bound to the South Sea, under the direction of the Royal Society?' (Someone had explained to Horatio what the Society was.) 'Several rich gentlemen go, skilled in Astronomy, Botany and Natural History. She is fallen down to Blackwall, and sails about mid-August. Pray Maurice, find out where she lies, make haste, she will be gone, and send me a description! We have been shown all the oceans on the globe. A ship from Greenland off Tinmouth had only nine fish, but 570 seals (do you remember the seal washed up at Overy?) and *four bears*! They are white and much taller than a horse when they stand upon their hind legs, the mariner from Mundesley told me, who teaches us Navigation. Has Sukey writ you, she likes her school. I do not mind it here, but I had rather be at home...'

'Now boys,' said Mr Jones one September Saturday in the parlour, 'who has read the song of the American colonists reported from the *Boston Gazette?*'

A few had, amongst them William and Horace.

'And what does it portend, boys? Have you understood it? Nelson major?'

'Not exactly sir.'

'It is about the duties imposed upon some of our goods, notably tea, going into the colonies; it is a proper tax we have a right to demand that they should pay, for the British government needs to raise the money to defend the colonies somehow from their enemies, does it not? This song finishes with a slur upon British justice, boys, listen to this:

That wealth and that glory immortal may be
If she is but just—and if we are but free...

They think the duties they must pay are unjust! But is it just, my boys, that *Britons* should pay from *their* taxes for the defence of the colonists? Is *that* just?'

'No sir,' came the required answer from most of his unthinking listeners.

'They owe all they have to this country, and a great deal of their wealth to their trade with us. Even their tunes are British! This song goes to *Hearts of Oak,* listen to the chorus!'

And Mr Jones launched into it in his musical tenor, one hand extended, enjoying an opportunity to hear himself sing:

' "In Freedom we're born and in Freedom we'll live
Our purses are ready,
Steady, friends, steady
Not as Slaves, but as Freemen, our money we'll give. "

Think you, why should they consider themselves slaves in having to pay a few duties? Are *we* slaves, that we pay our dues and taxes levied by our parliament? We may object, but we know we must pay.'

Horace reflected that the smugglers did not pay.

'Yes Paul, what have you to say?' Paul Johnson was the son of a gentleman at Runton, quite near at hand. He had come to school at the same time as Horace and William and was in the first class with them.

'If you please, sir, my papa says that the colonists would perhaps rather rule themselves and have their own parliament and decide their own taxes.'

Mr Jones was stunned into silence, and then resorted to sarcasm. 'Rule themselves, indeed! And a fine showing they would make of that! Unlettered men mostly, settlers, farmers and fishers! What time, what skill have they for sitting in parliament?'

'My papa says that they should have members in our parliament if it rules them.'

'Does he so? What, from thousands of miles away across the ocean?'

'If you please, sir, this is why my papa thinks they might be better off ruling themselves.'

'What, break away from us, and we lose all the trade we have built up? I suppose your papa was never a merchant?'

'My grandfather was, sir.'

'Then I should expect your father to wish to guard our trade.'

'My papa says he thinks free trade is best sir, and that they would not wish to lose the trade either, sir.'

Mr Jones snorted, finding himself out of his depth.

'Never, boys,' he said with unction 'be deceived into working against your King and country. In a few days we shall celebrate Coronation Day. Let it establish you in your fervour as Britons!'

Coronation Day was September the twenty-second. William's memory provided an immediate impression of the jolting of the wagon on a cool, sweet-smelling night, candles, a bonfire, toffee, Mamma holding Horace.

'Horace, do you remember Coronation night? We all went to Wells in the wagon?' he asked as they lay in bed.

Horatio frowned.

'Were the ships lit up?'

'Yes! And there were guns.'

'I think I do,' Horace said. 'I think I remember the ships lit up. But Mamma tells—told me about it too. How old was I, how long ago?'

William counted up. 'Seven years ago,' he said. 'You were almost three. I was four and a half.'

'I'll be ten next week.'

Horace reflected that he was glad to be ten, it was better than nine.

On Coronation Day Sir William Paston's scholars, granted a half-holiday, marched (some grinning foolishly but most in due seriousness) round the market square, led by William Booty. They halted at the market cross in the centre, an eight-sided structure of timber with a dome which had windows in it, where he unrolled his paper and declaimed his speech of loyalty to His Majesty, to the honour of God, and also of the founder.

Now various boys stepped forward, importantly fluttering papers on which were written odes of their own composition. William Nelson's had been chosen, a simple effusion wishing long life to His Majesty, which Horatio thought extremely clever. William pinned his paper with immense solemnity upon a grocer's doorpost. He was very good at occasions and processions and doing things well, thought Horatio. How pleased Papa would be!

The second red letter day came in Mr Jones's opinion inconveniently soon: yet which should give place to which, the King to the founder? Or the founder to the King? A nice point which he was not prepared to argue with Mr Harbord Harbord, Mr Thomas Durrant, Mr John Berney

Petre, Dr Yonge the Bishop and others whose names were not sufficiently grand for him to have mastered them: in short, the governors. In his own mind, the founder had precedence. If they did not honour Sir William Paston who on October the first, 1606 had founded their school, who would? So he had deputed his favourite pupil, Thomas Taylor, to make the oration for the founder. Thomas's speech was very splendid with its figures and its tropes, in praise of education and Sir William Paston. Horace listened hard (for he liked Thomas) but he was soon lost. After this, Thomas must read a long part of the school statutes, the Ancient Oration; even his lively and dulcet tones grew dull.

The oration over, the boys trooped into church for prayers, within view of the founder's splendid tomb in the sanctuary, right up against the altar. Sir William Paston, moustachioed, fashioned in alabaster, reclining peacefully upon his elbow, fixed a sad stare upon them. Their founder was the nephew and heir of that Sir Clement Paston who had built the magnificent house at Oxnead when the great family was rich and flourishing. Sir William's son Christopher had run mad in his father's time. It was said that a prior of Bromholme, crossed by some Paston of long ago, had laid a curse upon the family: *Since you are thus cruel and inexorable to us, and our brethren and house, you shall certainly from henceforth always have one of your family a fool, till it is become poor.* The ruins of Bromholme Priory lay between North Walsham and the sea, near the village of Paston whence the family took its name.

Papa wrote with news of the family: what a good darner of stockings was Ann: what was Miss Kitty's latest trick; how Edmund and Suckling, now six and four, were begun on their letters: and how he and Mr Allott had petitioned my lord the Bishop of Norwich for leave to take down the church of Sutton, the chancel, and sell the materials, together with the lead of Ulph church and sell it also towards the repairs of Ulph. Horatio remembered his father's anxiety about the churches: William thought how agreeable to be my lord Bishop of Norwich and grant faculties, as Papa called them.

Sukey wrote telling them of her lessons and her stitchery and how upon Coronation Day her godpapa, Mr John Berney, had taken them to a Rural Gardens without St Stephen's Gate illuminated with lanterns and with fireworks, as good as Vauxhall in London.

Maurice wrote; he had asked Uncle Maurice who was there when he visited them at Kentish Town, but he had been too late, the *Endeavour* had sailed. He told his brothers that at Uncle William's grand house there was a cheerful happy butler from the West Indies, who was very good to Maurice and Maurice loved him. His name was James Price and his people had come at first from Africa. Horace wondered if Uncle Maurice had conveyed him to England?

And then, at last, Christmas was coming. (Mr Jones was glad to see the vacation approach, there was smallpox in North Walsham.)

Sukey was home before them and the reunion was joyful. The rector could not help but be glad to hear their shouts and laughter, for the little ones seemed very quiet compared with Sukey's giggles, Horatio's boasts, William's bombast and appetite.

If only Maurice were there! But it would be all travel and no pleasure for so short a time. All were mutely aware of the sadness of the anniversary, that last year Mamma prepared the feast, that her place would never be filled.

There was smallpox in Burnham also: Peter Black and his wife and their four or five children were being inoculated and Peter came not into the parsonage. Horace would talk to him each day, calling from a window. Dr Suckerman had lately died and the shop and his house were to let in the market; young Mr Kerrich was all the busier. Smuggling had come to such a pass on the Norfolk coast that dragoons from Norwich were sent out to Blakeney and Cley, a piece of news Horatio related with glee to Maurice. And in the *Mercury* of the week before Christmas appeared a strange and most interesting notice.

'Pray Papa, did you read this?'

Horatio stood, the paper spread out, straining to see in the afternoon light.

'"Stolen or strayed from the Parish of BURNHAM WESTGATE, in Norfolk,"' he read, '"a COMMON belonging to the said Parish; as also a large quantity of GLEBE LAND, belonging to the Churches of Burnham Westgate and Burnham Ulph. Whoever will give intelligence of the above particulars so that they may be had again, shall be well rewarded for their Trouble; and the Discoverers of the Common, shall also have the Thanks and Prayers of the poor Inhabitants who are great Sufferers by the Loss of it." Papa! What does it mean, is it true?'

'There are those who think so,' Papa said.

'And who do you suppose has put it in, Papa?'

'I do not precisely know, Horace, but I can very well guess; cannot you?'

'Mr Allott?'

'I would not be surprised.'

'And who has stolen the land, Papa?'

'Mr Allott is of the opinion that the squire has ploughed in much of the glebe to his own, and overrun the common.'

'Papa! What will happen? Will not Squire Wilkinson be very angry?'

'Time will show, my boy.'

He noted with approval that Horace's reading was much improved.

CHAPTER TWENTY-ONE

The Ague

By the time the governors of Sir William Paston's Free School met at the King's Arms on Friday, the thirteenth of January, the smallpox seemed to be over. (Mr Durrant became the new treasurer, Mr Jones gave a report.) And when people from outside were still declaring North Walsham to be pox-ridden in the third week in February, the affronted citizens advertised that it had been for the last six weeks entirely free and was never known to be more in health.

The boys, back at the school house, seemed healthy enough as lessons began again in what looked like the middle of the night. And an argument broke out concerning the rights and wrongs of pressing sailors.

'Pray listen to this!' said William Booty, who had availed himself of the newspaper. 'It is from London. It says that press warrants are immediately to be issued "for the taking up all Vagabond Boys between the ages of thirteen and twenty, who are to be registered in the Dock Yards of Chatham, Portsmouth and Plymouth: five and twenty of them to be sent on board each of the Frigates now fitting out for Channel Service, the remainder on board the Guard ships..." It says it's thought that in St Giles' parish only, there are nine hundred boys that have no other subsistence but stealing and pilfering. This newspaperman is complacent! He says: "What a happy Nursery of Young Seamen will be thus formed!" I say they will continue to steal and pilfer and be beaten for it, and do their best to run away.'

'It's against the freedom of the people!' said Paul Johnson with some heat.

'Why should any boy go to sea against his will?' said someone else.

'But it might be better, it might be more agreeable than having no bread, and having to steal!' shouted Horace.

'Being forced to go to sea is not agreeable,' said Thomas quietly.

'Being forced to do anything is disagreeable,' said William Nelson.

'I should not mind going in a frigate upon Channel Service!' Horatio shouted again.

'Then that is very well! But these vagabonds may not feel as you do! No free man should be made a sailor against his will!'

'Wilkes and Liberty!' roared several boys together.

'It is better than starving perhaps,' shouted William Nelson in support of his brother: a statement greeted with a howl of laughter, for William's prowess as a trencherman had early made itself known.

'Happy Nursery indeed,' snorted Mr Booty. 'What nursery could be happy if the inmates do not wish to be there?'

'But if the country needs sailors, why should nine hundred vagabonds go idle, stealing, doing nothing for their bread?' yelled Nelson minor from the top of a desk. They were in the schoolroom.

'That is not the point at issue, young Nelson,' said Booty in a lordly way. 'You must needs think clearly and keep to the point: is it right for a free boy, a free man, to be forced to a profession he cares not for? Let him be given the chance by all means, but let him choose! If he be so foolish (as it appears you would be) as to choose a life at sea, that is his affair. But I declare press warrants are wrong!'

'As wrong as general warrants. Wilkes and Liberty!'

'I cannot see what Mr Wilkes has to do here,' Thomas put in, looking up from his work.

'Then you see no further than your nose and your grammar,' said Ashmul. 'Mr Wilkes fights for every man's freedom.'

Horatio sat thinking upon the desk. Booty watched him.

'Nelson minor, how if Thomas's papa took you by the scrag of your thin neck and said, "Get you into my workshop and be you a weaver!" Would you be a happy weaver, Nelson minor?'

Horace grinned, admitting he would not.

'But supposing there is a war and the King needs sailors?'

'A war is different. In any event a man must serve the King of his free will, to serve him well.'

'Britons never never never shall be slaves!' roared two or three boys together.

'That,' put in Thomas, 'means slaves to another country.'

But they thought not what it meant, only enjoying the noise they made.

Not long after this, early in March, William climbed into bed some time after his brother to find Horatio quaking and sweating beside him.

'Horace! What is it? Is it your fever?'

Horatio grunted, his teeth clenched, shivering.

William, to whom Horace's fever was not unknown, climbed out of bed again and padded off to the private wing of the house to seek help and Mrs Jones. Mrs Jones, thoughts of smallpox fresh in her mind, wrapped Horatio in a blanket and conducted him stumbling to a small room she kept for such occasions, far away from everyone else. Here she comforted him with hot water bottles, drinks and cool cloths upon his hot brow, and sent for the doctor in the morning.

'Are you subject to these fits, my boy?' asked the doctor.

Horace nodded from the hot, aching, throbbing place of his fever. His eyes hurt, his throat hurt, his mouth was dry, his lips baked and stiff. Sometimes he shivered with cold, sometimes he was suffocated with heat.

'Ay, the ague no doubt. 'Twill last three or four days. Let him drink as much as he will; keep him warm, let him not lie in a wet shirt. When did you last have it, my boy?'

But Horatio could not remember. Not at school. At home. Mamma would cool his head, stroke back his wet hair. He wished he were at home, he wanted Mamma. A sigh like a sob escaped. The doctor, enquiring his age, remarked that he was small and thin and needed care. Mrs Jones bade her husband write to his father. After a week, the rector came to fetch him.

Horace leaned against Papa in the chaise, weak but filled with joy. He felt better, he was going home: there would be firelight and candlelight in Papa's study, warmth in the kitchen, Ann and the children to play with. For a few days he went back to being a young child again with Mary to cosset him. After that the rector gave him some Latin in the mornings, and Dr Poyntz called with a book for them to read all about the island of Corsica, by a gentleman called James Boswell who had been there. Corsica was a matter of moment: the French were making depredations against it. The following Monday Papa had a wedding to take: he bade Horace dress up well and come with him, he could do with another witness. Horatio obeyed with alacrity for he loved to be Papa's companion in everything. They went up to Thorpe church on a blustery day of some sunshine, and there was churchwarden Jacombe who greeted Horace with his usual kindness, and a shy couple waiting to plight their troth. She was Elizabeth Spurgeon, marrying Thomas Massingham of Holt. In the register Mr Nelson filled in the date, '13 Mar', and added the figures '69' for the year (he forgot to put the '7' after the one thousand, a trick he was prone to). Then the couple signed their names, and Robert Jacombe signed his, and passed the pen to Horace. And Horace wrote 'Horace Nelson' neatly as Mr Jones had taught him. But when the others had gone Papa spoiled it by changing it to 'Horatio'.

'Your real name is Horatio, my boy. You must sign "Horatio" on public occasions,' his father said. And Mr Allott awaited them at home. He had heard that the parson had gone to fetch Horatio and he presented him with a small packet of peppermint humbugs from Mr Lateward's.

'And may I ask, how is the sufferer?' he said in his brisk kindly tones.

'Better sir. Oh thank you, sir!' said Horace receiving the striped sweetmeats with some glee. He offered them to his elders who refused them and then put one in his own mouth where it proved an effective silencer.

'And how do affairs progress between you and the college?' the rector asked, pouring his guest a glass of madeira. He had never taxed Mr Allott with the writing of the advertisement for the lost common: if he wished him to know, he would tell him. Now it appeared that the slow tale of the dispute between Dr Shepherd of Christ's and the reverend Mr Allott had taken a sharp turn. There lived at Snettisham a well-meaning young gentleman called Nicholas Styleman, son of the reverend Mr Armine Styleman who had married the heiress of the late Sir Nicholas LeStrange of Hunstanton Hall. This lady, his mother, was now dead but his father could distinctly remember his first wife telling him that her father (LeStrange) had had a lease with the college for certain rights at Westgate, in trust for the rector of the time. Mr Nicholas Styleman searched his mother's papers and found that the lease in question was for twenty-five acres of land and a moiety of the tithes of Burnham Westgate. When the rector died, Sir Nicholas had sub-leased the rights, first to a farmer and then to the next rector, Mr Henry Spurling, who had later had a direct lease with the college. Mr Styleman, full of an innocent desire to help enlighten a case which was becoming a scandal, set out eagerly to visit Mr Allott.

'So you see sir,' he had finished triumphantly, 'the accounts between Mr Spurling and my grandfather prove beyond possibility of doubt that the lessee was entitled to a full moiety of the tithes of Burnham Westgate as well as the twenty-five acres of land!'

Mr Allott sniffed, and strode about. This was not in the least degree what he wished to have proved concerning the tithes.

'That I could not say, sir, until I had examined them,' he replied shortly.

'Ah, well, I have written to Dr Shepherd...'

'You have written to Dr Shepherd, sir!' broke in Mr Allott. 'Here have I been three years or more at the utmost pains to discover the truth of the matter! I had rather you had come to me before you writ to Dr Shepherd!'

'Sir,' said Mr Styleman, very much puzzled, 'I have suggested to Dr Shepherd that the only way is to go to arbitration. I have promised to put all the papers before them.'

'And do these papers cast any light upon the disappearance of my rightful glebe? I have already admitted the college right to the twenty-five acres, sir.'

'That I fear they do not, sir.'

All this Mr Allott now retailed while young Horatio swallowed and gulped over successive humbugs.

'Well of course you will accept arbitration,' Edmund Nelson put in when he had the chance. 'It is the obvious way out of the difficulty.'

'I do not know at all that I am prepared to do so,' said Mr Allott. 'There may be no mention, do you see, of the two other parishes which I deem to have been consolidated with Westgate and upon which I base my opinion that Dr Shepherd is entitled to one third of the moiety of the lands now within that parish.'

'But,' said the rector, 'if there is no mention of them, and this but forty-five years ago, does it not suggest your case is groundless?'

It was the nearest he had come to trying to halt the impetuous clergyman.

Mr Allott looked sharply at him with flashing violet eyes and chose to disregard his remark.

'You remember the squire asserts that the clergyman following Spurling, one Thomas Groom, left all the land, the college glebe and his own, to *him* and that he has worked it ever since?'

'Yes, you did say so.'

'And it seems the late Mr Smith never bothered to recover it, for Mrs Smith assures me he never worked it, she knows nothing of such land. And listen to this, Mr Nelson, I have found a servant of the squire's ready to swear that just before and after Mr Smith's death he was required, nay ordered, to plough up the baulks which showed where the college lands lay alongside the squire's! Upon pain of dismissal!'

'Upon my soul! Have you dared to tax the squire with this?'

'He swears through thick and thin he knows nothing of any college claim and denies destroying the baulks!'

'What will you do now as to the church glebe?'

'Sue him, sir. Outright. If he refuses to part with my acres! How say you, Horace? Shall a rich man steal my land and I not fight for it?'

'No sir, I'll say not sir,' Horace spluttered.

So it appeared that matters had come to open enmity between the parson and the squire, an unhappy state of affairs for Burnham Market.

With the summer came Maurice. He came in the sweet of the year, late June, from London to Lynn and thence made his own way so that Papa need spare no horse or man from the hay fields. He came quite late in the evening when they were all up in the meadow at work: Horace had been on tenterhooks all day awaiting him and heard his halloo first.

'There he is! There he is, Papa!' he cried. All threw down their forks and hurried to meet him, Horatio running faster than any. He flung himself upon his now lanky brother and was clasped fervently in his arms.

'Huzzah! Maurice!'

'My turn, my turn!' Sukey laughed.

William ran at his brother, cheering and slapping his shoulder.

Maurice embraced each in turn, picking up Ann, patting the little boys, and last, clasping his father. He was almost taller than Papa; he was sixteen, his face thinner and pale for lack of country air and sun. Peter stood watchful and smiling, leaning upon his hayfork higher up the meadow. Maurice ran to him, took him by the arms to greet him.

'Well, bor!' said Peter shaking his head sideways, smiling a twisted smile. He loved Maurice. 'Yew look sumthen under ripe, we'll hev to get yew in the sun right quick.'

Maurice's eyes glittered with joy to be home. They bore him to the house to find food and drink. Two weeks, two whole weeks of paradise! But London had not been all loss, all dull. Maurice would tell them as they cut or tossed the hay some of his adventures: how Uncle William and Uncle Maurice had taken him to the first exhibition of paintings in the Academy in Pall Mall, an infant institution which owed its birth to His Majesty himself; and of Mr Horace Walpole's splendid entertainment at Strawberry Hill which Maurice had heard of; and of Mr John Wilkes' expulsion from Parliament not once but thrice, being re-elected by the people of Middlesex and re-expelled: since Mr Wilkes, said government, was incapable of sitting in the existing parliament. The rector, not very political, had been uncertain what to think and hoped his son might tell him.

'What do your uncles say?' he asked.

'Why Papa, that it is against the right of the people, who must elect whom they choose! Uncle Maurice told me that Mr Horace Walpole and all that family are strongly against general warrants which deny the right of the people: and this is just as much so!'

'Your mamma's cousin, Sir John Turner, was *for* general warrants and won the seat at Lynn again upon the issue. He is strongly for the King. This Wilkes was taken up at the first for seditious libel against the King!'

'Ay, so he was, and lately again for the same thing against Lord Weymouth, because my Lord used the soldiers last year against the mob. Uncle William thinks Wilkes a seditious rascal with some right on his side. But it is all stuff and nonsense, when one comes back to the countryside!' Maurice laughed, drank his mug down with the utmost enjoyment and gave a long sigh.

'And how do you like your work, my son? Is it too irksome to be borne?' said his father anxiously, at last finding courage to ask the question.

'I get on quite well, Papa, better and faster. I am more used to it now. They are satisfied with me. Perhaps I may take some lessons in a shorthand soon.'

'What is a shorthand?' Horace asked.

'A way of writing things down more quickly, signs for many words, a kind of new alphabet,' his brother explained.

Meanwhile, with his hay-making and his favourite newspaper to read, Maurice was happy. He would read it out as he used to do, to the family: in Norwich somebody's pet lark died at the age of twenty-three and was given an epitaph in front of the Duke Tavern in the Castle Ditches. And there was so great a plenty of mackerel in the city that they were cried by the bellman, two for three-halfpence.

Far too soon Maurice was gone back, dragged unwillingly from the fields and the sea (where he and Horatio had walked and talked with the fishermen): and Sukey was off again to Norwich; and William and Horatio faced their endless autumn at school.

After the midsummer holiday of 1769 there appeared the reverend Mr Hepworth, round-faced and friendly, a new curate in the town who now came in to help Mr Jones. He was a graduate of Queen's, Cambridge, twenty-two years old and an able mathematician. He was of a Yorkshire family and being young and less fiery than Mr Jones was soon generally liked. He was capable of teaching all branches of the mathematics and his most important pupils were William Booty and John Ashmul, destined for Cambridge this year.

William and Horace Nelson now saw the schoolroom from a different place. Both were moved up into the second class and took their places in the opposite corner of the room. Horace himself was against the wall, near the fireplace.

'Pray keep that youngest Nelson boy warm, Mr Jones,' Mrs Jones was to say as the autumn days came on. 'He is forever ailing!'

That summer, preparations had been on foot for a Shakespeare jubilee at Stratford-on-Avon under the direction of Mr Garrick, with the music in the charge of Dr Arne. Mr Jones celebrated the poet by a study of *King Henry V* with his boys.

'This prince, young gentlemen, was born at Monmouth: and if Monmouth is not in Wales, it should be, it lies upon the border. Now look you, what brave things come out of Wales!'

Horatio warmed to the story of *King Henry,* longed to declaim those fiery speeches to the soldiers, that band of brothers, when the great battle was won. But he was too small and too young. An older boy spoke them with ardour and courage: Horace never forgot the rising tones of his voice saying ruminatively '...*But if it be a sin to covet honour, I am the most offending soul alive.*'

At Stratford in September there were fine breakfasts and an ode spoken by Mr Garrick; assemblies and an oratorio by Mr Arne. There was a masquerade ball attended by the wealth and nobility, including Mr James Boswell habited as a Corsican chief. But the unusual wetness of the second and third days spoilt all. The fireworks died as soon as lit, most of the gentlemen wore dominoes, while the ladies must pick their way to their carriages upon planks.

Mr Garrick's ballad with its repeated refrain lingered for weeks in people's memory:

For the lad of all lads was a Warwickshire lad!

Early in November Horace was struck again by the ague and after four or five days Papa with some anxiety fetched him for a little recruit at home.

Once more there happened to be a wedding, upon Monday the thirteenth of November, and Papa and Horace trudged up to church to marry Hannah Pinner to Peter Dennis of Docking. On the way, they met Goody Black.

'Home again, Horatio?' said she, guessing the reason by the look of his pale face. The boy needed his mother, rest her soul.

'The ague again, Ann. I hope he does not go on thus for ever. Though mind, I remember I was much the same as a child,' the rector confessed.

'Ay, he'll grow out of it. How old be you now, master Horace, then?'

'Eleven.'

'That's the growing pains an' all. That's nuffen to worry about, you take my word for it.'

Hannah and Peter and Ann Scott, the sexton's wife (collected on the way for witness as she so often was, living near), were all unlettered and made their marks upon the register instead of writing their names. Horatio's name stood in solitary state: neatly written, the 't' to remain for ever uncrossed.

CHAPTER TWENTY-TWO

The Measles

North Walsham Academy (as those unimpressed with the Paston connection called it) seemed sadly the same to Horatio in the New Year of 1770; yet there were subtle differences. John Ashmul and William Booty were gone, who had lorded it not unkindly over the younger boys. Ashmul was the better scholar though Booty being two years older had made a stronger impression of character. (Horace never forgot his outburst upon the pressing of seamen). Both had gone as scholars to Caius College with which the school had early connections; for Sir William Paston, the founder, had been there when it was Gonville Hall and Dr Caius himself was a Norfolk man. Thomas Taylor stayed on at school, quiet, affable and studious, for which Horace was glad. Mr Hepworth, deciding that he must try to better himself for he wished to marry, started to look about him. Mr Jones was well satisfied with his sixty boys and his Cambridge scholars. M Moisson continued to teach the citizens of North Walsham French and fencing. William and Horace, now old hands at school, instructed the new boys in its geography and traditions: Nat Clarke, son of an ironmonger at Attleborough, and Richard Ellis whose papa was parson at Northrepps (and who remembered them at Norwich); Tom Deeker who lived at home, for his father was a linendraper in the town; and little Charles Mann who was only eight, son of a mercer of Norwich.

Gradually over the past two years William had established a kind of ascendancy over Horatio in school. For William enjoyed lessons, he relished Latin and history and mathematics and religious instruction, and pleasing Mr Jones. When it came to Greek, he was willing to master the characters, he was a plodder. To William, heavy, clumsy and physically lazy, to be sitting still comfortably at his books was preferable to being active. Moreover he could now see the advantages: he might go to college, become a lawyer or a parson, a judge or a bishop even! Knowledge increased his importance and his stature, all famous and important men were educated, Papa had often said so: and William now took it for granted.

But Horatio was no plodder where his attention was not engaged: Greek appalled him. Latin, though he knew he must master it, seemed to him no end in itself. Small, light, active to a noticeable degree, he was soon tired with study, longing to be up and doing, needing a change. He delighted in the games they played, the racing round, the forbidden sallies into the town and back unobserved; he liked nothing better than to be dared to climb this or execute that dangerous performance and be cheered and admired by the rest when he had done it. William had not Horace's physical courage, his seemingly total lack of fear: he would smile rather primly and let him be. He had his own compensation now and as far as his teachers were concerned, the superiority. He had the makings of a reasonable scholar, attachment, application and industry. Which is perhaps as much as to say that William lived more fully at school, Horace at home. William was content at North Walsham, usually actively happy; Horace seemed more alive in Burnham. His frequent slight illnesses did not help his schoolwork, for he missed lessons and covered up (with his quickness at grasping the gist of a thing) material he had never properly learned. William began to achieve the reputation of a worker, one who even might help a younger boy, but who liked his own way and usually had it, whose friends were those who were subservient to him. Even his greed was pandered to by some. William must be respected as he grew older: Horace was often loved for his spirit, his ideas, his bravery, his natural warm friendliness to other boys, a kind of open-hearted charm which he had always possessed. He did not much excel in the schoolroom and he dearly liked to excel. He looked upon school as a somewhat tedious interruption of real life. His powers to excel did not lie here. He wished to have adventures, to make money, or achieve fame and honour. Struck by the words of King Henry the Fifth, his daydreams put him at the head of armies, or leading explorers, or commanding ships like his uncle; or more modestly overcoming smugglers. He was nearer to all this at Burnham Overy Staithe, in Wells harbour, than in the schoolroom. Upon the whole, although he tried to please both Papa and his masters, he longed for the vacations.

The week after Easter that year, Mr John Wilkes was freed from the King's Bench prison. All over the country the people, convinced that this man (be he a scallywag) had in some important way upheld their rights, fell to rejoicings for his liberty. Burnham was no exception: Mr Allott, fire-brand that he was, could be relied upon to lead the huzzahs, though Mr Nelson and Mr Crowe might be more reserved and Canon Poyntz might excuse himself with his usual grace. In Norwich, a company of woolcombers issued at noon, wearing woollen caps of various colours representing the Cap of Liberty, and marched through the market and the principal streets. At King's Lynn the bells were rung, the guns were fired, many gentlemen gave elegant entertainments, and the day was ushered out with a great bonfire.

When they returned to school Thomas was there before them, conducting a new boy to his place in the dormitory.

'This is William Bulwer,' he said.

Horace nudged William, William stared at Horace with a slow smile spreading over his fat features.

'*Bulwer,*' Horace whispered. '"We are strong enough to do for you all so take care how you behave!"'

'"We will blow out your Brains and burn down your House over you..."' recited his brother with increasing loudness.

'"And if Buller or Durrant or My Lord send anybody to prison they shall meet with the same Saufe by God!"' finished Horace in a yell. And both Nelsons collapsed laughing upon their bed.

William Bulwer flushed scarlet, stood forward and raised his fists for a fight.

'I'll teach you to laugh at me, for whatever reason, you rude, boorish nincompoops, and as to your threats, I know not what you mean, but you shall hear about it very soon from my papa at Heydon!'

'Oh,' Horace assured him, 'they are not threats! We were only remembering a play we used to indulge in when we were infants. It concerned poachers who had written a letter to Mr Hearne of Heveringland, and my godpapa Lord Walpole at Wolterton was in it...'

'And so was Mr Bulwer. Your papa I presume?' put in William.

'I dare say,' admitted this fiery boy grudgingly. 'I am William Bulwer of Heydon. I do seem to remember something of the sort when I was a child.' He had lowered his ready fists and was prepared to smile.

Horace chattered on. 'Mr Hearne I remember was used to put man-traps in his woods: did they ever catch anyone? Where do you sleep? On, here, quite near us, we shall be able to talk in bed. Have you been to school before? We were in Norwich but learnt nothing so my papa sent us here where we learn a bit more.'

'I've had a tutor,' William Bulwer said. 'But I don't much care for lessons, I like hunting and shooting. My father has taught me, he says I am a fine shot for my age, though I will be better when I'm taller. I'd put a bullet through any poacher I saw on my father's land.'

'That would be murder,' William Nelson objected stolidly.

'May be, but nobody would know who did it.'

Such cynicism took Horace aback. 'They might find out,' he said, 'but I dare say you might conceal it. Though it would be disagreeable to have killed a man?' he questioned. He liked the new boy's spirit, but

211

was doubtful of the outcome. 'I should have it upon my conscience, would not you?'

William Bulwer sat down, scratched his head and began upon plans for the disposal of the body. Thomas Taylor left them to it with a smile more relieved than superior.

It was not long after the start of the term that Nat Clarke, reading the newspaper in the parlour, called out suddenly: 'Ho! Listen here, listen to this! It is dated the twenty-fourth of April, from Wy-mondham.'

'Windham!' shouted many a local boy present.

'Very well, as you please. "The reverend Mr Hepworth, Assistant in the Academy at North Walsham, being appointed Master of the…"(—ahem!—) "*WINDHAM* Free Grammar School, proposes opening the said school at Midsummer next, where Young Gentlemen may be conveniently boarded and instructed in the Languages, Writing, Arithmetic and every Branch of the Mathematics." So we are to lose our dear instructor! I shall weep bitter tears!' and Nat pulled forth a large, dirty handkerchief and proceeded to do so. A few younger boys played up to this: one of these now sprang to his feet, sobbed loudly, and waved a hand.

'Farewell, old Hepworth!' he wailed, using the word as a term between affection and abuse and with little relevance to age, as Norfolkers do. Before he spoke the door had opened.

Mr Hepworth strode in and possessed himself of a book. His amused glance took in the situation, most of the boys present having scrambled politely to their feet.

'Farewell, bor,' said Mr Hepworth, tweaking the blushing boy by the ear as he passed him.

A laugh of approval and delight filled the study.

'Sir, sir!'

'I say, sir…'

'We're very sorry you are going, sir!' said Horatio, with truth and charm.

'Thank you Nelson minor, and so am I in some respects,' said Mr Hepworth, departing.

He wondered about that little Nelson, always saying the right thing to his elders: was he a prig? Did he calculate the effect he made? Was he a toady? No. He had a fund of natural affection, amiable feelings, and the readiness to show them: a noticeable power to make people respond in the same way.

Sukey stood in Rust's the milliners, in the market-place in Norwich, where she had been purchasing for herself a new, very grown-up summer hat. Now she was looking for presents for the family. An array of large coloured jars contained lavender-water, Hungary-water, orange-flower water, rose-water, milk of roses. The children had best have Warren's original British teeth-powder, and a new brush each. Or Papa might well like some Warren's royal opiate for his teeth, which often ached. Fine lip-salve would be useful for everybody, and sweet almond soap at one shilling. How grand a powder-engine would be, but impossible to carry and much too expensive! And Papa did not use powder nor wig. Susannah was turned fifteen, she was going home for good now to look after Papa and the children; to help teach Ann, to care for Edmund and Suckling and mother Kitty. The boys would be home for their holiday, Maurice would come from London, there would be hay-making, and fruit-picking and harvest. She considered herself quite grown-up and though she would miss all the girls, to the dearest of whom she had promised eternal friendship, she had no sense of regret: to this good-humoured modest country girl the parsonage in summer seemed full of pleasures.

That summer, shortly after the children's arrival home, Edmund Nelson had news of the death of old Mrs Henley at her house in St Andrew's Street where she and her daughters had welcomed the boys so kindly from the Norwich school. Horace had an immediate memory of the pink-cheeked, smiling old lady upon her sofa, laughing quietly at his mimicry of Mr Simonds. She was ninety-six. The rector hoped the Misses Henley had been properly looked to.

That summer too, cousin John Turner had a visit from a gentleman named Mr Arthur Young, who had advertised his coming as 'The Farmer's Tour through England'. Sir John gave him details of the common husbandry around Warham and of his own experiments. Mr Young was duly impressed with Sir John's draining of his marsh: no sooner was the sea shut out, than the old creek was full of very fine fresh water, making acres of good grazing land. Sir John had for years cultivated sainfoin for fodder, and, more recently, lucerne, as summer feed for his horses. He had grown osiers on his marshland, and his use of sea ooze as manure Mr Young thought a brilliant device, proved by experiment. He declared that Sir John kept his land as clean as a garden. But he had his complaints: why could not these farmers long wedded to their turnips grow some carrots, so suitable to the sandy tracts? And why would they not learn to pleach their hedges? And why would they persist in ploughing in their stubble instead of chopping it for use as litter? Their breed of sheep he found contemptible but their cattle ('the little mongrel Norfolk sort') were excellent for the dairy. Sir John laughed heartily, recounting all this to Sir Mordaunt Martin at Creake, where he had gone to look at Sir Mordaunt's new crop of lucerne.

Young Horatio, his cheeks whipped with wind, felt for the first time the hull of a fishing boat answering to his hands upon the tiller: for a few seconds he held her, before the fisherman's brown hands came down again on his. 'She be too heavy for the likes of yew, bor.' How he longed to be the dashing Captain Fairlie of the Hector Cutter, off Yarmouth, whose flair in the recovering of brandy, Geneva and tea were heroic! Or should he speak to Charles Boyles' papa about becoming a riding officer? But he would of the two rather ride a ship than a horse.

Horace awoke puzzled in mid-afternoon in a room he did not know. It was not the dormitory at school; it was not the room he shared with William in the parsonage at home. There was sunlight in the window. His head still ached, his ear ached, his mouth was dry, his throat sore, he was very thirsty. Now he remembered: there was measles, several boys had it. Mrs Jones had said:

'Oh yes young Nelson, you were bound to take it, were not you, poor boy. What a very great pity, you returned so well after the vacation.' As if it were his fault that he was struck.

And Horatio had joined the latest batch of cases in a room hired in the parish clerk's house in the town, where the parish clerk's daughter, Mistress Gaze, was tending them. It was early August, not a happy time to have the measles.

Mrs Jones had been in a perfect panic at the first rash-covered, feverish boy for it could so easily be the rash that presaged the smallpox. But it was the measles: Mrs Jones soon had several invalids, quite as many as she had room for and could look after, with the help of extra girls and a nursing woman from the town.

The governors were appealed to by Mr Jones: what was he to do if the epidemic spread? Where was he to put extra boys? How could he stem the disease? He could not have the sufferers in with the healthy. His space was filled to capacity and his wife could do no more. A special meeting of the governors was called quickly and it was suggested that what was needed was a place within the grounds but without the house: what about that loft chamber above the stable? It ran the whole length above the muck bynn end as well: it could be emptied of hay, cleaned, aired and made ready with beds in an hour or two: indeed, said the enthusiastic purveyor of this plan, the hay could well make good palliasses for the boys and there was a window at the stable end to let in the blessed sunshine.

'And who,' said Mrs Jones, apprised of the plan by her husband, 'is going to traipse up and down that perpendicular loft ladder carrying water, possets, food, slops and other things? Not I, nor my girls, nor Goody Purvis.'

'I suppose that a new stairway up, safer, might be made,' said the master doubtfully. He himself hesitated to put his patrons' children over a smelling muck bin in August.

'And how long will that take, pray?'

'A day or two I suppose.'

'Means must be found now for any new cases to be looked to. Rooms must be hired, Mr Jones, if need be, in the town,' said she. 'Why, tomorrow there may be three more.'

Horatio was amongst the next cases. They were hurried to Mr Gaze's quite near at hand. He was not a rich man, he was glad to let rooms, and his wife and daughter were prepared to nurse the boys.

Horace now heaved himself up, blinking, and looked round. The occupants of the other beds still slept.

'Well, you've had a good long sleep, after that bad night last night. Do you feel better, my boy?' said young Mistress Gaze in a whisper.

Horatio smiled and nodded, deciding that he did.

'Are you hungry for a little dinner now?'

'Yes if you please, I think so.'

She brought him broth and some bread and sat by him while he ate it. She was a kindly young woman, and gentle. As he grew better, Miss Gaze and Horatio had long talks, when she was at liberty: he was more talkative than the other boys, an eager boy full of questions and grateful for all that she and her mother did. He would tell her about his family, and his dearest mamma who had died not long since, and his brother in London and his hero uncle in the navy; and she would tell him of the past happier days of her family, how they had lived at Bacton Abbey and how in the dreadful summer and autumn of 1758 the cattle began dying in this plague that strikes cattle and her papa lost all his beasts and was ruined.

'It was the year I was born,' exclaimed Horace.

'So 'twas then, if you are twelve.'

'I am just about to be,' said he. 'To be about to be, the gerund in Latin. I'll wager you don't know that, Mistress Gaze,' he chirped.

'No, I know no Latin,' said she laughing at him. 'Here, I brought you an old *Norfolk Chronicle*, you say you are a newspaper boy!'

'Oh thank you,' Horace said, falling upon the county paper with gusto. There was a new song greatly to his taste in this issue. He read it once, twice, several times. It appealed to his interest in seamen, his just dawning notions of romance. Yet he was aware it had some hidden meaning he knew not of. He must remember to ask Papa.

> Ye Captains and Admirals, mighty and brave,
> Who rear Britain's standard, and traverse her wave
> That each cruize may prove glorious, be sure you take care
> To carry a lock of her *dear little hair.*
>
> Your future High Admiral bids you do this,
> As something to play with, and something to kiss;
> Tho' his H -s expressly does not tell where,
> He cropt this sweet lock of her *dear little hair.*
>
> This lock was the dearest that ever was found
> No less did it cost him than ten thousand pound:
> Such a circumstance surely may serve to declare,
> Its right to the title of *DEAR little hair.*

(Mistress Gaze could have told him: the King's youngest brother had pursued Lord Grosvenor's wife and it was to cost this large sum, and more, in damages.) She always remembered Horatio's name when she had long since forgotten all the others.

The school trustees, meeting on the twenty-first of August at the King's Arms and partaking of their usual dinner at their founder's expense, discussed the matter of the so-called infirmary and decided to let it lie. The epidemic seemed over, no urgent need for a large sick-room was found.

Papa wrote that if Horace needed to, he should come home for a week or so to get strong. So Horatio found himself with two precious weeks of liberty in August which he spent largely upon the foreshore at Burnham, and which made his return to school the harder to bear. Papa gave him a smooth, deep wooden pencil-box with a sliding lid about seven inches long, made for him by Mr Dent. It was plain but serviceable. Horace loved it at once and vowed he should always keep it.

Chapter Twenty-three

'...the disturbance with Spain relative to the Falkland Islands...'

'Someone should undoubtedly go and relieve the master of some of those excellent pears,' remarked Paul Johnson (a large and forward boy for his eleven years) looking from the bedroom window in his night-shirt upon the dusk of a September evening. 'The hour is ripe.'

'You mean the pears are ripe,' some junior piped.

'Two people,' went on Paul ignoring him, 'cannot possibly with safety eat all those pears. It would be a kindness to take some.'

More boys gathered at the window. There was a prime view of the master's pear-tree from this window and the boys had watched the ripening of a handsome crop with increasing envy. Somebody had espied Mr Jones one evening gently handling a yellowing pear. Dessert pears, as everybody knows, must be plucked at precisely the right moment.

'But you must open the gate, it will click, he will be sleeping on the watch for any sound,' protested William Nelson.

'Why, just push through the hedge the lower end, there's a thin patch there,' said somebody well acquainted with the ins and outs of the master's garden.

'But the main trouble is the *door!* The door you goose, the house and back doors are locked and bolted!'

'The window, this window!' William Bulwer said, joining them.

'In full view of the Jones's bedroom?' asked Nat Clarke.

'It must be dark, wait till they are abed. We shall see the candle extinguished!'

'Then who jumps from the window?' demanded Bulwer.

'I might easily jump from this window,' said Paul, 'but how could I get back?'

'A sheet, or two sheets! Tied together. We can let you down and pull you up!' Bulwer exclaimed.

'And if the sheets tear?' Paul pursued.

'Mrs Jones will be angry at her sheets torn,' piped Charles Mann.

'Mr Jones will be far more angered at his pears gone. He'll half kill us!' Nat Clarke said.

'He cannot kill us if he knows not who did it. We must swear on oath to say nothing,' stated William Bulwer.

'Then who is to go?' said Johnson after a pause. 'It must be someone light: I should break any sheets and my neck as well,' he confessed.

' So should I,' said Nelson major who had no desire whatever to go.

'I durstn't,' admitted Charles Mann sleepily, afraid lest his small stature should single him out for the job.

'What goes on?' asked Nelson minor who had just appeared. 'What are you all looking at?'

'The pears, we're debating a raid on old Jones's pears. We're all too cowardly to go,' said angry William Bulwer, trying to nerve himself for the adventure.

'I'll *go,*' said Horace at once without thought. 'How am I to get down? It is something of a jump but I might hazard it,' he said peering out of the window.

'Sheets, we'll make them ready. Come on,' Bulwer said eagerly.

'What am I to carry them all in,' Horatio deliberated, dressing himself quickly again in his shirt and breeches. 'I cannot hold on to many pears all loose.'

'A pillow-case!' said Bulwer, who was now regretting it was not he who was to go and was raiding his own bed and Johnson's for sheets.

'Capital, have mine,' said Paul.

'I know how to knot sheets…' Bulwer shouted, already at the task.

'Just see to it you knot them correctly if you please. I have no wish to break my crown,' Horace called.

'Hush, such a din, quiet everybody. It's of no use to go until their light is out. We have hours to wait. We'd best go to bed,' young Johnson ordered.

'Then we shall all fall asleep.'

'I shan't fall asleep,' Horace announced. He was in a fever of excitement to be off, to achieve the goal and be back again. He strode up and down restlessly.

'Sit still and wait. I'll watch at the window. They must needs *both* be abed. The parlour lamp is still lit.'

It was a good half-hour before Paul announced that all was dark and quiet. The window was slid up and Horatio prepared to descend. At this moment the renewed movement brought in a deputation from next door. Here was a dilemma. They must be told of the plan and sworn to secrecy too. They were also promised some of the rewards.

Halfway down the wall, Horace kicked himself clear with his toes, let go the sheet and jumped. He landed lightly, picked himself up, and waved to his companions. Once inside the garden, his feet upon grass, he hurried for the pear tree. He could see little and could reach less. He must climb. He must take back a goodly number for fifty boys or more. He stood on an old seat, pulled himself up to the crutch of the tree, and out upon a branch. Feeling, feeling between the crisp, cold leaves, he found one pear after another. One or two dropped, most were silently captured, lifted up, detached, put into his pillow-case which one hand must hold, the hand which balanced him. The sack grew heavier and heavier as he picked and picked in a frenzy of speed and success. Now it was so heavy, so unruly, the pears rolled as if alive. There was nothing for it but to let it fall on to the grass. The pears fell with a thump, but no noise of alarm followed. He made his own way down and added more pears to his sack from the other side. Not many of Mr Jones's pears were left when Nelson minor had finished. A white thing dangled from the window looking like a body in a winding sheet. His fellows had employed the tedium of the wait in tying the sheets up to make a loop, a kind of bosun's chair.

'Sit in it,' somebody hissed.

Horace did as he was told, his free hand clutching the sheet, the pears clutched by the other hand upon his restricted lap. He was jerked upwards, his body bumping and scraping against the wall. At the window ledge he was grabbed by many hands, relieved of the pears, hauled inside. Bravos and huzzahs were whispered at him from all around. By the light of a candle the pears were shared between the eager boys, and a silence broken by juicy munching followed. Horace asked none for himself, indeed could not be rid of them fast enough. He was, now the deed was over and the acclamations received, impressed with the magnitude of his crime, and hoped to mitigate it a little by not partaking of the profit.

'Here come on, here's a splendid one, do not you eat one, Horace?' Bulwer said nudging him.

'No thank you,' said Horatio somewhat priggishly climbing into bed. 'I only took them because no one else would.'

'I say, have you cold feet, Horatio?' asked Paul through a mouthful of pear.

'Well it is stealing,' said Bulwer stoutly, who by now knew Horatio pretty well. 'He has a very tender conscience has Nelson mi. We shall not tell, we have all sworn!'

'That makes no difference,' said Horace into the bedclothes.

Silence fell. The sheets were unknotted, the stained pillow-case hidden, the candle extinguished, and all were in bed and asleep long before calmness came to Horatio.

What on earth would Papa think? He was a common thief! People were beaten in the market-place for less, for stealing a spoon! How ashamed his father would be if he were sent away from school in disgrace! He did not mind about getting a beating, but he minded disgracing the family. And although his school mates had sworn not to tell, who knew, who was proof against Mr Jones's anger, Mr Jones's guile? He might get the truth from someone, some toady or coward. Mr Jones might even ask each boy separately! How was he, Horatio Nelson, to add a lie to his thieving? Would he not show by his face that he was guilty? Would he not blush, or go pale? How was he to remain unmoved, to conceal his guilt? How was he *not* to confess? But was he so *very* guilty? He had eaten none of the pears, he had simply taken them because all the rest were afraid. They had suggested it, he had not thought of taking the pears. (He hurried over this lest he should realise that it was not strictly fair.) Very well then, he was not guilty in the true sense he told himself, it was as if someone else, not he, had done it. He was not a thief or a liar, he could not be, wrong acts were beneath him. At last he fell asleep.

Mr Jones thundered, he raged, he resorted to the most searing sarcasm, he persuaded, he wheedled, the intonations of his excited Welsh tongue filled the schoolroom for many minutes. Not a countenance changed, not a glance was passed. He even offered a reward to the boy who would tell, since the thief himself was so hardened a scoundrel as not to confess. Even at this, in the solidarity of his school mates Horace remained unmoved. It was not he, someone else had climbed and picked that tree. What was Mr Jones saying? A reward of *two guineas!* Two guineas? Had they heard aright? What could not a boy do with two guineas? But no sign of their longing was shown, their faces remained impassive. Mr Jones had thought he was safe to offer a substantial sum: and so he was, he would have no need to expend it. Now he would impose a heavy corporate burden and punishment upon them: they should lose two half-holidays, they should do extra Greek; they would have no need of ale, having eaten his pears, they should have water. These should be at once remitted when the culprit stood forth or some loyal boy told the truth.

Alas for Mr Jones, their loyalty was previously engaged: and the culprit had taken an early lesson in evading the torments of his lively conscience.

Mr Hepworth had gone at midsummer to Wymondham and in his place had come a young married man, one of his local acquaintances, Mr James North, as usher and to teach mathematics. While his anger lasted, Mr Jones affected a wounded coldness with his boys, and sent all special commands and communications to them through this Mr North, who was easy and pleasant enough, though had neither the intellect nor the command of Mr Hepworth. Mr Jones's coolness excepted Thomas Taylor who (perhaps fortunately for both himself and Horatio) had been at home in Norwich at the time of the pear-stealing following a late harsh attack of the measles. Had he been here, Mr Jones told him, such a disgraceful occurrence would never have happened: but if he ever learnt the culprit, no doubt he would enlighten his friend. Thus appealed to as his master's friend, poor Thomas announced to his school-mates at the earliest opportunity that he must on no account be told who stole the pears or he might find himself obliged to divulge it. The secret was kept. Little by little Mr Jones's manner returned to its usual brisk forbearance tempered with bouts of inspiring eagerness.

'Now then young gentlemen,' said he one day in October, twirling the globe with his hands, 'who amongst you can tell me where lie Falkland's Islands?'

Nobody knew: as indeed how should they, these remote Isles being only occasionally before the public eye.

'You may gather round and I will show you,' said he.

Horace was first at the globe, forgetting in his eager curiosity that he had lately avoided putting himself in a position to meet his master's eyes at close quarters. Mr Jones pointed out the small group of islands lying off the curved foot of South America.

'Who can tell me what is our present quarrel concerning these islands?' he went on.

'The Spaniards have captured our station there, if you please sir,' said Paul who had been told this by his father.

'So they have. We who have had a post at Port Egmont for years, have been forcibly driven out by an overwhelming body of Spaniards from South America! What must we do?'

'Send a force at once to recapture it!' announced William Bulwer.

'Quite so, but what if the Spaniards engage and our navy is dwindled to such meagre proportions that we are in no position to fight sea-battles and re-take stations? As so it is, we are told.'

'Build ships, sir!' Horace said.

'Enlarge the navy, find more seamen!' said Nat Clarke.

'My papa told me the navy has been let run down in a shocking manner since the end of the last war, sir,' stated Paul. There had been much criticism by the opposition of the neglect of the navy by Lord North's ministry. It was difficult to know the truth. Horatio reflected that his Uncle Suckling had been on half-pay for years.

'Such is the case, we are told. Few ships and fewer seamen. How are we to keep our colonies, protect our trade, enlarge our empire, put down those who insult us and seize back our possessions without ships, young gentlemen, ships and sailors? However, this is not my concern but the King's and government's. What I wish you to note is the importance of the position of these remote islands in the circumnavigation of the world, and as a port for British traders in the South Seas. Only take the trouble to read the papers, boys, and you will see how this particular quarrel unfolds. The King asks for seamen, the government protests to Spain, it is touch and go but we shall be at war with that arrogant country before we know it: unless a show of arms be enough to put them down.'

Returning to his desk, Horace was thoughtful. Did the King truly ask for seamen? At the first possible opportunity he made for the parlour, found the papers, and settled himself to discover what more he could about the quarrel over the Falkland Islands. Here was a paper, the oldest, dated the twenty-ninth of September, his birthday! His eye fell at once upon the first important item it contained, a proclamation by the King of September the nineteenth. The King, in order 'to give all due encouragement to all such seamen who shall voluntarily enter themselves into our service...' was offering, it appeared, a royal bounty of thirty shillings to each seaman. They must not be above fifty or under twenty, they must offer before the twenty-first of October (which was Uncle Maurice's day, their festival day: with what a strange shock the familiar dates struck him to the heart!) And ordinary seamen were to get twenty shillings each man. They were not to leave one ship and collect their bounty twice by joining another. Horatio fetched a deep sigh. If he were but twenty, would he not run to join the King's service? By the time he was twenty, it would all be over. Besides, Papa and Uncle Maurice would not let him go as a seaman, he must be a midshipman. The report concerning the Falkland Islands told how two Spanish frigates which arrived at Port Egmont had pretended to be surprised at finding the English and insisted they should evacuate the island. Captain Hunt had refused: upon which the Spanish landed, took possession and after a humiliating delay forced the English to sail home. The news had come in earlier in the summer: now the *Favourite* sloop of war was arrived, on the twenty-second of September, saying she had been permitted to come home and bring off the people upon condition that they should not serve against Spain if a war ensued. What the newspaper did not make clear was that the Spanish attack was an answer to a peremptory British demand the year before that the Spaniards should leave the Falkland Islands, which were the possessions of King George III.

'Our claim to the island,' read Horatio, his soul raging at the insolence of Spain 'is founded upon its having been discovered by one

Falkland, a native of our country.' Horatio never questioned the truth of this statement. 'The claim of the Spaniards to it is founded upon their having all the neighbouring continent, and a positive assertion of their own that we have no right in those seas.'

There was nobody to explain to a schoolboy the dubious rights of the case, nor to show him how the smaller quarrel was part of a larger, between Britain and the allied Bourbon powers of France and Spain. Since the Spaniards had been upon the islands since 1766, having had the post handed to them by the French, and since the French had established this post even earlier than the British had theirs (in 1764 and unknown to the French), the sovereignty of the islands was a matter of some complexity.

It was by no means obvious that they were the possessions of the British King: and the governor of Buenos Aires, who had been given permission two years since to displace the British station could he find it, had acted upon this, sending a Spanish force large enough to overwhelm the British. During that summer the ministers had played for time, for the British navy was not ready for war: and in any event Lord North hoped always for settlement. Like most other Britons he thought a show of arms enough, a threat of naval force sufficient to shake Spain.

And now Horace sat in the parlour at North Walsham Academy reading about the disturbance concerning the Falkland Isles: ten Spanish sail of the line and between three and four thousand troops were hovering about Jamaica and the Leeward Islands: such was the intelligence transmitted near three months since by Commodore Forrest a few days before his death. Commodore Forrest? Memories of Uncle Maurice and Cap François stirred in Horatio. 'Captain Forrest of the *Augusta*': the same who had led his uncle's squadron. So he was dead. From this he passed on to scan a list of sail of the line in the British Navy and the number of their guns. There was also an item which disturbed him since his conscience had been made aware of it by older school-fellows: warrants were being issued for the impressing of seamen, to whom the writer referred as 'stout, idle fellows'. The *Lynx* man-of-war had tried to press the people of the *Duke of Richmond* East Indiaman lying at Gravesend; but the people had seized the arms chest and resisted, one being killed, several wounded. The man-of-war had been forced to sheer off; the Lord Mayor was doing his utmost to resist pressing in the city. A great number of sailors had gone on shore from a fleet of colliers arriving in Yarmouth. They had refused to navigate ships for London because of the fear of pressing: they had become landsmen and tramped through Beccles and Bungay, and by the walls of Norwich, in their way to the northward.

The next week's paper continued to fan the flames of public rage over the affront to the British by Spain. Its leader had indeed caused Edmund Nelson to laugh aloud as he sat in his study at Burnham Thorpe while Kitty and Suckling crawled about the floor. 'The sword of war,' the rector read, 'like the sword of Damocles, hangs, we are told, as it were by a horse-hair.'

'Papa! Papa,' worried little Kitty at his knee, 'what are you laughing about?' and she shook him furiously.

But this was impossible of explanation.

The King went a step further and made a proclamation on October the twentieth for all seafaring men in foreign service to come home; he also offered rewards to those who would tell of seamen secreting themselves. This was uneasy, Horatio could well imagine what Mr Booty would have thought of *this*. And Mr John Wilkes (who had lately been given the Freedom of King's Lynn by his supporters there) was in no doubt about it: he had written an open letter declaring the opinion of the great majority of the common people, that the pressing of seamen was detestable. A citizen bearing the historic name of Walter Raleigh, junior, answered him: detestable it might be, but would Mr Wilkes think of some other way of manning the navy in an emergency? All the seaports of Britain did what they could: Lynn declared itself ready to add one guinea to the King's Bounty, to every seaman entering the service at that port. The City of London offered more, as befitted its wealth: every able seaman, forty shillings, every ordinary seaman, twenty. Bristol, Montrose, Edinburgh, Aberdeen, Campbeltown followed.

Horatio wrote to his papa that it was a great pity that he was not older, so that he could go to His Majesty's aid, and join the navy where he thought he would do more good than at school. Papa wrote back that he must wait a while yet; why, he was only just struck twelve (like the clock in the fairy-tale): and what his Majesty wanted was trained seamen, not raw boys. Horatio must attend to his lessons, or even Ann would out-do him, who read very well. He told his boys, too, that the reverend Doctor John Gardiner of Great Massingham had died (the much abused father of 'Dick Merryfellow') and was borne to his grave in the chancel supported by Horace's godpapa, Dr Hamond, and by their papa's reverend cousins, Mr William of Hillington, and Mr Edmund Nelson of Congham (amongst others): and their own papa was not of the number for he was neither grand enough nor strong enough. He was suffering, he was sorry to say, from a lingering sore chest and cough, which the cold and wet had done no good to.

As December drew on, all the talk was still of the possibility of war. In the *London Gazette* the King made a further proclamation (which the provincial papers repeated) to encourage land-men to enter themselves on board His Majesty's ships of war. Messages travelled back and forth from Madrid: the Spanish ambassador declared himself to be unable to give any answer to Lord North in less than a month, when he should have received further dispatches from his court. Lord Weymouth declared publicly that there would be no war (while secretly thinking the opposite); Lord Chatham disagreed, asserting that Britain should strike a blow first. Lists of the fleets for West India and the Mediterranean were published, with their commanders. Someone put about an inflammatory tale that three thousand British seamen had been taken by the Spaniards out of our merchant ships into slavery, upon the coast of Africa. The Watermen's Company were called upon to furnish five hundred men for the navy, the admiralty was commandeering ships, money was being raised for ship building and repairs, more and more seamen were moved for. Lord Chatham began to expatiate largely one day in the Lords upon the miserable situation of our fleet for a war, when a clamour immediately ensued which drowned his oratory. Upon which he exclaimed: 'If we are not to have the freedom of speech, but the ministerial majority are to load us with hisses and contumely, I have no further business here.' And hobbled out, seventy glorious peers in his suite.

William and Horatio returned home for their Christmas vacation to find Sukey still cheerfully in charge, Nanny a reserved young miss of ten, Edmund and Suckling hardened to the schoolboys' life in Burnham, baby Kitty a baby no longer but nearly four, walking, talking, with a finger in every pie: and their papa not very well. The rector had not thrown off his persistent cough and wheezing chest, the wet, cold autumn had worsened it. On the Wednesday after the boys arrived home, the nineteenth of December, a furious storm and gale with drenchings of rain again hit the country, and Norwich and the Isle of Ely, flooded the previous month, went under once more. Christmas passed in misery for many homeless people, despite the money collected for the flood victims. The rector of Burnham Thorpe struggled through his services, every breath a cold discomfort, often a pain.

'We cannot cure this chest,' said Mr Kerrich called in afterwards, 'in this foul climate. Can you not rest a few days, then betake yourself somewhere warmer? Bath, now: can you get to Bath, sir?'

Anxious about his children but more anxious about his symptoms, Mr Nelson did as he was told. Towards the end of the year he set off for London where his eldest son Maurice would succour him, and Bath.

The parsonage seemed rudderless without him. William knew not what to do without his books and devoted himself to helping Peter outside; the small boys quarrelled, Kitty pined and wailed and must be comforted by a harassed Sukey or a severe little Ann; Horatio (the weather being too bad for his usual jaunts to the harbour) had recourse to his father's study where he found comfort in sitting in Papa's chair, his feet upon Papa's footstool, reading Papa's papers. This one was dated December the fifteenth, 1770, the day they came home from school. It contained a letter from the port of Chatham dated December sixth, giving lists of all the ships lying in ordinary, as well as all that were commissioned, building and fitting out there. There was but one first-rate, the *Victory:* she was of one hundred guns. Horace read through the list, savouring their names. *Triumph* he liked, and *Resolution* and *Revenge* and *Panther.* Christmas and Papa's illness had put the war business out of his head. Here were the ships from the list which were already commissioned. There were only five so far. Slowly, he read their names and the names of their captains –

Barfleur	of 90 guns	Commodore Hill
Egmont	of 74	Captain Whitwell
Buckingham	of 70	Captain Hempenfelt
Orford	of 70	Captain Strachon

The last was called by an awkward name that he could not easily read and suspected of being French, *Raisonnable,* 64 guns: and with a shock which went through him like a hot wave, Horace saw that her captain's name was Suckling. Captain Suckling, *Uncle Maurice!* He read on, disregarding for the moment his sense of shock and its meaning. Chatham yard was astir with activity. 'Our artificers,' he read, 'work two tides a day extra each; except the sailmakers who work three quarters of a day extra; rope makers work half a day extra; and the Blacksmiths work a quarter of a day extra.'

Horatio's mind faced the reason for his shock of excitement, almost of apprehension. Uncle Maurice was commissioned to this ship (whose name was so awkward): Uncle Maurice could take him to sea even at his age if he would, as a midshipman. The whole agitation of the autumn, the impending war, the King's proclamation published upon his birthday, the pressing of men, the building of ships, all seemed to lead up simply and clearly to this. *This* was his chance, he must act upon this. He sat quietly for longer than he realised, thinking of it.

CHAPTER TWENTY-FOUR

'I should like to go with Uncle Maurice to sea.'

If only, if only he had seen this, Horatio thought, before Papa was gone! How strange that Papa himself had not noticed it, it proved his feeling unwell: they liked news of Uncle Maurice, Mamma had always welcomed it and rejoiced. (Or had he seen it and said nothing?) They must write to Papa and he must write to Uncle Maurice or it might be too late. Who knew when Uncle Maurice might leave Chatham in this ship. This account was three weeks old. Or he might have sufficient midshipmen without Horatio. The idea having struck him with such force, Horace could not bear to wait or to be deterred. Besides, what was the use of returning to school next term if he were to go to sea? He would like this, he was yearning for change and adventure. He leapt out of Papa's chair, ran through the parlour, across the hall and the dining room, the doors banging behind him. He burst into the kitchen, waving the paper.

'Sukey! William! Mary, where's Sukey?'

'I'm here,' said she, coming in from the pantry. 'What's the matter?'

Horace ran to the back door and bellowed into the garden. 'William! Come here, pray come here, brother William! There is something in the paper you must hear!'

William came at once, inspired by Horace's urgent tone.

'Look here, read this! Read the list of ships commissioned. Read it out to Sukey and the others!'

William was not slow in doing so: then thinking some celebration called for, he waved the paper and danced a ponderous jig.

'Uncle Maurice! Commissioned to a ship! Huzzah!' Uncle Maurice had been on half-pay since long before Mamma had died.

Sukey clapped her hands. 'How pleased Mamma would be!' she said.

Ann clenched her hands beneath her chin and jumped. The small boys ran in from the yard demanding to know what was the excitement. Susannah caught sight of Horatio standing still and quiet, his eyes very bright, his cheeks flushed, his lip stuck out. He saw her looking at him.

'I must go!' he burst out. 'I must go with Uncle Maurice to sea! My father has often said he promised to look to one of us when Mamma died. This is the chance, now! Do, brother William, write to my father at Bath and tell him I should like to go with Uncle Maurice to sea!'

'Horace!' Sukey exclaimed stricken. 'You are too young, you cannot! And you are not very strong or big! Oh, what would Mamma say!'

'Mamma? Mamma would be glad! Mamma always said she would like one of us to follow my Uncle Maurice, I remember her saying it! Oh pray William, write for me!'

'But why cannot you write for yourself?' William asked. He had been struck silent at Horace's suggestion.

'You write better and more easily than I. Also,' Horace hesitated: 'I have wrote to Papa before about this.'

'And what was his reply?' Susannah asked.

'That I must stay at school and mind my lessons until I am older. But then it may be too late, the war may be over, Uncle Maurice ashore again!'

'The war has not yet begun,' William objected. He was not at all sure that he wanted Horatio stealing a march on him, going off into the navy. Horatio was younger than he was.

'You can persuade Papa, William. You can tell him I do not much excel at school. You know I don't. And only think, Papa is ill. It will be better for him that another of us should be away and looked after!'

'Oh master Horace,' Mary burst out unable to help herself. 'Bless your little heart, you be too young and so often sickly!'

'But Mary I long to go, it may make me stronger! My mother used to say a life at sea would make or mar a man!'

Mary shook her head but did not smile. She was still little more than a girl herself.

'After all I am twelve, I am very nearly grown-up and a man!'

There was silence for a minute while Sukey settled to peel the spongy apples she had brought from the store room: and William wondered how Horace could like to go to sea and to the wars rather than to stay peacefully at school. Sukey was thinking of what Mamma might do.

'Horace,' she said at last, 'have you long felt like this, have you had it in your mind to go to sea when you grew up for some time?'

Faced with this question, Horatio reflected: and it seemed to him that there had never been a time when he had not felt the sea pulling him. But his knowing about it had begun that autumn, awoken by opportunity: the threat of war, the King's call and now Uncle Maurice having a ship. He tried to explain all this to Susannah. Her mother, she thought, would have applauded him, encouraged him, even while she wept to lose him.

'William,' she said, 'since Horace knows so well what he wishes to do, and since it is good and brave of him to think of assisting Papa in this way, and since my mother would be proud of him, go you to the study with him and write to my father! You have missed today's post but it will go on Monday,' she finished, ever practical.

William jumped up, waved his arms and shouted: 'Huzzah! Horace shall go to sea, we shall have an admiral in the family! I shall be a bishop, Horatio shall be an admiral! Come Horace, let us be about composing this letter now, as old Jones would say.'

Edmund Nelson could scarcely believe it, but the magic which pertained to Bath in the minds of all fashionable people, and which he had secretly tended to ridicule, seemed to be having its effect. The journey to London had tired him greatly and he had scarcely been easy to occupy his son's narrow bed while that good son cheerfully stretched upon the floor. Good, patient Maurice, now eighteen and in a room of his own; perhaps soon he would earn more, better himself, achieve more comfort. Yet he did not seem to put himself out or aspire to greater things. He had cared for his father famously, laid in food and wine at who knew what expense and had ready some particular warming posset for his chest. There his father had sat all of Sunday, answering Maurice's eager enquiries about the family and Burnham. Reaching Bath and finding his lodgings and his landlady all that they had been recommended to be by Mrs Poyntz, the rector relinquished all effort and found himself so weary that he entertained lowering thoughts of never seeing his family again. Yet the next morning when this gentler air blew upon his cheeks and he drew his breath more easily he began to admit the beneficence of the place. He would rest utterly for a few days, he would go neither to the pump room nor the assembly: he had no wish to see couples figuring, he had a positive fear of being quizzed by dowagers from behind fans, of being discovered to be widowed, of being thought to be melancholy and interesting enough to deserve attention. His cloth, alas, would not protect him.

Three years, it was now three years! He knew that this spell of ill-health was largely due to the griefs of these lonely years without his wife. But his life was now her children. He must recover quickly, that he could finish his task, and see them all established before he could join his beloved. There were seven more to set up in life somehow.

William's letter with the suggestion it contained was both a profound shock and an incitement. The shock did its work first. Horatio! To sea! His loving companionable spirited Horace to sea, so young! Why, he was so sickly with his fevers and his coughs, just as he himself had been: each year at school something had struck him, the ague, the measles.

Surely the rigours of life at sea would kill him, he would never survive them. The parson could never quite get over the notion that to send a boy to sea was a kind of punishment for misbehaviour or irregularity. There was his cousin William, Uncle Thomas's son, sent to Eton, did no good, packed off to sea. There was his own brother John, but he disappeared into the army, to be sure. Again and again one had heard of black sheep, sent to sea to be lost all sight of. It would break his heart.

Yet, yet: Horatio, in the strongest possible terms as written by his brother William, wished to go. William reported that Horace's masters at school did not put him in the top rank for scholarship, that he (William) was counted the better, that Horace longed to lead an active life (their papa smiled, thinking of the two boys concocting this letter together). That here was an opportunity: that Uncle Maurice had offered help: that he, Papa, was overwhelmed with them all needing support (William, his papa thought, had some eloquence already): that Horatio would be bitterly disappointed if the chance were lost. That their dearest mamma had ever hoped for one of them to follow their uncle.

Edmund Nelson knew it was all true. He could imagine Horace's impatient eagerness, it was no more than the natural consequence of his earlier remarks about serving the King. And when he was well in the summer, down by the Staithe, how bold and active and concerned he was with the ships and their gear. And Catherine? Catherine would be delighted, he heard the ringing tones of her voice full of love saying the boy's name and at the _well_-remembered sound tears flooded his eyes. He let the thought of her pleasure raise him up, stimulate him. He reflected upon Horace the midshipman for the rest of that day, and in the morning wrote to his brother-in-law.

Captain Suckling received Edmund Nelson's letter in the midst of his somewhat blind and baffling preparations for the fitting out of his ship. The business of the war was still all in the balance, rumours in London were strong on both counts, one knew not yet what to believe and he was no politician. However, there were all the usual steps concerning stores and men that a captain commissioned to a ship took, and upon these he was begun. Now came this letter from sister Catherine's husband about Horatio. He supposed that this was as good a time as any to fulfil his duty to his sister. But Horatio! Why, the poor boy was always ailing: never did he meet Maurice or hear from Burnham, but Horatio had been ill. In his general offer to help Edmund Nelson with one of the boys, he had never entertained thoughts of *Horatio.* Yet he now thought about him. He could always *remember* Horatio as he searched his mind for memories of his early visits. He seemed to see Horatio, rapt, following the tale of Cap François when he was barely more than a toddler. He had a sudden vision of a sharp, eager, flushed face at his sister's table. At her death, the poor boy had clung to him as it appeared for a kind of comfort. And it seemed that Horatio *wished* to go to sea. This was a great thing, if his heart were in it. And if he himself were to have no son, as now he had given up hope of, would it not be a pleasant circumstance to rear up a nephew in the service? If the boy survived at all, he might do well. They would be awaiting his reply. But he must see they faced the hazards and the hardships that were in store for a boy at sea, the rector must not put his boy into it unawares, nor must that boy come blind to the perils and the cost. He did not want a nephew who fell by the wayside. He composed a bluff, brusque letter (he was not an easy writer) which should put the matter plainly. They had time to change their minds.

When Mr Nelson received Captain Suckling's answer he was feeling much better and more than ready to travel. He had been two weeks away, his cough was gone, his chest cleared. His brother-in-law's acceptance of Horace was a further cure, despite its terms, for he could well imagine Horatio's pleasure. He felt almost excited himself at the idea of another bird about to fly, and he had already told Maurice in London of the day he hoped to travel. His first visit to Bath, however, had done him nothing but good and he thought of the town already with affection.

Maurice was quiet, hearing his father's news: his father almost wondered if he were envious. But he said:

'I hope, Papa, that he understands what he is in for?'

'I shall see that he does, to the best of my ability. At all events, there is to be no war they say. By the time he sees action he will be older and hardened.' For the news of a probable settlement with Spain was beginning to reach the papers.

'That is true. And I shall see you when you bring him to London?' Maurice's pale face lit up with pleasure at the thought.

'Most certainly. I hope perhaps your Uncle William may accommodate us.'

'Oh, yes! How soon will it be?'

'All seems uncertain, except that Horace is to go.'

'Bold Horatio!' Maurice said fondly.

Bold Horatio's impatience was consuming him by the time his father reached Burnham. He arrived in the afternoon one day, in time for dinner. Peter had been to fetch him, the children all bore him in with shouts and affection. Sukey had had Mary light the fire in the parlour, William took his cloak, Horace his bag, Mun his hat, little Kitty clung to his gaiters. He was tired but happy, he had spent the night before with Mr Pyle and Horace's god-mamma in Lynn, he had told them of the plan. Horatio watched his face eagerly in silence, received his kind smile, hoped, wondered, but knew he must not ask when a traveller was tired. Sukey brought Papa a glass of wine, relieved that he seemed so much better.

Edmund Nelson did not tantalise his son for long.

'My dear Horace, you need not tell me what is uppermost in *your* mind!'

'All our minds, Papa,' Susannah put in.

'Very well then, the answer is yes, Horace may go...'

Immediate uproar greeted the news, William cheered, Horace joined him, they jumped and roared together, Sukey and Ann laughed and clapped, even Edmund and Suckling showed their approval by butting their brother with their heads. Kitty sat in her father's lap, laughing. It was a family, a corporate triumph.

'But,' went on Papa, 'he is to ponder well, to weigh up the hardships, to realise the hazards. Fetch me my bag. So. Here is the letter. I will read it to you.'

Their father passed quickly over the usual courtesies which begin a letter and went on:

"What has poor Horace done, who is so weak, that he above all the rest should be sent to rough it out at sea? But let him come; and the first time we go into action, a cannon-ball may knock off his head, and provide for him at once."'

This sally was received in the jesting spirit in which it had been written, and drew roars of laughter from the boys. But Kitty, quite old enough to understand the words but not the mood, burst into tears.

'Not...knock off...Horace's head!' she roared in anguish.

'Hush, hush, Kitty-katty,' said Horace, well-pleased to play the hero. 'I'll not have my head knocked off. You'll see, I'll knock off the Spaniards' heads I promise you!'

The rest of the letter was read, the plans discussed, the settlement with Spain agreed to be no bad thing, the dates of his starting pestered for by Horatio: indeed, far from causing his son to reconsider in seriousness his dauntless notion, the rector saw that the letter had settled and inspired him. Dinner passed with an unwonted accompaniment of prattle on all sides: and Papa had not the heart to quell it. He surveyed his family with tenderness, hearing Horatio's boasts, William's taunts, Sukey's admonishments and flights of fancy with a sense of rich gratitude. He realised he felt well, he was happy, he was hopeful of his son's future, it was as if Mamma were beneficently here with them. William had found some horrifying tale with which he sought to terrify his brother, about the pressmen. This poor wretch, he related, dashed into a clock-maker's to escape the press-gang and the clock-maker hid him in a clock-case: but one of the gang saw his face peering out through the glass, and asked what that might be? It is a damned ugly dial-plate, let us look at the guts of it! And accordingly he opened it and conveyed the poor fellow on board the tender. But even this tale, which petrified Ann for days afterwards, did not dismay her brother. Until William asked him how he would like it, if he were set to press poor wretches to the ships?

'I own I should not care for that occupation,' said Horatio, suddenly serious.

'Let us pray you will never be enjoined to do it, my boy,' Papa said.

After all this, Uncle Maurice's next letter came as a shocking anti-climax, saying that as the *Raisonnable* was not yet ready for sea, it were better for Horace to return to school and wait till he were sent for. In vain Horatio pleaded: his father knew the value of discipline. However stern he might be, a boy at home would be more lax than a boy at school. No, Horace must go back with William; and William at least was pleased when the next Saturday, the nineteenth of January, a day that brought more news of the conciliation with Spain, they set out as usual together early in the morning.

Horatio soon sought out William Bulwer and told him of his future; in reality, he was already a midshipman! William's reception of his boast was not altogether what he had expected.

'Well, I would not be you for all the tea in China,' said the young man decidedly.

'Why not?' said Horatio, taken aback.

'Terrible things happen at sea,' William said. 'But perhaps you like the sea very much?'

'Yes, I do. Besides, I am going with my uncle.'

'That makes a difference I grant. You are to be an officer and not one of these poor pressed wretches we hear of.'

'They are not all pressed, the seamen, you know! Some choose it, they like it!'

'Well, I should not. Now if you had told me you went in the army, I might have envied you.'

'Is that what you will do, William?'

'I very well think I might. Yes. Battles! Shooting and charging and leading my men!'

'But I shall have battles! Sea-battles! Boom!' Horace roared, with a dim memory of Cap François. 'And I shall lead a line of ships!'

'You are looking ahead somewhat,' Bulwer remarked smiling, thinking how small Nelson minor looked to be a midshipman. But he was a plucky little fellow all the same. Either that, or he simply knew not what he was in for. A parson's family, William supposed, lived very quietly, knew very little of things of the world. That was it, he was what his lady Mamma would call unworldly.

So the news of Horatio's departure was soon round the school.

Horatio long remembered the unsettled temper of his last few weeks at school, of the fluctuations he suffered between excitement and apprehension, between hope and dread, caused not only by the opinions of his school-mates but by his own moods and feelings. The high-hearted determination of his decision in the early days must now battle with wild wonderings, fearful imaginings, and insidious second thoughts. When these depressed him on his own account he fell back upon the notion of his duty, instilled into them all from their earliest days by their father. His duty to help his father and his family was no small part of his plan. He wished now ardently upon grey February mornings to be away, to be started upon the task.

At last the ship of Horatio's fate caught the wind again. Papa wrote saying that he had informed Mr Jones that Peter would come for Horace very early in the morning of next Friday and that Horatio should be ready, his bag packed, his farewells taken. For his Uncle Maurice had written that his ship would be soon fitted. They would travel to London at once to Uncle William's house, so that Papa would have the few days necessary to fit him out with all he needed.

Horatio, stunned at first, soon became full of glee.

'There,' he said, putting his books away at the end of that week, 'I shall not need you, or you, or you again to be sure. But I shall take my notebooks and my pencil box, and this, and that...' and he began collecting up all those much loved oddments, of little use or none, which a schoolboy amasses. His friends gathered round him, caught up in his excitement, some wondering how he could be so pleased, whether it were courage or mere simplicity: many sorry to see him go and aware that they would miss him.

'You show every sign, Horace, of being delighted to leave us, I must say,' remarked Paul Johnson gloomily surveying his friend's busy activity.

'I have to confess I am,' Horatio answered laughing. 'I have waited about long enough, it has well nigh killed me!'

'All I can hope is that this desperate life you have chosen, Nelson mi, will come up to your fantastical expectations,' said Bulwer, who was beginning himself to feel severely tried by the inactivity of school life. 'At least you have the courage to act on your inclinations, you do not lack guts, to put it vulgarly my dear Horace.'

'I think he's not only brave but very dutiful,' put in Thomas Taylor quietly, for he had received a good deal of Horatio's confidence in the past weeks, 'and I wish him all the good in the world.'

'Hear, hear!'

'Certainly!'

'Three cheers for our brave midshipman, to launch him upon the waves!'

'Huzzah! Huzzah! Huzzah!'

'Rule Britannia, and so forth!'

All laughed, many pummelled the hero, who defended himself breathlessly. Despite their banter their farewells that evening were heartfelt and full of good will.

But it was brother William who took the departure the hardest. Horatio, wrapped up in his own eager plans and expectations, nerving himself to be full of anticipation and to feel no repining, had scarcely noted how glum and silent William had become. Now as they lay in bed, Horace's possessions all packed and only a few hours to go, poor William's sorrow emerged as complaint.

'Why am I to be left here, why am not I to be launched upon some exciting career as well? I might have gone to sea if you had not had the idea first, Horace, I am older than you, it would be more proper that I should be going!' he whined.

'But William, would you like to be going, would it please you to be going to sea?' Horace asked, startled. He was near enough to his brother to realise his sadness, he tried to imagine how it would feel to be left behind. He felt guilty not to have foreseen how William would feel.

William grunted.

'I might find it more agreeable than being left here,' he muttered. 'If we were going together now, how capital that would be! I shall miss you!' he whispered crossly. He was dimly aware of himself at school, bereft of the warmth both of Horace himself and of Horace's reflected popularity.

'Oh William I shall miss you too!' Horace answered with perfect truth. 'You never said you would find it agreeable, a sailor's life! How would you fare, climbing the rigging and roughing it at sea?'

'I cannot tell unless I try. I might like it very well,' his brother argued.

'But you have never wanted to climb trees much or come with me to Overy or go fishing with the men! You would miss your books, William. You are good at your books. You know you would like to go to Cambridge; you are going to be a lawyer or a bishop, brother, you have often said so!'

'But why could not I at least come home with you tomorrow, wish you God speed? Why must Papa decree I stay here?' William grumbled.

'No doubt Papa thinks you should not miss any lessons,' Horace said sagely. And unaware of the irony of the situation, he set about comforting his brother for his own imminent departure, who should himself (one would have supposed) have been in need of some comfort. William sniffed and argued and whined unwilling to be comforted, and at last fell asleep. Horatio slept little, wide-eyed with excitement and roused to sorrow by his brother's feelings. When he was awoken in the early hours, it seemed as if he had hardly slept at all. Ready to go, he hugged his brother and wished him goodbye. William clutched at him, still half-asleep.

'What is it? Are you gone? Is Peter here?'

'Not yet, but I am to have a little breakfast,' Horace whispered.

'Go you down, I shall come to see you off,' William said yawning.

Horatio doubted this. But sure enough, as he stood in the parlour listening to Mr Jones's formal good wishes, feeling Mrs Jones's kindly hand upon his shoulder, there was a fumbling at the door handle and in burst William in his dressing gown, come to see his brother away. William did not lack love for Horatio, though his love be still bound up with a kind of dependence upon him.

Almost at once came Peter's knock. The front door was flung open by the master, that door by which they had entered school together three years ago. An icy gust of morning air smelling of frost blew in, and Peter's shape was seen in the light of the lamp. Before Horatio went out into the cold dark morning, the two brothers hugged each other without words. William hurried back to his empty bed, dived beneath the blankets and wept upon his pillow.

CHAPTER TWENTY-FIVE

The House in Kentish Town

'There, my boy, look your last on the noble old South Gate of Lynn, for it may be some time before you see it,' Edmund Nelson said.

Horace was more impressed with his father's notion that he should be long away than with the antiquity of the gate in the wall.

'How long shall I be away this first time do you suppose, Papa?'

The rector was not insensible of his son's feelings. He laid his hand reassuringly upon his knee as he continued:

'The gate is medieval. It is handsome I think, do not you? As to when you will see it again, you must not take your papa's remarks too much to heart.' His kind eyes twinkled down at his son. The occasion had presented itself to him as dramatic, this beginning of a new epoch for Horatio, who had reached an age to be setting off for sea. But his fatherly instinct bade him minimise the drama. 'Midshipmen no doubt have their times of freedom like anybody else. And if you're to be in home waters awhile you may well be able to arrange to come home with Maurice, who knows!'

Horatio nodded, pleased, and sank back into his hard dusty corner. They sat close together to keep warm, for the weather continued cold and bleak. Sixteen hooves and the creaking of the wood and the complaining of the leather: two passengers were soon snoring, two more nodding. Papa and Horace chatted companionably for a long time. It was a journey Horatio would long remember.

'You will like to see the colleges, my boy. You have not been through Cambridge before?'

'No, Papa. I long to see it. But I had rather be going to sea than going to college,' he said with conviction.

His father was pleased at his determination.

'Since you know so well what you wish to do, I see no reason why you should not be highly successful,' he said. 'It is the putting of one's whole heart and mind into a thing which is required for success. Never forget it.'

'No Papa.' Horatio paused a minute before his next question which fell upon his father's ears as full of pathos. 'But do you suppose that I shall like it, Papa,' he wondered, 'shall I enjoy life at sea?' He sounded puzzled and uncertain.

'There will be times you will enjoy and times when you will be miserable. As with every man in every calling,' his father said slowly. 'If it is intolerable, you are young enough to abandon it. But out of your good heart you have taken this chance to help your father and your family. Is that not the case?'

Horace nodded soberly.

'Well then, you go to do your duty my good son, and that in itself will succour you in times when you like it not.'

Horatio most fervently believed this to be true.

'And perhaps, Papa, when I'm a captain I shall take prizes and make money and bring you all back riches,' he said.

'Money is not very important, one is better to be totally disregarding of money. Nevertheless,' he went on, 'it is a useful commodity and we shall all accept it with joy when you produce it. Never fear Horatio, the poor of Burnham may well live to bless you!'

Horace laughed, knowing he was twitted.

'But I hope I shall not ever have the task of pressing men,' he said next, 'for I could not bear it.'

'There is talk that they will soon recall all the press warrants, matters being adjusted between ourselves and Spain. But your uncle thinks they intend to keep ready a greater number of ships and seamen than of late, for which we should rejoice upon yours and his account.'

'Papa,' Horatio began after a sleepy pause, 'shall you miss me, do you suppose?'

'Yes, my boy, indeed I shall,' the parson said vigorously. 'Partings, you know, are amongst the sad things of life. And you are young to be going forth…And will your school-fellows miss *you*, my boy?' he went on, smiling.

Horatio looked up confidently. 'Yes. At all events, some said they would.'

'Then you are fortunate, are you not, to bear their good opinion. Too high a conceit of oneself is never a good thing.'

Horace nodded, chastened. 'Papa,' he remarked next with a transference of thought which his father noted with amusement, 'how does Mr Allott these days, is he still hammer and tongs against the college?'

'He sent you his heartfelt good wishes, by the way. There is much that is most loveable in him. But I fear he may be a ruined man if he goes on thus.'

'What is he about?'

'Why, the same. Fortified by becoming a bachelor of law last year, he has no intention of accepting arbitration as was suggested. He simply keeps the case dangling and the doctor in suspense. And meanwhile he pays not these dues which will mount up terrifyingly.'

'But Papa, do you not think right is on his side?'

'I am very much afraid not. But he is a splendidly active friend to your papa, in the arrangements concerning the refurbishing of Ulph. The roof is repaired. Thomas Thurlow is busy about the rotten window ledges, the floor, the new seats.'

'Good. And is Sutton destroyed?'

'Ah, Sutton has had its day. We have stripped off the chancel lead and sold it. The elements will now do the rest. Alas, for Sutton!'

'It is melancholy when a church goes into ruin.'

'It is, Horace. But there is not the money in a small parish like Sutton to build up so ruinous a church. We shall call Ulph Sutton-cum-Ulph, I think, to preserve the name. Building, you know, is an expensive business. We have not the whole country to draw upon, like the founders of the hospital in Norwich. I understand that even your schoolmaster Mr Jones was in the list, as well as all our friends and relations.'

'Good old Mr Jones,' Horace said flushing suddenly scarlet. (For with a twinge of horror he had remembered the pears.) 'Did you subscribe Papa?'

'Yes, I sent my humble guinea. Did I tell you that I heard my cousin William of Hillington has gained the rectories of Redeham and Strumpshaw? Worth five hundred, I believe. Unto him that hath shall be given,' Mr Nelson said with some irony. 'It is all a question of knowing the right people. Interest, Horatio, you will constantly meet with in the world. It is of great value when it is offered, as your Mother's good brothers have offered it to us. But I would be uneasy to have to seek it out. However, so the world goes on, so posts and pensions and parishes are distributed, I concede. By the by, I meant to tell you sooner. There was some idea his father told me of putting young Charles Boyles to sea as well.'

'Oh, he has always liked the sea!' Horace exclaimed, pleased. 'What do you think, Papa? Shall we be together?'

'I never heard the outcome. But you will know soon enough.'

'I should greatly like his company!'

In conversation and reminiscence, in sleep, even in dreams, the long day passed (Horace ran wildly along a dark quayside at Lynn with Mr Jones pursuing him, cane in hand). Nearing Ely, they saw the cathedrals twin towers rising up from the leaden fen, mysterious in silver rain. In Cambridge, Edmund showed his son Magdalen College and the bridge across the river Cam, St John's and Trinity and the gabled courts of Caius where he himself had lived, standing down beside the Senate House. And so out into King's parade where Horatio took his first astounded look at the chapel of all chapels. The begowned young men he eyed with interest and no envy. The coach fetched up in Petty Cury and turned into the Red Lion yard. Here they dined, and stretched their legs into the market-place to see Thomas Hobson's handsome stone fountain enclosed with its iron palisade, folk going and coming continually to draw water from it.

Leaving the towers and spires behind, the coach sped along, raised above the fen on their right hand, Hobson's stream bubbling upon their left. Horatio soon fell asleep once more: but Edmund Nelson was consumed with anxiety. Suppose that they should not be met, though he had informed Mr William Suckling and his good son Maurice of the time? It would be quite dark. All his precepts to his innocent son, yet here he sat, as nervous as a tabby! He decided it was fatigue and sorrow. Horatio looked so young, so unprotected, so unworldly, to be thrust rudely into so harsh a life. His father prayed: and thus calmed himself and fell into a doze.

They both awoke to the lights and bustle of an inn-yard. Some young voice was shouting up to the guard, some voice the parson recognised.

'Have you my father with you? The reverend Mr Nelson from Burnham? And my brother? You come from Lynn do you not?'

Horace leapt to his feet. 'Maurice! That's Maurice,' he shouted.

'Papa, Horace! Get you down here, I will see to your boxes,' Maurice cried, putting his head in at the door.

Horace flung himself upon his brother and leapt out, jumping with relief. His father descended more circumspectly. 'Where are we, then? In Cornhill?'

'Cornhill! No, Papa,' Maurice laughed, embracing him.

'Cornhill is miles further on. You are in Kentish Town, where you alight for Uncle William's, it is but a step or two, I will carry Horace's chest. Horatio, pray take Papa's bag and follow me. They all await you. I am bidden to sup too and lie here tonight!'

Dear God, the joy, Edmund Nelson thought, of the end of an anxious journey, the arrival at home! For it was home, here was loving, cheerful, faithful Maurice telling them they were looked for. 'Home' was simply where love was. He stumbled after his two eager sons, his eyes suddenly blind with tears. Maurice's 'step or two' was a ten minutes' walk, some part of which was up Uncle Suckling's handsome carriage drive, but none minded.

'You will approve this house, Horace. Papa, have you in truth never seen Mr Suckling's house? It is very fine, almost as grand as Wolterton, not so large indeed, of fair red brick. There, you may see the lights at the steps. When folk are expected, Price is bidden to light them! Is it not handsome, that stone stairway to the door?'

240

The rector raised his eyes to a new, square, spacious-built house, lights shining from the windows. Horace counted the wide stone steps as they mounted them. Fourteen. Maurice pulled upon a jangling bell. The great door was flung open instantly (Price must have lurked behind it) to reveal a large hall, candles in the sconces, a handsome staircase. But Horace's eyes were on Price. Here he was at last, the black butler with the gleaming white smile of whom Maurice had spoken.

'Welcome, welcome, enter and welcome young master, reverend sir,' said good James Price softly, bowing and smiling and handing them in. 'You travel well?' he said in his gentle voice. Horace smiled into soft, friendly eyes.

'Very well, I thank you,' he said.

Price knocked upon a door to the left, opened it, said, 'The reverend Mr Nelson and his sons,' and retreated. Then formality was at an end, several doors opened at once, Uncle William Suckling strode from the drawing-room, Madam swayed heavily from the parlour, the two cousins whom Horace had never met flung themselves down the wide staircase to greet their favourite Maurice and see his brother. They were William and little Benjamin seeming very much like Edmund and Suckling at home: but much more grandly dressed.

'There now, here is a new coz for you and a midshipman to boot! How do you do sir, you journeyed well I trust. Madam, my poor sister's spouse, Mr Nelson, who I think you have not met before. Madam has arranged for us to dine to suit you travellers. You are heartily welcome, to be sure. We dine when you are ready. Young Maurice, you are too thin, you suffer from the lack of Madam's care. What a cold night, you must all be parched with it, there's a capital fire down here!'

Price had re-appeared with a maidservant and had picked up the bags and, to the sound of Uncle William's cheerful talk, Horace followed his cousins up the stairs, slightly subdued by the grandeur of the balustrade, the pictures, the furnishings, but his heart expanding with the warmth of his uncle's welcome.

In the days that followed he explored every corner of the handsome house in the company of his cousins and grew to love it; and realised how pleasing are space and loftiness and light and colour allied to gracious furnishings. William would try to tell him who all the people in the portraits were. Many of them were Townshends, for the whole collection from the parlour of Admiral George Townshend (who had lived in the house in Hanover Square where Uncle Maurice had stayed at the time of his marriage) had come to Uncle William upon the admiral's death in 1769: they were second cousins and William Suckling was the admiral's executor. Horatio tried to remember what relationship was his to Admiral George. For a boy about to be a midshipman did well to have an admiral amongst his relations, however distant, as well as a captain for his uncle.

'How was Admiral Townshend related to us, Papa? To me?' he asked his father.

Mr Nelson frowned, sipping Madeira, and looked at his brother-in-law.

'It is upon your grandmother Suckling it depends...'

'Why yes, Horatio, listen here. My mother (that's your late Granny Suckling) and the admiral were first cousins: for their mothers were sisters, Mary and Dorothy Walpole. Dorothy married the second Viscount Townshend. Please to fetch that gold snuffbox, fetch the picture of Dorothy Viscountess Townshend, and you shall see.'

Horace picked up the little golden box with his 'mother's picture in it' which the admiral had left to William Suckling. A sweet, buxom, rosy lady with the hair dressing of fifty years ago looked out at Horatio. Dim memories of his granny's talk about Houghton and Walpoles and Townshends came back to him as he looked.

'Uncle William, did she die of the smallpox sir?'

'She did my boy, alas she did. When her sons and daughters were very young. George was but eleven, he used to say.'

'I was but nine when my mamma died,' Horace stated.

'So you were, to be sure.'

'Now Horace, your coz, Charlotte Townshend (that is the family we know best),' Papa put in, 'is niece to the admiral, is she not, Mr Suckling?'

'She is, yes. Daughter of Edward Townshend late dean of Norwich, the admiral's youngest brother. And Charlotte is the youngest of his four.'

'Sukey visited them and their mother when she was at school in the city.'

'Did she indeed. How is Miss Sukey?'

'Very well, and a good mother to her brothers and sisters,' the rector said. 'Not to speak of her ageing papa.'

'Come, come,' said Mr Suckling bridling. 'We are not old yet.' He was just turned forty himself and liked to be thought young. But Edmund Nelson approached his fiftieth year and made no bones about it. He smiled quizzically at his brother-in-law and said naught.

Out of doors, Uncle William's estate was equally exciting, for there were five acres of garden and shrubbery and wood and wild to explore; and along the west side of all this, a row of fine elms added a sense of park-like grandeur. Horace had little time to traverse it all for there was much else to see to.

There was all his fitting out. Captain Maurice had sent a list to Edmund Nelson with the names of the proper shops and the right tailor to go to. Young Maurice was given a day off to guide the innocent Norfolkers. Horatio stood, rigid and excited, to be measured for his blue tailcoat. It was to have a white silk lining, this uniform coat (he had never had a coat with a silk lining before).

'Pray stand easily and natural young sir, not drawn up, that is better, so. He is not big, your honour, is he, he's perhaps small for his age?' the tailor surmised in a quiet voice, taping Horatio at every point.

'He has always been small but he will fill out, now. And he has a big heart,' the rector added, smiling at his son.

Horace had working breeches and waistcoat of jean, and smart ones of white nankeen. He had shirts of frilled white linen, and a scarlet waistcoat of kersey-mere for wild weather. He had a frieze watch-coat, which went over all when need be, the garment which he knew from Norfolk fishermen as a slop. He had a black silk kerchief for his neck and a high three-cornered hat with gold loop and cockade.

'Let him not take too big a supply, sir,' the tailor advised quietly. 'They will be "borrowed" that is I believe "stolen", by his less fortunate fellows. So I have been told sir, by my many customers,' he added.

'I am certain the tailor is right,' put in Maurice. 'I have heard exactly the same...'

The clothes accumulated in his chest (which Papa had had Mr Dent make him). Horatio had never in his life had so many new clothes at a time before. The hat he tried often, striking an attitude, his hand upon his dirk before the long mirror on Uncle William's first landing. Ben and William watched with cries of admiration.

'Oh Horace, that hat makes you look a regular blood,' William shouted. 'I wish I went in the navy!'

'May I put the hat on? Please may I put the hat on!' roared Ben.

But the hat which looked huge enough upon slim Horatio extinguished Benjamin. William and Horace could only shriek with laughter.

Beneath the clothes lay his tin wash basin, his knife and fork and spoon and china, his pencil-box, his pocket book, his letter paper, his prayer-book, his penknife, a set of favourite marbles and the copy of *Gulliver's Travels*. Papa's copy.

Captain Maurice Suckling's message had been vague enough. A few weeks before Easter he had said, send the boy down before Easter. That was all Mr Suckling or his father knew. Mr Nelson planned to depart; father and son it was decided should go their different ways upon the same day. Horace walked to the inn whence Maurice had collected them a week ago carrying his father's bag. He was to put his papa upon the diligence for Lynn early in the morning. He was not uncheerful, but sober: he seemed to his father to have grown in stature already. They embraced each other with their usual warmth.

'Goodbye my son, I shall think of you ever, and pray for you. You will do well, you are eager and dutiful. Always seek help from your uncle if you are in trouble. Goodbye!'

'Goodbye dearest Papa, goodbye. Take my love to Sukey and William and the children!'

'I shall do so! Farewell, my bold Horatio!' Papa said, hiding under jocularity the true pain he felt at the parting.

Horace stood back to wave till the flutter of Papa's handkerchief showed no more. He gulped, turning for the house again. How he would miss Papa! Only now did he realise it. He would miss Papa more than them all. It was much worse than being away at school, it was so much the further away. He frowned, stuck out his lower lip and strutted forward, swinging his arms to invoke his courage.

CHAPTER TWENTY-SIX

The Raisonnable *at Chatham*

Uncle William had conveyed Horatio into town in his own chaise and at the customs office handed him over to Maurice: Mr Suckling's coachman was driving them towards London Bridge. The brothers talked happily.

'There Horace, look at Saint Paul's from here, is it not imposing? How went Papa away, in good heart? I hope you feel more cheerful than I did stepping forth in life!' And Maurice laughed ruefully. Nothing had altered, London was still exile, the office still a prison, only he was grown used to it. He felt for Horatio, remembering the long-drawn agonies of those early hateful days.

'Perhaps I am more fortunate than you, Maurice. I love the sea, I have always admired sea captains and Uncle Maurice, I feel excited at the attempt. And I shall not be on my own, I have Uncle Maurice to look to, as you had Uncle William. Would Mamma be pleased do you think, to see me go?'

'I'm pretty sure of it. I envy you the air and the sea. I suppose Uncle Maurice will send a man to take you aboard?'

'I do not know. I shall find my way, don't be anxious. I have a tongue in my head, and I shall smell the river out!' Horatio said gaily.

Maurice looked doubtful, gripping his brother's small shoulders before he entered the coach. 'Have you anything to eat?' he asked finally.

'Eat? I have breakfasted as well as I could with Papa.' Food never detained Horace much.

'How much money have you?'

'I have enough to tide me over. I can buy food and ale if I need it,' Horace laughed at him. 'I shall be able to care for myself, never fear!'

But Maurice embraced him with a sad heart, despite his smiling face. He was so young, so small, so unaware of all that might happen.

'If you're to be in Chatham for some time, we may be able to meet! Goodbye, brother. I know you do this partly to help Papa and I hope you will get your reward. I quite envy you the journey. Goodbye!'

Horatio waved, smiling while he could see his brother. Then he sat back clutching his hat on his knees, his mouth pursed, his face stern. Papa was gone. Maurice was gone. He was alone. But Uncle Maurice would be there at the other end and this was comforting. He sat still, intent upon garnering and preserving his diminishing courage and high spirits.

As the fields appeared, with dark bushes and tight-lipped trees waiting for spring, Horatio began to feel more composed. The countryside was fair enough even under the dumb hand of winter, and they were often within sight of the river. At Greenwich he had time to climb down in the gusty cold wind and look back towards London. At Gravesend the river seemed so wide and the ships so many, that one must be a good navigator indeed to bring in a great vessel. Would he ever be trustworthy thus? Papa would say it depended upon him. His heart swelled with ambition to do well, to please Uncle Maurice, to be highly thought of, to master all the difficulties of seamanship. He let out a sigh which was partly weariness and partly impatience. He longed to begin.

Now they turned south over chalky uplands, past hop-gardens and cherry orchards untouched by spring, down towards a river valley which he was soon informed was the Medway. A cheerful and noisy woman had joined the stage at Gravesend, whose bulk had caused Horace to shrink to half his exiguous size, but for whose warmth he was not ungrateful. Having eyed his hat and his uniform for some time, she now addressed him.

'Going to sea, young sir, are you?'

'Yes,' he replied. 'To Chatham. To my uncle's ship.'

'Ah, I thought you was, I figured you was bound for Chatham. Been before, have you?'

'Oh no, this is my first day, my first...I am just set forth as a midshipman,' he said.

'Oho, a right youngster. I thought as much. See now, just as we turn this bend, from the top of the hill...' Her great arm, pointing, eclipsed all Horace's view. But at the next bend in the road he saw laid out below a view he would long remember. There was the broad Medway and the bridge spanning it to the chalky mound where a cathedral and a castle stood. To the east a great loop in the river made a silvery basin dotted all over with ships; small ships and large, three-masters, skiffs, lighters, cockle boats, ships with bare masts, ships wearing sail. At the far shore of the river he saw a stretch of buildings like huge warehouses, while beyond the valley the land rose again to chalky uplands. The view was gone in a few seconds, but he had seen it like a picture of his future. He was suddenly exhilarated and inspired.

'See the castle, did you? Ay well, that's Rochester, and the cathedral beside.'

'Then where is Chatham, ma'am?'

'On beyond. All part and parcel. First we come to Stroud village, I live there. My husband's in the oyster trade. Then you'll be over the bridge, Rochester Bridge. And straight on, for Chatham. Did you catch sight of the ships? Ay, a fine sight. I wonder which is yours.'

He bade her politely farewell, touched by her kindness, and soon found they were crossing the very bridge he had seen. The oyster-woman looked after the coach and wondered what was in store for the lad, a brave young boy with his smart hat and gentle manners. She shook her head.

At Chatham all the passengers climbed down and soon dispersed, while Horace claimed his chest, put on his hat, brushed down his uniform, and waited cold but confident, looking about him for Uncle Maurice: Captain Suckling, as he must now call him.

Or perhaps a seaman, Captain Suckling's servant.

'Be you the Captn's nephew, young sir?' he would say.

He was expected, of course. Somebody would come soon. From here, he could look back upon the cathedral and the great castle from the other side. He could feel the cold wind from the river and smell the water, a smell he loved. Perhaps he had arrived at an awkward time when all were busy in the ship. He stamped his cold feet and took a turn or two. The smell of the midday ordinary from the inn close by made him conscious of hunger. There would be a meal of some sort he supposed, upon the *Raisonnable*. He did not know what the time was.

Where were the ships, where was the *Raisonnable*? Probably he was expected to find his own way. He was a midshipman now, not a child. There was no one to meet him, why should there be. All were too engaged. He had boasted to Maurice that he would find his own way, yet had thought to be conducted. He now picked up his chest and sat it upon his head, carrying the hat beneath one arm. Then he looked about him, and turned down to the waterfront.

It was colder right beside the river, and a north-easterly wind met him smelling of the sea. The wind, the ships floating in the basin, the wharf side, transported him suddenly to Overy Staithe, miles and miles away. Were he but walking along hailing the fishermen, and soon to mount the pony and ride for home! An ache spread all through him from his heart to his eyes. He put down the chest, shook himself, and looked out over the blurred water. No ships were very near, he could make no guess as to which was his. He now saw half a mile away the imposing row of dock buildings he had noticed from the coach and decided to walk along and see them. He picked up the box again and started off.

'If you please, can you tell me where the ship the *Raisonnable* lies?' he asked some fishermen. But none recognised the name nor knew of it. Horatio felt their eyes upon him as he marched on.

He was approaching the dock buildings; workmen came and went, some of the great doors stood open. He remembered suddenly the account in the newspaper of the busy dockyard at Chatham. The account that had determined him to come to sea, had brought him to be thus walking forlornly by Chatham water front seeking a ship of which nobody knew.

He turned around and began to trudge back the way he had come. He was by now very cold.

A sea captain emerged from the commissioner's office in the dock buildings behind Horatio, and saw the slight figure carrying the sea chest wandering ahead of him. A youngster he supposed, just arrived and feeling lost. When the boy stopped, put down the box and gazed out over the river towards the distant craft, the man overtook him.

Horace heard footsteps approach, turned, saw the uniformed figure and for one glorious moment thought it was Uncle Maurice. Then his smile faded.

'Are you awaited, my boy?' the officer asked kindly.

'No sir, I think not sir. I am come to join a ship called the *Raisonnable*.'

'The *Raisonnable*? Ah, Captain Suckling?'

'Yes sir, if you please, sir. He is my uncle!' Horatio gasped in the profoundest relief.

'Is he so? But I think he is not in Chatham for a day or two. He is an acquaintance of mine. I can tell you where the ship lies. Have you but just arrived?'

'About an hour ago sir, on the stage from London.'

'Have you eaten, my boy? Are you hungry?'

'Yes sir, I am a little hungry. I have had nought since breakfast,' Horace admitted.

Breakfast! What an age, an eternity, since he and Papa took breakfast! Breakfast was in another life.

'Come home with me, my lad, and have some refreshment. Then I will see about getting you out to your ship.'

'Oh thank you, sir. You are very kind.'

The whole day, the very quality of the wintry light, the brave ships on the brisk water, changed from the colour of melancholy to that of hope. By the time the sea-officer had shared his dinner with Horatio, questioned him, finding him eager and apt, encouraged him and set him at his ease, he was a bold midshipman again, ready for anything.

'Well now if you are ready, Mr Nelson,' said the officer 'we shall walk along to the docks, for I can show you the ships and warehouses and it is all on the way to where your ship lies in the Chatham reach. My servant shall bring your box down.'

Horatio was delighted. They explored the Old Dock first, where he saw huge pyramids of balls stacked up inside a barn.

'Oh! Cannon balls, sir?'

'Ay, this is used now for stores and ordnance. Those will blow the Spaniards to destruction, will not they?'

'I thought we had made peace with Spain sir?'

'So we have boy, but who knows when another scrap will arise.'

Now they turned about and headed for the Royal Dockyard where the officer had first found Horatio wandering and made their way past sheds and storehouses stacked with masts and miles of rope, with rigging, hemp, flax, pitch, everything needed for building and equipping the ships; past the huge sail-loft crammed with rolled canvas, the smith's shop where separate fires burned and many men hammered anchors and chains and ironwork. There were docks for repairing and slips for building new vessels: the place was in an active flurry, the more so that evening fell. Here shipwrights, carpenters, caulkers and their mates hastened to finish before the light faded.

The small midshipman became aware of huge wooden walls towering above him. They had stopped in the shadow of a ship. From one of the open galleries at her stern came the sound of hammering, and a workman came towards them along her side.

'How is the lady now?' called the officer.

'Oh she be fit and ready sir, all but. We be only titivating here and there where disuse has harmed her.'

'Come Horatio, you'll like her figurehead,' his friend said, leading him up beyond her bows so that they could look back. Fresh paint had picked out sharply the intricate group of figures at her head.

'There's His Majesty in the middle. This is old Britannia on his right with her lion. The other side's Victory with her laurel crown, and behind her Fame, blowing her trumpet. All neat with new paint. She's been lying in ordinary some years.'

Horatio narrowed his eyes at the carved figures. 'What ship—' he began. Then, 'Is she the *Victory*, sir?' he suddenly said.

'Ay, she's the *Victory*. You know of her?'

'I've read of her. How old is she, sir?'

'Let me think. She was ordered 1758—'

'The year I was born sir!'

'Then you and she were conceived together,' said he, winking.

'Keel put down that great year, 1759. They launched her in 1765, so far as my memory goes. So she's your age Mr Nelson, is the *Victory!* Fine ship.'

Horace gazed at the ship, saying nothing. The officer noted his pinched face and red nose. An eager boy who should do well, but not strong.

'Come, it is too cold to linger here. We'll get down to the water now and find a boat to take you out.'

It appeared by good fortune that one of the *Raisonnable's* cutters was alongside, about to cast off having loaded some stores. Aboard her Horatio was hustled, his box after him, the jerk of her oarsmen almost spilling him as he turned to wave.

'Goodbye sir! Thank you heartily!'

'Goodbye lad, the Lord be with you!' And the good Lord will he need thought the officer, watching the small swaying figure turn and sit amongst the casks and the grunting people and the brusque mate giving them their time. Horatio realised with regret that he knew not the officer's name, had been too shy to ask and at the last too hurried. But Uncle Maurice would know. The cutter had a double bank of oars and made her way fast over the channel. They were quickly alongside the middle of a ship.

'Let this lad up first now. Up you go and look lively, do you see the battens? Hold to the ropes. We'll heave your chest up.'

In the fading frosty afternoon light Horatio climbed to the upper deck of the *Raisonnable*, clutching his hat in one hand and the side rope in the other. His pale face and wild wispy hair appeared above the gunwale like a wraith. A midshipman and several seamen stared at him.

'Who is this in Gawd's name, where's this sprung from?'

'The Captain's nephew, if you please.'

'The devil he is. Heave, oh. Aft, and report—'

'My chest—'

'Here't be. Report to the officer of the watch.'

'Where is he, if you please?'

'Up aft, on the quarterdeck. Out of my way!' A cask had already followed Horatio's chest. The purser's mate untied it.

'Here you, boy, show this younker the whereabouts!' said the midshipman who was counting in the casks.

Horace picked up his chest and followed the boy thus summoned past a sentry in a red coat, and up the ladder to the quarter-deck, where a lieutenant stood on the watch, his glance sliding to all quarters of the deck in turn and back to the people unloading the casks, the deck-log open before him.

'The Captain's nephew hif you please,' said the boy, who had heard the new arrival speak.

The officer was the fourth lieutenant and his name was Mr Faithful Adrian Fortescue. He brought his glance to rest at last upon the new midshipman with a teasing smile which aroused a spark of anger in the forlorn child.

'Very well, take him aft, show him the gunroom, show him all he needs to know, be quick about it,' he commanded. 'Carry the midshipman's chest, boy,' he added.

Horatio followed the boy across the quarter-deck again, down the hatchway once more to the upper deck, and down again to the lower deck and the room right aft of it which was to be his home: the gunroom, the dim domain of the gunner, where also abode the ship's arms, and which lay (as Horace later discovered) below both the captain's quarters and the wardroom where the officers lived. The gunroom appeared now to be empty. Here the boy downed the chest.

'You 'ang yer 'ammock 'ere sir,' he said.

'Where is my hammock?'

''Ammocks piped down at four bells. From the nettin's. 'Long the sides. You'll see.'

He then at Horatio's urgent request showed him the necessaries and the piss-dale, and hurried away, leaving him to his own devices and unsure of his way back to the gunroom. He regained it, however, and slumped down upon his chest, his arms dangling across his knees, assailed by that horridest of panics, the loneliness one feels in a crowd that knows not that one exists, nor cares. The ship was full of folk, officers watching and commanding, mates shouting orders, seamen and midshipmen performing them, marines standing guard, boys dashing hither and thither, their feet thudding: all knew their duty and ran to do it, like ants in their nest. Save only Horatio, who knew neither where to go nor what to do, as he piteously told himself.

Some stern voice in his mind, akin to Papa's voice, braced him up. At least it is no good to sit here, he said to himself. How shall I see what goes on and what I must do, if I linger here? He leapt to his feet. As he came out of the gunroom the ship's bell was struck, sharp, loud and clear. Horatio counted. Eight. Eight bells, it was called. It meant the time of day, he knew enough to know that. He thought it was four o'clock. The sound came from far forward and above him, on the forecastle. He had edged forward by now and was by the main capstan, surveying the length of the lower deck divided into sections by red gun-carriages. Scarcely had the bell's tone ceased when a pipe tune followed, a merry tune.

The lower gun deck was almost at once peopled. From every direction men appeared, hurrying and eager. Some seized vessels and pots and ran past Horatio in a jostling procession to the hatchway behind him down which they disappeared yet further into the belly of the ship. Others were hooking down narrow boards from the beams which they proceeded to fix as trestle tables in the little rooms between each gun. Benches appeared too, and tableware, plates, knives, mugs. From leather barrels in the ship's sides some sailors were producing small wrapped morsels which they put upon their plates. Very soon the procession of mess-cooks re-appeared with bread, cheese, butter, precariously piled, which they delivered each to his mess. From a barrel on the deck grog was being served to each mess-cook. Horace saw the food and drink welcomed in and shared out and the men fall to; and the cheerful sight made him ache with loneliness and turn away. Up the ladder last came the boy who had conducted him, laden with provisions. He saw Horace, and cocked his head in the direction of the gun-room; Horatio slid after him. Several men now sat at the top of the table, one in a blue coat, the others in varying strange garments. The man in the blue coat glanced at Horatio with his mouth open, showed some surprise, but being in the middle of a sentence to his mates did not trouble to address the pale-faced newcomer.

'Plate. Mug,' muttered the servant boy at the end of the table. Thus welcomed, Horatio unlocked his chest and took out these articles, for some instinct told him not to refuse his food even when he could not eat it. Then he sat down upon the chest and nibbled at the bread (it was good shore bread, not hard biscuit, about which he had heard such tales), trifled with the butter and cheese, and drank a sip of his ale. Watching what the others did, he carefully wrapped up his leavings in his handkerchief and stowed them in the barrel the boy pointed out. When he turned back to the table, his mug was empty and both boys grinning, as they cleared away the crumbs and prepared to wash the plates.

The ship's bell struck again, but once. It was drowned soon by the roll of a drum.

'Muster,' said somebody.

Horace followed the rest out and up to the quarterdeck. An officer sat at a table with a large red-stained marbled book, from which he called the muster roll rapidly, for there were nearing two hundred souls aboard and it took a long while. Horatio listened intently, but his name was not called. His mind went back to his first day at Norwich School when the master knew not who they were. Here, they knew not even that he was present. He longed, suddenly, for brother William.

But the men were all dispersing, hurrying off to different quarters, to their stations, each knowing what he did.

'Any new men, Mr Fortescue?' said Mr Edward Leigh the purser to the fourth lieutenant who had now been relieved of the watch.

'Yes, a youngster. Where is he?' said Mr Fortescue, looking about to see what dregs were left after the tide of men had gone.

'If you please sir,' Horatio said.

'Ah here he is, to see the purser,' said Mr Fortescue, leading Horatio forward by the ear. The purser held his pen over a piece of rough paper, for he would not sully his book until his facts were clear.

'Name?' he said.

'Horace Nelson if you please sir.'

'Ah, so. He appears at last, Mr Nelson. On the books since January. Rank?'

'Midshipman, if you please sir.'

'Whence?'

'Burnham, sir. Burnham Thorpe in Norfolk.'

'Burnham? Near Wells, isn't it?' said the purser not looking up.

'Yes sir,' Horace said eagerly. 'Very near Wells.'

The purser wrote Wells. Everyone had heard of Wells.

'That's all,' he said to Horatio's disappointment.

He was cast loose again to wander up and down where he chose, the magic names of Burnham and Wells which had momentarily warmed him lost in silence. The purser had nothing to say to him: feeling not well at the time. Horace surveyed the activity on the lower deck. Officers and a midshipman or two went the rounds of the men inspecting them, inspecting their gear, seeing the gun-carriages pulled out (there were no guns), inspecting the pumps, intent upon their task. Horatio walked back and forth also intent, partly that he should seem to be not only composed but learning by observation, partly to keep himself warm. For it was now very cold and the light gone. The dank air smelt of river and frost. Lanterns had been lit upon their own and other ships, flares came and went upon the dock shore. From here he could just see by lantern light the ship's bell in her tower, as the master's mate struck it.

Four bells. Followed by the pipe once more. The servant boy said something about four bells and the hammocks.

Sure enough there began a procession of men up to the quarter-deck, and all along the sides of the waist, where each was receiving from the master's mate on duty a tightly rolled brown bundle which must be his hammock, tossed to him from the nettings where they were stowed. Horatio lingered until all were dispensed, then explained his case and received a clean hammock and scant words from a seaman. The accomplishment of this necessary task gave him the first small satisfaction since his arrival. He carried it to the gunroom where, by careful observation of one of the other boys, he succeeded in slinging it. He had already put his chest back against the side where he had noted other chests to be. He now took from it what he needed. One or two smaller boys had turned in already, but the gunner's servant and his friend played at marbles on the boards by a glim in a bottle. Nothing more seemed to be required of him. He undressed and swung himself into his unaccustomed bed, where he allowed himself at last with frowning face and sternly bitten lip to think of his papa, who would by now be in Lynn or even home; of Maurice, whom he had left in London and who had been right as it proved to think of his brother's arrival with concern; of Uncle William and Madam and the children in Kentish Town who had welcomed and warmed him; of brother William and his friends at Walsham left only one week ago, the longest week, surely, in his life: of Sukey and the children and Kitty-kat. Of Mamma. His thoughts were at the same time his prayers. He screwed his courage to its sticking point. He had chosen this life, to help Papa, to help the family. He prayed for himself, that he should acquit himself well. All would be well, he repeated in his mind, when he was grown used to it; when he knew what he must do; when Uncle Maurice arrived. He fell asleep utterly exhausted. If they had asked him to run up the rigging, to take an oar in the cutter, to swarm up a mast, no courage would have been required. Circumstances had tested him to his particular limits by meting out cold indifference. The child had not failed the test.

When the gunner came below to turn in nigh on eight bells, he noticed the unaccustomed hammock, remembered the new midshipman at supper and peered at him with his taper.

'Who is he, any road?' he asked the servant boy, who watched him with one eye open.

''E said 'e's the Cap'n's nephew, sir!'

'Then I hope you looked after him proper,' grunted the gunner guiltily.

In his cabin the Master, Mr William Clark, who wrote his own journal while in port, pondered over the day's notes from the deck-log. He had not seen Horatio arrive, being down in the hold with the purser, ready to examine the new casks and stow them behind the few remaining old. Who was this, then, who had arrived? *N.E.* he wrote in the appropriate column for wind, and against the day's date: *D⁰ weaʳ, pm recᵗ, 1 man and 902lb of beeff, the muster master mustered.* What a tongue twister it was, he had put 'master' twice. He corrected it, wondering who the man was who seemed of so much less consequence than the beef.

The bitter north-easterly blew from the bleak North Sea as it had ever done and ever would. It frisked the waters of the basin into brisk little waves, pretending to be playful as they slap, slap, slapped the side of His Majesty's ship: rocking all the souls inside her with who knew what sweet or sinister intent.

THE SEQUEL

A Thorough Seaman

The Ships' Logs of Horatio Nelson's
Early Voyages Imaginatively Explored

Pauline Hunter Blair

£16.95 ISBN 0-9536317-2-0
Available from Church Farm House, Bottisham,
Cambridge, CB5 9BA

Before Horatio Nelson was eighteen, he had sailed towards all points of the compass: as captain's servant, coxswain of the captain's gig, able-bodied seaman, foretop man, and midshipman.

After Chatham, he sailed to the West Indies on a sugar ship, the *Mary Ann*, when he must have first revelled in the glorious trade winds. Her captain was a trusted naval friend of his uncle's, now commanding this merchantman, for whom perhaps the boy developed a loving admiration which almost caused his naval ambitions to falter. Safely back in the Medway and Thames, he learned their tides, channels, sand banks and landmarks or points of departure: on one occasion very probably under a Lt Boyles, who sounds like his old friend of Burnham days.

When news of an Arctic voyage to seek a north-east passage to the Pole fired his imagination, he was off in a converted bomb-ketch, aptly named the *Carcase*, to foggy, frosty wastes, encountering floating structures of ice, padding white bears, walrus, and a million sea birds. Six tempests on the way home initiated him into the buffeting manners of the rough North Sea.

HMS *Seahorse* then carried him south, round the Cape, across the Indian Ocean to Madras, and the Bay of Bengal to Calcutta; then to Ceylon, to Bombay, and up the Persian Gulf. They were once involved in a minor but possibly explicable exchange of fire, off the Malabar coast, with some ships of one Hyder Ali, out from Mangalore; his first taste of a skirmish.

HMS *Dolphin* and her kind captain carried him home from Bombay, a sad victim of malaria, and not expected to make England. But on the way, miraculously, he recovered, as we all know.

Logs of all but the first of these voyages exist, so that we can follow the events. Of his relations with captains, officers, masters and friends we know less and must imagine more.